P9-DEK-882

TAILSPIN

A sharp crack occurred underfoot as he shifted to face her. He felt himself sinking, dropped the metal, and scrambled for purchase on the ledge. "I've got you," she called. Steadied, he was able to slide one foot onto a sounder board and pull the other free of the broken wood. With a lunge, he reached the main dock and safety.

His heart hammered, he could barely catch his breath, and a burning throb was developing in his foot. But what filled his awareness as his senses cleared, was the feel of Celeste Ashton pressed tight against him . . . so close that he could feel her heart was beating fast, too.

That wave of adrenaline drained, leaving in its place a confusing flush of heat. He looked down into her upraised face—luminous skin, delicate features, generously curved lips . . . Soft, she was so *soft* against him . . . everywhere . . . his chest, his loins, his thighs, his arms. And everywhere she was touching him, something seemed to be melting . . . his resistance to her, his clothes, his very skin.

It should have raised an alarm in him. But as he looked into her large, dark-centered eyes and felt the warmth of her body seeping into his chest, he couldn't think of a single reason to let her go . . .

THE
MERMAID

Betina Krahn

 BANTAM BOOKS

New York Toronto London
Sydney Auckland

The Mermaid

A Bantam Book /September 1997

ISBN 0-553-57617-8

Published simultaneously in the United States and Canada

Bantam Books are published by Bantam Books, a division of Bantam Doubleday
Dell Publishing Group, Inc. Its trademark, consisting of the words "Bantam
Books" and the portrayal of a rooster, is Registered in U.S. Patent and
Trademark Office and in other countries. Marca Registrada. Bantam Books,
1540 Broadway, New York, New York 10036.

PRINTED IN THE UNITED STATES OF AMERICA

OPM 10 9 8 7 6 5 4 3 2 1

For
Matthew and Linda Stone
who introduced me to the beauty of the
underwater world

One

Oxford, England
July 1884

"NOTHING MORE STIMULATING than a juicy new heresy, eh, Thorny my boy?"

Titus Thorne stopped short in the doorway to the faculty meeting room, causing a chain reaction of collisions among the black-robed dons filing in behind him. Grunts and exclamations of surprise trailed down the long black line, a testament to the ambulatory peculiarity of the professors of Cardinal College . . . who habitually walked with their heads bent, studying their shoes as they pondered the great questions of the age.

"*New* heresy?" Titus stared at Sir Parthenay Fenwick's twinkling eyes. "What heresy is that?"

"This aquatic personage." Sir Parthenay, the college head, pulled him out of the doorway so that the rest of the dons could shuffle in and take their places at the large rectangular meeting table. "Creating quite a stir, I understand. Has all London awag. Been in all the papers."

"Haven't seen any London papers of late. I came straight from Newcastle—that Viking-artifact debacle," Titus said, his interest piqued by the prospect of yet another scientific boondoggle in progress. "What 'aquatic personage'?"

"This 'mermaid' creature. Saved a copy of the *Gazette* for you." Sir Parthenay hurried across the Gothic oak-paneled room and snatched a newspaper from under another aged don's bespectacled nose. He handed it to Titus and waited eagerly for the younger man's reaction.

HUMAN MERMAID CARRIED AWAY BY DOLPHINS

Titus's jaw tightened as he read the account of a young woman on the southern coast of England who claimed to have been befriended by dolphins and taken into their watery world. The article dubbed her "the lady mermaid," called her recently published book "absorbing," and made tittery allusions to the "romantic" nature of her revelations.

"Pure nonsense," he said, tossing the paper onto the nearby meeting table.

"*Popular* nonsense," Sir Parthenay corrected, rescuing the article.

Titus frowned and continued toward his seat at the end of the long oak table. "They will do anything to sell books to a gullible public. Dolphins and mermaids. Ridiculous. It won't last." As he passed Sir Isaac Ellis, he stooped out of habit to lift the venerable old don's foot onto his gout stool. Sir Isaac responded by thrusting a stack of news clippings into his hand.

"That first article came out more than a fortnight ago," the old fellow wheezed, pointing a gnarled finger at the newsprint Titus held. "These followed."

"Since then, it's been an endless stream of mermaid-this and mermaid-that in the news," hoary old Sir Mercer Gill declared from across the table.

"A number of faculty from other colleges and even the chancellor himself have inquired as to *your* response to the matter," Sir Parthenay added.

"My response?" Titus scowled at the expectation in their faces.

A mermaid craze. Stranger things had happened in recent years. Two-headed farm animals promoted as oracles . . . people claiming to contact spirits of the dead . . . reports of sea monsters in lakes . . . faked antiquities from bogus archaeological digs . . . spurious miracle cures . . . cults bent on saving the human race by making people into living lightning rods . . . he had been there to unmask and expose the lot of them. In the last five years he had become Britain's resident skeptic . . . the leading investigator of hucksterism and "quack science."

Now it was a mermaid. It wouldn't have been the first time he'd battled a mythological creature, but he had learned from experience that such things were seldom a matter of science. No matter what evidence he uncovered to expose such preposterous claims, some would refuse to be convinced. They simply wanted to believe. And he had no time to waste on lost causes; not when there were so many more worthy battles to fight in the name of truth and reason. He tossed the stack of articles onto the table, unexamined, and sat down.

"It's a pile of bunkum. It has nothing whatsoever to do with science."

"Well, I'm afraid the Oceanographic Society is of a different opinion," Sir Parthenay declared in a challenging tone. "They've set aside this month's scheduled speaker in favor of an address by this 'mermaid' personage. *And* they've invited the Zoological Society to sit in for a joint session."

Titus's eyebrows shot up.

"The hell you say."

An invitation to address the royal societies was tantamount to an offer of membership . . . the academic equivalent of a royal patronage . . . reserved for scientists, naturalists, and explorers of major accomplishment.

"See for yourself." Sir Parthenay passed a printed meeting announcement down the table to him. "Seems all a bit reminiscent of that Atlantis business, back in '82. What was that American fellow's name again?"

"Donnelly . . . Ignoramus Donnelly," Titus muttered, taking the paper.

"Ignatius," Sir Mercer corrected.

"Whatever. And look how that turned out. Every Tom, Dick, and Herbert climbing into a toga and claiming to be the lost royalty of the long-lost continent . . ." As Titus stared at the written confirmation of Sir Parthenay's news, his stomach began to heat. After all his work with shark and large-fish feeding habits, he himself had been invited to join the Oceanographic Society only a year ago. And now, to have this absurd scientific pretender—this flimflam artist in a phony fish tail—invited in to address a meeting of not one but *two* major scientific societies . . .

Small wonder the chancellor was disturbed and his fellow faculty members were up in arms, demanding to know what he intended to do about it.

"It's an outrage," he said, retrieving the spurned news articles and glancing from headline to headline. "Elusive," "romantic," and "mysterious" . . . characterized the early opinions, but farther down in the stack, the words "perceptive," "painstaking observation," and "revolutionary thinking" crept in. He shot to his feet.

"Who is this absurd female? What credentials could she possibly have?"

"No academic training, of course. But her grandfather was Sir Martin Ashton, an archaeologist of some reputation," Sir Mercer declared. "Cambridge man. Solid fellow. Did work in the Azores and the Canaries, I believe."

"She's apparently something of a sailor," Sir Harold Beetle added. "Claims to have been researching aquatic populations in a bay near her home when a dolphin sought her out and tried to talk to her."

"Lunacy," Titus declared.

"No, clicks and squeaks," gravel-voiced Sir Milton Ruckers put in. "Says it's their language. Got up the nerve to climb right in the water with the thing, and it hauled her around for a ride."

"Bullfeathers."

"Not necessarily." Sir Parthenay raised an excepting finger. "There are documented cases of sailors being saved by dolphins . . . towed to shore and safety. She experienced several such 'rides' and seems to think such behavior is intentional. That dolphins are curious about us. That dolphins . . . think."

"*Think?* Horse manure!"

"No," came a reedy objection, "don't believe there were any horses in the book . . ." Old Sir Isaac was puffing for breath, struggling over the arm of his chair to reach something that had slid from his lap onto the floor. Titus rounded the table, picked it up, and found himself holding a sea-blue book with a dolphin embossed in gold leaf on the cover. His eyes widened as he read the title on the spine. *The Secret Life of Dolphins,* by Miss Celeste Ashton.

"You've read this?"

Sir Isaac looked unrepentant.

"Had to see what all the fuss was about," the old don insisted, huddling back in his chair.

Titus stalked back to his seat, observing that the cover of the book looked rather worn. As he flipped through the well-thumbed pages, they fell open to an oft-read passage on pages ninety-three and ninety-four. Scanning the print, his gaze fell to a line containing the words "frequency of romantic behavior." A bit farther down, the phrase "astonishing variety of mating techniques" caught his attention. At the top of the second page, "continuous and fascinating sexual play" positively leaped out at him. Stiffening, he dived into the flowery prose, and before he realized it, he was reading aloud.

" 'The lotharios of the deep, dolphins spend most of their nonfeeding time engaged in courtship and romantic displays. Not unlike males in some human societies, dolphin males must compete for dolphin females' attention and favors. Since the traditional land-based methods of attracting a mate—preening and self-decoration—are impossible in their watery world, behavior is their only recourse for courtship. They use every method of persuasion possible . . . sound, acrobatics, and a surprising variety of physical contact. First, they serenade their chosen ladies with a series of clicks and coos not unlike the songs of human minstrels. *"Click, click, click, click . . . screee, screee"* is a common refrain in courting songs . . .' " He glanced farther down the page.

" 'It was only after I saw Prospero courting a female of the group that arrived later, that I realized that the behavior he had shown toward me was essentially courtship behavior. He had approached me as if I were another dolphin. Perhaps that is why he and the others permitted me to move so freely among them. It is possible that they considered me an adopted dolphin.' " He raised his head. "Courted by a fish? The woman's mad."

"Strictly speaking, dolphins are not fish. They are mammals of the genus—"

"I *know* what they are, Sir Mercer," he growled. "I also know that most of what is supposedly 'known' about the creatures is nothing short of mythology!" He glanced back at the open book and his eyes narrowed.

"Listen to this: 'The females are usually coy at first, like haughty debutantes pretending not to notice the romantic attentions of their ardent suitors. The lovely Ariel, Prospero's intended, was no exception.' " He looked up. " *'Debutantes,'* for God's sake. And 'suitors.' It's anthropomorphism run amuck." He might have laughed if it hadn't been so alarming. By all accounts, the royal societies were swallowing this drivel and asking for more.

" 'After a while, Ariel allowed him to swim by her side, tickling and stroking her with his fins and poking her seductively—intimately—with his long nose.' " He gave a snort of disbelief. " 'They were consistently playful, even while engaged in overtly sexual behavior. Prospero repeatedly rolled Ariel onto her back beneath him and she escaped numerous times, seeming to want to romp and to draw him into her play, before the actual coupling occurred.

" 'I observed at least thirty-two separate incidents of actual mating, and in each, Prospero insisted on being directly above his lady during the process. Concerned that I might be led astray by one dolphin's amorous preference, I determined to observe other pairs during mating and discovered, to my gratification, that Prospero was no more or less inventive than the other males of his group. They universally attempted to roll the females beneath them, in a 'belly-up' position . . . which necessitates the females holding their breath for long periods. More than once, I observed an exasperated female breaking off in the middle of mating and wriggling away to the surface for air, leaving her clumsy swain to dive into the depths to hide his shame.' "

Titus glanced up with fire in his eyes.

"Randy dolphins . . . this absurd female plunging into the water to watch them mate—in the missionary position, no less . . . The woman's either a colossal liar or seriously depraved!"

"No, no, truly—read on," Sir Mercer demanded, waving his hand. "It gets even better."

"Better?" Titus looked at the old fellow's ruddy face and glowing eyes, shocked to find the aged don enthralled by that ridiculous prose. Then his gaze strayed to Sir Isaac's reddened face . . . Sir Parthenay's, Sir Mercer's, and Sir Harold's.

All around the table, eyes were glistening and aged cheeks were ruddy with unseemly heat. He glanced down at the well-used book in his hands, then up at their faces. It still took a moment for him to make sense of what he was seeing.

"You've read it, Witherspoon? Sir Parthenay? Sir Mercer? Sir Milton? Good Lord—*all of you*?"

After an uncomfortable silence, Sir Parthenay cleared his throat. "Purely in the interest of science, of course. We felt it best to . . . keep up on the latest developments."

Titus stared at them, thinking that the time he had long dreaded had finally come. It was mass senility. The old boys' garters were all snapping at once . . . even Sir Parthenay, who at sixty was several years younger than the rest of the Cardinal College faculty. Titus was the only don in the room who still had all his own teeth, didn't have to pluck his ears, and could still "take wine" in the traditional Oxford manner without suffering an attack of the gout.

The old boys had offered him the chair in ichthyological studies several years ago, when he was yet a fledgling scholar. They had taken him immediately into their midst and into their confidence; he was never treated as "junior," as new faculty were in other colleges. They had given him the benefit of their experience, their time-ripened judgment, and the deep understanding they had accumulated over lifetimes. They were men of science and letters . . . renowned, even brilliant minds who had written many a theory and text. Now, to see them caught up with some absurd scientific boondoggle—mermaids and sex-mad dolphins, for God's sake—was nothing short of painful to him.

He had to do something. For the sake of his beloved mentors, for the integrity of his college, and for the dignity of the royal societies, he had to confront this fishy tart and expose her sham of scholarship. He rose and gathered up the book and newspaper clippings, tucking them under the arm of his black robe.

"I intend to look into the matter," he said curtly. "I shall take the 3:03 to London tomorrow and attend this 'mermaid' fiasco on Friday. If you need me I shall be at the Bolton Arms in Knightsbridge."

The old dons exchanged glances as they watched him exit. When the echoes of his footsteps faded in the hall, Sir Parthenay sighed and settled back into his chair. "He's off and running again."

"Feel a bit guilty, setting him on that 'mermaid' creature." Sir Harold wagged his head. "The boy does tend to get a bit wrought up about these things."

"Well, someone has to guard the gates." Sir Parthenay rubbed his chin. "If only he would loosen up a bit . . . allow for the unexpected or unorthodox in the process of discovery . . . he would be a much better scientist himself."

"And a better candidate for the Head, when you retire,"

Sir Harold mused, inhaling deeply from his nasal atomizer. "I fear for us all when he takes over."

"It's what comes of poring over fish guts for years on end," Sir Mercer Gill announced with a frown. "I've tried and tried to get him to take out an expedition . . . do some study in the field while he's still young enough."

"Won't have none of it," old Sir Isaac said with an asthmatic wheeze. "Don't need it, he says. Odd thing. Never seen a young man so rigid and hidebound."

"Oh, I don't know . . ." Sir Milton pulled out his leather tobacco pouch and began to tamp his trademark pungent blend into a meerschaum pipe. "The boy isn't entirely hopeless." When the others looked at him with puzzlement, he clamped the stem of his pipe in his teeth and grinned. "Somewhere along the way he's picked up an understanding of what is meant by the term 'missionary position.'"

The Savoy Hotel
London
Friday morning

"WE SIMPLY CANNOT have our Sacred Virgin gallivanting about all over the city without proper escort," Lady Sophia Ashton declared.

"I am not your—" Celeste Ashton thought better of that particular objection to her grandmother's declaration, realizing where words traded on that subject would inevitably lead. Here and now—standing in the doorway to her hotel suite, only minutes away from addressing a joint meeting of two of the most prestigious scientific organizations in Britain—she didn't need a recitation of all the reasons she had been proclaimed "Most Revered and Sacred Virgin" of the Atlantean Society of Pevensey Bay.

Taking a quiet breath, she averted her gaze to keep it from settling too pointedly on the swaths of embroidered linen that hung from great golden brooches on her grandmother's shoulders, the gold circlet that wrapped around the old lady's sensible bun, the ample brown leather handbag she clutched fiercely before her, or the embroidered pink kid gloves she wore . . . relics of a former life and a former fashion sense. She didn't want to have to explain her grandmother's eccentric dress to a score of Britain's leading scientific minds, and she certainly didn't want her grandmother explaining it. *"Of course this is just my everyday wear. You should see my ceremonial chiton and himation . . ."* and *"No high priestess worth her salt would be caught dead in the street without proper gloves, you know . . ."* Celeste could just imagine the looks on their faces.

There was only one way to ensure that such a thing didn't happen.

"But I do have an escort, Nana." Celeste smiled warmly at Brigadier Penworthy Smythe, who waited just outside the door of the suite, resplendent in his old regimental uniform. She was grateful that the old fellow had taken to heart her comment that he looked so dashing in his uniform, it was a pity he didn't wear it any more. "I have the society's sergeant at arms with me. The brigadier is more than equal to the task of escorting me in and out of carriages and making introductions. So you see, you really *don't* have to go. I shall be perfectly fine."

Lady Sophia took in the brigadier's distinguished silver muttonchops and military bearing, and scowled . . . not yet willing to abandon what she saw as her grandmaternal duty.

"How can you possibly be fine? Look at you." The old lady waved a hand at Celeste's garments. "That stuffy wool skirt and jacket . . . starched pin-tucks and a Windsor tie . . . all cinched and boned and buttoned and hooked. Tsk. Near strangulation. You should appear in something free and flowing, something better befitting your exalted status as—"

"An author, a researcher, and an invited speaker," Celeste

declared firmly. "This is precisely what they would expect a serious scientific thinker to wear."

But there was a bit too much force in the way she smoothed the peplum of her blue tailored jacket and a tremor in her fingers as they flitted over her pristine starched collar and striped silk tie. In truth, she had no idea what the august gentlemen of science she would soon face might expect of her. To her knowledge, the Royal Oceanographic and Zoological societies had never before invited a woman to present a paper. The thought was more than a little intimidating.

It was also thrilling. This was the chance she had dreamed of for as long as she could remember: the opportunity to follow in her beloved grandfather's footsteps, the chance to be recognized and accepted as a person of letters, a scholarly mind, a researcher of merit. How could she have guessed when she bundled up her journals and sent them off to a London publisher—hoping for a bit of money to keep the household afloat—that they would be published straightaway and have the good fortune to attract the attention of renowned scientists?

"I still cannot see what's so important about looking scientific and having those old fogies knight your work," her grandmother continued stubbornly. "Your grandfather didn't give a fig what they said about *his* work."

"He did in the early days," Celeste reminded her. "While he was at Cambridge he presented frequently at the Archaeological Society. It was how Grandfather made his reputation. You know as well as I do, Nana, that 'presenting' is how one makes a reputation in—" She halted, noticing the smudges of fatigue visible under her grandmother's lively gray eyes.

With coaching delays, baggage mix-ups, and the confusion of arriving in London a day late, in the dead of night, and on a noisy train filled with Portsmouth sailors fresh from long months at sea, the trip from their home on the south shore had been nothing short of a disaster. Clearly, now was not the time to resume their ongoing debate over whether her future lay in scholarly pursuits or in more mystical ones.

"You look tired, Nana." She reached out to stroke her grandmother's velvety cheek. After a moment, Lady Sophia's determined posture softened.

"I suppose I am wearing a bit thin."

"That settles it." Celeste slipped an arm around her grandmother and turned her toward the bedroom and the comfortable four-poster waiting inside. "You'll have a lie-down. I'll deliver my talk. And we'll be back from the hall in time for tea in the hotel dining room. Mr. Cherrybottom says their tea cakes and sandwiches are the best in London." She smiled at the light that appeared in the old lady's eyes. Her grandmother had a weakness for cucumber sandwiches. "Then we'll have a lovely dinner this evening. I've promised Mr. Cherrybottom that you will tell him all about the society and your work."

Moments later, Celeste and the brigadier descended the sweeping marble stairs into the palatial lobby of the hotel, and paused near the bottom to scan the forest of palms and hanging ferns for a glimpse of her publisher. She finally spotted Edgar Cherrybottom through the bustle of elegantly clad patrons and of uniformed porters trundling baggage to and fro. He looked up, as if in response to her gaze, and a second later was hurtling across the lobby.

In the few hours since she had met him on the platform at Paddington Station, Celeste had formed the impression that Edgar Cherrybottom proceeded through all of life at a gallop. His movements were bold, his speech fast and bombastic, and his smile faintly cherubic. He was a good-natured typhoon that caught you up, spun you about, then set you down again in what seemed new territory.

"There you are!" he called out as he approached, beckoning them down the last few steps. "Thunderation, don't you look splendid, Miss Ashton!" A grin spread across his broad face as he took her extended hand. "If you'll excuse my saying so, the gentlemen of the royal societies are in for a double delight this afternoon: a tantalizing tickle to the intellect and a veritable feast for the eyes."

Before she could think how to respond to such bold flattery, he had placed her hand in the crook of his arm and was drawing her toward an out-of-the-way corner of the lobby. "My carriage is just outside, but first . . ." When they parted the small crowd of hotel guests that had collected, Celeste was surprised to see a photographer and a whole complement of photographic equipment arrayed before an ornately carved chair set on a draped platform. Her eyes widened.

"Didn't think you would mind . . . we've had so many requests for your likeness . . . newspapers, journals, popular sketch artists, and the like," Cherrybottom barreled on. "Great interest in you and your work, you know. Capital opportunity. So I said to myself: 'Edgar . . . why not just arrange for a few photographs on the way out the door?' Only a minute or two, and we'll be on our way." He flashed a contagious smile. "Wouldn't do to have you late for so momentous an occasion."

Photography. She was instantly intrigued. It had been years—more than a decade—since her grandparents had taken her to have her picture made at a Portsmouth photographic studio. The rigors of the process she had quite forgotten, but she had always relished the resulting image of herself in braids and a ruffled smock . . . barefoot . . . with an adventuresome glint in her eyes. The prospect of having another photograph to mark "so momentous an occasion" delighted her.

She was ushered into the chair, stripped of her hat, and posed with a quickness and purpose that belied the supposed spontaneity of the sitting. The photographer and Edgar Cherrybottom stood behind the camera, heads together, peering over and under the black camera drape, murmuring approval. Alert and focused, her curiosity alight, Celeste watched every motion and visually examined every bit of equipment, framing a score of questions to ask.

The brightness of the first flash and the smell of burning powder caught her by surprise, but she had no time to ask about them. Cherrybottom quickly suggested she lean toward one arm of the ornate chair and place both hands on its cool, polished surface.

It registered in her mind that the arms of the chair were made in the shape of leaping dolphins and she traced the dark, thick carvings with surprised pleasure . . . noting that the images were unusually authentic. As she looked up, the powder flashed again, blinding her momentarily. She squeezed her eyes shut, trying to recover, and the photographer bolted forward and removed some of the pins from her hair.

That unexpected intimacy, the fellow's abrupt withdrawal, and the slide of her hair down her neck so surprised her that she didn't know quite how to react. Turning her face aside and bending slightly, she raised one arm to retuck her hair. Again, the powder flashed.

"Wonderful!" Edgar Cherrybottom strode forward to offer her assistance down from her perch. "Nothing short of perfection, eh, Brigadier?"

The old soldier harumphed about "newfangled nonsense" and inserted himself determinedly between Cherrybottom and Celeste.

Nonplussed, the garrulous publisher led them through the crowd of curious hotel guests, to the front doors and the enclosed carriage waiting beyond. They were three blocks away before Celeste reclaimed her senses enough to repin her hat and once again concentrate on her mission.

"Oh, my bag—my charts and equipment!" she said, looking frantically over her shoulder.

"In the carriage boot," Mr. Cherrybottom assured her, looking very pleased as he balanced both palms on the head of an ornate walking stick. "I had my driver bring them out while you were being photographed. You needn't worry about a thing, my dear. You need only tell your story, as you did in the book, and then respond to a few questions.

They'll be charmed, I'm certain, just as the rest of London has been."

"The rest of London?" She frowned. She hadn't a clue what Mr. Cherrybottom was talking about.

The publisher sat forward. "I was saving this to announce at dinner, but . . . we've passed sales of twenty thousand copies and there's no end in sight. Just yesterday, I struck an agreement with French and German publishers to issue translated editions. Scarcely a day goes by without an article in a newspaper somewhere, remarking on the 'dolphin craze' initiated by your book. You're a smashing success, Miss Ashton."

The news stunned her. A dolphin craze. Twenty thousand copies. Why, if she had sold *one* thousand copies, she would have been delighted. Imagine . . . *twenty thousand* people reading about her dolphins, learning about the ocean and its marvelous creatures, discovering some of the joy she had felt at being permitted a glimpse into the mysteries of the deep. That was her hope, her dream . . . her mission in life . . . to research the sea and somehow awaken people to the wonders it held. She thought with awe of thousands of people sitting at night by their lamps and hearths, reading about Prospero and Ariel and the others . . . imagining themselves gliding through the sea-green waters with her . . . their eyes and hearts opening to the beauty and majesty of the sea . . .

It took a moment for her to realize that twenty thousand copies also meant larger-than-expected revenues. *Money.* Her eyes widened. She would have enough money to replace the entire roof and pay some long-overdue grocer's and butcher's bills. She might even have enough money to take Nana back to the Azores, where they had lived when her grandfather was doing archaeological work . . . where she had first met dolphins! Her mind began to race and her heart began to pound. Why, she might have enough money to buy a larger boat . . . to build better equipment to use under water—

"Bloody Duke of Wellington!" The sound of the brigadier swearing by his favorite military hero interrupted her spiraling expectations. She looked up and discovered the carriage was slowing and the old general was staring out the window in alarm. Sliding across the seat, she peered out over the brigadier's shoulder, while Cherrybottom raised the shade on the window across the way. The publisher's face lit with a broad smile.

Swarming toward the coach was a noisy throng of men in bowler hats and rough woolen coats. Most had pencils stuck in their hatbands or tucked behind their ears; a few bore sketchpads. The instant the coach stopped they clambered onto the wheel spokes and carriage steps and strained to peer through the windows, calling out questions.

Cherrybottom seemed not the least bit distressed. Smiling, he straightened his tie and readied his high-crowned hat for donning as he left the carriage.

"Who are these cheeky blighters?" the brigadier demanded indignantly.

"I sent word to one or two news writers that Miss Ashton would be arriving by this entrance," Cherrybottom told him, with a glance in her direction. "I expect word got around. They all want a glimpse of the Lady Mermaid."

"Lady Mermaid?" She scowled. "Who on earth is the 'Lady Mermaid'?"

Cherrybottom thrust open the door, knocking one intrepid fellow from his perch on the carriage steps. As he exited, he cast a grin and two words over his shoulder.

"You are!"

Two

CELESTE EMERGED FROM the carriage into the brigadier's arms and a storm of voices. Here and there in the pushing, jostling crowd, someone waved a copy of a newspaper bearing a drawing of a dolphin and a grotesque figure that seemed to be part fish, part human. As Mr. Cherrybottom and the brigadier made a way for her through the crowd, she tussled with the unfamiliar bulk of the skirts she wore and caught snatches of what they were saying:

Could she really breathe underwater like a fish? Where did the dolphins take her? How did she say "I love you" in dolphinese? And—surely she hadn't heard right—a request that she show them her "tail"!

It was unsettling to say the least, and her first coherent thought, once they were safely inside the Gothic dignity of the Athenaeum Hall, was that she was glad that Nana hadn't had to run that awful gauntlet with them. Her second was bewilderment that those pushy people seemed to think her work was somehow linked to a bizarre mythological sea creature. And her third was that Mr. Cherrybottom not only seemed to know of that unfortunate connection, he seemed dashed pleased about it. Clearly, there was more here than met the eye.

But she had no chance to quiz the publisher, for at that

moment a pair of massive doors at the center of the lobby opened and a reedy older fellow in a dark suit came hurrying out, headed straight for them.

"Miss Ashton?" His pasty face colored with relief at the sight of her. "I was so concerned that you wouldn't be able to get through that hideous mess outside. Insufferable, these news writers . . . we've had to evict a number of them from the hall already this afternoon. So pleased you've gotten through."

"Sir Hillary Hockstetter, Miss Ashton." Mr. Cherrybottom introduced the fellow. "General secretary of the Royal Oceanographic Society."

The fellow took her extended hand with a harried nod, then used it to usher her toward the doors from which he had just emerged. "We're not quite assembled, as yet. This was our usual dinner meeting and what with hosting those zoological fellows"—he flicked a nervous glance toward the staircase across the lobby, then overhead—"most of our members and guests are still in the dining room, upstairs. If you will just follow me."

The oak-paneled lecture hall was nothing short of cavernous. Ornately carved oak arches supported a high, vaulted ceiling that enclosed space for well over three hundred seats. Arched windows with accents of stained glass and oak-paneled walls lent a cathedral-like air to the place. Ranks of wooden chairs filled virtually every inch of floor space, all facing a stage draped in dignified gray velvet on the far end of the room. On that stage—awaiting her arrival—were several chairs, a table, an easel, and a speaker's podium. Celeste's knees weakened at the sight of it. She followed numbly as the secretary seated her escorts near the back, then led her down a side aisle and up onto the stage.

Did they truly expect to fill all of those chairs? She had spoken numerous times before the fledgling Pevensey Bay Conservancy Society and occasionally before her grandmother's Atlantean Society. It hadn't occurred to her that a royal "scientific" society would be comprised of consider-

ably more than just a score or two of individuals. With growing uneasiness, she began to hang her charts and to arrange
her equipment on the table for display.

After a few moments a rumble rose at the back of the hall
and grew steadily louder. She took refuge in her seat just as
the doors flew open and in rushed a garrulous tide of dark-
clad, Windsor-tie-wearing humanity. The gentlemen of science. The distinguished fellows of the royal societies.

Her mouth went dry. There were literally *hundreds* of
them.

Her first impulse was to run for her life. Her second was
to close her eyes and fight the first impulse. And her third—
the one that always came to her rescue—was the urge to
seize what had caused her to quail, examine it, experience it,
and ultimately make it yield up some sort of benefit. Knowledge, confidence, joy, adventure . . . her grandfather had
taught her there were treasures waiting beyond the forbidding barriers of the unknown. And if there was anything
Celeste Ashton loved, it was an adventure with a promise of
treasure.

Grappling with the blend of tension and excitement inside her, she watched the royal societies streaming into the
hall, and was stunned to realize that they were all men. A
veritable tidal wave of men. No, she told herself, these were
scientists—real scientists. They shared the same love of learning, pursued the same goal she did . . . truth. They
weren't so different from her.

But as they shook hands and slapped shoulders and roared
greetings at one another, she was struck by the uniformity of
their dress—black or charcoal suits, starched collars, and silk
ties denoting old school affiliations—and by the preponder-
ance of silver or missing hair among them. In fact, there was
only one full head of dark hair in the first several rows of the
audience. Her eyes lingered on that head for a moment,
registering that it was higher than the others, then moved
on. Up from her assembling audience wafted a mélange of
scent: stale tobacco, recently imbibed port, a peculiar tart,

sweatlike musk, and the occasional whiff of mentholatum. Foreign sounds. Foreign smells.

Her stomach tightened. These might be fellow scientists, but they were also unequivocally men. And just now she had never felt more aware of the fact that she was a woman. The only woman in the room.

Most of the seats were filled by the time the society secretary called the meeting to order. When he welcomed as guests both the fellows of the Royal Zoological Society and their esteemed speaker, every motion and every utterance in the hall stilled.

Celeste took the podium, clutching her notes and a copy of her book, and stared—cotton-mouthed—at several hundred serious male faces. The scattered and desultory applause caused a disconcerting thud in her chest. She sipped from the glass of water on the stand.

"I am honored, indeed, to be asked to address this meeting of two distinguished royal societies. I bring to you a body of observations on the nature and habits of bottlenose dolphins, made over a number of years and in two distinctly different climates and locations."

She could have sworn she heard someone mutter: "A number of years? She's scarcely been alive that long."

Rattled, she glanced at her notes, pretending not to have heard. "Perhaps it would be helpful if I detailed something of how I came to learn about aquatic life. From a very early age, I accompanied my grandfather, Sir Martin Ashton, to the locations of his archaeological fieldwork in the Azores and Canary Islands. While there, I was required to maintain a strenuous daily regimen of studies, but I still frequently found myself with too much time on my hands."

More mutters. "I'll say" and " 'At's what comes of permissiveness with young females" seemed to come from everywhere and nowhere in particular.

"Our cook was a wonderful Portuguese woman, who took me to the markets with her and introduced me to her brother, a local fisherman. At first, he allowed me to watch him and his crew sort their catch and answered my questions. After a while, he permitted me to help them do the sorting. Before long, I was allowed to accompany them on short fishing trips. It was from that generous and knowledgeable fisherman that I learned the basics of sailing and navigation, the practice of diving, and something about the habits of common commercial fishes. However, when I reached the age of twelve years, I was dry-docked by my grandmother."

"About time," and "What was the silly woman thinking—letting the child run wild like that?"

Irritation shot up her spine, straightening it.

"But by that time"—she raised her voice a determined notch—"I knew enough to carry on my investigations from the beaches near the house we had rented. With my grandfather's advice and support, I began to observe and catalogue the habits of crabs, mussels, starfish, and the numerous fishes in the bay. It was there that I encountered my first dolphin."

There was a flurry in the third row, and she poured her concentration into her notes and tried to ignore it. It would not, however, be ignored. She had spoken no more than another sentence, when she was interrupted by determined throat clearing. She looked up to find a thickly upholstered older gentleman standing with his arms crossed and his several chins tucked in disapproval.

"Yes?" she said, affecting a graciousness she little felt.

"I believe that I speak for the majority of the members when I say that we are all quite capable of reading of your 'unique' personal history for ourselves. What we are truly interested in, young woman, is sorting out just what truth may be gleaned from these published 'observations' of yours."

The secretary's gasp—"Most irregular"—might have been an echo of the one inside her head.

"I assure you, sir, there will be time for questions," she responded.

"I should say there will be." A second silver-haired fellow

rose behind the first, tugging down his vest and glancing at the faces about him as if to garner support for his actions. "Answer me this, young woman: do you stand before this august gathering of scientists and assert that you personally have been carried by dolphins to their home, far under the sea?"

"I do not, sir," she said, surprised by both the question and the tone of accusation. "Nor did I say so in my published observations. All of my dealings with dolphins have taken place in coastal waters of twenty- to thirty-foot depths. I have never stated, nor would I support the notion, that dolphins have a common 'home' somewhere beneath the sea. The entire sea is the dolphin's home."

A third gentleman rose, farther back in the audience. "You've made a great deal of the lascivious and wanton nature of these creatures. As a young woman . . . how can you be certain that the 'behaviors' you supposedly observed between these dolphins were indeed 'matings'?" There was an eruption of murmurs and half-audible exclamations, which seemed to spur the questioner on. "For that matter . . . how were you able to determine the gender of these individual dolphins? Is it not perfectly possible that you've mistaken other behaviors for courtship and mating? Dominance displays, perhaps . . ."

Her face flamed in spite of her. All around the hall, the gentlemen scientists were nodding and muttering agreement. Until that moment, it hadn't occurred to her that her sex or age might have any bearing on the acceptance of her work. She couldn't have imagined that true men of science would consider her painstaking observations and reporting of dolphin behaviors to be somehow improper or indel—

Indelicate? The heat in her face ignited her pride. They implied she *shouldn't* know the very rudiments of reproductive behavior, simply because she was a young woman?

"I am not at all mistaken," she said, perceiving at last the magnitude of the skepticism she faced. "I am fully acquainted with dolphin physiology, sir, including the reproductive parts. While it is true that determining the gender of a dolphin is not easy, time and patient observation invariably remove all doubt."

The questioner's sputter of indignation led yet another wave of negative commentary.

"Positively indecent . . . immoral . . ."

". . . should be ashamed to admit such in public!"

Suddenly, society members were popping up all over the lecture hall, calling out questions in challenging tones.

"How could you possibly stay under the water long enough to see how dolphins and fish behaved?"

"Why would a decent woman voluntarily subject herself to witnessing such depraved and revolting behavior in animals?"

"If dolphins did have a language, pray, what would the dimwitted creatures have to talk about?"

"Have you no discernment whatsoever . . . investing these creatures with silly, female notions of romance, and calling it science?"

For every question there were resounding cries of "Hear! Hear!" and a half-dozen quips and comments. Members began heated discussions among themselves, leaving their seats and spilling into the aisles to debate their points. Order and civility were degenerating at an alarming rate. From the back, she could have sworn she heard a slurred: "Hey, m-mermaid—ssshow us yer tail!"

In the midst of the confusion, Sir Hillary appeared at her side, calling futilely for order and civil attendance. But the members' attention shifted instead to someone sitting in the third row . . . a younger man . . . the dark head she had seen towering above the silver ones. Members of both societies were calling on the fellow, urging him to join—or lead—the questioning.

"Here, Thorne, do something! This is *your* bailiwick—"

At length, he rose, tugged his vest into place, and glanced about him with steely disapproval.

"Gentlemen, please," the man called in deep tones that

had the effect of oil on troubled waters. Quiet spread outward from him like ripples in a pond, until the hall was virtually silent. He turned to the stage with a muscle flexing visibly in his lean jaw.

"Miss Ashton, may I apologize for what may appear to be rudeness on the part of our members? The familiarity of long acquaintance and the dogged pursuit of truth sometimes lead us to overstep the bounds of general decorum."

She stared at the tall, dark-haired order-bringer, uncertain whether to be irritated or grateful that he had just taken over her lecture. There were no clues to his intentions in his tall, angular frame, his gentlemanly garments, or his cleanly carved features. She took a deep breath and made herself look away.

"I believe I . . . understand."

Looking around the lecture hall, she was indeed beginning to understand. She had considered their invitation to speak as an honor, and seen it as a coveted offer of membership in the societies. But, in fact, she had not been summoned here to *join;* she had been summoned here to *account.* They had issued her an invitation to an inquisition . . . for the grave offense of publishing research without the blessing of the holy orders of science: the royal societies.

"Perhaps if I restated a few of the questions I have heard put forward just now," he said, glancing at the members seated around him, "it would preserve order and make for a more productive exchange."

She nodded, taking note of the way the others seemed to relax back into their chairs, now that he had taken up their cause. A bad sign, she decided. Despite his handsome smile and mannerliness, her instincts warned that here was no ally. He produced a card from the inner pocket of his coat, studied it for a moment, then looked up with a pleased expression.

"Your writings, miss, raise numerous questions for us scientists. Your methodology, for instance. You state that most of your observations have been made while you were in the water with the creatures, themselves." As he spoke, he made his way to the end of the row, where the others in the aisle made way for him to approach the front of the stage.

"That is true," she said, noting uneasily the way the others parted for him.

"If I recall correctly, you stated that you sail or row out into the bay waters, rap out a signal on the hull of your boat, and the dolphin comes to greet you. You then slip into the water with the creature—or creatures, if he has brought his family group—hold your breath, and dive under the water to observe them."

"That is precisely what happens. Though I must say, it is a routine perfected by extreme patience and long experience. Years, in fact."

"Just so." He strolled closer, watching her reactions and measuring her resourcefulness as keenly as she did his. "You further state that some of the male dolphins in your group, including the one you have labeled 'Prospero,' are ten to twelve feet in length and weigh three to four hundred pounds." He paused just to one side of the podium, where he had a clear view of her tailored form. "And how much do *you* weigh, Miss Ashton?"

"I beg your pardon?"

"It is a pertinent question, I believe. You expect us to believe that you, who must weigh—what?—a hundred pounds, dripping wet—"

"One hundred twenty at least," she declared furiously.

"Truly. And a formidable one hundred twenty it is." He shared an indulgent smile with his fellow members, who muttered derisively. "Nevertheless, you must admit to being greatly outsized by even one of these creatures, much less an entire family of them." He folded his arms and leaned back on one leg, changing directions yet again. "What is the average temperature of the ocean in the vicinity of Pevensey Bay, Miss Ashton?"

"In summer . . . often sixty-five degrees," she answered, her mind racing.

"And in winter, at least twenty degrees colder," he asserted.

"I do not dive in winter, sir. Don't be preposterous."

"Yes, please. Let us *not* be preposterous, Miss Ashton." His tone sharpened, though he maintained his casual posture. "You expect us to believe you not only call these creatures at will, but that you voluntarily . . . single-handedly . . . climb into frigid water with any number of these monstrous large beasts, and that you swim underwater for hours on end to observe them?" He straightened, glancing at the others as he readied his thrust. "That is a great deal indeed to believe on the word of a young woman who has no scientific training and no formal academic background."

His words struck hard and sank deep. So that was it. She was young and female and intolerably presumptuous to attempt to share her learning and experiences with the world when she hadn't the proper credentials.

"It is true that I have had no formal academic training. Precious few of my gender have; women are not permitted the luxuries of stipends, tutors, and lectures and examinations at Oxford and Cambridge. But it is patently untrue that I have no scientific training. I studied and worked with my grandfather for years; learning the tenets of reason and logic, developing theoretical approaches, observing and recording." She stepped out from behind the podium, facing him, facing them all for the sake of what she knew to be the truth.

"There is much learning, sir, to be had *outside* the hallowed, ivy-covered walls of a university. Experience is a most excellent tutor."

She saw him stiffen as her words found a mark in him. But a moment later, all trace of that fleeting reaction was gone.

"Very well, Miss Ashton, let us proceed and see what your particular brand of science has produced." His words were now tightly clipped, tailored for maximum impact.

"You observe under-water, do you not? Just how do you *see* all of these marvels several yards beneath the murky surface?"

"Firstly, ocean water is not 'murky.' Anyone who has spent time at the seaside knows that." She moved to the table and picked up a pair of goggles. "Secondly, I wear these. They are known in sundry forms to divers on various continents. I have reconstructed these particular goggles to improve the seal that keeps out water." She held up the handmade leather contraption so all could see the glass lenses, then held them out to him. He headed for the steps and in several athletic bounds was on the stage with her, inspecting the gear firsthand.

She took the goggles back to demonstrate the fit over her eyes. He bent down to investigate, giving a tug with one long finger and finding the apparatus secure against her face. He scowled.

"Very well, it might work. But several obstacles still remain. Air, for instance. How could you possibly stay under the water long enough to have seen all that you report?"

She looked up at him through fiercely narrowed eyes.

"I hold my breath."

"Indeed? Just how long can you hold your breath, Miss Ashton?"

"Minutes at a time."

"Oh?" His eyebrows rose. "And what proof do you have?"

"Proof? What proof do you need?" she demanded, her hands curling into fists at her sides. "Shall I stick my head in a bucket for you?"

Laughter skittered through their audience, only to die when he shot them a censuring look. "Perhaps we could arrange an impromptu test of your remarkable breathing ability, Miss Ashton. I propose that you hold your breath—right here, right now—and we will time you."

"Don't be ridiculous," she said, feeling crowded by his height and intensity. He stood head and shoulders above her and obviously knew how to use his size to advantage in a confrontation.

"It is anything *but* ridiculous," he declared. "It would be a demonstration of the repeatability of a phenomenon. Repetition of results is one of the key tests of scientific truth, is it not?"

"It would not be a true trial," she insisted, but loath to mention why. His silence and smug look combined with derogatory comments from the audience to prod it from her. "I am wearing a 'dress improver,' " she said through clenched teeth, "which restricts my breathing."

"Oh. Well." He slid his gaze down to her waist, allowing it to linger there for a second too long. When she glared at him, he smiled. "We can adjust for that by giving you . . . say . . . ten seconds?"

Before she could protest, he called for a mirror to detect stray breath. None could be found on such short notice, so, undaunted, he volunteered to hold a strip of paper beneath her nose to detect any intake of air. The secretary, Sir Hillary, was drafted as a timekeeper and a moment later she was forced to purge her lungs, strain her corset to take in as much air as possible, and then hold it.

Her inquisitor leaned close, holding that fragile strip of paper, watching for the slightest flutter in it. And as she struggled to find the calm center into which she always retreated while diving, she began to feel the heat radiating from him . . . the warmth of his face near her own . . . the energy coming from his broad shoulders. And she saw his eyes, mere inches from hers, beginning to wander over her face. Was he purposely trying to distract her? Her quickening pulse said that if he was, his tactic was working. To combat it, she searched desperately for someplace to fasten her vision, something to concentrate on. Unfortunately, the closest available thing was *him*.

Green eyes, she realized, with mild surprise. Blue-green, really. The color of sunlight streaming into the sea on a midsummer day. His skin was firm and lightly tanned . . .

stretched taut over a broad forehead, high cheekbones, and a prominent, slightly aquiline nose. Her gaze drifted downward to his mouth . . . full, velvety looking, with a prominent dip in the center of his upper lip that made his mouth into an intriguing bow. There were crinkle lines at the corners of his eyes and a beard shadow was forming along the edge of his cheek.

She found herself licking her lip . . . lost in the bold angles and intriguing textures of his very male face . . . straining for control and oblivious to the fact that half of the audience was on its feet and moving toward the stage. She had never observed a man this close for this long—well, besides her grandfather and the brigadier. A man. A handsome man. His hair was a dark brown, not black, she thought desperately. And as her chest began to hurt, she fastened her gaze on his eyes and held on with everything in her. This was for science. This was for her dolphins. This was to teach those sea-green eyes a lesson . . .

The ache in her chest gradually crowded everything but him and his eyes from her consciousness. Finally, when she felt the dimming at the edges of her vision, which spelled real danger, she blew out that breath and then gasped wildly. The fresh air was so intoxicating that she staggered.

A wave of astonishment greeted the news that she had held her breath for a full three minutes. All she could think was that it seemed an eternity. Waving off an offer of smelling salts and the suggestion that she "have a lie-down," she collected her composure and turned again to her inquisitor.

"Are you now satisfied that I am capable of holding my breath during underwater activity?" she demanded, still breathing hard.

"Very well. We must give you that." He stepped back, his countenance dark. "But there is still the matter of swimming." His gaze slid over her in blunt assessment. "How could a young woman of such delicate frame and constitution possibly keep up with such large creatures in their own element?"

"I swim exceedingly well," she declared hotly. "And when I must dive or cover distance quickly, I grab onto a dorsal fin and ride along. Dolphins are quite accommodating in that regard."

Argument broke out throughout the hall on the plausibility of "riding along" on a dolphin. But the intensity of the debate meant that at least some of her audience were ready to give her words credence. The faces of those clustered around the stage and those standing on chairs to see over them were flushed, animated, eager. Somewhere between answering questions and holding her breath, she had made some of them believe her observations were possible.

"Very well." Her inquisitor tugged down his vest. "Given that you could actually perform such observations in the sea . . . we must turn to the substance of these 'investigations.' You maintain that these dolphins come to your signal . . . like dogs to their master."

"I am hardly their master, sir, but they do come. Sound carries well under water, and they are very swift."

"As quick as you are with your answers?" His smile owed nothing to good humor. "You have studied this particular group of dolphins for some time now and have even given them names. How is it, Miss Ashton, that you can tell one dolphin from another under-water?"

"Each dolphin has its own identifying characteristics. Some are darker, some lighter; some are thinner, some fatter"—she gestured to their audience—"just as humans come in varying sizes and shapes. In addition, some bear rake marks from other dolphins or scars from encounters with predators. And, of course, each dolphin has its own individual character. Some are bold and curious, some are too shy to approach humans, some are mischievous, some are annoying . . . just like *certain* humans." Her scowl left no doubt as to just which human she had in mind.

"Ah-ha!" He stepped closer, towering over her, forcing her to bend her head back in order to continue meeting his gaze. "Therein lies one of the prime flaws in your work

. . . this annoying tendency to attribute human qualities to these creatures. You would have us believe that these creatures are little more than humans in costume . . . thinking, playing, helping each other, *courting* one another—" He straightened with a look so smug her palm itched to smack it. "You present your work in such cloying, anthropomorphic prose that it is impossible to separate reality from your romantic imaginings."

"My romantic—" The words stuck halfway out, burning her throat.

"Although calling it 'romantic' might be putting too polite a face on it," he muttered, then once again raised his voice so all could hear. "Science is the collection of facts in the revelation of truth, Miss Ashton. Repeatable, verifiable facts. Your work reads more like daydreams. And daydreams—especially a *mermaid*'s daydreams—are not subject to scientific verification."

Mermaid's daydreams. His words echoed about the hall like the sound of a gavel falling . . . as if she had just been found guilty and sentenced to a life outside the hallowed halls of science.

Snatches of the news writers' questions as they arrived and Edgar Cherrybottom's declaration that she was the Lady Mermaid came rushing back to her. Her grand inquisitor knew about the unfortunate title that had been bestowed on her in the common press. She looked at the troubled and expectant faces around her. They all did, and it fed their outrage that a young woman aspired to some sort of intellectual accomplishment, to a scientific endeavor. The connection went beyond just a sketch in a penny newspaper; it had gone so far as to prejudice them against her work and even now was threatening everything she hoped to do with her life.

For a moment she wavered, feeling beset and uncertain. How did she fight something as amorphous as an idea of what a young woman should or shouldn't do, or a crude, ridiculous image printed in a newspaper?

As she shrank from the horror and humiliation of it, she again ran headlong into the core of her grandfather's determined teachings. "Fear is a coward," he had always said. "Take it by the tail and it will flee for its life, every time." Slowly, she squared her shoulders. There might not be much she could do about the wretched newspapers, but she was not about to go meekly into scholarly exile because of their lies. She seized the outer layers of her fashionable skirts and yanked them aside as she advanced on him.

"Who are you to dismiss my work because of the scratching of news writers and the dribbles from cartoonists' pens?" She was virtually nose to nose with him before he finally yielded and backed a step. "My observations *can* be verified." She poked his chest furiously with one finger. "And I challenge you, sir, to be the one to verify them!"

Without time to consider fully the idea forming in her head, she was at the mercy of her instincts. And just now her instincts were telling her that there was only one way to repair the damage to her scholarly reputation: she had to prove to the royal societies' leading skeptic that her work was genuine and make him publicly confirm her findings.

"What? Me?" He gave a twist of a smile that said what he thought of her challenge. "Don't be absurd. It is impossible to verify *anecdotal* evidence."

"Ahhh!" She inched closer and he backed another step. "But you can see the dolphins with your own eyes . . . watch me interact with them . . . swim with them yourself. As you said, the ability of another researcher to repeat results is the keystone of good science. *You* can repeat my experiences with the dolphins yourself and write about them. That will be all the verification I need."

A storm of controversy broke around them. Arguments pitched back and forth, some vehemently for and some furiously against her proposal. But the gentlemen scientists soon came to see that there was no other way to settle the matter. Gradually they registered support for the idea; advising, urging, and then insisting that he accept the challenge of

ferreting out the truth about the "mermaid" and her dolphins, once and for all. Celeste noted with rising spirits that
the more they insisted, the more unsettled her inquisitor
looked.

"I cannot possibly take the time, not with the new term
mere weeks away." He glanced around at the sea of faces
ringing the stage and clogging the nearby steps. "Someone
else will surely have to—"

"Nonsense!" a voice called from the rear. He looked gen-
uinely startled, pivoted, and faced a genteel, bespectacled
gentleman making his way to the edge of the stage. "You
needn't worry about the coming term, my boy. Sir Mercer
can take your lectures and I shall be pleased to meet your
tutorials."

Titus Thorne stared in ill-cloaked dismay as the head of
his college paused at the apron of the stage, beaming cooperation and largesse. He had no idea that Sir Parthenay had
intended to come to London for this meeting. And what was
the old boy doing—insisting that he get involved even
deeper in this mermaid nonsense? Before he could think of a
rebuttal—

"Excellent," she said with a vengeful glint in her eye.
"Then there are no impediments to your spending time at
my home, learning about dolphins and confirming my findings. A fortnight should do."

He was caught. Like a flounder in a dragnet.

"Furthermore, I think it should be agreed that when you
have verified my work," she continued, "you will publish a
detailed confirmation in the Oceanographic Society's quar-
terly journal."

"Oh, absolutely," Sir Hillary declared, nodding eagerly.

"Absolutely *not!*" Titus erupted, then had to scramble for
a plausible reason for his objection. "The society's journal is
for the publication of original research, not verification of
results already announced elsewhere."

"I could publish them as an addendum to Miss Ashton's
book!" When they turned to see who had spoken, a ruddy-

faced Edgar Cherrybottom was pushing his way through the crowd on the steps. "I am Miss Ashton's publisher—I would welcome the chance to present the public with a scholarly review and endorsement of her work."

"Capital!" Sir Parthenay put his stamp of approval on the scheme.

"That assumes there is anything to review and verify." Titus turned a scathing look on Sir Parthenay, who merely rocked up and down on his toes, looking rather pleased at the turn of events.

"Oh, I can promise, you'll have plenty to write about, Professor . . . You have the advantage of me, sir," Miss Ashton declared, with a look in her eyes that warned it would be the last time such a thing would happen. "My credibility as a researcher has just been placed in your hands, and I do not even know your name, much less your qualifications for judging my work."

"Oh— Thorne." Sir Hillary hurriedly stepped in to make the introduction. "Professor Titus Thorne. The chair in ichthyology at Cardinal College, Oxford."

Her eyes glinted briefly, then she turned aside and began to collect her equipment. "Then you must be well acquainted with the sea. Do bring something to swim in, Professor Thorne."

SHE MANAGED TO WAIT until they were outside the hall, waiting for the carriage in the warmth of the early afternoon sun, before turning on Mr. Cherrybottom with fire in her eye.

"The Lady Mermaid? Where on earth did they get such a ridiculous notion about me?" But her pointed glare said she had already guessed where the blame should lie. Cherrybottom's fleshy face reddened and he fumbled with his watch.

"I haven't the faintest . . . except . . . there was some talk of using a mermaid instead of a dolphin on the cover of the book." He pocketed his timepiece and resettled his hat on his head. "Well, however it came about, it has generated a great deal of interest in your book." His trademark grin reappeared. "I say, Miss Ashton, outstanding performance in there. Went toe to toe with that professor chap, and not even a blink. Most impressive. Bound to get a full column in the *Times*."

Celeste was stunned, totally at a loss for words.

"Now we have a marvelous excuse for another whole edition," he rattled on as he waved to a cab waiting down the street. "People who bought and read the first book will want to see what the controversy is about—and to read the professor's confirmation of your work." His eyes glowed as they darted over unseen vistas of profitability. "Excellent. Just excellent."

The clearing of a throat behind Cherrybottom caused the publisher to turn abruptly. There stood a man of moderate height, dressed in an exquisite charcoal coat and pinstripe trousers and a silk top hat that glinted in the sun. He spoke to the publisher but his gaze was fastened on Celeste. And such a gaze . . . blue as the Aegean and quite as warm, set in a face that was as handsome as it was manly.

"I do not wish to intrude," the man said with a decided drawl. "But I was hoping, Mr. Cherrybottom, that I might persuade you to make good on your promise to introduce me to the celebrated Miss Ashton."

"Ah, Mr. Bentley." Cherrybottom beamed and offered his hand to the fellow. "Miss Ashton, may I present a new acquaintance, a gentleman I met while waiting for your lecture to begin. An American, from Virginia, and a gentleman of great scientific curiosity. Mr. P. T. Bentley."

"At your service, miss." He bowed with a hint of extravagance. "And may I say, my admiration of your work is now fully equaled by my admiration for your beauty and courage. I am enthralled by the thought of a living mermaid, swimming with those noble and fascinating creatures of the sea."

She scarcely knew how to respond. Total strangers now accosted her on the street expecting to see her garbed in fins and scales! "Th-thank you." Unsettled by the way every-thing seemed to be spiraling out of her control, she retreated to the familiar support of the brigadier's arm and turned a narrow look on her publisher. "I would greatly appreciate it if you would change our tickets so that we may return home on tomorrow's train, Mr. Cherrybottom. Now, if you don't mind, we really must get back to the hotel . . . before my *fins* dry out."

"'ATA BOY, THORNY!"

"Good work! Got her right where we want her, eh?"

"She'll be quakin' in her scales, a'fore you're through with her."

Titus strode out of the Athenaeum Lecture Hall on a tide of congratulatory fustian and male bombast. To hear his esteemed colleagues tell it, he had just been tapped for the greatest honor since the Almighty charged King Arthur with the quest for the Holy—

"There you are!" Sir Parthenay caught up and fell into step beside him as he strode along Cromwell Road. "Well done, my boy."

"You must be joking," Titus growled.

"Not at all. Excellent opportunity here. Haven't seen such interest in marine science since that Verne fellow published that story *Twenty Million Leagues*—"

"Twenty *thousand*," Titus grumbled. "Submarine boats and rampaging giant squid. Had everyone terrified to stick a toe into the water for fear of being strangulated by a sea monster."

"Ah, yes." Sir Parthenay shook his head fondly. "Interesting stuff." Then he came back to the matter at hand. "Just think. You'll be away from the rut of routine . . . sleeping in the fine sea air . . . not to mention swimming with a very fetching 'mermaid.' You know, of course, that Sir Isaac will be green with envy." When Titus stopped in his tracks, glowering, Sir Parthenay chuckled. Clapping one hand on the younger man's shoulder, he hailed a cab with the other. "I'm off to the train station. Have to be back for a meeting, first thing in the morning, or I'd stay over and have dinner with you." As he swung up into the carriage, he grinned. "Can't wait to hear your report."

Titus was left standing on the corner of Cromwell and Gloucester roads, staring after the cab, wondering how in hell he had gotten himself into this mess.

He had come to this wretched "mermaid" meeting with the noblest of intentions: confronting and discrediting a scientific sleight-of-hand artist, a fraud in a tawdry fish tail. He had read her preposterous book and prepared to confront her with its obvious flaws. But from the moment he walked in the door nothing had gone quite as he had anticipated.

He had expected the old boys in the royal societies to fawn, toady, and welcome Celeste Ashton with open arms. They didn't. He had expected a lively, perhaps even heated, discourse on the scandalous claims and observations made in her book. There wasn't one. He had planned to lead the attack on her ridiculous notions. He found himself calling a halt to it instead.

His disillusionment had begun at dinner, where he heard exaggerated recountings of passages from her book . . . stories bearing no semblance to anything she had written . . . which he found exceedingly strange, since what she *had* written was quite sensational enough. It soon became apparent that only one in ten had ever set eyes on her work, but nine out of ten considered themselves experts on it. Then as the port was passed around for a third time, there was ribald speculation about the young woman herself— conjecture on her worldliness and experience—and on the best way to "clean and scale" a mermaid.

By the time they filed into the auditorium, the "gentlemen of science" were in anything but a gentlemanly mood. Some of the old cods at the back were downright pie-eyed. Their subsequent disrespect and crude, ill-informed questions were nothing short of an embarrassment to the scientific community.

His irritation with his fellow members' behavior, however, was equaled by his dismay at the unexpected nature of Miss Ashton herself. In the short time he had studied this "mermaid problem," he had grown accustomed to picturing her in terms of the sketches in the newspapers . . . as a leering spinster, a fish-tailed siren of the sea, a voluptuous fishwife, or a bluestocking with webbed feet and the face of a trout.

But this Miss Ashton didn't look the slightest bit like a cartoon Lorelei or a virago with gills. He closed his eyes and there she was again . . . just inches from his face . . . blond and blue-eyed . . . curvaceous . . . well-spoken . . . intrepid beyond imagining. And there he was, again, staring at her . . . embarrassingly aware of every part of his body in proximity to every part of hers . . . feeling a peculiar warming in his skin and an alarming itch crawling up his inner thighs.

Just thinking about it, he was starting to feel warm and slightly irritable.

Halting in his tracks, he glanced desperately around and found a cab. Settling back in the worn leather seat, he gripped his knees and took several deep, calming breaths. Never mind how he'd got into this mess—how the hell was he going to get out of it? What was he going to do, stuck for God knew how long—perhaps a whole fortnight—in the seaside lair of the determined and potentially treacherous Miss Ashton?

He took several deep breaths and soon felt calm and reason returning.

He was going to prove her wrong; that was what. He was going to demand that she produce her damnable dolphins and make them do a few tricks. When she failed to do so, he would quickly decamp, hie himself back to Oxford, and write a carefully reasoned and utterly lethal assessment of her lunatic ideas. Before he was through, she would rue the day she ever stuck her appallingly provocative nose into the hallowed halls of science!

That settled, he relaxed back against the seat and looked out the cab window just as they passed a sign advertising seaside cottages and holidays in Brighton.

Seaside. Her last words to him came rushing back to him, and he found himself instantly back on the edges of his nerves.

"Something to swim in, my arse," he muttered. "I'm not going anywhere near the damned water."

Three

ASHTON HOUSE WAS an old stone manor house built around the ruins of a medieval keep. It had been built atop an ancient stone cairn that was revered by the early people who populated the south of England. It was the air of mysterious history about the place that led Sir Martin Ashton—archaeologist and incurable romantic—to purchase that particular property more than twenty years earlier. But it was what lay just beyond the house that made Sir Martin and his family come to love their home.

To the rear of the sprawling manor, below the rocky cliff that nature had fashioned into a set of broad steps, was a sheltered cove containing a beautiful, sandy beach. And crashing onto the barrier rocks that protected the cove and lapping at the beach was the sea itself.

Broad and mesmerizingly blue . . . constantly in motion . . . capricious, secretive, and alluring . . . the sea was a mystery far deeper than any pile of stones mere humans could erect. It was an unimaginable force with an entitylike will that shaped every bit of land it touched, pounding and tearing away the rock and then gently carrying the pieces back to shore. It filled the air with the taste of salt and the lulling sounds of breaking waves. It colored the daylight, moderated the weather, directed the morning and evening breezes, and nourished a unique community of sea birds, tidal creatures, and humans who lived by its changeable edge. And it had cast a spell on the mind and heart of the youngest Ashton the first time she set eyes on it.

That bit of magic was renewed each time Celeste stood watching from the top of the cliffs, the widow's walk on the roof, or the flower garden at the side of the house. This morning, she stood with a basket of freshly gathered flowers, watching the clouds out at sea, drifting over the water's surface. From here, the water looked serene and the clouds resembled wisps of cotton wool. On each side of the cove, green fields ran to the very edge of the cliffs, and the rocky escarpments below them bore striations of brown, gray, and chalky white. Every texture, every interplay of color, light, and surface, made her feel as if this were the one place on earth that she belonged.

With a sigh, she started for the front doors. She still had a number of things to do before the professor arrived that noon. Halfway to the entrance, she looked up at the house and slowed, seeing the mossy gray stones, the warped and rickety windows, the sagging roof, and crumbling chimneys as her reluctant guest undoubtedly would. It wasn't an especially inviting picture. But then, the wretched man wasn't coming to rate the accommodations, she told herself irritably, he was coming to verify her writings about dolphins. And after his pomposity and arrogance at the lecture hall, three days ago, he was fortunate indeed that she didn't leave him to find his own lodgings.

Holding on to that defiant thought, she hurried through the arched entry doors and stopped in the center hall, where her resolve melted. Pulling a cloth from the pocket of her apron, she hurriedly removed a spiderweb trailing from the stairs to a seldom-moved bench, then gave the carved banister an additional pass before stepping back to evaluate. It was no good. A few fragrant blossoms would never compensate for the creaky old house and threadbare furnishings.

A hint of a memory—a tall form, hot-eyed and somewhat

forbidding—teased her inner senses, setting them on edge, and she quickly suppressed it. He might be a pompous, over-bearing, arrogant wretch, but he was a *gentleman* wretch and she dreaded the disdain she was certain to see in his face when he beheld her home. Whatever had possessed her to demand that he come to Ashton House for a whole fort-night?

She sighed. Her instincts. And her instincts were seldom wrong.

As she hurried toward the kitchen stairs, her grandmother called to her from the hallway to the left. Following the blur of white disappearing into the library, she found her grand-mother in the middle of the room, bent over a littered work-table on which sat a half-assembled vase and sundry pieces of fired clay.

"Come look!" Lady Sophia beckoned excitedly with the magnifying glass in her hand. "Tell me if you don't think this is a royal trident." Shoving a piece of the earthen pot into Celeste's hands, she pointed to a figure carved into the clay. "See . . . there . . ."

Celeste squinted at the image of an elongated, three-pronged spear. "Definitely a trident, Nana, but as to whether—"

"It's from Poseidon's temple, of course," Nana declared, glowing. "It has to be. Look at the elegant lines and the intricate pattern of the glazing. And there are two more just below. You see? *Three*. Poseidon was always associated with the number three."

"Well, I suppose it could be—" Celeste's gaze fell from the shard of pottery to her grandmother's clothes: a loosely draped chiton, fastened at the shoulders with brooches, and a himation draped around her and over one shoulder. "Nana, you're not dressed!"

"Don't be silly, dear. I'm wearing clothing," Lady Sophia said.

"Not regular clothes . . . from this century."

"I know, dear, but it's been years since I wore a corset

and I was thinking . . ." Her grandmother turned to her with a look of stubborn hopefulness. "If this professor is such an intellectual sort, then he surely must find some of the society's work on the lost culture of Atlantis rather interesting. And if—"

"Ohhh, no." Celeste set her flower basket on the littered desk and quickly put her arm through her grandmother's, ushering her toward the door. "He won't find your theories interesting, he'll find them insupportable. According to what Mr. Cherrybottom was able to learn about him, Professor Thorne is narrow-minded, unbending, and notoriously hard-nosed. He's made something of a career of discrediting and dismantling other people's ideas."

She urged her grandmother out the door, down the hall, and up the main staircase, where the old lady slowed and gradually drew her to a halt.

"Celeste, dear . . ."

"We talked about this, Nana," she insisted, "and you promised."

Lady Sophia scowled, then, after a moment, continued on up the stairs. At the doorway to her bedroom, she gave Celeste a searching look. "I know your dolphins mean a great deal to you, dear. They mean a great deal to us in the society, too. But I doubt very much that my wearing a corset and stifling under layers of petticoats will secure a good report from him for you. If he's as objectionable a man as you say, then I say . . . scuttle and sink him!" She waved a dismissing hand. "You don't need him to continue your work."

Celeste groaned. It wasn't as if she hadn't considered that possibility.

"Nana, he publicly challenged my work . . . as much as accused me of making up stories. It was humiliating. And if I don't prove my work is genuine science, everyone will believe he was right. Who would dare publish my work then?" She bit back the question of how they would live if she didn't publish.

Lady Sophia studied her face, then reluctantly conceded. "I suppose . . . if it is that important to you."

"Thank you, Nana." She gave the old lady a brief hug before heading once again for the stairs. "And remember, no lectures on Atlantis or the Atlantean Society." She looked back just long enough to see her grandmother nod, then continued down the steps, missing the old lady's knowing look.

"And I suppose 'science' is the reason you've been cleaning house all week like Attila the Hun," Lady Sophia muttered.

ONCE ON THE main floor, Celeste paused to recall what she had intended to do and remembered her flower basket. She hurried back to the library to retrieve it and her attention was snagged by the glazed jar taking shape under her grandmother's expert hands. Nana had an uncanny knack for finding the right pieces and putting them together. Give her a box of jumbled, nondescript bits of pottery and she would resurrect a work of art. It was a remarkable talent. And how poignant that she had come to it so late in life, only after her beloved husband had died.

Celeste set her basket back down and ran a hand over the cracked surface of the vase, tracing the patterns, wondering at the beauty of the pattern and quality of the colorful designs. For the thousandth time, she surveyed the objects and artifacts that were the fruit of her grandfather's lifelong search. Huge stones, pedestals, brass plates, great shells, carvings, bronze castings . . . many of them intriguing, some perfectly astonishing. But did they truly tell the tale that her grandmother had woven from her devotion to them and to her deceased husband?

To have known such a love and to live with such a loneliness and longing . . . then to channel that love into a passion for re-creating the good of a civilization . . .

For the thousandth time, she rolled those questions from

her shoulders and once more battled down the guilt she felt at asking Nana to refrain from revealing her work and her views on Atlantis before the professor. It couldn't be helped. One scientific inquisition at a time was enough.

TITUS THORNE ARRIVED late that afternoon in an unsprung pony cart driven by the grizzled local blacksmith. The train down from London had been on schedule, but he had stopped to pay a call on a former student now serving a vicarage outside Brighton. By the time he arrived at the coaching station, the three o'clock coach to Pevensey Bay had already departed. Hiring a horse was out of the question, for he had never learned to ride. With the help of the livery-man at the station, he located a freight hauler traveling east and hired space on the wagon bed . . . hoping it wasn't an omen that he was listed on the wagoneer's bill of lading as "live freight."

But his journey derailed once again when the freight wagon broke a wheel just outside the sleepy little village of Cardamon. He and the teamster were forced to walk through the afternoon heat to the local smithy, where once again he benefited from the good graces of a local Samaritan. It seemed the aging smith, Ned Caldwell, was "goin' thataway, meself," and was willing to give him a ride.

According to Ned, Ashton House was a "roight old place," and "them what lives there is fine wimmen." Those pronouncements apparently exhausted the smith's conversational repertoire, for he rode the rest of the way to Ashton House in glowering silence.

The sun was sinking toward the sea when they rounded the last turn and headed up the rutted road to Ashton House. It was a larger place than he had imagined and was nestled around an impressive old Norman tower. But, as they neared, Titus saw that the house was older than it had first appeared, and seriously neglected. By the time the black-smith let him off by the front entrance, he had assessed the crumbling mortar, paint-bare doors, and beggarly windows, and was regretting that he hadn't made his own arrangements for lodgings.

He was met at the door by a houseman so bent with age that Titus watched anxiously as he struggled to pick up Titus's bag and totter inside.

"Wait 'ere, sir. I'll tell the mistruss," the old fellow wheezed, then disappeared with his valise.

Titus glanced about the once impressive hall, then strolled over to peer through the open doors on either side. They were huge rooms . . . Elizabethan in style, with arches, nooks, and carved finials everywhere . . . heavy, old Jacobean furnishings, threadbare rugs, and dim, sagging tapestries. The dark wood of the hall and main stairs was worn thin from literally centuries of foot traffic. But on the center table was a large vase of brilliant flowers that included every color and variety imaginable in a summer garden. Their vitality and freshness posed a stunning contrast to the rest of that moldering pile of rocks. Delphinium, roses, asters, foxglove, coreopsis, showy phlox, verbena, daisies . . .

"Welcome, Professor."

Jerking his nose out of the flowers, he turned to face a genteel-looking older woman with thick silver hair and rosy cheeks. She came forward with an outstretched hand and he found himself momentarily mesmerized by a pair of timeless blue eyes that looked somehow familiar.

"I am Sophia Ashton, Celeste's paternal grandmother. We were expecting you earlier in the day. I hope you haven't had a mishap on the road."

"Not at all." He straightened his aching spine. "Uneventful journey, really."

"Good." She turned smoothly at his side, inserted her arm through his, and urged him toward the stairs. "Dinner is in a quarter of an hour. I'll show you to your room so you can freshen up."

The old lady showed him to a spacious but stuffy chamber on the second floor and advised him to ring for whatever he might need. As she turned to go, he was startled to see that her proper gray dress had been left open in back from neck to bustle, exposing a shocking expanse of white muslin.

He puzzled over that for a moment, then shook his head.

Strolling around the room, he gave the large tester bed an experimental poke, ran a hand over the writing table—came up without the expected dust on his fingertips—and then headed for the window. He parted the worn lace curtains and struggled to turn the rusty handle and open the aged window. The metal finally gave with a scrape and a creak, and the frame swung open. He stood in the opening, inhaling the salt air, then focused on the sight of the bay.

For anyone but Titus Thorne, the view would have been breathtaking—gilded sky . . . glittering blue-green sea . . . a stretch of pale sand . . . the white foam of waves breaking on rocks and beach. He tensed and curled his hands into fists. He had to go through with this, he told himself, staring down at that restless water. There was no backing out now.

Dolphins. Why did it have to be *dolphins*? Why couldn't she have studied birds, or exotic plants, or even archaeology like her old grandfather?

He turned away from that disturbing view and began unpacking. In the middle of his starched shirts was that blue-green book with a dolphin on it. He picked it up and couldn't help leafing through it . . . pausing wherever his eye caught on a line. Invariably the lines that caught his eye contained the words "sexual," "coupling," or "mating preferences." He snorted and tossed the book on the bed. He didn't need to look at it to recall what it said; her inflammatory prose was virtually scored into his brain. The more he read and studied it, the more annoying it became.

Here, he had finally understood, was a diabolically clever work. Her presentation of her research—if it could be dignified with that title—was crafted to appear to be a scholarly work, while appealing to the lowest, basest impulses of the masses. It was pure sensationalism . . . sex and sea creatures . . . hedonism cloaked in scientific terms.

She had been canny, indeed, in selecting her subject. Dolphins were familiar to all levels of society, were largely unexplored by legitimate scientists, and were something about which the general population had a natural curiosity. And her methodology—direct underwater observation—was so unprecedented and so difficult to repeat, she probably believed she was all but assured of no direct challenges to her conclusions.

Even her style of writing—at first glance amateurish and infuriating—now appeared nothing short of brilliant. She had combined scientific terminology and titillating romantic prose in a way that stimulated the reader's libidinous impulses without triggering any feelings of guilt or moral outrage. *It was just animals, after all,* he imagined her saying. *All done in the name of science.*

Science, hell. It had all been done in the name of *profit.* A calculated grab for money and notoriety. A masterpiece of scientific hucksterism.

He had to give her credit, though; she was a shrewd one. This "Lady Mermaid" idea was positively inspired. She had somehow managed to fill both the papers and people's heads with visions of half-naked women wearing fish tails and swimming about the ocean, seducing exotic secrets from the deep itself. One look at her—blond hair, blue eyes, country fresh and ripely curved—was enough to give a tantalizing hint of flesh to the fantasy. The portrait that appeared in yesterday's *Gazette* had been nothing short of sensational.

He sat down on the bench at the foot of the bed and pulled the clipping from the back of the book. There she was . . . seated on a chair composed of carved dolphins, her body curved over one of the arms, her eyes bright and unabashedly provocative as she caressed the wooden dolphin she rested on. She certainly earned points for audacity, presenting herself before Britain's finest scientific minds, lecturing *them* on marine science. Annoyed, he crumpled it and stuffed it in his coat pocket.

She was not to be taken lightly, that was easy to see. Confronted, she had defended herself quite capably, and backed into a corner, she had proved dangerously resourceful. Her challenge that he come to her home and verify her work had seemed straightforward enough . . . until he studied her work again, in the light of her brazen attitude and bald manipulation of public opinion. She had something clever in mind, he was certain of it.

The task she had set for herself was formidable, indeed: conjure up a small herd of dolphins, climb into the water with them, and convince him that she and they were practically blood relations. The task was so formidable, in fact, that he couldn't help wondering how she meant to pull it off.

Or *if* she meant to pull it off.

But then, faking such a demonstration would be no trivial matter, either. He was an ichthyologist, for heaven's sake. It wasn't as if she could just draft a few barrel-chested fishermen, strap a fin on their backs, and set them to swimming back and forth in the water. She had promised him firsthand experiences . . . a close, personal look at her subjects.

A smile spread slowly across his face. It would be interesting to see how she handled it all.

DOWNSTAIRS, CELESTE STOOD looking out the seaward windows in the drawing room. She was dressed in a gathered blue cotton skirt and matching blouse, and her hair was pulled back into a simple chignon. They were the best clothes she owned, aside from the proper woolen suit she had worn the day she gave her ill-fated lecture. At a sound from the door, she turned to find old Stephan showing her reluctant guest into the room. The professor, looking tall, dark, and disdainful, paused just inside the doorway. Something deep inside her responded with a quiver. Dread, she told herself and stood straighter to compensate.

"I see you found the way," she said, trying not to let her thoughts show in her face as he came forward into the light. This was her arrogant professor? She was surprised by how different he was than she had remembered. He was tall, but not gargantuan; a bit on the angular side, but not rawboned or cadaverous. His nose was actually quite normal-sized and his eyebrows didn't really meet in the middle. His garments were well tailored, and his dark hair was perfectly groomed. He didn't look at all like the monster she had remembered him as being. He was physically impressive, striking of countenance, and blatantly, unmistakably *male*. Which made her worry about just which of her instincts had made her challenge him to come to Ashton House for a fortnight.

"My grandmother was concerned you might be lost," she said coolly.

"Lost?" He gave a huff of amusement. "Hardly. I have an unerring sense of direction. Nothing, my dear Miss Ashton, would have kept me from this appointment."

"A pity you couldn't have arrived earlier in the day. The wind was perfect for sailing. We shall just have to hope for fair weather tomorrow as well." She looked pointedly at his starched shirt and elegant silk tie, then had to force her gaze away from his broad shoulders. "I hope you brought something less formal to wear when meeting the dolphins."

"*If* I meet dolphins, Miss Ashton, I doubt they shall be interested in what I am wearing."

"Oh, you'll meet them, all right."

She jerked her errant gaze up and it collided, head-on, with his. She recalled with sudden, breathtaking clarity those sea-green eyes, that dark hair, the bold curve of his lips, the sun-bronzed texture of his skin. It all came back in a rush that heated the air she drew into her lungs. Don't stare, she told herself. But it was impossible not to; his gaze held her like a magnet did a needle.

"Dinner, missy," Stephan announced from the doorway.

Freed unexpectedly, Celeste headed for the door with her heart racing and heat tingling in her cheeks. He might not be a monster, she realized, but that didn't mean he wasn't dangerous.

The dining room was a large, paneled hall, furnished with a venerable walnut table, ringed with heavy, intricately carved chairs, and two well-worn Jacobean sideboards laden with covered dishes that vented wisps of fragrant steam. The walls were hung with elaborate old tapestries faded by time. The only things that had been added to the room in more than a century were the two sizable mirrors hanging over the sideboards and the rose-tinted light provided by the lowering sun.

"Welcome again, Professor." Nana beckoned him to the seat on her right, leaving Celeste to take the chair across from him. "I hope you don't mind that I didn't wait. Old bones must be humored, you know." She flashed him a flirtatious smile as he took his seat. To her granddaughter, she said, "Celeste, my dear, he is even more dashing than you said."

Celeste looked up from settling her napkin, her face flushed with color. Had her grandmother somehow read her mind? "Nana! I never—"

"His eyes." The old lady squinted at him. "Just the color of the sea on a summer's day. You were absolutely right. And I do believe 'aristocratic' quite sums up his face." Celeste groaned silently and Nana relaxed into an impish grin. "But I should have known. Our Celeste doesn't miss much, you know."

"Do tell," he said, flicking Celeste a look that warned *he* didn't miss much, either.

"Oh, yes. She is quite the observer. Of course, she hasn't had the chance to observe many *gentlemen* at close range."

"Nana!" Her face flamed now. "Pay no heed, Professor. My grandmother can sometimes be a bit . . . direct."

"Like grandmother, like granddaughter?" he asked tartly.

"Oooh. And a touch of humor. You didn't mention that, Celeste." Lady Sophia chuckled at Celeste's ill-concealed distress and leaned over to pat her hand. "Well, Stephan, I believe we're ready for Maria's soup." She turned to the professor with a confidential air. "Oyster, you know. It's our Maria's specialty."

"Your Portuguese cook?"

"Why, yes. How did you know?"

"It was in Miss Ashton's book," he said, shifting his broad shoulders to one side to allow the old butler to serve him.

"You recalled that from my book?" Celeste asked, grateful to move on to another topic, any other topic.

"I have made a thorough study of your writing." His voice was noticeably cooler. Their gazes met briefly and she felt a ripple of uneasiness, wondering what sorts of conclusions he had drawn from her work, and hoping she hadn't revealed more in her book than she intended.

"In my sort of work," he continued, "it is important to be well prepared."

"Your sort of work?" Lady Sophia said. "Tell me, Professor, what is your field of study?"

"Ichthyology, madam," he responded.

"*Fish science.* How interesting. Not my cup of tea, of course. I'm far more interested in—" She caught Celeste's glower and—scowling back at her—changed direction. "In more artistic endeavors. And travel. Not that I get to do much, these days. Do you travel much, Professor?"

He looked up from his nearly empty soup dish. "When the occasion calls for it. But I spend most of my time in Oxford." He paused, considering something as he looked at Celeste. "I just returned, not long ago, from a stay in Newcastle."

"Newcastle?" Celeste frowned, thinking instantly of coal, iron ore, smelters, and hot, sulphur-laden air, and wondering what a skeptical "fish scientist" could possibly find of interest in a notoriously rough and dirty industrial town. "What were you doing there? Collecting specimens?"

"Hardly. I was researching and exposing an archaeological fraud." He ignored the clang of Celeste's spoon dropping in her dish, and looked at Lady Sophia as he continued. "It seemed a fellow in that city claimed to have unearthed a Viking ship covered with magical runes. He set up a tidy little business, charging for viewing it. After a while, he began to claim it could effect miracle cures. For a fee, people with dire illnesses could spend a night in the ship and be healed."

"And were they?" Lady Sophia leaned forward. "Healed?"

"Despite his claims," he replied with obvious satisfaction, "I was unable to locate a single person who had been cured of anything but false hope or a fat purse. Most of the charlatan's patrons returned to the boat night after night until they were drained of resources."

"Were you able to stop the blackguard?" Lady Sophia asked eagerly.

"With some effort. A survey of his former clients exposed the shameful number of failed cures, and could not bring to light one verifiable healing. After careful study, I was able to determine that the carvings were neither ancient nor authentic. All that remained was to discover who had actually done the carvings on the boat and bring the fellow and his accomplices to justice."

"But how did you come to investigate Viking artifacts?" Celeste asked, thinking of the artifacts her grandmother had packed into every available inch of the library and breakfast room. "Archaeology is not your field."

He looked at Celeste speculatively. "I am called upon to investigate a wide range of inventions and discoveries which seem a bit 'fishy.' "

"How appropriate. Who better to investigate a 'fishy' situation than an ichthyologist?" Lady Sophia called for their next course.

Her grandmother obviously hadn't heard the veiled threat, but Celeste had. What could possibly be more *fishy* than a "mermaid" . . . especially one who wrote about her underwater experiences with dolphins? Coupled with what she'd heard from Mr. Cherrybottom about him, his declarations were nothing short of ominous. He was a crusader against shoddy and fraudulent science, a self-appointed arbiter of truth, a one-man justice and jury in the courts of scientific opinion. If there had been any doubt in her mind that he had come here to discredit her, he had just dispelled it.

"You are a professional skeptic, then," she said tautly.

"I am a scientist first and foremost, Miss Ashton. As a scientist, I am devoted to the search for the truth. And as a seeker of truth, it is my duty to unmask falsehood masquerading as scientific progress." That echoing pronouncement brought dinner conversation to a total halt.

Celeste had lost her appetite. In contrast, Titus Thorne systematically demolished Maria's oyster soup and Spanish paella . . . closing his penetrating, sea-green eyes to concentrate on each bite. By the time he sampled the braised sole with capers and ginger butter, and pronounced it "surprisingly light and delicate," it was all she could do to keep from launching herself across the table at him.

The wretched man analyzed and evaluated everything around him . . . passing judgment as if he had been put in charge of standards for all of humankind. Nothing escaped him. She watched him mentally cataloguing flavors and deciphering ingredients in the food, fingering the worn table linen, scrutinizing the crystal, running his hands over the edges of the plates, as if examining them for chips. She found herself staring raptly at those hands . . . large, neat hands, long, slender, supple fingers . . . She finally looked up and found him watching her. Her face heated defensively.

Judging her now, was he? She could just imagine what he was thinking. *Poor desperate, deluded creature . . . living with an eccentric grandmother in a crumbling house. Small wonder she believes she can talk to dumb animals.*

It was during the raspberry trifle that Lady Sophia finally resurrected the conversation. "Tell us, Professor, what sorts of 'fish' things do you study?"

He cleared his throat. "I specialize in the feeding habits of large fish . . . the saltwater varieties. Swordfish, sharks, marlin, tuna, sunfish, and the like."

Nana beamed. "Then I imagine you must fish a great deal, Professor. How fortunate you are. Not many men manage to combine their vocations and avocations."

"Oh, I never fish," he said, finishing the last bite of his trifle and settling back in his chair. "That would be a deplorable waste of time."

An ichthyologist who wouldn't waste time fishing? "If you don't fish, how do you get your specimens?" Celeste asked pointedly.

"I contract with certain parties to secure them for me."

"What parties?"

"I have a standing arrangement with certain fishing-boat captains who operate out of the London docks." He spoke succinctly, with a hint of annoyance. "I give them a list of the specimens I need and when they haul one in, I go around to the wharf and collect it."

She frowned, thinking of some of the large fish she had encountered, trying to imagine how he could handle and study seven- to twelve-foot specimens in captivity. "Then what do you do? I mean . . . I should think keeping them in a tank would be terribly difficult—not to mention costly and dangerous."

"A tank?" He looked briefly puzzled, then gave a short laugh. "Hardly. I put the specimen in the back of an ice wagon and take it to the London School of Medicine. They allow me to use their operating theater."

"For what? Surely, by then, the creature must be *dead*."

"Of course it's dead." He adopted a professional air. "I perform a dissection and analyze the contents of the creature's digestive tract. Whatever the fish has eaten in the last six to eight hours is evident. Most large fish swallow their prey whole . . . with the notorious exception of the shark, which will also bite and tear away pieces of much larger prey. But even then, one can still usually identify bits and pieces as belonging to . . ."

That was it? Celeste sat stunned, listening to him recount his gruesome technique. *That* was how he researched the feeding habits of fish? He dissected their stomachs and examined the debris?

"Let me see if I have this straight," she interrupted, sliding to the edge of her chair. "You claim to be an authority on the feeding habits of fish, but you don't watch them feeding in the wild . . . never see them capture or eat their prey . . . and never have more than one or two fish at a time to study?" Her voice rose along with her indignation. "You simply go down to the London docks, buy the odd carcass, cart it off, and cut it open to see what's inside?" She paused, struggling to contain her outrage. "A fishmonger could do as much!"

He reddened. "It is hardly that *simple,* Miss Ashton."

"It is hardly more complex, Professor," she countered, gripping the edges of the table and rising. "And it is hardly science!"

He shoved his chair back and sprang up. "It is certainly better science than if I claimed I swam about in the ocean, leering at animals, then concocted tawdry stories about their sexual habits." He raised his chin. "At least when I cut open a fish, there is no question about what it has ingested. It's there or it isn't. I deal in pure, undeniable fact, not dubious tales or lurid conjectures."

"That's what you think, is it? That I've just made it all up?"

"I believe that is what I'm here to determine."

"So, you'll decide if I am a liar and a charlatan, or just some poor deluded little ninny who wouldn't know a dolphin mating if she saw one!"

His voice lowered so that it set her fingertips vibrating.

"Oh, I don't doubt that you'd know a *mating* if you saw one."

She looked straight into his sea-green eyes and was suddenly engulfed in treacherous waters. Undertow. It took a moment for her to catch his meaning.

That again . . . the intimation that she knew more about such things than a young woman should know.

"The real question here, sir, is: will *you* know one when *you* see it?"

He straightened, a vein suddenly visible in his temple, and she rounded the head of the table to confront him.

"And there is no better time to find out than now. Come with me."

"What? Now?" He gestured to the lowering light coming from the window. "It's practically night."

"Dolphins don't sleep . . . at least not like we do. It's in my book, remember?" She headed for the door.

Appealing to Lady Sophia with an incredulous look, he received only a beatific smile in response. He gave his vest a violent jerk downward and followed Celeste.

The old lady sat for a moment, her eyes glowing as she studied the doorway where her granddaughter and the professor had disappeared. Then she clasped her hands together and broke into a laugh.

"She has needed someone for so long . . . And such magnetism. Such dynamic opposition. Together, they positively radiate sacred energy!" Her gaze darted over unseen possibilities as she considered what to do, then gradually narrowed upon a course of action. Moments later, she reached for her wine and finished it with a flourish.

If things went as she hoped, soon dolphins might not be the only things "mating" around here.

Four

CELESTE LED HIM through the house, through a cavernous stone kitchen—where she paused to thank a rotund, dark-eyed woman for dinner—and then along a worn gravel path that ended precipitously at the edge of a cliff. Titus's heart thudded when she veered from the path and disappeared over the edge of the cliff.

Hurrying to the edge of the cliff, he glimpsed a stepped path leading down the side of it, and reluctantly followed. He was still burning from their confrontation, and fixed his gaze on the swaying blue skirts ahead of him.

Infernal female—having the temerity to disparage his work and compare him to a *fishmonger*. He was a respected researcher, a professor who held a chair at Oxford. The list of his papers and presentations was as long as his arm. True, his method of inquiry wasn't dashing, or adventuresome, or wildly romantic. Why was it that people—even some who should know better, like his colleagues on the Cardinal College faculty—persisted in promoting the myth of the great romance of discovery? The old boys talked about research in grandly overblown terms, as if it always involved sailing up the Nile or wading through Amazonian swamps or being bitten by some exotic vermin in some exotic climate. Yet another symptom of encroaching senility, he was convinced.

They had forgotten the details of their earlier days and now simply made some up.

The truth was, real science involved precious little glamour. Real science was methodical, exacting, and sometimes even unpleasant. Real research employed grit and determination in the dogged pursuit of elusive but critical details. The study of ichthyology didn't require sailing the seven seas, and it certainly didn't require making oneself *into* a fish in order to study fish!

His eyes narrowed.

Celeste Ashton clearly hadn't the first idea of the methodologies of legitimate scientific investigation. If she did, she wouldn't be dragging him down to the water in the dark to witness God-knew-what. Then it struck him like a thunderbolt: she was hauling him down to the water at dusk . . . declaring dolphins don't sleep . . .

She had something up her sleeve. He could just feel it.

He took a deep breath and rolled his aching shoulders, forcing them to relax. Forewarned was forearmed.

The beach was a pale crescent at the heart of a large, rounded cove. To the right, a rocky finger of land jutted out into the sea and formed a protective barrier that kept the water of the cove more placid than that of the surrounding shoreline. When they reached the bottom of the cliff, she struck off across the beach and he trudged through the soft sand after her, wondering briefly if she meant to charge straight into the water, clothes and all. But, with a glance back over her shoulder, she corrected her course.

"Where are you taking me?" he called out as she climbed several rocky steps to a path.

She pointed toward a dock and boathouse near the mouth of the cove.

"A boathouse? You cannot mean to go out in a boat now . . . tonight . . . with darkness coming on?"

"It wouldn't be the first time I've gone out at night."

"This is idiocy," he muttered, following her up the steps

with an eye on the water breaking against the rocks just below his feet.

"I prefer to think of it as *determination,*" she shot back. "I am experienced at sea . . . you would be perfectly safe with me at the tiller . . . day or night."

Her at the tiller. His teeth ground together. Wouldn't she love that?

He stalked along after her, so intent on his thoughts that he didn't watch where he was putting his feet. When a board cracked underfoot, he jumped ahead to a sounder plank, then turned to look in horror at the splintered wood and the darkness beneath it.

"Oh, and do mind where you put your feet, Professor." He couldn't see her face, but could somehow tell from the sound of her voice that she was smiling. "Some of the wood isn't quite what it used to be."

"See here, Miss Ashton . . ." He drew up behind her as she opened the rough planking door to the tumbledown boathouse. Smells of rotting algae, damp wood, and musty canvas rolled out of the boathouse onto the evening air. "Either you have these dolphin creatures at your beck and call, or you don't."

"It is not quite as simple as that." She entered the darkened boathouse and slid a hand along the wall, feeling for a shelf and then along the shelf until she found a lantern and matches.

"It isn't?"

"This is not a safe, predictable laboratory, Professor. This is the sea."

"Science is science, Miss Ashton," he declared, tugging his vest irritably. "Either you can do what you claimed or you cannot."

A light bloomed in the darkness. He ducked inside and saw her standing in the center of it, holding up the lantern. He stood silent for a moment, taking in her heart-shaped face, framed in a halo of glowing golden hair . . . cheeks brushed with warm, rosy tones . . . big, dark-centered eyes . . . lips that seemed indecently full and red and almost . . . *edible*.

He suddenly realized she was speaking again.

". . . more than one way to call a dolphin."

She thrust the lantern into his hands. Then she lifted a large sheet of corrugated tin that had rope attached at two corners, and a pair of wooden dowels that had been made into mallets. Skirting him, she ducked out the door, and he was left staring at the glowing flame of the lamp, trying desperately to remember what objection he had meant to raise.

Something about calling dolphins . . . at night . . .

It was nothing short of absurd, he thought. The brazen chit . . . showing him dolphins in the dark . . . where they couldn't be seen clearly except by *her*. This was her clever plan? Did she really think him that gullible?

He exited the boathouse and found her where the dock formed a ledge along the side of the crude building. "This way," she said, flattening her back against the boathouse and edging along that narrow decking. He lost track of her after she rounded the corner, until he heard her call, "Aren't you coming, Professor?"

Expelling a ragged breath, he pressed his back to the wall and slid his feet along that narrow ledge. At the far end of the boathouse, the dock continued at full width for several feet before dropping off into the watery abyss. He inched his way along until he could slide around the corner, onto the relative security of the wider dock. There, he sagged against the boathouse wall to catch up on the breath he had missed in transit.

She had sunk to her knees on the decking and was hanging the large piece of tin between two of the dock posts, so that it was half suspended in the water. Then she settled on the edge of the dock herself, took a mallet in each hand, and began to rap on the tin: five short raps, a pause, then a single lower-pitched rap. After repeating that pattern several times, she paused.

"You'd better have a seat, Professor," she said, looking up at him. "This may take a while."

She was calling her dolphins, he realized. *Supposedly* calling. In her book she had said that she rapped on the side of the boat . . . a pattern of sound that the dolphins recognized as coming from her. *Allegedly* recognized.

"Very well," he said, approaching the edge of the dock and kneeling down stiffly on the splintery boards. "I suppose I have nothing better to do."

The deepening crimson of the sunset slid gently into purple, then almost imperceptibly into the last dark blues of twilight. The sea darkened for a while, then seemed to brighten, as if drawing the last available light from the sky itself. The regular lapping of the water and the measured pounding of her makeshift drum complemented each other, producing a curiously agreeable rhythm.

The longer he listened, the more pronounced and compelling it seemed. Slowly, it invaded his senses, vibrated along his nerves, and founded an unsettling resonance in his blood. Tension built in him, a persuasive sensual imperative . . . making him uncomfortably aware of his body. Then the drumming ceased and only the soft, expectant whispers of lapping water could be heard.

He scanned the surface of the cove for signs of a curved triangular fin, dimly aware that he was holding his breath. When the waters merely glistened and flowed on undisturbed, he turned to her. She was watching him. A moment later, she had returned to her drumming. Like waves piling on a shore, the seductive pattern of that primitive call accumulated in his consciousness, pushing his awareness of her steadily higher . . . to the point of true arousal.

After a time, he found himself seated fully, gripping his upraised knees with whitened fingers, staring heatedly at the hazy blue ribbon of the night horizon. His jaw was clenched, his legs were beginning to ache, and his trousers felt suddenly tighter.

"No dolphins," he declared thickly, and cleared his throat.

"They don't just swim around the dock, or even the cove, Professor. They have a very wide range . . . miles, perhaps even scores of miles."

"Then what makes you think pounding on a piece of tin could possibly reach them?"

"They have an exceptionally keen sense of hearing and sound carries under water for surprisingly long distances. And, of course, this is summer. They like to summer here, along this coast, with me."

"With you?" He raked a critical glance over her blatantly feminine form, wondering if dolphins could possibly be as susceptible to blond hair, big blue eyes, and generous curves as human males generally were. "And what makes *you* so irresistible to dolphins?"

She watched him sitting there with his back ramrod straight and his chin raised well above his stiff collar so that he could look down his patrician nose at her, and she was seized by an overwhelming urge to shock him.

"I'm a lot of fun," she declared firmly.

He made a choked sound, as if the word were a foreign concept. *"Fun?"*

She smiled with defiant cheeriness. "Dolphins put a premium on fun, and I think of novel things to do and introduce them to games and objects they've never seen before. That . . . and . . . when I get into the water with them, they get to laugh at my flukes and flippers."

"Laugh at your . . ." He glanced involuntarily at her lower half.

"Well, they are rather unusual." She hauled her skirt up to her knees and plopped first one, then the other foot up onto the dock. Fitting her heels together, she waggled her feet as if they were flukes. "Much too small . . . from a dolphin's perspective, anyway. And I expect they probably think my nose is pathetically short and my eyes are much too close together. Imagine"—she crossed her eyes—"what we must look like to them."

He produced a strangled sound that might have included a laugh.

"We're a strange sort of pale pink and white all over," she continued. "We have only these long, unwieldy flippers"—she demonstrated, wiggling her hands—"and have to thrash and dig our way through the water to keep up with them. Not very promising creatures, we humans. Although"—her eyes widened in mocking interest—"they might find you more promising than most."

"Me?"

"*Your* flukes"—she nodded to his feet—"are quite large."

He seemed to stiffen a bit more, but it was hard to tell for certain in the dim light. She rolled up to her knees and held out the mallets to him. "Your turn."

"My turn? Don't be absurd."

"It's not difficult. Five raps along the upper edge, a pause, then a single lower rap in the center."

He folded his arms. "I am merely an observer. There is objectivity to be maintained. My participation might muddle or taint the results."

She continued to hold the mallets out to him. "Oh, I doubt you would taint the results, Professor. Unless, of course, you have no sense of rhythm."

"That is beside the point, Miss Ashton—"

"Dolphins can hardly know who is calling them across miles of ocean . . . as long as the signal is properly given. And if you are to repeat my results, surely you must repeat my methods."

Cornered by her logic and his own pride, he grabbed the mallets from her and scooted awkwardly across the dock to take her place. She moved back and leaned against the post, arms crossed. It took an effort to keep her smile from turning into a taunting grin.

He began to pound the tin with jerky, self-conscious motions.

"That was only four," she interrupted.

"It most certainly was not." He looked up with his nostrils flaring. "It was five and then one, just as you did it."

"It was four," she insisted. "Perhaps you'd better count aloud."

"I will not." He rapped out another set, a bit louder and steadier this time, but still lacking discernible rhythm. She could see in his face that he was counting mentally, but his third attempt was not much better.

"Goodness, you really don't have much of a sense of rhythm, do you? Perhaps I should do it, after all."

"I am perfectly capable," he insisted, and applied the mallets to the tin with greater determination.

Eventually, he settled into a creditable rhythm. His face seemed to soften and his grip on the mallets became freer and more natural. He no longer held himself so rigidly, and his shoulders began to flex slightly with each lower tone. The familiar rhythm took on a whole new sound to her.

Her gaze was drawn to his profile: his long, straight nose, his prominent cheekbones, his high forehead and the lock of hair that hung over it. Looking away, she searched the cove for a glimpse of a dorsal fin. But again and again she came back to his hands, gripping those mallets . . . large hands, long, powerful fingers, and square, neatly trimmed nails. She recalled them tracing the edges of the plates and goblets at supper . . . gentle, authoritative . . .

Nana was right. She hadn't examined many gentlemen at close range. No doubt that accounted for this strange urge to stare at him, to study his movements and the nuances of his speech and expressions. It occurred to her that she knew more about dolphin males than human ones. And here was a prime specimen, practically at her fingertips . . .

"There, I've repeated your procedure, Miss Ashton." He paused, his eyes glowing in the dimness. "Still no dolphins."

"As I said, Professor, it may take them a while to get here." Her voice sounded oddly constricted to her own ears.

"And how will you know they're here?"

She pulled her gaze from him and looked down at the moonlit water at their feet. "They usually come to the dock and stick their heads up out of the water. If I'm not here, they sometimes swim around in the cove and leap out of the water to let me know they've arrived."

"They *leap*. Out of the water. To get your attention."

"They do."

He eyed her skeptically. "Because they 'like' you."

"I can't think of any other reason they would return each summer. Occasionally I give them a treat, but I'm not much of a soft touch when it comes to food. They eat prodigiously . . . it would be far too expensive."

"You honestly believe these creatures capable of 'liking' someone? Of the higher feelings of regard and affection?"

"I certainly do." Her voice came soft and earnest. "We have not the slightest qualm about crediting land mammals with such attributes. For example, we say dogs 'like' to be petted, because they seek it out. And we insist that they *love* a good game of fetch or a juicy bone, since they wag tails and leap for joy, and even appear to smile at us at times. Then why is it so difficult to believe that dolphins, who possess brains much larger than those of dogs—brains similar in size and structure to our own—may share at least those same fundamental feelings and attributes?"

He expelled a breath tinged with disgust and looked out at the sea. "Very well, just what sorts of things do dolphins 'love'?"

"They love to be with each other, they're quite social beings. They love to investigate things. They are very curious and easily fascinated by anything new or different. They love to play and, of course, to court each other and mate. But what they love the very most is . . ." When she paused for effect, he looked at her so intently that she smiled. "*Mackerel*. Much like human males, their affections seem to be tied closely to their digestion."

"Oh?" He laid the mallets on the dock and slid back from the edge. "And what would you know of the affections and digestion of human males, Miss Ashton? More than your grandmother is aware, perhaps?"

She glanced at his mouth, then away, and became suddenly aware of the threads of moonlight piercing the clouds drifting overhead, the *shoosh*ing sound of the waves breaking on the nearby rocks, and of the fact that she was very much alone with him on the dock.

"I was merely referring to the old saw: 'the way to a man's heart is through his stomach,' " she replied, dismayed to find her voice breathy.

"Were you, indeed?" He cocked his head and eyed her.

It took her a moment to realize that he meant her knowledge of human males probably came from more immediate sources, which, of course, meant that he believed she knew more than she should about— *That again!* When only a moment before she was thinking that there actually could be a human being buttoned up somewhere inside that stuffy, overbearing—

"Knowing the facts of dolphin life and reproduction does not make me an immoral person, sir," she said hotly. "No more than poking about in a dead shark's belly makes you an expert on the feeding of large fish!"

She grabbed the mallets, scrambled to her feet, and slid the ropes that held the sheet of tin up and over the posts.

"I believe it has yet to be established that you know the facts of anything, Miss Ashton." He stood up and brushed his trousers. "What happens if the dolphins appear and we're not here to see them?"

"Then they will simply wait until morning." She raised that unwieldy sheet of corrugated metal and shoved it against his chest.

"Hey!" He barely caught it before it bit into the toes of his well-polished shoes. By the time he straightened and bettered his grip on it, she had already retrieved the lantern and was making her way around the boathouse. As he started along the ledge, both she and the light disappeared at the far end. Balancing the sheet of tin against him as best he could,

he pressed his shoulder blades against the boathouse wall and slid his feet along the ledge, which felt even narrower than it had earlier. He was nearing the end, muttering furiously to himself, when she reappeared with the lantern and glowered at him.

"There you are. I was beginning to wonder if—"

A sharp crack occurred underfoot as he shifted to face her. He felt himself sinking, dropped the metal, and scrambled for purchase on the ledge. Failing that, he grabbed wildly at the rough boathouse wall for something—anything—to hold on to. Then one foot went through a rotted board and he began to fall.

"Aghhh—"

The light disappeared and the next instant his coat caught on something and checked his fall. As he straightened, he felt Celeste Ashton seize his wrist, and realized belatedly that it was she who had caught hold of his coat. "I've got you," she called. Steadied, he was able to slide one foot onto a sounder board and pull the other free of the broken wood. Then with a lunge, he reached the main dock and safety.

His heart hammered, he could barely catch his breath, and a burning throb was developing in his foot. But what filled his awareness, as his senses cleared, was the feel of Celeste Ashton pressed tight against him . . . so close that he could feel her heart was beating fast, too.

That wave of adrenaline drained, leaving in its place a confusing flush of heat. He looked down into her upraised face—luminous skin, delicate features, generously curved lips . . . Soft, she was so *soft* against him . . . everywhere . . . his chest, his loins, his thighs, his arms. And everywhere she was touching him, something seemed to be melting . . . his resistance to her, his clothes, his very skin. It should have raised an alarm in him, but as he looked into her large, dark-centered eyes and felt the warmth of her body seeping into his chest, he couldn't think of a single reason to let her go.

She looked up into his face—those bold, angular features,

penetrating eyes, and expressive mouth—and a wave of un-expected pleasure broke over her. Her first thought was that he was surprisingly flat and hard wherever she was pressed against him . . . her chest, her abdomen, her thighs. She had no idea that men had such firm and planar bodies. It was like being held against a wall.

When he lurched onto the dock and grabbed her, it had seemed the most natural thing in the world for her to open her arms to steady him. And now that she could feel the satin back of his vest beneath his coat, the heat of his waist, and the intriguing thickness of his shoulders, she was caught hard in the grip of discovery and hadn't the slightest thought of removing herself.

Looking up into his darkened eyes, she watched his face lower toward hers, degree by tantalizing degree. Her lips parted as his head tilted. The moist warmth of his breath bathed her lips, sending trickles of expectation wending along the underside of her skin. Another inch. Just one more inch and their mouths would meet in a . . .

He felt her quiver of anticipation, felt it migrate into his body. He was finally going to know if those lips really tasted like ripe cherries. That wayward but tantalizing hypothesis had lingered at the edge of his awareness since the first moment he set eyes on her. Red and lusciously moist, bursting with a tart sweetness—

His lips closed over hers and he finally knew; she tasted of honey mingled with salt . . . like the nectar of seaside flowers . . . like salty, sun-warmed apples. He absorbed the satiny resilience of her lips as they molded to his, discovering the provocative wet heat between them as they parted. He traced that tantalizing crevice with his tongue, exploring her ripening response and the lush sensations of sweetness and warm flesh and intimate oral contact. He pulled her tighter against him, absorbed in the way her body seemed to fit so naturally against his . . . her curves filling his hollows, her softness molding to his strength.

Against the background of the pounding surf and the soft

silver moonlight, it was all so perfect that he felt not the slightest disappointment that she didn't taste quite like cherr—

Cherries? The thought intruded, then doused his over-heated passions with an icy blast of reason. He was *tasting* her?

His eyes widened with recognition, focusing on her face, her closed eyes. *Kissing her.* He jerked his head up, breaking that alarming contact.

Sensing his withdrawal, she pulled from his arms and lurched back a step.

He tugged at his vest then shoved his hands into his coat pockets; she brushed at her skirts then thrust her arms behind her.

"Really, Miss Ashton," was all he could think to say at first, and disdainful was the only tone he could seem to say it in.

"Really, Professor," she echoed, her face brightening in moonlight.

"That was . . . most . . ." Then his speech mechanisms kicked into gear and began to run on by themselves, without any interference from his brain. "In future, Miss Ashton, please find another subject on whom to practice your repertoire of *human* mating rituals."

"Practice my—" She fell back a step, then glared at him as if he had just crawled from under a rock. She turned and made straight for the beach.

Pain shot up his leg when he tried to follow.

"Infernal dock is a death trap—damned lucky I didn't break something." He shoved his hands into his coat pockets and hobbled down the path. "Perhaps that's her plan . . . lame me and then lavish me with tender mercies so I'll be—"

So he would be what? Agreeable? Beholden? He scowled. He felt something in his pocket and drew it out. It was a crumpled piece of newsprint . . . that picture from the *Gazette* portraying Celeste Ashton as a sensuous siren of land

and sea. Even in the moonlight he could make out the suggestive outline of her body, the invitation in her posture, and the challenge in her expression.

She was a woman who knew the facts of life, that picture said, and who used them to get what she wanted.

The devious little piece! Dragging him down to the dock—alone, in the dark—on the premise of looking for dolphins . . . she wasn't trying to lame him, she was trying to *seduce* him. Thinking of the way she had flashed him a peek at her "flippers," thrown herself at him bodily, then kissed him within an inch of his sanity, he groaned.

How dense could a man be? She probably didn't have a clever plot or a prime bit of fakery in mind—she didn't expect to need one. Why should she go to such trouble if she could get his urges and desires to do her work for her? Once embroiled with her in some tawdry carnal escapade, he'd have a devil of a time exposing her fraud without exposing his own indiscretions.

He winced at the ease with which she had managed to get her arms around him, at how brazenly she had melted against him, and at just how close he had come to sampling her opportunistic charms. Fortunately, he had had the presence of mind and the moral fiber to interrupt her little game before she managed to inveigle him into a compromising position.

He stuffed the picture back into his pocket and limped toward the cliff.

She might be clever, his slippery Lady Mermaid, but he had made a career out of dissecting bigger fish. It wouldn't be long before he had her pinned to the board before him, her secrets bared and dubious claims exposed.

IT WAS A LONG and sleepless night for two of the inhabitants of Ashton House. When dawn finally broke, Celeste slid with relief from her bed, pulled on her clothes, and hurried down to the cove. She was disappointed to find the rolling blue-green waves undisturbed by dorsal fins and airy white "blows." Thinking of the long morning in store if she couldn't produce a few dolphins to verify her claims, she went out to the dock, rescued her makeshift drum from the rocks bared by low tide, and began rapping out her call once again.

Her mind drifted back to the sea-softened darkness, the fascination of watching Titus Thorne's hands wield the mallets, and the unexpected delight of being held against his body.

A swirl of warmth and ocean sound and moist lips recurred in her senses. She had been kissed, really kissed, for the first time in her life. And it had been marvelous. Soft and slow and deliciously compelling . . . For years she had observed and catalogued dolphin mating behaviors, and had wondered what it was like for humans. The closest thing to a description had come from the few "romantic" novels she had secreted from her grandfather's library. She knew all about sexual activity from a scientific standpoint, but hadn't a clue how it truly felt, until last night.

Then Titus Thorne had ruined it all by accusing her of "practicing" on him. The wretch.

She thought about that for a moment. What was so wrong with exploring the pleasures of human mating? If a body had to live as a human, her grandfather had said long ago, he or she might as well know the basics of how they came to be one. With her grandfather's and grandmother's sage instruction, she had learned those basics in theory. Her dolphins, who mated frequently, eagerly, and shamelessly, had taught her the more practical applications.

Everything in nature seemed to be sorted into mating pairs . . . including humans. Surely a man of science would understand the natural process of—

A man of science. She shook the lingering sensual fog from her mental faculties and made herself look at it logically. Titus Thorne was a man of reason and intellect, a man too absorbed in delving the secrets of the universe to bother with trifles like mating and pleasure. She thought of his pride and superior airs. No doubt he considered himself above such nonsense.

But then, a more empirical bit of evidence intruded. He hadn't *felt* like a juiceless prig when he pulled her tight against him, slid his hands over her body, and teased her lips with his. True, she was a novice at such things, but at the time, he seemed to be enjoying it as much as she did. And if afterward he was appalled . . . why would a man dislike having made pleasure, if it felt good?

Because he didn't like the person with whom he made that pleasure. *Her.*

She propped her chin on her hand and scowled as she looked out to sea. He believed she was either a fraud and a liar, or a young, idiotic female who confused her days with day*dreams* and infused her observations with all sorts of ridiculous female longings . . . neither of which would appeal to a man of logic and reason, who considered himself the guardian of the Gates of Truth. The thought caused a hollow, empty feeling in her chest and she sent a hand to massage it.

A moment later that telling motion annoyed her and she jerked her hand away. She was a scientist, for heaven's sake. Why was she spending precious time and energy worrying about what would appeal to Titus Thorne? She didn't have to have his approval or his blessed kisses; she only had to have his verification of her work. In writing.

Glowering, she took up her dolphin call again.

IT WAS WELL PAST dawn when Titus sprang up in the middle of his bed, wild-eyed and sweating, feeling the sting of phantom fish tails against his face. He'd been dreaming again. After a night of tossing and turning and finding every lump and button on that torture rack of a mattress, he had finally sunk into exhausted slumber just before dawn. And he soon found himself entangled in both damp sheets and disturbing dreams.

It wasn't the first time fish had appeared in his dreams. In London, the morning after he first encountered Celeste Ashton, he had awakened with his hands flailing about his face, pushing away the fish tails that were swarming around him. Virtually every night since, his beleaguered mind conjured up some strange vignette or other involving fish, whose tails usually ended up in his face.

Last night there were fish eating other fish. The big ones that were doing the eating turned and winked at him. Then they blew him kisses with huge, cherry-red lips. When he didn't respond, they grew irate and began to chase him. The chase ended when he stumbled and scraped his leg, and they all took turns swatting him in the face with their tails.

"Damned silly dreams," he muttered, hauling himself out of bed and throwing open the window for a bit of fresh salt air. His injured ankle was too tender for his usual morning calisthenics, so he settled on the floor for a few push-ups instead. As he completed twenty, he realized he was doing them in rhythm . . . five quick ones . . . and a longer, slower one. He paused and sat for a moment, hearing that same infectious rhythm he had drummed out last night, and thinking for a moment that it was his heart beating that way. Grabbing his chest in alarm, he soon realized that it was coming from *out*side, not *in*side.

It was *her,* calling her dolphins again. The sound was drifting in through the open window.

After breakfast in the dining room with an inquisitive Lady Sophia, he found himself ushered through the house and out the kitchen door, his hands filled with food and drink for Celeste. When she was on the trail of a discovery, Lady Sophia had declared, her granddaughter could be forgetful of her health and well-being. Thus, he had to make his way down the stepped cliff, across the soft beach, and along the rocky path to the dock while juggling a covered metal bucket, a cloth-draped basket, and a plate of warm scones.

"Miss Ashton!" he called, from the edge of the dock.

Her head popped out the boathouse door.

"In here!"

When he ducked inside, the far wall swung open and he nearly dropped the things in his hands. He located her several feet below dock level, standing in a sailboat somewhat larger than a dinghy, struggling with the boathouse's other door. One final heave sent it swinging back, where it banged against the outside wall and set the entire structure vibrating.

"Come on, get in," she called, ducking under a boom draped with canvas.

"You cannot mean now, this minute," he said, feeling his chest contract about his lungs as he eyed the modest craft. "Your grandmother sent your breakfast down with me."

"Good, I'll eat once we're under way. Hand it down and climb aboard."

A moment later, she was balancing against the mast, in the bow of the boat, and reaching up to take the food from him.

"I thought you said you could call the dolphins from here, Miss Ashton."

"I called again this morning and they still haven't arrived. If we go and meet them, it will save considerable time."

"I am in no hurry," he said.

"Are you not?" She used the dock to pull herself and the boat closer to him. "Well, I am."

He looked down at the dark algae-filled water beside the boat, then at the weathered boards of the hull and the cracked planks that formed the seats. With paralyzing alarm, he realized that the boat was likely of the same vintage as the boathouse itself, and probably in the same dire need of repair.

"Well?"

With effort, he focused his eyes and found her standing with her hands on her waist, looking up at him with a scowl.

"I—I'm not a sailor," he managed to get out.

She folded her arms. "Well, I am. This is my methodology, Professor. You publicly questioned the plausibility of my going out in a boat, alone, to dive and swim with dolphins. I must insist that I be given the chance to prove myself."

Her chin was up and the gauntlet was down.

He had no choice.

Five

WITH EVERY STEP down the rickety ladder, Titus expected to hear the crack of the wood giving way, to feel that dark water closing around him. It took a supreme act of will to tear his gaze from that ominous water and lower himself onto a splintery seat in the middle of the boat. He gripped the wood of the seat with one hand and the boom with the other. He tensed, shutting his eyes, feeling the air around him suddenly chill and knowing—dreading—what was coming.

The boat began to rock, and the rocking grew until the craft was heaving and bucking wildly. He was frozen; his hands were so icy he could scarcely feel the ropes or the railing in his grip. There was fierce noise and violent water everywhere, lashing him, stinging his eyes and face as it slammed in giant waves over the boat. Everything was filling with water—he could feel the cold rising around his legs, the treacherous waves pulling at him as he struggled to remain upright—

"You're not sitting there?" Her voice penetrated that storm of memories. He managed to pry one eye open and looked up. She stood near his shoulder with her hands on her hips . . . warm and clear-eyed and reassuringly real. "You're too tall. If I have to tack, you will be knocked into the water. This is only a catboat . . . mast in the bow, sailed from the stern. The sail has to have room to swing." She suggested the motion and range of the sail with a hand. He looked back at the mast, then at the height of the boom in relation to his shoulder, and promptly lowered himself to a seat on the very bottom of the boat.

Maneuvering the boat out into the cove with practiced ease, she took the wind direction and, with a graceful economy of movement, hoisted the triangular sail. When the breeze filled the canvas, she wrapped the lines around a cleat on the rail beside her and settled into the stern seat, propping a foot against the tiller.

The professor sat in the damp bottom of the boat, staring at her unladylike pose and struggling to maintain his own rigid posture. He flinched at every roll of the boat or errant splash of water. As they left the cove and encountered the larger waves of the open sea, his hands grew white on the seat at his back and the rest of him turned a ghastly shade of green.

Sick, she realized with mild surprise. He was prone to seasickness. No wonder he'd been so reluctant to go out with her in the boat. She offered him a bite of a jam-slathered scone and grinned when he closed his eyes and wrenched his face away. She poured herself a mug of tea from the earthen jug in the bucket, and sat back in the stern to enjoy the rhythm of the waves against the bow, the play of the wind in the sail, and the arrogant professor's seagoing misery.

As the land shrank behind them, she turned the boat to follow the coastline, pointing out familiar houses and landmarks that he refused to turn his head to see. When they reached the place she intended, she struck sail and pulled a pair of mallets from the tack box under the stern seat. As the boat rocked gently, she rapped out her dolphin call on the hull and paused periodically to scan the bobbing waves for a dorsal fin or leaping dolphin.

After an hour of intermittent rapping, the caw of gulls

and the swoop of terns were still the only signs of life outside the boat. There weren't many signs of life inside the boat, either. She looked at Titus Thorne's braced form and tightly shut eyes and at the water collecting in the bottom of the boat around his rear quarters and outstretched legs. "Wouldn't you be more comfortable on a seat, Professor?"

"I would not." He opened his eyes to a narrow squint.

"I thought you might feel warmer if you weren't sitting in a puddle."

He looked down at the pool he was sitting in, apparently perceiving it for the first time. He scrambled up and grabbed the boom, struggling against the pitching of the boat— which he himself was causing. "Water—we're taking on water!"

She flung her arms and legs against the sides to steady the craft. "All boats take on some water—we're in no danger . . . unless you keep thrashing about. Sit down, Professor, or you'll tip us over!"

He sat down abruptly on the center seat, still hugging the beam. "How can you go to sea in this—this—wreck?"

"One makes do with what one has, Professor." She settled back onto her seat. "This is the boat I learned to sail in. My grandfather taught me when I was six or seven, and I've taken this boat out by myself since I was thirteen."

"Six or seven?" he bit out testily. "You expect me to believe you've been doing this since you were little more than an infant?"

"I was practically born on the water. My father was an avid sailor—he and my mother were out in a boat and they barely made it back to land in time for my birthing. I'm told they taught me to swim before I could walk."

"That explains a great deal," he muttered. "Salt water has a notoriously corrosive effect."

She studied his foul humor. "I take it you don't like the water."

"What is there to like?" he said, avoiding her gaze. "It's wet, cold, deep, and treacherous. If the Almighty had meant mankind to spend time sloshing about in water, he'd have given us webbed feet."

She smiled defiantly. "He gave us *boats* and *sails* instead. Look around you, Professor." She swept a hand around the glittering, sunlit expanse of water. "Isn't this much better than being cooped up in a smelly little room somewhere, poking through fish entrails?"

A hint of color appeared in the gray of his countenance. "The air may be a bit better, Miss Ashton, but from what I can see, the *science* certainly is not. There is nothing informative or enlightening about sculling around out here in a leaky old bucket, hoping to catch a glimpse of a fin or a fluke. By your own account, six- and seven-year-olds can do as much."

Stung, she shot him a glare. "Sailing is hardly child's play, Professor."

"Nor is it science, Miss Ashton. Science is meticulous, methodical, painstaking—sometimes backbreaking—work. It isn't the least bit glamorous or exciting. True research requires slogging through the minute, often messy details of the natural world, and then piecing those bits and details together into a coherent picture."

"But science is also about pushing back the limits of knowledge, taking risks, trying new things, combining ideas and experiences in fresh, new ways."

"Is that what your grandfather taught you, Miss Ashton? That science is some grand and romantic quest?"

"My grandfather taught me a good many things, Professor, including open-mindedness . . . a lesson that *your* grandfather apparently forgot to include."

Something flickered briefly in his eyes, but after a moment it was gone and he was again his acerbic, professorial self. "There you are wrong, Miss Ashton." He smiled sardonically. "I never had a grandfather."

She caught herself staring at him, wondering what lay beneath that casual, caustic tone. Unsettled by her incurably personal interest in him, she forced her attention back to her dolphin call.

Half an hour passed before he spoke again, surprising her with a question. "What happened to your parents?"

She hesitated, but could think of no reason to refuse to answer. "They were lost on an expedition to Tibet, researching the religious and social customs of remote villages. My father was something of an anthropologist and my mother's work complemented his. She studied women's work and child-rearing practices wherever they went: Africa—the Gold Coast, Persia, India, Tibet. Adventure apparently runs in Ashton blood. Or maybe it's just a contagion that we catch from one another. We're always going somewhere and investigating something."

She rose and busied herself unkinking a knot in the sail lines. "What about your family? What do they do?"

"Don't have one."

"But you must have had . . . at least parents."

"They died. Long ago." He looked decidedly uncomfortable.

"Well, what did they do before they died?"

"Breathed, I should imagine." He shifted his glare to the mallets lying on her seat. "Shouldn't you be calling your finny friends, Miss Ashton?"

Irritated by his dismissal of her question, she turned back to her calls and pounded the side of the boat with considerably more force.

After what seemed a small eternity, she peeled herself upright, rolled her aching shoulders, and stared at the unbroken waves around them. Under the professor's accusing glare, she was forced to face the unpleasant facts. Her dolphins weren't anywhere nearby.

She raised the sail again and headed for the cove with a gathering sense of doom. If this kept up, Titus Thorne would be publishing an account of her methods that would make a complete fool out of her and everything she'd been trying to accomplish.

She considered tipping the boat to give him a good drenching, but settled for turning the boat slightly more across the wind, so that the hull bumped as it cut across the waves. Noting his white-knuckled grip on the side and seat as the bow smacked the water again and again, she consoled herself with the thought that his churning stomach and wet clothes were probably quite uncomfortable.

Discomfort was the perfect description for Titus Thorne's condition, on every possible level. The wool of his trousers had wicked so much water that his entire seat and legs were now sopping wet. His collar had absorbed moisture from the spray and lay drooping, the dampened starch in his shirt was sticking to him beneath his coat, and his hair was virtually standing on end. His limbs were aching with cold and the strain of keeping him upright, and his stomach was doing agonizing somersaults each time they crested a wave and sank again.

But those conditions, vexing as they were, could not obscure the fact that Celeste Ashton did indeed know how to handle a boat. Leaning against the sway, casually weaving her wrist in a spiral to take up the line as if she'd done that small maneuver a thousand times before, facing into the wind as if drawing energy and pleasure from it . . . she behaved as if she had indeed spent her whole life on the water. Even the way she was dressed—a pale blue skirt and simple peasant blouse, her hair pulled back into a single, utilitarian braid—seemed perfectly suited to seagoing adventures.

Despite his efforts to blunt awareness of this whole, wretched experience, he also had managed to notice that her cheeks were wind-kissed and rosy and that her eyes shone with delight at being on the water and sailing her own small boat. She belonged here. The insight disturbed him. Her claim of sailing and being out on the water alone was absolutely *true*.

But as they nosed back into the cove's calmer waters, and he returned to a less harried state of mind, he reassessed the importance of that conclusion. She might indeed be some-

thing of a sailor, but that was a long way from diving unassisted in the open ocean and being adopted by a roving herd
of hedonistic dolphins.

With his skepticism battered but still functional, he
stepped out of the boat on wobbly legs, jerked his damp vest
down into place, and resisted the impulse to fall to his knees
and kiss every rotten board in that decrepit dock.

AFTER LUNCHEON, CELESTE excused herself to her rooms
for a time and Lady Sophia excused herself to the library.
Titus was left to his own devices and found himself consumed with dread at knowing that Celeste intended to go
out in the boat again that afternoon. After futile attempts at
resting in his room and making notes in his damp journal—
the ink bled into fat, fuzzy letters, an exercise in frustration—he escaped his room to prowl around the venerable
old house.

Even in the unseasonable warmth of the afternoon, the
old halls were serenely cool and shaded. Wandering the paneled corridors, he investigated a number of portraits, hang-
ings, and aged but exotic furnishings. There were paintings
on silk from the Orient, carved chests and cast-bronze lamp
stands in Middle Eastern motifs, and screens of camphor
wood inlaid with ivory. Clearly, in earlier days, Ashton
House's residents had been persons of wealth and world experience. After a time he found himself strolling down a side
hallway on the main floor, heading for a column of light cast
on the wall by a door left ajar.

Stealing to the opening and peering inside, he saw library
shelves stuffed with oddly shaped stones, reassembled vases,
ancient-looking wooden chests, stone obelisks, massive
shells, and bits of corroded bronze resembling round shields.
Around the edges of the room were crates and stacks of
books that served as stands for artifacts, piles of cotton wool
used for packing, plaster castings, and trays in which lay
shards of crockery and bits of bone.

He gave the door a nudge. As it swung back he saw that the rest of the room was even more cluttered . . . with boxes, chests, larger inscribed stones, eroded statuary, and a few odd iron and wooden pieces that might have been either artifacts or furnishings.

Bathed in bright sunlight from the tall, leaded windows and bent over a cluttered worktable, was Lady Sophia, dressed in her customary gray dress, open entirely down the back. He must have made a sound because she turned, spotted him, and produced a smile that could have melted polar icecaps.

"Professor! Do come in." She beckoned with the shard of pottery in her hand.

"I don't wish to disturb—" But his curiosity got the better of him. "What the devil is all this?"

She beamed with proprietary pleasure at the motley collection around her. "This is my work, Professor. I'm continuing my late husband's studies of the artifacts and culture of the Lost Civilization." Seeing his frown deepen, she clarified: "Atlantis. Surely you know of the legend of the lost continent . . . sunken in the Atlantic . . . spoken of in Plato's dialogues . . ."

"Of course I know it." Indeed, there was scarcely a boy who got through grammar-school Latin without hearing the tantalizing legend. He looked from her to the maze of crates, objects, artifacts, and equipment stacked higgledy-piggledy about the room. "You mean to say you're working on . . . that these objects supposedly come from—"

"Atlantis." She folded her hands and rocked up on her toes, glowing like a young girl. "My Martin devoted his life to finding evidence of that great uncharted civilization. After his untimely death, well, I simply couldn't allow his whole life's work to go for naught." She smiled fondly at the stacks of crates and stones, sketches, trays, and plaster impressions. "And since I was with him on all his journeys and excavations, and was sometimes drafted to serve as his secretary, who better to interpret his journals and continue the analysis of his findings?"

"Atlantis. The lost continent in the Atlantic Ocean. Sir Martin found *factual* evidence, of the existence of Atlantis?" He scowled at the crowded and chaotic room. The place looked as if someone had set off a bomb in the basement of the British Museum. "And this"—he gestured to the artifacts—"is that evidence?"

"It is, indeed." Lady Sophia clasped her hands to contain her excitement.

"That is absolutely . . . without a doubt the most . . ." He halted, struck powerfully by the old lady's silver hair, lively blue eyes, and gently aged face. "It's simply . . . utterly . . . inescapably . . ." Curious . . . how the light in her countenance made her seem both very old and very young at the same time.

Titus Thorne had never been a man to peer too deeply into his fellow beings. The inner workings of even the most rational members of the human species had always seemed to him to be messy and appallingly unpredictable. But just now, without trying to or even wanting to, he could see the old lady's entire inner landscape, laid out before him like an open book. He saw a lifetime spent at her husband's side, the affection and respect born of those many years, her immense grief at his passing, and the determination to carry on his work that had become her own reason to go on living. It was all so clear and so personal that he felt like a bloody window peeper.

He shifted his feet, felt his collar suddenly grow restrictive, and wished he could somehow block out those unsettling impressions. But it was too late; that unsought knowledge of who and what she was had already insinuated itself into the equation of his reaction. He groped for a way to complete the sentence he'd left hanging and found himself declaring her assertions to be *"fascinating."*

She beamed. "Come, I'll show you some of our treasures."

Taking him by the arm, she led him through a stack of crates to where a bizarre-looking stone-and-bronze object sat warming in the afternoon sun. It had a large, flat, carved stone base that resembled a hefty bench, with three enormous bronze spikes attached along the far side, forming something resembling a pitchfork. Along two ends were clumps of what appeared to be bronze rope rounded into arches, some strands of which had been beaten flat and twisted into odd, undulating ribbons. He bent for a closer look.

There were carvings on the bench itself: shells, fish, stylized waves, clearly a nautical motif. The designs were simple, even primitive, but the closer he looked at them, the more he perceived the delicacy of their craft. The gray, flecked stone was cool and surprisingly smooth to the touch . . . granite, he guessed, and highly polished. Examining the spearlike projections, he suddenly recognized them as the points of a trident. Of course, he thought. A marine motif . . . it was Poseidon's scepter. The curious bench was in fact . . .

"A chair," he announced, glancing at Lady Sophia.

"A very special chair." She fairly giggled with excitement. "A *throne*."

"Throne?" He stepped back to take in a fuller view and banged into an obelisk. He wheeled, caught it just in time, and found himself holding a tapered stone column about shoulder height, engraved with all manner of spirals, stylized waves, and fish. Not *fish*. He squinted and bent closer to examine them. *Dolphins*. He jerked his hands away.

When he looked up, Lady Sophia was gazing fondly at the piece. "It's one of the crowning jewels of our collection, you know. From the temple of Poseidon, probably in the heart of the great capital city of Atlantis. Not quite grand enough to be intended for Poseidon himself. More likely a priest's or priestess's. Women figured quite prominently in their religious orders, you know. As did all things from the sea."

She led him to a number of beaten-copper and bronze
shields, stacked on boxes and propped against the walls. He
had taken them for arms, but now saw that they were too
broad and thin for military purposes and were covered with a
sort of pictographic writing.

"At first, we couldn't imagine how these were used." She
lifted one and offered it for his inspection. "But we eventually realized they were covered with descriptions of the temple in which they once hung. They depict images of the
sacred rituals of the people of Atlantis." She waved a hand
indicating the circular shape and then narrowed in on the
spirals and circles on the edge of the disk. "Waves, circles,
and spirals seem to have held great meaning in their culture.
Completion, perhaps. Or connection. Return. Celestial
rhythms. So many interesting possibilities in a circle. And
waves actually are really circles in disguise, you know. My
Martin used to try to explain the theory behind that to me,
but, I confess, I never quite grasped it."

She introduced him to several other pieces, watching intently his handling of the artifacts. Then, as he peered into
several other crates, she turned to a small polished chest on a
nearby shelf, and produced something wrapped in black velvet and tied with a golden cord. He pulled his attention from
the large stone carving on a pedestal in the corner . . .
another damnable *dolphin* . . .

"This is something I've been working on for some time,"
she said with a pensive frown. "Ingenious bit of workmanship, I'll say that. We found it in the remains of a degraded
wooden box, preserved in a large marble catafalque." She
opened the cloth reverently to reveal what appeared to be a
set of notched silver sticks, each about six inches long, some
of which were intricately angled on the ends. Each bore
markings that looked like a combination of Scandinavian
runes and Egyptian hieroglyphs.

"I believe they're some sort of ritual puzzle, like the
Urim and Thummin of biblical days. Created to give celestial advice to mortal decision makers. But"—she gave a wist-

ful sigh—"I have never been able to put it together properly.
I don't even know what shape it is supposed to be."

Scowling, he looked from her hopeful gaze to the bundle
of rectangular metal rods and reached for the cloth. Picking
them up, one by one, he held them up to the light and
examined their workmanship and curious markings. It was
highly doubtful that these silver jackstraws, however unusual,
were the "holy dice" of the lost continent of Atlantis. But he
had to admit he'd never seen anything even remotely like
them. As he examined one after the other, he found himself
growing strangely absorbed in the challenge of their mystery.

"Are you certain they're all here?" he asked, experimen-
tally fitting the end of one to the end of another.

She shrugged. "How can one ever be certain with an
artifact?"

Pursing his lips, he retreated to a seat, spread the cloth on
his lap, and began to join the ends of the sticks together at
various angles, matching angles and patterns of the engrav-
ings in what he hoped were logical configurations.

Half an hour later, Celeste hurried into the library with
her face flushed and eyes stormy. "Nana, have you seen the
professor? He seems to have—"

She stopped at the sight of her grandmother pressing a
finger against her lips. When the old lady stepped out of her
line of sight, Celeste beheld Titus Thorne sitting on what
they all had come to regard as "Poseidon's throne," contemplating the half-assembled skeleton of a silver sphere.

Her stomach slid toward her knees as she glanced around
the cluttered library and realized that for the professor to be
sitting there, contemplating Nana's special puzzle, Nana
must have told him all about Atlantis. This was all she
needed: his scientific outrage aggravated by her grandmother's impassioned lectures on the world's desperate need
for the resurrected culture of the lost Atlantis.

"There you are." She strode briskly around the worktable
to stand before him with her hands on her waist. "I've been

searching everywhere for you. We have to put out soon or we'll lose the light coming back."

"Sorry, dear." Nana slipped around the table. "The professor wandered in, and I couldn't resist showing him some of your grandfather's finds."

"It must fascinate him, I know," she responded tightly. "But we have another scientific issue to settle first."

He shot up from his seat, reddening. "I should—indeed—" He looked at the half-assembled artifact in his hands as if wondering how it got there, then quickly glanced about for a place to dispose of it. Nana came to his rescue, and as he transferred it to her hands, it collapsed once more into a jumble of sticks.

The old lady watched her granddaughter usher the professor from the library and then lowered her smile to the pile of "sacred jackstraws" she held. In her mind's eye, they became once again the skeletal orb that had begun to take shape as the professor worked on the puzzle. Moisture collected in the corners of her eyes as she rolled them heavenward.

"It's *him*, Martin. Our 'Man of Earth.' He's finally here."

Six

THE WIND HAD GENTLED, giving the sea beyond the cove the smooth, satiny appearance of rain-soaked pavement and puffy white clouds had sprung up to block some of the strong afternoon sun. She stayed ahead of him by a pace or two as they approached the path down the cliff.

"So . . . your grandfather discovered the remains of the lost civilization of Atlantis." When her step faltered briefly, he continued: "You Ashtons certainly are an inventive breed, I'll give you that. But then you said as much, earlier."

"Inquisitive." She halted and turned with her eyes narrowed, forcing him to stop as well. "I said we are inquisitive. We *discover* things, we don't *invent* them." After a moment, she proceeded down the path. But the heat of his first gibe didn't have time to dissipate before he fired another salvo.

"Well, perhaps you should take a lesson from your grandmother . . . be certain you have plenty of evidence of your 'discovery' on hand before you write a book about it."

She turned back with rising anger. "How dare you suggest that my grandmother and I make false claims and manufacture evidence?"

"I made no such charge. I merely observed that your grandmother at least has something tangible to present as evidence to substantiate her claims." A glint appeared in his eye. "She even has several *dolphins*."

Celeste's cheeks caught fire, but she refused to give way to his goading. "You'll see evidence of my dolphins soon enough. Until then, may I remind you that you are here to verify my writings, nothing else. My grandmother's work is not open to examination."

"And why is that?" he demanded. "Because you don't believe her claims about the artifacts are true?"

"Because it isn't relevant." She struggled to contain her temper as she wheeled and started down the steps again.

"What isn't relevant? Her work or the truth about it?" He hurried down the steps behind her. "Or perhaps you're just being pragmatic . . . saving her work for the next book . . . the next tidy bundle of cash."

She stopped dead. Money? Was that what he thought this was about? Reversing course, she stalked back with her shoulders braced and her chin up.

"Look around you, Professor," she commanded, flinging a hand toward the house, part of which was still visible above the edge of the cliff. "Our roof sags, our windows are warped, our floors need bracing, and our furnishings have scarcely been so much as rearranged since Tudor times. We draw all our water from an outside well; we have the luxury of an icebox only in winter; our household linen is near a century old; and there isn't a decent 'necessary' on the place. Does it honestly look to you as though we're getting rich from the proceeds of the 'clever fraud' I've perpetrated?"

She looked directly up at him. His lean features were taut, his body radiated an intriguing mélange of heat and male scents, and in the depths of his eyes she glimpsed a shimmering distortion like that which rises above a hot blue flame.

In spite of her better judgment, she lowered her gaze to his parted lips.

The memory of being caught in his arms, pressed tight against his body, and kissed until her knees melted, materialized in her senses. There was yet another aspect to Titus

Thorne's nature, she realized, something less intellectual, less controlled. Something passionate. It was evident even to her untutored eye. She could see it in his movement, hear it in the huskiness of his voice. And when he looked at her, she could feel it with every exposed inch of her skin.

She whirled back around and headed down the path on wobbly legs.

When they reached the boat, Titus Thorne looked down at it with disdain.

"I see absolutely no sense in my putting out in a boat again," he declared stiffly, folding his arms over his chest. "You've proven that you're a sailor . . . I'll give you that." He untucked a hand to give a dismissive wave. "Just go fetch your blessed dolphins and haul them back to the dock. I'll wait here."

She bristled at his high-handed manner.

"And give you reason to doubt my methods and harbor suspicions that I've somehow 'manufactured' my dolphins? No, sir." She narrowed her eyes and lowered her voice to the bottom of its register. "Climb down into the boat, Professor."

With that she turned on her heel and headed for the boathouse. He was left staring after her, watching her skirt swish the dock with each irritable stride she took. Pulling his gaze from that absorbing sight, he studied the boat for a moment. After a brief but intense struggle between his pride and his instinct for self-preservation, he forced himself to take hold of the ladder and swing around onto the first rung.

In spite of his determination, he felt the blood draining from his extremities as he lowered himself to the boat, steadied himself on the boom, and eased onto the middle seat. Lord, how he hated water and boats. He swallowed hard and then swallowed hard again, fighting to keep the memories at bay. But everything around him was only a reminder . . . the damp wood of the hull, the scent of the salt water, musty canvas, ropes . . .

The roar came first, then that sudden, paralyzing chill that invaded his limbs. Everything darkened in his vision, and grayed. Then he felt the boat beginning to roll and pitch under him, as memory confounded present sense, making it seem he was again in motion. Everything was wet. Even the air was filled with water—plunging, battering waves and vicious spray.

The roar grew deafening and he cried out, inside his own head, to the man struggling with a sail stuck halfway down. With icy hands, he gripped ropes he could no longer feel. That horror, so distant in time, still held him as he felt the boat give a violent heave beneath him and saw the boom break free. And he watched, as he had a thousand times in memory, his father's coat disappearing beneath a huge wave. He had been a boy of seven . . . too young, too small to do anything but hang on to the lines his father had tied around him. A brief summer squall. And his life had changed forever.

He battled those disturbing visions back to the periphery of his soul and shook his head to clear it. Damned boats. Damned water. He took a heavy breath. Why did it have to be *dolphins*?

When he finally looked up, Celeste was casting off the line and starting down the ladder. Her free arm was full of something, but after she lifted her skirt to climb down he glimpsed bare flesh—from trim ankles all the way to shapely knees.

When she stepped from the ladder and released her skirts, it took a full minute for him to recognize that they weren't the same blue cotton she had worn that morning. Somewhere along the way, she had changed into a long smock or duster of some sort . . . a heavy, shapeless dark green affair with large sleeves and no collar.

Neither spoke as she maneuvered out into the cove, then onto the wide, open waters of Pevensey Bay. The wind and sea were so much calmer that they seemed to float along on top of the water as she steered them along the same course they had sailed earlier in the day.

Braced in the bottom of the boat, Titus stretched his neck to peer over the side at the placid waves. Surprised by the calm sea, he felt his stomach with one hand and released his death grip on the seat and edge.

"Feeling somewhat better, I take it," she observed.

"Somewhat." He looked up. "Considerably. A great deal better, in fact."

"A pity." She gave an exaggerated sigh of resignation. "I was rather looking forward to watching you turn forty shades of green again."

"Sorry to disappoint you. Perhaps you can amuse yourself by watching me drown in this blasted bilgewater, instead," he responded, shifting irritably in the water collecting around his hindquarters again.

"You might try sitting on a seat," she proposed, looking down her nose and smiling. "Revolutionary idea, I know."

Unwilling to test his good fortune and risk upsetting his stomach, he folded his arms, making it plain that he intended to stay where he was . . . until he looked up and spotted two blankets stacked on the stern seat, a yard away. He scooted a few inches along the bottom, stretched mightily, snagged them, and stuffed them beneath him.

They sailed on for a while, listening to the caw of the gulls, the quiet rush of water past the bow, and the occasional rustle of canvas as it caught the uneven wind. It didn't take Titus long to realize he'd made a tactical mistake in choosing to sit in the bottom again. His only view was up and to the rear . . . a vista occupied entirely by Celeste Ashton and her wind-teased hair, flashing blue eyes, and bare ankles showing as she propped her feet up on the seat.

Lord. Did she have to sit like that? Knees raised, bare flesh showing . . . He found himself staring at the hem of her baggy smock, recalling the shapely contours of what lay beneath it and feeling himself warming to his thoughts. Suddenly the wet chill in his nether regions took on a disturbingly erotic feel. He shifted to a less stimulating position and glared at the cause of his discomfort.

"So . . . you don't believe your grandfather found evidence of Atlantis," he said in a challenging tone. "That's why you won't discuss it."

She gave him an abrupt, piercing look. "I've said all I have to say about that. It has nothing to do with my work or the reason you're here."

"Very well. Then tell me, Miss Ashton, what is your real purpose in bringing me out here, sailing fruitlessly back and forth, and wearing my patience and my health down to bare tacks?"

"I should think that was obvious, Professor," she said, still busily scanning the horizon. "To make you see and experience what I do. To give you a taste of my methodology as well as a glimpse of my dolphins."

"Come now, Miss Ashton. Neither of us was born yesterday." He folded his arms and leaned back against the seat. "You've concocted a clever scheme here. Downright ingenious. But you and I both know, we could sail around out here for weeks without spotting a single seagoing mammal outside this boat."

He gave her a smile intended to draw her into an air of confidence, and watched with anticipation as she lowered her feet and shifted to face him.

"I doubt it will take that long, Professor."

"For what? For me to lose all track of reality and begin seeing pink dolphins leaping around? Or perhaps *blue-eyed mermaids*?" When she slipped the tie rope over the tiller arm and abruptly made her way forward to lower the sails, he came to attention, feeling he had somehow touched a nerve.

"I have to admit," he continued, "the 'mermaid' idea is nothing short of inspired. You certainly have the looks for it." That caused her a moment's pause; he could almost see her ears straining for more. "And using portraits as a rebuttal for all of those ridiculous cartoons . . . a master stroke. Truly." He leaned forward. "What's next? Pear Soap adverts?"

"What?" She turned, bracing against the mast.

"You know . . . Pear Soap advertisements. The company contracts with professional beauties to lend a face and a name to their advertising notices." He gave her a tart look of appraisal. "I can see you now . . . hair undone . . . wearing strategically placed cockle shells . . . stuffed into a sequined fish tail . . ."

"I had nothing to do with that 'mermaid' nonsense," she declared, reddening and turning back to lower the sail with a smack. "It was merely an idea of Mr. Cherrybottom's that somehow got into the newspapers and then got totally out of hand. I've told him I want it stopped, immediately."

"Ummm. And you were so opposed to it that you posed for portraits portraying you as the sultry-eyed siren of the sea." He smiled. "Interesting sort of protest."

She flushed crimson. "Mr. Cherrybottom had a photographer set up equipment in the lobby of the hotel and I merely sat for a few moments while the fellow took a few—" She sat down on the edge of the stern seat, gripping her knees. "What's this about portraits?"

"One was published in the *Gazette* the day I arrived." He studied her surprise, deciding it was probably genuine. "I take it you haven't seen it. Capital likeness. Definitely highlights your best attributes."

He leaned back against the seat, and swept her with a look. "Take a bit of friendly advice, Miss Ashton. If you think your little mermaid charade is going to work on me, you're quite mistaken. I'm here to see your dolphins, not your"—his gaze dropped to her skirts—"*flippers*. And I won't settle for anything less."

"You'll see dolphins, all right," she declared, scanning the waters around them.

"I know . . ." He leaned forward, his eyes glowing. "Why don't you just slip into your tail fins, dive into the water, and go *look* for them, like a good little mermaid?"

She stared at him for a moment, then, to his surprise, threw him a half-smile.

"Excellent idea, Professor." She stood up and reached for

the buttons of her smock. "You obviously won't be satisfied until you've seen the *Lady Mermaid* at work." One button gave, then a second . . . "So, why not show you how she works?" A third . . . a fourth . . . a fifth . . .

His jaw loosened. His attention fixed frantically on the parting button placket of her smock. Good Lord—he'd called her bluff and now she was taking off her clothes! He swallowed hard, feeling his senses springing to life, focusing in spite of himself on the white muslin being bared before his eyes. Then she bent to reach the lower buttons and he glimpsed a rounded bit of flesh down the front of her . . . what, shift? Shirt? Oh, who the hell cared what they called it?

He almost groaned aloud when she straightened, ripping those erotic curves from his sight. But then she stood for a moment, her smock completely undone, her eyes heated, her thick golden braid draped over her shoulder. For a moment, the sun lit her hair from behind and he realized he was doomed.

She was going to slide that smock from her shoulders . . . and stand there in all her seductive, golden-haired glory, tantalizing him. Then she was going to come to him and glide down atop him . . . and he was going to lose every shred of objectivity and integrity he possessed. He was going to make mad, passionate love to her on a bed of blankets oozing bilgewater.

Oh, God . . . why couldn't he just have been seasick?

CELESTE STOOD COLLECTING his attention, prolonging the suspense, letting him wonder, making him wait. With a deliberate air, she peeled back her long smock and let it slide down her shoulders. She paused in her short, knitted cotton combinations, giving him a glimpse of what a "mermaid" really wore. Then she bent down to pick up the goggles from her tackle box, stepped up on the seat, and dove in a graceful arc, straight into the sea.

The chill of the blue-gray water was both familiar and welcome against her burning skin. The sea closed around her like a caress that covered every inch of her being, massaging away her tension and much of her anger. She surfaced briefly to don her goggles, then filled her lungs and dived in earnest . . . leveling at a modest depth and circling in a spiral pattern . . . searching the blue-tinged depths for the silver flash of a fin or fluke, and alert for the prickle in her skin caused by the clicking sounds her dolphins produced . . . never far from that dark, rectangular shape bobbing on the surface, overhead.

TITUS SAT FOR a minute, blinking at the place where she had stood an instant before. She was gone.

Overboard—she'd gone *overboard*! Abandoned ship!

Abandoned? He'd been abandoned?

"Aghhhh!" He scrambled up onto his knees, grabbed the side, and peered over it at the endless expanse of swaying water. "Miss Ashton?" he called, his voice suddenly hoarse. "Miss Ash— Celeste! Where are you? Don't be absurd—you can't just plunge into the ocean!"

But she had indeed taken that plunge, and now wasn't anywhere to be seen. He swallowed hard and turned his head enough to see that she wasn't visible on that side. She had probably gone to the other side. Yes, that was it—she swam around the boat! It took Herculean effort for him to peel his cold fingers from the edge and make his way to the other side, where he wrapped his hands over the edge and pulled himself up.

No mermaid.

"Miss Ashton," he roared, "this is *not* amusing!"

His heart was hammering so loudly, he wasn't sure he would hear her if she did answer. After a moment, anxiety and frustration got the better of him.

"Dammit, Celeste—get back here and get back in the boat!"

The only response was the gentle, laughterlike lapping of the water on the sides of the boat. His anxiety bloomed to true panic.

He wrenched about, craning his neck, trying to determine his location. Blood drained from his head at the sight of the distant shore. Thousands of yards. A mile. Maybe two.

He looked up at the bare mast and then at the tiller, realizing just how little he knew about sailing. He glanced back at the shore. What did it matter how far? He'd never get there. He had sworn, long ago, to never ever set foot in a boat again. And here he was, at the mercy of a merciless sea once again.

Wild thoughts began to streak through his mind. He could drift out to sea and never be seen or heard from again. She was probably swimming for shore, leaving him to fend for himself in that leaking wreck . . . figuring that if he was lost at sea, her problem was solved. Who else would dare to challenge her work, if her first investigator met an untimely end? Wait—another boat—there had to be fishing in the area—somebody would see him—eventually—

He edged toward the bow and searched the water between the boat and shore for sign of her. Nothing. With waves and reflection, he couldn't be certain of anything more than a few yards away.

CELESTE SURFACED FOR the third time, resting and drinking air gratefully into her starved lungs. She had stayed down as long as she dared, searching, checking every glimmer she saw, but she had nothing to show for it. She swam the few yards to the boat. As she reached the side, she halted, treading water. She had a problem.

She removed her goggles, hung them on her arm and looked down at her wet combinations, seeing altogether too much of herself through the now-translucent knit. In her pride-driven determination to demonstrate her diving prowess and continue her search for her dolphins, she hadn't reckoned with having to climb back into the boat with him, dry off, and then sail all the way back to—

Suddenly, she thought of the blankets sopping up water in the bottom of the boat and she groaned. The boat rocked and dipped and Titus Thorne's widened eyes appeared over the side.

"It's *you*!" He sounded relieved. For a moment. "Where the bloody hell have you been? How dare you just plunge off into the bloody perilous ocean and leave me here in this rotten death trap of a boat—without a single word of warning or a plan for getting back into shore if—if something should happen? Dammit, anything could happen! There are huge fish . . . sharks . . . rampaging squid strangulating people out here! In case you hadn't noticed—this is the bloody treacherous *ocean* you're poking around in!"

If it hadn't been for his thunderous volume, she would have sworn he was hysterical.

"I was searching for Prospero and the others," she replied calmly. "I dive all the time, Professor, in the bloody treacherous ocean." She took hold of the side of the boat. It dipped under her weight, and he flung himself backward to offset the force.

"What the hell are you doing?" he yelled. "You'll swamp us!"

"It takes a good bit more than me climbing aboard to swamp this boat," she said, feeling her chin starting to quiver. "Professor—I have a problem."

"On that, we most assuredly *agree*," he declared, seeming a bit more in control. "But now is hardly the time to discuss your mental competence. Climb in the damned boat!"

"Well, that *is* the problem, actually. I'm used to diving alone and when I'm all wet . . . well . . . Could you close your eyes, while I climb in? I'm starting to get cold."

When he poked his head over the side to stare down at her, his eyes widened in comprehension, and he quickly retreated. There was a pause, and a bit of muttering that sounded faintly profane.

"All right. Climb aboard," he called out.

She grabbed the side, hoisted herself up, levered herself onto her chest, then swung a leg up and over the side, as she had done a thousand times before. In a moment, she was standing in the stern, dripping wet, trying to brush water from her skin and wring it from her braid and the abbreviated legs of her combination. She grabbed her smock and thrust her arms into it. Fortunately it was made of heavy, absorbent cotton. Unfortunately, it was soon soaking wet. And the evening wind was rising.

"All right," she said, finishing her buttons and rubbing her sleeves vigorously over her arms. When he opened his eyes, she had settled on the stern seat and was trying to rub some circulation back into her lower legs and feet.

"That is positively the most idiotic thing I have ever seen a human do in my entire life," he declared with quiet fury. "Jump out of a perfectly safe, perfectly dry boat—"

"I d-do it all the time," she said, beginning to shiver. "It's my research m-method . . . remember? And it's not id-diotic, it's perfectly safe when d-done properly." She wrapped her arms around her waist. "The b-biggest danger is staying down too long and blacking out . . . or perhaps losing too much b-body heat." She smiled ruefully. "That's why I don't usually s-stay down as long as I am capable of. I c-come up regularly to breathe and warm up. Only, this time I was so busy searching . . ."

Her face felt cold, her lips felt clumsy, and her shivering was getting steadily worse. She really had overdone it this time.

"So . . . if something doesn't eat you, crush you, or rip you to shreds down there, you're just as likely to snuff it from drowning or exposure," he said, summing up the hazards of her work. "Forgive me, Miss Ashton, but you're either the most heroic human being I've ever met, or you're a complete and utter lunatic. And right now I'd put my money on *lunatic*."

"I'm not a m-madwoman. I'm always v-very careful. I

always use a diving line and make c-certain I have something hot to drink and plenty of blankets to w-warm up in."

"Unfortunately, you don't seem to have thought ahead this time."

"Yes, I d-did," she said, hugging herself tighter. "But my blankets are . . ."

His eyes followed her gaze to his soggy pallet on the bottom of the boat. His expression changed to one of chagrin.

She shivered massively and began to rub her arms and legs briskly again. "Strange . . . I don't usually have this m-much trouble w-warming up."

Titus looked up at her pale face and blue-tinged lips and felt a fresh surge of anxiety. She was quaking so much she could scarcely rub her feet and legs. He closed his eyes against that disarming sight, and up came the image of her standing there, dripping wet, with that flimsy garment clinging to her like a second skin. He groaned privately. It wasn't his fault, he told himself. The woman wasn't rational.

But it was his fault the blankets were wet. And it would bloody well be his fault if she succumbed to some grisly form of consumption and died as a result of this little episode. He'd be infamous throughout England as the wretch who *drowned* the Lady Mermaid.

"The hell I will," he muttered, struggling up onto his knees and ripping his coat from his shoulders. "Here, put this on," he ordered, wrapping the garment around her. Then he settled on the bottom beside her and pulled a bare foot onto his lap.

"R-really, Prof-fessor . . ." She tried to draw it back, but he glared up at her and she relented. "I'll be fine soon, r-really."

But several minutes of briskly rubbing her feet and lower legs had little effect. When she shivered again, he pulled her off the seat, onto the driest part of the bottom of the boat, and into his arms.

"R-really, Professor, this is hardly nec-ces-s-s—" She couldn't quite get it out for the chattering of her teeth. He

took advantage of her arms being trapped inside his voluminous coat and pulled her bodily onto his lap.

"Make no mistake, Miss Ashton, this is prompted by
nothing less than desperation. If you swoon or wilt or whatever it is females do when they're totally out of kilter, I shall
be stuck out here for the rest of my life." She didn't look
convinced, so he added: "If there were any other sort of heat
available, do you honestly think I'd be offering you *mine*?"

It was probably a comment on her estimate of his character that she accepted that argument and stilled on his lap. He
wrapped her chilled curves in his arms and tried to think
warm thoughts . . . which wasn't especially difficult with
her sitting smack in the middle of his lap. All he had to do
was close his eyes and allow the feel of her against him to
conjure up the image of her as she climbed into the boat
. . . more naked than nakedness itself. Her full, rounded
breasts with their darker rings and erotic bumps at the tips
. . . her curvy waist and rounded hips and long, sleek legs
. . . which he now knew from experience to be surprisingly muscular. Then there was that tantalizing little vee at
the top of her legs.

Damn him for peeking. Now he was going to have to live
with that sight every night for . . . He popped his eyes
open.

Her head lay against his shoulder and, as he turned to her,
she raised it and opened her eyes. Huge blue pools of feminine mystery that could do terrifying things to his insides.
Her color seemed to be returning. Her shivers were abating.
But her breathing remained irregular and her lips still seemed
a shade darker than usual. Luscious lips, he thought, and was
utterly undone by his intimate knowledge of how they
would taste.

He closed his eyes, knowing he was in trouble, and lowered his head. His breath stopped as his lips touched hers. It
was like plunging into a steaming bath on a frosty winter
night. Heat surged through his face and slid down his throat,
collecting there. He shifted, pulled her closer, and poured

every bit of hunger in him into one long, blistering kiss that
pulled an unexpected intensity from her.

She opened to him, yielding him her softness at first, then
gradually asserting her own demands, exploring his mouth
with increasing eagerness and mastery. She stroked his lips as
he had hers, toyed with his tongue, and tilted her head to fit
her mouth to his in ever-changing combinations.

There was just room on the dry part of the bottom for
him to slide her bottom from his lap and lie back, tucking
her against him, half covering her with his body. When that
stunning kiss ended, he had more ready and carried them
lower, along her throat and shoulder, then back up to her
ear. She was soft and tasted salty and cool against his burning
lips. Drifting downward, across her chest, he nudged fabric
aside and dispatched buttons. He dropped kisses over every
inch of skin he could reach, and every bit of her he claimed
made him want more. He was suddenly driven to consume
her, to absorb her through his very skin . . . to bury himself deep inside her . . .

She arched and wriggled beneath him, making soft mew-
ing noises and gasps of delight. Every part of her was aching
for his touch, for the same attention he was showering on
her lips and face and breast. With subtle movements she
directed the flow of his kisses to untouched areas, and then
she stilled to drink in the new sensations.

Pleasure. It was pure, undiluted pleasure. How strange,
she thought, her thoughts now heated and fuzzy, that he
seemed to want to touch her as much as she wanted to be
touched. "What a lovely arrangement," she marveled, unaware that she had spoken aloud until he raised his head.

"Arrangement?" he echoed.

She looked into his glowing sea-green eyes. "That you
seem to enjoy doing this as much as I enjoy having you do
it." She smiled. "Nature certainly is clever to have set things
up like this."

A soft rumble came from deep in his throat as he slid a
hand beneath his coat and swept a caress up her side, from

hip to breast. "Clever Nature. Clever indeed." He watched her shudder of response with a banked heat in his expression. He kissed her gently, almost playfully on the lips, and then pushed up onto his elbow above her.

"Are you warm enough now?" He shot a glance down her disheveled, half-open smock, letting it linger briefly on the damp cotton clinging to her breasts. Curiously, she felt not the slightest urge to cover herself.

"Warm-*er*," she said, watching his gaze fasten on the tip of her breast and feeling a strange tingling, drawing sensation in it. "The air is getting cooler."

"So I see," he murmured, watching her nipple contract against the chill of her damp garment. Then he rubbed that brazen little bump with the back of one finger and stopped the breath in her throat. Her reaction must have registered in her face, for he smiled . . . a wry and deliciously dissolute expression of intent. Then he turned his hand over and fitted it possessively over the entire mound of her breast, causing a shudder of pleasure through her.

"Better?"

"Yes," she whispered, closing her eyes to trap those elusive sensations in her head long enough to commit them to memory. "Much better."

A moment later his lips closed over hers once more. This time her arms slipped around his neck and shoulders and pulled him closer. And before long, she was learning a corollary to her earlier discovery: it was as pleasant to touch him as it was for him to be touched.

Clever. The word circled back into his awareness, dragging with it his earlier assessment of her. *Clever girl.* He sat up, propped one arm on an upraised knee, and ran his hand back through his hair. She'd said something about an "arrangement" and seemed damned pleased. Something about how clever it was of nature to have set things up such that— he looked down at her, lying beside him, warm and flushed from his attentions—such that his own unruly passions would do her work for her! He blanched. What in hell was he doing getting entangled physically—*amorously*—with her?

She watched him withdraw, saw his mood change abruptly, and guessed what must be happening in him . . . probably the very opposite of what was happening in her. She sat up, pulled her smock together, and began fastening buttons and examining the dampness and wrinkling of his coat. Her head felt oddly light and her lips felt curiously naked.

When she looked up, there was a flush of embarrassment in her cheeks. "I'm sorry about your coat. I'll have Stephan see if he can rescue it. He used to be my grandfather's valet, years ago."

"You are making a dent in my wardrobe. Two pairs of trousers and now my best coat . . . Savile Row, you know."

"I warned you to bring clothes suitable for the water," she said with a rueful smile. "It's your bad luck that you chose not to believe me."

He pulled her braid and she rolled away and scrambled to her feet. She shoved her arms into his oversized sleeves, carefully rolled them up, then set about raising the sail and making for the cove. He watched, hearing her last words repeating over and over in his head. ". . . *Your bad luck . . . you chose not to believe me.*"

He *had* chosen not to believe her. He had gone well past objective and rational, had even defied logic not to believe her. He didn't want her to be right. And for all his pride in his own perception and in his integrity in pursuit of the truth . . . he had pursued an agenda of confrontations with her that made a mockery of his own vaunted principles of objectivity and sound scientific practice.

Grimly he observed her competence on the sea and admitted that she showed equal mastery beneath the water as well. She was out of the boat for at least ten minutes and was definitely not thrashing about at the surface. *Under water* was the only place she could have been. His reluctance to admit it, even in the face of irrefutable evidence, disturbed him.

Why was he so reluctant to admit the truth? She was one hell of a sailor. She could and did dive in the open ocean, unassisted and at considerable risk to her own health and safety. He glanced up, catching her in profile for a moment. Those two facts alone made her the most unusual woman he'd ever known. And the most courageous. Hell, he didn't know any *men* who would attempt what she apparently did with regularity!

His heart began to thud as he watched the land grow in his field of vision and realized the stakes he was playing for had just enlarged as well. It was no longer just a matter of pride or his reputation as an academic and a scientific skeptic. It had gone beyond that, somehow. In admitting that she truly did sail and dive, as she claimed, he now had to admit at least the possibility that she was telling the truth about the rest of it as well. Dolphins. What if she really had seen and studied dolphins?

He stole a glance at her and saw her give a small, single shiver. The tension that simple motion generated in him made him realize that, whatever happened, he was not going to get out of this unscathed. Something deep and fundamental in his being had been engaged, had involved itself in her fate. He closed his eyes and suffered a keen awareness of the lingering heat in his loins. And he hoped against hope that a bit of *heat* was all it was.

FAR ABOVE THE COVE, on the rampart of the old Norman tower, Lady Sophia and a few of her closest friends stood watching Celeste's boat put in to the dock. They observed in silence the familiar motions of Celeste tying off the boat and the pair of figures climbing up the ladder. The professor went first, then turned to extend a hand to Celeste, which she seemed to ignore.

"Wait—" the brigadier said, squinting and cocking his

head at a different angle to get a better view. "Is that his coat she is wearing?"

Lady Sophia beamed. "It most certainly is."

"And look at how they're walking," came another feminine opinion. "Close, but not too close."

"Not in much o' a hurry," was the assessment from a coarse male voice.

"They look quoight roight together," came a third female judgment. "But then, it's quoight a dist-ance, ain' it?"

"Have to see 'em close up," the brigadier declared, stroking his chin.

"Oh, we will," Lady Sophia said, gazing fondly at the pair ambling across the beach in the lowering light. "We most certainly will. At dinner."

Seven

A WARM BATH, a change of clothes, and a cup of Maria's rich coffee, laced with something from old Stephan's special shelf in the wine cellar, did wonders for Celeste's chilled spirits and aching body. She soaped and soaked and sipped, relishing the sudsy warmth between her bare toes and recalling the afternoon.

She had made her scientific point. Now Titus Thorne had to admit that she was a diver and was capable of carrying out the research she had published. That should secure her a few days in which to locate her truant dolphins. But the wisp of a smile on her face and the hum in her body had nothing to do with dolphins or diving or science at all . . . unless one considered human mating rituals to be a field of scientific inquiry. She had also made her personal point. Titus Thorne had kissed her and touched her because he wanted to. While he clearly still harbored misgivings about her work, it was now abundantly clear that he didn't find her *person* distasteful at all.

Her thoughts settled on his reaction after their "warming" session in the bottom of the boat. He had distanced himself from her again, become cool and professorial, although with noticeably less hostility toward her. As she thought about why, trying to see it from his perspective, she finally concluded that he was loath to involve himself personally with her because he still expected her work to be fraudulent.

She sank deeper in the water. As long as he disbelieved her, he couldn't allow himself to become entangled with her, no matter how pleasurable it was. She sighed. What she wouldn't give for a few friendly dolphins, just now.

By the time she had rinsed, dried, dressed, and emptied her bathwater herself, she just had time to give her hair a good toweling, powder her sunburned cheeks, and put a pair of tortoiseshell combs in her hair. The sound of the clock in the hall chiming eight sent her hurrying down the main stairs, where she ran into Stephan showing an equally refreshed and refurbished Titus Thorne into the dining room.

She tried to resist the temptation to stare at the glint of his dark hair, the contrast of his sun-burnished face to the pristine white of his collar, and the changeable sea-green eyes that seemed to be searching and evaluating her as well. With her cheeks reddening under his scrutiny, she fell in beside the old servant and vowed to make Titus Thorne admit, aloud, over supper, that she proved her "method" today. But when they entered the dining room, she stopped halfway to the table, horrified to find a number of the chairs already occupied . . . by the Atlantean Society of Pevensey Bay.

"There you are!" Lady Sophia called from her chair at the head of the table. "I hope you don't mind, Professor. I invited a few friends to dinner and . . . what with all our creaky limbs and achy joints . . . we thought it best to wait for you in comfort." She gestured to the others at the table, all of whom had survived to an age of at least sixty years, and they nodded agreement, smiling at Celeste and the professor, who had stopped beside her.

Celeste came to her senses and proceeded to her chair, watching in quiet desperation as her grandmother launched upon the disaster of the moment.

"Permit me to introduce several members of our local

society," Lady Sophia continued, clearly in her element as hostess. "Brigadier Penworthy Smythe, Royal Army, retired . . . Miss Penelope Hatch, our local postmistress, retired . . . the Reverend Marcus Altarbright, retired vicar of Cardamon . . . Misters Hiram and Bernard Bass, proprietors of a local fishing concern . . . Mrs. Anabelle Feather, milliner . . . Mr. Darwin Tucker, retired haberdasher . . . and of course, you have already made the acquaintance of Mr. Ned Caldwell, our local blacksmith."

Celeste could only watch in dismay as Titus Thorne shook the men's hands and nodded politely over the women's. He seemed perfectly obliging, as if he dined with hatmakers, postmistresses, fishermen, and village blacksmiths on a regular basis. But she recalled too well that his mannerliness could be a prelude to far less pleasant behavior.

"Really, Nana"—she gave the old lady an emphatic, pleading look—"Professor Thorne cannot possibly be interested in our local *society*."

"On the contrary, Miss Ashton," he said as he took his seat opposite her. "I find things to interest me in the most unlikely places. The mark of a true scientist, curiosity."

"Ah, yes. Professor Thorne is a scientist, you know," Lady Sophia informed the others as she beckoned old Stephan to begin the serving. "An *ichthyologist*. One who studies fish."

"Do tell," one of the Bass brothers said, leaning over his plate with widened eyes. "Bernard and me"—he jerked a thumb at his hulking, ruddy-faced brother—"we be 'fish men' ourselves."

"Know ever' shoal and shaller, ever' school and big'un in these waters," Bernard declared with pride as he tucked his napkin firmly into his collar.

"How interesting." The professor's face was a polite mask as he flicked a narrow glance at Celeste. "Then perhaps you've seen Miss Ashton's dolphins?"

"Oh, aye." Hiram Bass eyed with eagerness the tureen

making its way toward him on the serving cart. "Dozens o' times. Ever' time we have our Sacred Dolph—"

"How is your soup, Professor?" Celeste hurriedly broke in, knowing full well that he'd not yet had time to taste it. "It's turtle. A great favorite of ours. Compliments of the Bass brothers. They provide us with a marvelous bounty of fish."

"We see 'er dolphins now an' then," Hiram continued gamely. "Miss Celeste don't like us to take our boats too close to the cove, on account of it gets 'em all wrought up." When he saw the frown flicker across the professor's face, he explained: "They chase th' boats, y'see. Ride th' bow waves. And if we ain't careful, they get all fouled up in our nets."

"And have you ever heard one of her dolphins *talk*?" Titus Thorne asked, eyeing the garrulous old brothers.

"Aye. If ye can call them clicks an' screeches talkin'," Hiram answered.

"Don't be silly, Mr. Bass." Miss Penelope, the postmistress, spoke up. "We all know they talk. We've all heard them at one time or other."

"You have?" Thorne sat forward, now completely focused. "Can you understand them? What do they say?"

"Ohhh, they speak of mysteries, sir," Miss Penelope answered smartly. "Things too deep for human ken."

Celeste groaned privately, knowing just where the conversation was heading. This was precisely what she had hoped to avoid.

"They are the messengers of the deep," Miss Penelope went on, "who carry with them the secrets of ages past and the promises of glories yet to come."

"Well"—Titus Thorne seemed to be suppressing a smile—"how annoyingly inscrutable of them."

"Oh, it ain't in-scroodable, sarr," Mrs. Anabelle Feather said in tones of East End London. "It's parfectly understandable to them what's in the know."

"I think we may be having oysters for a second course—

have you ever studied oysters, Professor?" Celeste tried desperately to derail the conversation.

Titus Thorne gave her a look that said he intended to
hear it all, precisely because she was trying to distract him.

"In the know? About what?" he asked the coarse-spoken
milliner.

"And I believe Stephan and Maria may have made spiced
pears for dessert—" Celeste tried again.

"Atlantis, o'course," Anabelle Feather responded, glancing at the others, clearly pleased at the prospect of ex-
pounding on their common passion. "Th' lost continent.
Th' *ante-de-luvian* world." She leaned forward to earnestly
explain: "That means 'sunk under th' ocean.' "

Her answer took Titus by surprise. He blinked, then
chuckled. "Atlantis? Dolphins speaking to human beings
about the sunken continent of *Atlantis*?" He glanced at Lady
Sophia, then at Celeste as if to say that he held her responsible for such nonsense, then returned to Anabelle Feather.
"The possibility of dolphins speaking of anything at all is
exceedingly remote . . . but the possibility of them knowing and speaking of the secrets of a civilization that has been
gone for three thousand years . . . well, that is nothing
short of . . . ludicrous."

Silence fell over the table and he looked from one wary
and unsettled face to another, discovering he had just tres-
passed an unrecognized boundary. After an increasingly uncomfortable pause, he glanced again at Celeste, who looked
at her grandmother with a firm expression of *I-told-you-so*.

"We don't think it is ridiculous at all, Professor," Lady
Sophia responded, warming the suddenly chilled atmosphere
with a smile and an air of maternal indulgence. "Of course,
we couldn't expect you to know about it or to appreciate
such a discovery, yet. It has been kept rather close." She
gestured to those seated down the table. "Known only to us
in the Atlantean Society."

"The . . . Atlantean . . . Society?"

"Th' Atlanteen Society o' Pev'nsey Bay. That'd be *us,*" Anabelle pointed out.

"In our research," Lady Sophia went on, "Martin and I discovered that dolphins figure prominently in the tablets, vessels, and carvings of Atlantis. You may recall seeing some of them in the library this morning. We have a goodly number in our collection. Dolphins were obviously revered by the people of Atlantis. That is why, when Celeste became interested in dolphins and they seemed to show such an affinity for her, her grandfather and I encouraged her to study them."

He looked from Lady Sophia to Celeste, frowning, obviously trying to fit this piece into the puzzle of what was happening here.

The Reverend Altarbright cleared his throat. "A number of us local folk have followed Sir Martin's and Lady Sophia's work from the outset . . . as well as Celeste's. We have become convinced that what the world desperately needs is the wisdom and harmony of Atlantean culture."

"They were an exceedingly enlightened people," Miss Penelope added. "They had an exemplary system of communication—regular mail delivery."

"Their clothing was free-flowing and graceful, while completely practical." The dapper little haberdasher, Darwin Tucker, poked his finger beneath his collar and gave it a tug. "Unlike today's miserable garments."

"Top-notch sailors," the brigadier said gruffly. "Excellent navy."

"Hot an' cold water piped into each an' every house!" Ned the blacksmith put in with unabashed admiration.

"And they give proper due to th' sea an' to their fishermen," Bernard Bass declared. "Thought right highly of 'em."

Hiram Bass's head bobbed agreement. "Built 'em temples an' such."

Titus listened to each member who spoke then turned to

Lady Sophia. "So, you have discovered all of this . . . from *dolphins*?"

"Oh, dear, no." Lady Sophia chuckled. "Not from dolphins. From sound archaeological evidence. From the artifacts and the work that Martin and I have done."

"Then you don't claim to actually talk to the dolphins . . ."

"Heavens, no. Much too complex a task for us mere mortals," Reverend Altarbright answered for them, garnering nods of consensus.

"The beasties talk. We jus' listen," Anabelle clarified.

The professor scowled. "You *listen* . . . to the dolphins . . ."

"Maria will be heartbroken if we allow her turtle soup to get cold without even tasting it," Celeste broke in loudly. She raised her spoon, smiled emphatically, and plunged it into her bowl.

With Celeste's determined navigation, they managed to negotiate the soup course, oysters, and a salad before Titus Thorne was able to steer the conversation back to the topical shoals of "Atlantis."

"You mentioned listening to dolphins," he said as he was being served a generous portion of walnut-crusted sea bass. "What do they say?"

The reverend smiled, ignoring Celeste's covert entreaty to caution. "Well, since none of us can rightly decipher the dolphins' tongue, each of us has his or her own ideas about what messages they bring." He leaned back in his chair and took hold of his lapels. "I personally believe that dolphins bring us prophetic warnings about our wasteful, prodigal ways."

"Naw." Hiram Bass lowered his knife and fork, but kept them standing in readiness on each side of his plate. "That ain't it. It's the sea, ye see. We say"—he motioned with his knife to his brother, who nodded agreement since his mouth was full of buttered roll—"they come to show us how to use the sea to meet folks's needs . . . to keep 'em from goin' hungry . . . give 'em honest work."

"All very 'useful' to be sure," Miss Penelope said with a delicate wave of her fork. "But it is clear to *some of us* that the dolphins carry with them the history and culture of that ancient people. Sir Martin's and Lady Sophia's treasures tell of temples built by the water's edge and how the great kings of Atlantis talked to the priests and the priests *talked to the dolphins*."

She halted with an arch little smile and a glance at the reverend. "Did I say priests? I meant priest*esses*. The sacred daughters of Atlantis. Dolphins only talk to young, virtuous women, you see. That's why they talk to Celeste." She smiled with pride at Celeste. "She is our Most Revered and Sacred Virgin."

Celeste flamed. There it was. The revelation she had dreaded. Now she was not only an audacious, eccentric female who claimed to research dolphins by swimming with them, she was also the center of a daft archaeological cult populated by sexagenarians who believed she was their anointed "virgin" . . . chosen by the fates to prize the secrets of the ancients out of talkative sea creatures. She could see that his professorship was having as much trouble swallowing that as he was swallowing the huge bite of sea bass in his mouth.

"Really, Miss Penelope, you know that I cannot 'talk' to my dolphins or understand what they say any better than anyone else," she said firmly. "As Mrs. Feather said, they talk . . . to each other . . . and all I can do is listen. It would be a great enough achievement if I could merely convince the scientific world that dolphins are capable of systematic communication—language—amongst themselves."

"I would be interested to hear some of this dolphin language," the professor said, his lips quirking up on one side. "Of course, to do that I would have to *see* some dolphins, first—"

"You'll see them, Professor," she responded sharply. "Perhaps as soon as tomorrow."

Blessedly, that put an end to all talk of dolphins and Atlantis. But the silence that followed was filled with tension. Lady Sophia exchanged looks with her guests; they exchanged wary or opinionated glances among themselves. Celeste cast her grandmother a look of worry and warning; her grandmother shot back a look of unshakable serenity. Celeste sent Titus Thorne a glare. He returned her a look that was some part evaluation, some part denunciation, then turned his probing eye on her grandmother.

She watched him evaluating Nana, no doubt analyzing her quest for the secrets of Atlantis through his mercilessly objective standards, and remembered how proud he was of having exposed that fraudulent Viking ship. Was he sitting there, even now, planning how to destroy her grandmother's work the minute he finished with her?

Righteous indignation rose in her. How dare he sit at their table, eating their food in company with their friends, and make veiled threats toward her grandmother's precious work? Her blood began to heat. She picked up her fork and stabbed the spiced, wine-poached pear in the dish before her, wishing with all her heart it was a piece of Titus Thorne.

Conversation slowly began again, in subdued tones. Local talk, remarks on recent weather and the quality of the local fishing. She looked up at her grandmother's twinkling eyes and grew steadily more furious at the prospect of seeing the joy in them dimmed by some callous, pigheaded self-appointed guardian of science. When she could stand it no more, she shoved abruptly to her feet and steadied herself against the table.

"A lovely dinner," she announced, aware she was bringing it to a premature end. "I'm sure the professor is tired, after such an exhausting day. But before he retires, I think a turn about the flower garden might do him some good. We have a lovely moonlight collection. Will you join me, Professor?"

He looked up in surprise, then down at the half-eaten pear in his dish, and relinquished his fork. Her invitation had all the warmth of a naval conscription notice, but, as she had intended, he could not refuse.

Bidding the others a good evening, she led him out through the hall and front doors, then down the gravel path to the garden. A warm golden disk of a moon hung above them in a deep blue sky and the mingled scents of grasses in bloom and garden flowers in abundance swirled around them on a light breeze. In the background, the ever-present sound of sea meeting shore provided a soft, pulselike beat of anticipation.

She squared her shoulders and set a brisk pace, concentrating on what she had brought him out here to say. But soon she realized he had fallen behind and turned to find him halted by a patch of oxeye daisies that glowed a luminous blue-white in the moonlight. Taking a deep breath, she strode back to him.

"We aren't here to examine the flora, Professor."

"I would imagine not." He looked up with eyebrows raised. "Still, it is a most unusual sort of pigmentation. I never would have guessed daisies could glow like that at night. But then"—he straightened and produced a knowing smile that sent a spurt of heat up her spine—"I suppose nothing is impossible in the domain of a *most revered and sacred virgin.*"

Taunting was probably inevitable, she told herself, Titus Thorne being the vile combination of insufferable male and science snob that he was.

"Nor are we here to discuss the society's peculiar notions of me."

"A pity. I was all set to inquire as to whether 'virgin' was a genuine requirement of your exalted role or merely a part of the title."

She forbade herself to blush and planted her fists at her waist.

"You're here to 'discredit' me, to prove me a fraud and my work a pack of nonsense. I know that and I am prepared to accept it and deal with it. But I will *not* accept your interference with or condemnation of my grandmother's ideas." She advanced two paces and punched a finger into his immaculate shirtfront.

"I don't care if you think her ideas on Atlantis are as dense as plum duff—she's perfectly entitled to them. If she wants to organize her friends into a 'society' and to believe I may someday talk to dolphins, that is *her* business and no one else's. Her theories may not be pristine science, but they keep her busy and vital and alive, and that's just the way I want her. Alive. She very nearly grieved herself to death when my grandfather died. It was only the prospect of carrying on his work that kept her on this side of the Shade. And I intend to see that she goes on patching up artifacts and spinning grand theories until she cocks up her toes and gets carried out in a box!"

Halted by the need to draw breath, she realized she was practically stabbing him with her finger. She stared in dismay at that intrepid digit and shoved her hands behind her back.

"If there is any charity or humanity in you, you will ignore everything you saw in the library and heard tonight. You'll pretend her work doesn't exist."

"But it does exist," he declared quietly.

"Only for Nana and the members of the society." She began to feel the heat radiating from him and backed a step. "No one else knows of it."

"Except me." He took a step forward. "There are the artifacts, materials that appear to have come from archaeological digs."

"Of course there are. My grandfather opened several productive dig sites in the islands, and some of the artifacts are quite remarkable. But my grandmother is convinced they could come only from Atlantis—"

"And *you* are not." His eyes seemed to shimmer in the moonlight.

"I . . . am not." There it was, spoken aloud for the very first time. Her admission of doubt made her feel every bit as guilty as she had always feared it would. "I am not convinced they are Atlantean. But it doesn't really matter what I think, as long as it keeps her busy and gives her something to live for."

"So, the truth of her work doesn't matter?"

"Not to me."

Her pronouncement hovered, unchallenged, on the air for a long, uncomfortable moment, then she looked up and searched his moonlit features, hoping to find some glimmer of understanding in him. She saw nothing to encourage her in his guarded expression, but she saw nothing to discourage her, either. She would have to take a chance, lower her defenses to speak from her heart, and hope that the man who had warmed her and kissed her so tenderly that afternoon was still present inside the tightly buttoned and rigidly rational academician standing before her.

She looked away, wishing she could escape those eyes. "The truth wears many faces, Professor. Who is to say that what she believes about my grandfather's work—her work— is *not* true? Don't you see? Right now, she has something to care about and believe in. Something to live for." She lowered her head and swallowed, as if the words stuck in her throat. "I don't want her to be hurt."

Titus stared at the top of her head for a moment . . . opened his mouth . . . then closed it without speaking. She honestly thought he would pounce on her cherubic, silver-haired grandmother like some crazed scientific zealot and attempt to destroy both the old lady and her life's work in the name of Truth. But then, he told himself with appalling insight, why shouldn't she? That was precisely what he'd vowed to do to her and her work, at the first opportunity.

"Miss Ashton," he said tightly, "if I were half the vengeful, unscrupulous cur you believe me to be, I would never have come here in the first place. I'd simply have watched the good gentlemen of science disassemble you in that lecture hall and then joined them for a celebratory round of port after."

He edged closer, watching her eyes widen. He thought of the sparkle in the old lady's eyes as she showed him her precious artifacts, of the hope he read in them that had prevented him from airing his skepticism about her conclusions. Praying he wasn't being influenced unduly by the moonlight, the sweet, pollen-laden air, and the proximity of Celeste's much-too-memorable curves, he made a decision.

"I'm here to learn the truth about you, Celeste Ashton. Nothing else."

He couldn't resist brushing a wisp of hair back from her cheek.

Relief melted her features into a smile that was part confusion, part pleasure. His blood began to warm. His pulse began to quicken. Suddenly all of his penetrating reason, sophisticated logic, and finely honed powers of deduction melted helplessly into a single obsessive thought. That title the old birds had bestowed upon her. Was she truly a "Most Revered and Sacred—"

"Are you?" he said, his voice now low and resonant.

"Am I what?" she whispered, swaying ever so slightly toward him, her head tilting up.

"Their Virgin?"

She ran her tongue over her reddening lips as her eyes slid to his mouth.

"I'm . . . not . . . sure."

"About which part?" he whispered huskily, lowering his head. " 'Their' or 'Virgin'?"

For a moment the question hung on the night air around them, unacknowledged. He watched her responding to the heat rising in him, and felt himself equally drawn to her warming. Mere inches and he would feel her soft, pliant lips again. A simple contraction of muscle and his arms would close around her supple, shapely form. A small relaxation of control and he would again experience the pleasures that had made mincemeat of his self-possession only hours before.

It would be so easy to make that first motion, just a fraction of an inch, just a hint of movement.

So very easy.

Then the sense of his question finally struck her.

"Are you asking if I am a—a—"

She raked him with a look of outraged dignity, and headed straight for the house.

As he watched her stalk down the garden path toward the hulking outline of the house, he wondered what the hell was the matter with him. He rubbed his hands down his face, then shoved them into his trouser pockets. Then, he forced himself to continue around the rest of the oval garden path.

Asking her if she was a . . . What would possess him to ask her something that idiotic? He paused, glaring at a patch of lilies glowing serenely silver and white in the moonlight. Curiosity, he realized with some alarm. He asked because he wanted to know. Wanted? Hell, he was consumed with the need to know.

A moment later, his intellect justified his desire. Of course he had to know. His entire objection to her work, his view of her work as a coy parody of scholarly writing, and his expectation of being seduced into approving her scheme had all proceeded from his assumptions about her worldly, calculating character. It never occurred to him that she could be anything but a clever, contriving female with a wealth of sexual experience . . . who obviously had used her own exploits as the basis for her eroticized accounts of dolphin behavior. Her personal sensuality had been there in every blessed line, every titillating phrase of the book.

How could she possibly be a *virgin*?

He sat down on a large rock at the turnabout in the path, determined to think this through.

What did he truly know about her? He counted off her

attributes on his fingers. Clever, literate, determined, knowledgeable, resourceful, and unafraid to jump into the blessed ocean at a moment's notice.

Annoyed, he tried again.

She was bright enough and brazen enough to stand before some of Britain's finest scientific minds and insist that she—a totally uncredentialed female—had done creditable scientific work, and was competent enough and courageous enough to sail a boat by herself and to dive unassisted in the open ocean.

He gave a huff of disgust and tried a third time.

She was infuriatingly opinionated and self-possessed for a young woman of . . . what? twenty? twenty-two? . . . and she made a point of flashing him a peek of her blessed "flukes" whenever possible.

Flukes. He pressed fingers against the inner corners of his eyes, trying to massage away the memory of her wriggling feet.

The *truth* was that she lived in a decaying old manor house at the seaside with a dotty grandmother who wandered about half dressed and dreamed of resurrecting the culture of a mythological civilization. The truth was, she had lived here for years and there probably wasn't a human male capable of providing her with unbridled sexual escapades within twenty miles of the place. The truth was she was desperate for money . . . not for luxuries and fast living, but for bread and eggs and a few new tiles to patch a rotten roof.

The disturbing truth was that she was no longer a faceless huckster in a fish tail or a lurid caricature in a newspaper. In the past two days she had become a living, breathing woman to him, a person with virtues as well as faults, strengths as well as weaknesses. She was a young, intelligent, attractive woman with a passion for the sea, more than her share of pluck, and a fierce and compassionate loyalty to her grandmother.

His tension melted into a much warmer feeling as he

thought of her standing in the moonlight . . . a loving granddaughter . . . willing to forfeit his approval and risk his censure to protect the old lady's dreams.

Whatever deception she had practiced, he now understood, it hadn't been out of greed or a desire for notoriety. More than likely, it had been done out of an honorable but misguided desire to follow in her grandfather's footsteps, or the need to hold her crumbling household and dwindling family together.

He stood up, gave the gravel in the path a thoughtful kick, and started back to the house himself, sensing that this bit of revelation had just made his task here all the more difficult. How was he going to tell the truth about her and her "research" without destroying her in the process?

FROM A DARKENED WINDOW in the little-used morning room, the Atlantean Society peered down into the moonlit garden, watching the dim outline of Titus Thorne perched on a rock. In avid silence they concentrated on his figure, trying to make out whether he was rubbing his head or talking to himself. After a time, they saw him leave his seat and amble along the path with his hands jammed into his coat pockets, kicking gravel along the way.

"I tho't he was gonna kiss her," Hiram Bass whispered, scowling.

"Should have, the blighter," the brigadier declared, drawing his chin back in annoyance. "Dashed waste of good moonlight."

"He's a gentleman," Miss Penelope said, beaming approval. "He would naturally approach these matters with a certain gallantry and restraint."

" 'E's a bit of a dry stick, I say," Anabelle Feather declared, planting a hand on one ample hip. "Ye sure he's the one, Sophie? I mean, he ain't put th' whole puzzle together, yet. Mebee he ain't our Man o' Earth."

"Oh, he's the one, all right," Lady Sophia said, watching

Titus Thorne's troubled form. "Even his name, Titus. A variation of Titan, of course. And you saw the way she looks at him, and the way he looks at her. They're like dry tinder, awaiting a spark."

"And when they finally get 'em a spark, wot then?" Bernard Bass asked.

Ned Caldwell elbowed the burly fisherman in the ribs. "Whaddye think, Bernie? You ain't that old."

"I believe he is referring to the prophecy, Nedwin," the reverend put in, turning to Lady Sophia. "And a good question it is, too. What does happen after they're bonded in eternal bliss?"

One by one, they turned to their "high priestess" as she stood by the window. She sighed and gave a rueful shrug. "The prophecy is regrettably vague on the specifics. But the outcome is perfectly clear. 'When the Man of Earth and the Woman of Sea join in spiritual and physical union, a new era will be born on the earth. The sacred dolphins will speak and the spirit of Atlantis will be released in the world once more. From their union shall come a transformation that will renew the face of the earth and bring about a new life, giving union between land and sea.'"

"We know that Celeste and her professor will lead us into this new era." The reverend came back to the question at hand. "My only question is, how will they know what to do?"

Miss Penelope gave a "tsk" and wagged her head. "Really, Reverend. The dolphins will speak and tell them what to do. While they are 'joining' we summon the dolphins by our Sacred Dolphin Ceremony. By the time they've finished 'joining,' their ears will be opened and they will understand the dolphins' speech."

"They will need help, of course," Lady Sophia added. "That is our task. To render them whatever counsel and aid we can."

There was a harumph from the brigadier's direction.

"Still think we should write the queen. Dashed bad form, not informing one's superiors."

There was a chorus of disagreement, since they had long ago decided that issue. "We all agreed t' let the ol' gal find out about it like ever'one else." Hiram spoke for the rest of them. "No sense worryin' th' dear ol' thing."

Eight

MIDMORNING, THE NEXT DAY, Celeste trudged across the sun-warmed beach with her shoes in one hand and her thin cotton skirt held out of the way in the other. When she reached the steps up the cliff, she paused to brush her feet and don her slippers before starting the climb. She had just spent three long hours pounding a tin sheet, calling her dolphins, and all she had to show for it was a knot in her middle and a faint ringing in her ears.

It had been a relief, at first, that she didn't have to face Titus Thorne's smug skepticism at the crack of dawn. She had risen early, given Stephan orders to let the professor awaken by himself, and hurried down to the cove alone, intending to locate Prospero and the others before he appeared. But as the sun climbed steadily higher over a serene and empty cove, fresh worries rose with it.

The time was slipping by. What would happen if she couldn't produce Prospero and the others in the next few days? How long could she keep Titus Thorne sailing around in the bottom of a boat and pounding a piece of tin? What choice did she have? As long as it took to find her dolphins.

She headed for the house, determined to insist that he join her in the boat for another dolphin-hunting foray. When she entered the kitchen she found Stephan sorting table linen, and learned that Titus Thorne had last been seen in the library with her grandmother.

Hurrying through the house with visions of still greater disasters looming in her mind, she found her grandmother ensconced cozily at her worktable, studying an inscription on a stone jar with a magnifying lens. She was wearing her Grecian chiton again, complete with a flowing himation draped around her. Celeste halted in the doorway and closed her eyes against the sight. Was there no end to the humiliations she would suffer?

"So there you are," Lady Sophia said with a note of cheeriness. When she opened her eyes, the old lady was coming toward her. "I heard you calling your beasties. Are they here, yet?"

"Nana, you promised," she said plaintively, picking up a fold of Lady Sophia's voluminous wrap and giving it a half-hearted tug.

"Well, that was before the professor learned about the society and my work. What harm can it do to have him see me in my normal clothing, now?" The old lady threaded an arm through Celeste's and drew her along toward Poseidon's throne. "Anyway, the professor didn't seem to mind."

There he sat . . . on the throne in the strong morning light, the sheen of his dark hair creating the arresting impression of a halo about his head. His face fairly glowed with intensity as he regarded the object on the black velvet drape spread over his lap. It was a ball-like lattice made of glinting silver rods . . . Nana's special puzzle, now assembled into some sort of geometric figure. He was so immersed in studying the skeletal orb that he didn't notice them at first.

Celeste stared at him. Even in his impeccable Oxford-proper suit, starched collar, and silk tie, he looked as if he belonged in that chair. As she watched, he contemplated the ball from all angles, watching the play of light and shadow on its interior and running his fingertips over the inscriptions that lined the sides of the squared rods. Her gaze fixed on his hands as he rolled the ball deliberately from one palm to the other. Those large hands and lean, supple fingers that were both skilled and tender . . . for one breathtaking moment, she recalled the feel of them gliding across the bare skin of—

"Oh, my." Nana scurried toward him with her hands raised in delight. "Professor, you've done it—you've assembled our sacred puzzle!" She took it from him and lifted it into the light. Reverently, she turned it over and over, examining it from all sides. "It's wonderful . . . magnificent."

He rose with a dent of apology in his brow. "Well, I'm not certain it's magnificent, or even that it is the correct configuration. You see, I seem to have one piece too many." He held out his hand and in his open palm lay one final silver rod. Celeste, like her grandmother, was drawn close to take a look at the unused piece. It bore no markings or symbols at all.

Nana picked it up, looked it over, then gazed analytically into the many-sided geometric figure he had created. "But of course." She smiled. "It's perfect, don't you see? One lone piece. It's an axiom among students of antiquities that ancient puzzles were often made with extra pieces or pieces missing." When he looked at her in bewilderment, she gave his arm a pat. "Well, I shouldn't be surprised; you weren't trained as an archaeologist, after all.

"The practice was common in old civilizations," she continued. "The workmen intentionally introduced an imperfection into the object or work they were creating, in deference to the divine and as a caution against human pride. The lesson intended was that we humans must never think ourselves complete unto ourselves. We must never begin to think we or our creations are perfect and without need of celestial guidance and support." She turned back to the silver orb and seemed to be searching for a proper description. "Although, this seems nearly perfect. It's a marvel, a regular . . . a . . ."

"Dodecahedron," he supplied, folding his arms and settling his gaze on it. "A twelve-sided figure. It was the odd combination of angles at the ends of the pieces that gave it away. And, of course, twelve is considered a holy number in many civilizations and religions. What better for 'holy dice' than an orb with twelve sides?"

Just then Stephan peered around a stack of crates, squinting and searching for Lady Sophia. "Callers, ma'am."

"Oh?" Lady Sophia turned at the sound of his voice and clutched the silver orb to her bosom. "Who is it, Stephan?" When the houseman presented a card, Lady Sophia read it, made a soundless O, and handed it immediately to Celeste.

"Mr. Cherrybottom? Here?" Celeste looked up from the card with fresh anxiety washing over her. "What could he possibly be doing here?"

But in truth, as she hurried for the door with Nana and Titus Thorne not far behind, she realized that there could be only one reason for him to abandon his demanding business and journey all the way from London. He was eager to get on with preparations for his new edition of her book, and had come to see how her "proof" had been received. She wilted inside. What on earth would she tell him?

She paused in the arched doorway, finding not one but *two* male figures awaiting her.

The portly publisher turned from the sea-facing windows with a hearty smile and met her halfway across the long room. "Miss Ashton! How wonderful you look—the very picture of health!" He pressed an exuberant kiss on her hand, then drew her back toward the window and his traveling companion. "Isn't she simply the loveliest, most adorable creature you've ever seen, Bentley?"

"The very most adorable," came the reply, in soft, masculine tones that were both unsettling and familiar.

"And here is Grandmama." Cherrybottom deposited her hand in the stranger's and hurried over to Nana. "Lady Sophia. Radiant, as always. And of course our splendid professor."

Celeste searched both the stranger and her memory, feeling a bit flustered under his admiring gaze. She finally recalled the face, if not the name, as he led her toward her grandmother and Cherrybottom in the middle of the chamber.

"I don't know if you will remember Mr. P. T. Bentley," Cherrybottom said. "I introduced him to you as we were leaving your marvelous lecture in Knightsbridge. He's an American, deeply interested in marine science. We've dined together twice since that fortuitous meeting, and when I mentioned that I had half a notion to come and see your dolphins for myself, he would not rest until I agreed to bring him along." The publisher beamed in impish apology. "I could scarcely say him nay and disappoint your most devoted admirer."

"Mr. Cherrybottom flatters me." Bentley's blond head poised over her hand with a perfect blend of restraint and eagerness. "But in truth, I have thought of little besides your work, since the moment I purchased your book, more than a month ago."

"Welcome, Mr. Bentley," Lady Sophia declared with a twinkle in her eye. "You'll stay with us for a few days, won't you, Mr. Cherrybottom? I won't hear of you saying no."

Arrangements were made for his room, and Lady Sophia called for refreshments to wash the dust from their throats. By the time the lemonade arrived, the old lady's offer of hospitality had been expanded to include Bentley, and the American had installed himself discreetly at Celeste's side.

"Well, what do you think of Miss Ashton's dolphins, now, Professor?" Cherrybottom asked as he settled his bulk into a sturdy wooden chair.

She froze in the midst of a sip of lemonade and peered over the rim of the glass at Titus Thorne.

"My opinion has had little opportunity to change," he responded with a wry smile. "Miss Ashton's dolphins seem to have taken an extended holiday."

Cherrybottom looked to her in some confusion. "Holiday? What? Do you mean to say—"

"They aren't here," Titus answered.

"They usually don't travel far from Pevensey Bay in summer," she said calmly. "It's just taking them a bit longer than usual to get here."

"But they will be here?" Cherrybottom prompted.

"Of course they will," Lady Sophia declared. "Naughty beasties. It wouldn't surprise me if they were out in the cove this very minute, playing hide-and-seek."

"Do you intend to call your dolphins again today, Miss Ashton?" Bentley asked, engaging her attention a bit too directly and holding it for a bit too long. She felt her cheeks reddening under his potent admiration.

"Yes, I do. Perhaps out in the boat."

"You'll go sailing?" Bentley slid one of his hands over hers as it lay on her lap and lifted it as if it were a great treasure. His voice dropped to a soft, penetrating rumble. "I would consider it one of the highlights of my life if you would permit me to accompany you, Miss Ashton."

When she nodded assent, Bentley turned to the publisher with his eyes silvering with excitement. "This is too much to credit, Cherrybottom. To join the famous Miss Ashton on a genuine dolphin hunt . . ."

"Scarcely a 'hunt,' sir," she said, lowering her eyes.

"Nothing quite so thrilling," Titus Thorne put in with a sardonic edge. "But then, some men are more easily amused than others."

"My boat is not large. I'm afraid I cannot take everyone." She glanced at Titus Thorne. "Perhaps, Professor, you would stay behind and permit Mr. Bentley to take your place."

"Absolutely not," he replied vehemently. They all stared at him in surprise. "As you have so often pointed out, Miss Ashton . . . in order to appreciate your work, I should be there to experience every aspect of it."

"But I thought, in view of your unfortunate—"

"A temporary inconvenience." He dismissed the subject of his seasickness with a wave.

In the end, it was the accommodating Cherrybottom

who decided to stay behind. By the time they started down the cliff path, a quarter of an hour later, Titus was wondering what had possessed him to volunteer—nay—*demand* to hazard life and limb once more in Celeste's pathetic sieve of a vessel. The salt air must be corroding his mental faculties at an alarming rate.

He glowered as he watched the dapper, drawling Bentley sprint ahead to catch Celeste and use the uncertain footing of the soft sand as a pretext for claiming her arm. He watched the way she smiled at the handsome American and the way their shoulders sometimes brushed as they trudged along. It set his teeth on edge.

Here, he told himself, was the true Celeste Ashton, the wily, alluring mermaid. Her seduction hadn't worked on him, but Bentley was another story entirely. The man was already besotted. Just look at him; hanging on her every word, gazing at her as if she were some decadent sweet, and using every excuse to put his hands on her. Wait until he'd spent three hours in her leaky boat, on a heaving, churning sea, with the wind and spray lashing him, Titus thought, smiling. He wouldn't look so eager then.

Bentley offered to cast off the line and Celeste thanked him, then climbed down into the boat. Bentley joined them in the boat, planting himself on the middle seat.

"You really ought to move, old man," Titus finally said from his seat in the stern. "You'll be knocked off if you sit there."

"I shall be fine here, Professor," Bentley said with a faintly superior smile. "I'm quite accustomed to dodging the boom. I run a sloop at my home on the Chesapeake, a vessel considerably larger than this. But I learned to sail in a catboat much like this one." He smiled at Celeste, who was nudging the bow out to catch the breeze. "This rather brings it all back to me."

The annoying American proved to be as good as his word, anticipating the boom's movements and adroitly ducking from one side to the other when Celeste made a change to sail across the wind. Titus's spirits sank as they hit the rougher waters of the open sea and Bentley remained untroubled by the boat's heaving motions.

Worse, yet, when Bentley tried his hand at rapping out her dolphin call, the blasted American had no trouble picking up the right rhythm. And he seemed equally adept at pulling soft smiles and admiring comments from her.

"Still no luck?" Titus said, when he could bear watching no longer.

Celeste stood up, shaded her eyes, and searched the water for some sign of her dolphins. When it became clear that the trip would end in disappointment, she sank down on her seat and gave Bentley an apologetic smile.

"I'm sorry to have disappointed you."

"Think nothing of it, my dear Celeste," Bentley said, putting his hand over hers on the tiller. "It has been a pure delight, being out here with you."

"We can try again tomorrow, Peter," she said, her face rosy with pleasure as she gazed at his hand, atop hers.

"Celeste" and "Peter" now, were they? Titus thought. The bounder had known her for all of four hours and already they were onto first names, while he was still calling her Miss Ashton and she addressed him as "professor" when she could bear to speak to him at all. Out of sheer stubbornness he refused to give up the middle seat to Bentley, and doomed himself to spend the inward journey either ducking, crouched in anticipation of ducking, or with a sail flapping in his face.

Mr. Cherrybottom and Lady Sophia met them at the dock, eager to learn the results of their trip.

"Not a single dolphin? How disappointing," Cherrybottom said in dismay, as he watched first Bentley, then Celeste climb the ladder. Then Titus started up, and the publisher rushed to assist. "Here, Professor, let me lend you a hand."

"I am perfectly fine," Titus snapped.

Cherrybottom backed off with a dubious look and Titus made an athletic leap from the last rung onto the dock and straightened. Sensing they were staring at him, he ran his hands back through his hair. It was standing on end. And his borrowed sweater—which had managed to collect a good bit of spray—was sagging badly. Bentley, however, had not so much as a hair out of place.

"Are you sure you're—" Celeste began, with a slight frown.

"I am perfectly fine, Miss Ashton." He clamped a hand over his stomach. "Never felt better in my life."

They were halfway across the beach before it struck Titus that he had spoken the truth. Lagging behind the others, he halted and felt of his stomach. He did feel perfectly well. In fact, other than a few internal rumbles as they had gotten under way, he had felt fine the entire time they were on the water. He hadn't been seasick at all.

The realization stunned him. He had been so busy concentrating on Celeste and the attention the irksome Bentley was showing her, that he temporarily forgot about being ill. He paused halfway up the cliff to look back at the boat and the serene waters of the cove, feeling mildly alarmed. Three boat trips with Celeste Ashton had made more of an impact on him than he could ever have imagined possible. If three days and three boat trips with her had that much effect on him, what else might be happening to him?

DINNER THAT NIGHT was pleasant enough. The conversation was genial, the food plain but delicious, and there was only a passing reference to Atlantis . . . which gave Lady Sophia a chance to explain to Bentley her preference for classical garments. It was only when Mr. Cherrybottom expressed some concern over the missing dolphins, and pressed Celeste for some estimate of when they might make themselves available, that things became a bit strained.

Celeste shot a glance at her grandmother and strove to appear unconcerned. "We, who are accustomed to dealing with nature, learn early on that there are some things that cannot be rushed. Dolphins, it would seem, are among them. All we can do, Mr. Cherrybottom, is call them and wait."

Her combined scientific wisdom and air of assurance was apparently convincing enough to end that line of questioning. But, inside, Celeste felt as if she had just confessed to being a felon. She had studied and observed and swum with dolphins for years . . . more than half of her life. Suddenly none of that mattered; it was as if those hundreds of hours were all a sort of pleasant but irrelevant dream. She couldn't produce the creatures now—this very minute—before the scrutiny of the scientific world and her impatient publisher, and she felt like a total failure.

She managed to swallow a few bites of food and tried to listen to Mr. Bentley's description of his home in Virginia. But as the minutes dragged by, all she could think about was what would happen if her dolphins didn't come in the next day or two. She had precious few days left with Titus Thorne.

Then she looked up from her plate and found him staring at her, his brow knitted and his mouth tight with disapproval. Her heart sank even further. It was no longer just a matter of validating her scientific methodology. More than anything, she wanted to prove her truthfulness and integrity to him. She wanted to see surprise melt his skepticism when Prospero came leaping out of the water . . . to see delight warming his chilly authority when Ariel towed him across the cove . . . to witness his resurrected awe at the spectacle of Thunder and Echo rising up out of the water on their flukes and "walking the water" in perfect synchrony. She wanted to expose his skeptical nature to the magic of encountering her beloved creatures in their own element. She wanted to see that special joy in his sea-green—

"W-what?" She blushed, aware they were all staring at her. "I apologize. I'm afraid I was gathering wool."

Bentley smiled adoringly. "Your grandmother just suggested that you show me something called a 'moonlight collection' in your garden."

She forced a pleased expression. "I would be delighted to do so."

"I'll have Stephan bring our coffee into the drawing room," Lady Sophia said, beaming in her most inscrutable way. "Join us when you come in."

The garden was bathed in both moonlight and dew by the time they set out along the path. Titus Thorne had risen from the table to accompany them, but was diverted by her grandmother, who insisted he join her and Mr. Cherrybottom in the library for a look at some of her artifacts. Celeste saw his dark look following her as she led Bentley to the front doors, and the suspicion in it stayed with her. There she was, that look said, pulling Bentley off into a darkened garden for a bit of whatever it was lascivious mermaids did in the dark.

So potent was that accusation, that when Bentley took her hand and pressed an ardent kiss on it, she made a point of spotting an Asiatic lily with a rather unique luminosity. Exhibiting true sportsmanship, he released her with a glimmer of disappointment in his handsome blue eyes. For some reason, all she could think about was the strange quivery feeling she got in her stomach whenever she stood this close to the irascible Titus Thorne in the moonlight.

THERE WERE FISH all around him: big fish, small fish, brightly colored fish, fantastically shaped fish. They darted in to peer at him with scowls on their faces, then, seeing it was him, turned tail and swam furiously away . . . some giving him a swat with their tails in the process. Then suddenly a very large fish tail appeared in the water before him . . . luminous, multicolored, feathery . . . shimmering as if lighted from the inside. Beautiful tail. Remarkable. Like nothing he had ever seen. He reached out to touch it as it swayed and undulated, and at the moment of contact, their watery surroundings dissolved into the operating theater at the medical college, and he suddenly had his arms wrapped around that huge specimen and was wrestling it onto his dissection table.

When he finally plopped it onto the table, it stilled and he was able to back away and give it a look. Even out of the water that magnificent tail shimmered with extraordinary colors, as if each and every scale were a tiny prism that focused a light inside that fish into brilliant rainbows outside the creature. He stood in awe for a while, then gave in to the urge to touch it. The surface felt smooth and sleek and it seemed to glow especially bright wherever he touched it. Such magnificent colors. Such beautiful light.

A fish with a light in its tail? His scientist mind jolted back into operation. He had to investigate this. Determinedly, he picked up a scalpel and started to make an incision. But the tail flipped up powerfully and knocked the blade from his hand. Then the curvy fish sat up, glared at him, and gave him a resounding smack in the face with its—

Titus lurched up in bed with his heart pounding and his face stinging on one side. When he finally registered the sight of his room in the light of early dawn and got his bearings, he slid from the bed on unsteady knees and staggered to the washstand to splash his face with water.

Fish tails *again*.

Damnable dreams.

AT THAT VERY MOMENT, Celeste was making her way down the cliff to begin calling her dolphins again. Every step was compelled by the knowledge that her time was most certainly running out. If she couldn't produce a specimen or two in the next day or so, Titus Thorne would have every right to pack his bag and head for Oxford, proclaiming the falsehood of her research every step of the way. If that happened, she knew, she would never see him again.

Then her impatient publisher would hie himself back to

London, wash his hands of her and her "fraudulent" work, and she would be left in her crumbling house, disgraced, an academic pariah . . . coping with an increasingly decrepit household, struggling to find a way to pay the butcher and grocer.

Halfheartedly, she began to pound her tin, hoping against all odds that somewhere, somehow, her dolphins were hearing her call and responding.

"WELL," CHERRYBOTTOM DECLARED, shifting his portly frame up from the side of the listing boat, "this is all quite fascinating." He meant "boring." He turned to Celeste with a frown and handed her back her mallet. "Perhaps I don't do it properly . . . that's why they haven't come."

"No, truly, you did it all just right," she responded, her heart sinking a bit more with each restless sigh and guarded look from the portly publisher. He tapped his knee repeatedly with his fleshy fingers and scanned the watery horizon. He was a man used to brisk activity and instantaneous results and he was stuck on a leaky boat in the middle of nowhere, just sitting and waiting . . . endlessly waiting.

Across from Celeste, Bentley gamely tried to keep up a conversation by asking her to recount experiences that hadn't been recorded in her published work. She complied, but produced somewhat spiritless narratives that quickly lost their appeal. Eventually the gentlemanly Bentley quit asking.

The only positive aspect of the entire morning was the fact that Titus Thorne hadn't been there to nettle her already sore spirits with his prickly skepticism. He had given up his place on the boat to Mr. Cherrybottom, and now she couldn't help wondering if that meant he was giving up expectations of ever seeing her dolphins, as well.

When she finally brought the boat in, there was Titus Thorne waiting for them on the dock, standing with his feet braced apart and his arms crossed, looking like the embodiment of Final Judgment.

He confronted them with a cool smile. "Well? Did you see them?"

"Not so much as a tail fluke," Cherrybottom said with disgust.

"Contrary beasts must be hiding somewhere," Bentley said with a sympathetic glance at Celeste. "Sooner or later they'll appear. I'm sure of it."

Cherrybottom was apparently less convinced, for as they headed for the beach and the path up the cliff, he cleared his throat and began a litany of all the projects awaiting his attention in London.

". . . working on a marvelous new edition of Homer, an anthology of heroic sea stories, some new volumes on home economy and hygiene . . . also preparing a bid to publish Professor Dobson's latest work. His 'Alice' books have been a raving success . . . every edition a sellout. I really must be getting back."

Celeste felt as if someone had just pulled the dock from beneath her feet. "But you only just arrived, Mr. Cherrybottom."

"I know, my dear, but I do have other obligations. Probably shouldn't have come on such short notice. Next time I'll write ahead . . . so you can have your dolphins on hand for . . ." He tugged at his collar and gave her a guilty bit of rationalization. "Besides, I shall be able to read it all in the professor's report."

Titus scowled at the publisher, who ignored him, gave Celeste a perfunctory tip of his hat, and headed for the beach at a quick pace.

"I suppose I should join him, Celeste," Bentley said, taking her hand between his and giving her a look of such melodramatic longing that Titus, just outside her line of vision, rolled his eyes. "I fear our presence here has put you under considerable strain. And, my dear, I would not add one ounce to your burdens. Just say you will permit me to call upon you again, someday."

She nodded woodenly. "You will always be welcome, Mr. Bentley."

The American pressed a kiss on her hand, then turned reluctantly away.

Titus watched them go through a haze of rising anger. The wretches. They'd been here all of one day and they were deserting her. He on the other hand had spent four interminable days enmeshed in her fruitless search for dolphins and growing steadily more enmeshed in the puzzle of who and what she was. And as he stood there, watching her disappointment, he finally understood.

She had sailed and swum and dived for most of her life. The sea held a special allure for her, afforded her a special link with her dead parents and grandfather. Once caught up in its mystery, she must have begun to embroider glimpses and observations of marine creatures into full-blown experiences. Deception was probably the furthest thing from her mind, at first. An honest glimpse of a dolphin somehow grew into the story of a close encounter with one while diving. An encounter became an intentional meeting and eventually personal interactions. With a fertile imagination and a great desire to emulate her beloved grandfather . . .

He watched her square her shoulders and rally her sagging spirits, and wanted to pull her back into his arms and hold her until her disappointment passed. He wanted to tell her that he understood . . . that she needn't pretend any longer . . . that he would find a way to make his report as benign as possible. He wanted to protect her from the censure and legal consequences her overactive imagination might bring down on her.

An aching hollow opened in the middle of his chest. He pressed his hand over the spot, alarmed that she had the power to affect him so.

Anxiety crept up his spine and shortened his breath. His unwavering principles, the very cornerstones of his academic life, were caving in at an alarming rate. For the first time in his entire academic life, he was actually considering *ignoring* the truth. He was allowing his passions and his messy, irrational emotions to dictate the content of his scientific decisions.

How in bloody hell had things gotten to such a state?

Panic set in. He watched Cherrybottom and Bentley trudging toward the cliff and felt an overwhelming urge to flee with them. Every moment he spent with her jeopardized his ability to maintain his intellectual and moral integrity. He turned back to her and felt a strange ache spreading through his chest at the look on her face.

He could no longer deal with her on a rational, scientific basis. And he had no idea how to deal with her on any other basis.

"Well, Miss Ashton, I cannot say my time here has not been educational." He intercepted her as she started along the path and she stopped dead, staring at him. "I've seen quite a bit already, and I doubt my continued presence here would serve any constructive purpose."

"You're leaving, too?" She paled.

"If you like, I will draft my statement for the Oceanographic Society before I leave tomorrow. That way you will be able to see what I have to say. I can promise you, it won't be accusatory. I intend to stress that I was able to verify your sailing and diving abilities, but that the time and season didn't permit me to stay long enough to duplicate your work with the creatures themselves."

"But you can't. You can't leave before you've seen Prospero and the others. I told you it might be several days or even a week or more. You haven't been here a full week yet—you have to stay—"

"I'm afraid that won't be possible, Miss Ashton." The pain visible in her face made him feel like the world's biggest cad. All the more reason for him to pack it in and head for Oxford as fast as he could go. "I have a number of obligations at the university and I cannot see that my lingering here would serve either of us."

He struggled with the temptation to say something per-

sonal, something more reassuring, but knew there were pit-
falls along that path. After a painful silence, he extended his
hand to her. When she placed hers in it, he felt her trembling and couldn't keep himself from looking up. Moisture
had collected in her eyes, making them into luminous blue
prisms that tugged at that empty spot in the center of his
chest. And her lips . . . slightly reddened, full and soft
. . . lips that would taste of salt and honey . . .

"Perhaps if it had been another time, another circumstance . . ." He released her and, allowing himself one last
indulgence, ran his knuckles down the side of her cheek.
Then he turned away.

Stunned, unable to respond for the crushing weight of
emotion in her chest, she watched his long legs and the rigid
set of his shoulders as he strode across the beach. All she
could think was that she would never see him again. Titus
Thorne . . . her prickly professor . . . her tantalizing
skeptic with the tender hands and wicked wit and sardonic
smile. She brought her hands to her middle, trying to find
and assuage the void she felt.

She managed to put one foot before the other, feeling
mercifully numb as she followed the departing source of her
womanly awakening.

The sun was no longer warm, the sky was no longer blue,
and the sea had ceased to rush and roar. Failure and heartache deadened all her senses. But as she trudged, head down,
along the gray, flat, textureless sand, she still somehow managed to hear the sound of that splash.

She froze, fighting her way through the fog settling over
her being. And as she strained to listen against the sudden
pounding of her heart, it came again.

Splash!

Nine

CELESTE WHIRLED AND rushed to the water's edge, her senses at full alert, straining for a sign of a dolphin. Her knees trembled, but her gaze was bright and steady as she held her breath and scanned the waves.

Suddenly a cylindrical form broke the water at the center of the cove and vaulted through the air in a graceful arc, followed by an ephemeral trail of spray and foam. By the time it pierced the water's surface again, a cry was working its way up her throat. Half a shout of triumph and half a prayer of thanks, it split the somber peace of the cove like the joyous peal of a bell.

"They're here!" She spun about, waving and calling, "They're here!" Then she began to run toward the center of the beach, her arms open wide, leaping into the air as she ran. "Look, Professor—they're here!"

Titus was just starting up the cliff, Bentley was halfway up, and Cherrybottom was just disappearing over the edge when her cries halted them in their tracks. Each turned, searching both the disturbed water and Celeste's buoyant form running along the beach below. Each watched in astonishment as a glistening, silver-gray dolphin launched from the water in the center of the cove, spun lengthwise in a graceful spiral, and dove back into the water with a tremendous splash.

Cherrybottom rubbed his eyes. Bentley squinted and stepped back, training his vision on the foamy circles left in the dolphin's wake.

Titus was already in motion, running back down and across the beach toward Celeste. His heart was pounding and something in his chest was swelling, making it hard for him to breathe.

"Did you see?" she shouted, running with her skirts raised and her feet barely touching the wet sand. "Did you see him? It's Prospero! He's come!"

"I saw *something*," he declared, catching her shoulders to steady her.

"Something?" She laughed at his stubborn skepticism. "It's *them*—I told you they would be here!"

She looked past his shoulder, toward Bentley and Cherrybottom, who were scrambling back down the cliff as fast as they could. Grinning at the sight they made, she whirled and scanned the waves for a familiar shape.

"There!" she called, pointing to the triangular shape of a dorsal fin, then looked back at him with her face glowing excitement. "A dolphin, Professor."

With an exultant laugh, she darted to the water's edge, jerked off her shoes, and threw them back up onto the beach. Then, fixing her gaze on the center of the cove, she fumbled with the buttons of her skirt.

"What are you—" Titus's eyes widened as she pulled her skirt down over her hips and tossed it in the same direction as her shoes. In horror he glanced over his shoulder at the approaching Cherrybottom and Bentley. "Good Lord, woman—you can't just strip your clothes—"

But she *was* doing it. Now. Here. His jaw dropped then worked soundlessly as she jerked her blouse up and over her head and tossed it onto the pile. No decent petticoat or proper stockings—she was left in only that thin, short-legged "combination" she was given to wearing. His protest died a conflicted groan in his throat as he watched her shapely legs plunge over and over into the surf, until she stood waist-deep in water.

"Good God." Bentley's winded voice came from nearby.

"Come out of there, Miss Ashton! Are you mad? There's a beast of some sort—" Cherrybottom bustled down to the water's edge and tiptoed frantically back and forth, dodging incoming waves as tried to decide how to retrieve her.

"No, she's not mad," Titus declared, to himself as much as Cherrybottom. He watched with rising emotion as she waved, turned, and dove into the water. "Nor, it would seem, is she devious . . . distressed . . . or seriously deluded."

Bentley hurried over and stood beside them, staring at the place she disappeared and speaking for them all when he said with stark wonder: "By God, it's true—she does have a dolphin!"

Again the dolphin breached the water and dove back in, making screeching sounds and noises that in human parlance would have been termed laughter. Then as they watched, transfixed, they saw Celeste crash through the surface, clinging to the dolphin's fin, joining it in its upward arc, separating, and diving back into the water nearby.

The men looked at each other, each verifying what he had just seen by the startlement in the others' faces.

"By Jove, she's done it! Called the blessed creature right to her very doorstep!"

Cherrybottom was so full of excitement that he looked as if he would burst if he didn't release it. He grasped Bentley by the shoulders and they began to laugh and hop around like delirious children.

Titus stalked to the very edge of the water, anticipating her next appearance and feeling his world beginning to tilt crazily underfoot. He could barely make sense of what was happening before his eyes. She not only sailed and dove, she actually *swam* with a dolphin . . . touching the blasted thing, hanging on to it and letting it drag her about just as she had reported. She had told the truth. And, unless he'd gone delusional himself, that meant that something he had considered ridiculous, absurd, and scientifically impossible . . . *wasn't*.

That conclusion was nothing short of staggering. He had been so certain, so adamant that it was all a fraud, that now it was difficult to admit the evidence of his own senses. A part of him clung desperately to the security and superiority of intellectual doubt. It could be a fluke—a passing dolphin investigating those rhythmic sounds she produced. Before he truly would be convinced, he had to see the beast at close range, touch it himself—

She popped up in the water, some thirty yards out, waving and calling for them to watch. Then she dove beneath the surface and he found himself holding his breath until her head reappeared fifty yards out, and she rose straight up out of the water, with the dolphin underneath her, propelling her upward. In a twinkling, she extended and arched her body and dove into the water, and the dolphin disappeared. Titus, Cherrybottom, and Bentley were left with the searing image of her nearly naked form—extended and moving with effortless grace—burned into their vision. They were snapped back to reality, moments later, when the dolphin itself jumped out of the water, turned, and landed on its back with a tremendous splash.

"Did you see that?" Bentley cried, pointing wildly. "She was standing on its head! The thing lifted her up out of the water!"

"Have you ever seen anything like it, Professor?" Cherrybottom rushed over to grab Titus by the arm and give him an ecstatic throttling.

"Never," Titus answered, unable to take his eyes from the place she had gone into the water.

There were more leaps and splashes and she was launched by the dolphin into a dive three or four more times. Titus's desperate theory of "the passing dolphin" was utterly demolished by their spectacularly intentional cooperation.

They swam and dived together. The dolphin towed her around the cove, and for one brief pass along the surface, she mounted it and rode sitting up, as if it were a horse. They were behaving like boisterous playmates. There was only one possible explanation: the creature knew her, and knew her *well*.

As the reality of it sank in, Titus, Cherrybottom, and Bentley sobered and watched intently every flash of a fluke, every bob of her head, every bit of contact between the woman and the dolphin. After several stunning displays of partnership in motion, her head popped up beside the dolphin's in the middle of the cove, and they saw her direct a hand toward the shore. In an instant, the pair was headed for the beach, the dolphin towing her as she gripped its dorsal fin. In the shallows they slowed and stopped, and Celeste crouched on her knees so that only her shoulders were above the water.

"Come and meet Prospero!" she called, beckoning broadly.

Bentley began ripping off his shoes and stockings, but rotund Cherrybottom tried in vain—stretching and puffing—to reach his expensively clad feet. In the end, he plunged determinedly into the water with Bentley, natty footgear and all.

Only Titus held back. He watched from a distance of thirty or so feet while they approached the dolphin and jumped like startled rabbits when it screeched unexpectedly and splashed them.

"Come in, Professor!" She beckoned to Titus. "He won't bite."

"I can see very well from here, thank you," he called hoarsely.

Cherrybottom and Bentley moved still closer and, after some coaxing, Bentley put out a hand to touch the dolphin. He drew back giggling, then did it again. Cherrybottom followed suit and was soon laughing as well. Celeste said something to "Prospero," clapped her hands twice, and the beast rolled onto his side and began to slap the water with a flipper. Bentley and Cherrybottom lunged back to keep from getting wetter than they already were, but continued to laugh and exclaim how remarkable it was to "meet" such a creature. After a few moments, they retreated to the beach and stood dripping and grinning with schoolboy delight at their adventure.

As the three watched, she gave the dolphin a hug, rose, and started for the beach wearing nothing but her all-but-transparent combination and a glowing smile. She was glorious; her curvaceous hips swaying, her light eyes sparkling, her breasts with their cold-hardened tips— Titus choked out a groan, ripped his coat from his shoulders and thrust it up to shield her from the others' eyes.

"Miss Ashton, really!" He met her halfway, in ankle-deep surf, and flung his coat around her.

"You didn't come to meet Prospero," she said, looking up as he enveloped her with both his garment and his arms.

"There will be plenty of time for that, Miss Ashton," he said gruffly, unable to resist the temptation of sliding into the shimmering pools of her eyes.

"But you're lea—" Understanding lighted her face. "You're staying?"

"Of course I'm staying," he said in a tone she had never heard from him before. "I have a good bit of scientific work to verify." It was a softness, she realized, a tone of intimacy that sent a chill through her. "Potentially groundbreaking work . . . like nothing I've ever seen before."

"Like nothing *anybody's* ever seen before!" Cherrybottom crowed as he and Bentley rushed over to join them.

Titus released her long enough for her to slip her arms into his coat, then pulled her toward her discarded clothing. While he gathered her garments, thrust them into her arms, she shivered and huddled in his coat.

Feeling light-headed and having her teeth chatter with cold were minor inconveniences in view of what had just happened. In the space of half an hour, her reputation, her academic possibilities, her entire future had changed. She had just proved that her work and her word were based on genuine experience, not girlish daydreams or clever manipulations. But, as important as all that was to her, the thing that sent a delirious wave of warmth through her was the fact that she was once again wrapped in Titus Thorne's generous coat.

Her prickly professor wasn't going anywhere.

LUNCHEON THAT DAY was a festive occasion. Maria opened some of her brandied peaches and made a special cold prawn salad. Old Stephan managed to find a bottle of French champagne in the cellar, and Lady Sophia insisted on serving the entire thing on a folding table in the middle of the garden. Instead of having a centerpiece of flowers among her guests, she said, she would make her guests the centerpiece among a bounty of fragrant flowers.

When Celeste had bathed and dressed again in a simple gathered skirt and long-sleeved blouse, she joined them for a toast and a delicious meal in the drowsy peace of the warm summer afternoon. Throughout the luncheon, Mr. Cherrybottom and Mr. Bentley recounted over and over their experience with Celeste's dolphin and plied her with eager questions.

What did the creature eat? How much could she see under the water? Hadn't it frightened her at first? Was she ever worried that the beast might hurt her? Did the dolphins ever get overexcited, and how would she calm them down if they did? How did she communicate with this one? What sorts of signals did she use? Did she understand what it meant by its clicks and screeches? What new tricks was she teaching it?

It was late afternoon and the sun was starting to sink when they made their way down to the water for another demonstration. Celeste had Titus and the others sit on the edge of the dock while she maneuvered the boat out into the middle of the cove by herself. With whistles and hand claps for signals and a small bucket of fish for rewards, she and Prospero demonstrated that he had learned how to jump through a hoop, retrieve a painted cork float, and skitter across the surface of the water on his tail flukes. The dolphin returned to the boat each time for a treat and a rub around his head or back. Once or twice he rolled on his back, offering her his belly, and she pushed him away and refused to give him a treat.

Each "trick" drew applause or gasps of appreciation from her audience. When she ran out of fish, she clapped her hands and Prospero stuck his head up out of the water. She sang several notes of a musical scale, and by the third tone, the dolphin sang with her. The tones were flat and lasted only a short while, but no one hearing them could doubt the dolphin's vocalizations were an attempt to imitate her singing.

A standing ovation welcomed her back to the dock, where Bentley appropriated her hands and attention, and gushed over her achievement. Cherrybottom predicted a sellout for her second edition and an ever-greater swell of public interest in her dolphins. And Titus Thorne acknowledged that she had a unique rapport with the creature. Every comment was like a salve for her battered faith in herself and her work.

As they started for the beach, Cherrybottom declared genially, "I envy you, Professor."

"Me?" Titus gave him a puzzled look.

"Of course. You get to swim with those magnificent creatures, yourself." He made Celeste blush with the teasing grin he aimed her way. "And with the loveliest *mermaid* in all of the seven seas."

Titus's smile faded.

Celeste caught that change in his expression and watched him as they made their way up the cliff to the house. Since those first few delirious moments on the beach, he had grown increasingly distant, and Mr. Cherrybottom's comment seemed to have sunk him into a foul mood. She couldn't believe he would really be so stubborn or mean-spirited as to doubt the proof of his own eyes. Could he still disbelieve her work? Or was it—she made herself admit the possibility—that he was so rigid and unbending that he couldn't bear to admit he had been wrong?

She chewed the corner of her lip, thinking about the fact that he had refused to greet and touch Prospero and remembering his adamant views about science. Now that he knew her observations were genuine, was he determined to label them as irrelevant and unscientific? Would he still insist that his precious laboratory work was the only real kind of research? More importantly, would his intellectual pride keep him from experiencing the joy of the discoveries that awaited him?

That evening, over coffee and brandy in the parlor, Peter Bentley settled an acquisitive gaze on Celeste, watching her glowing countenance and graceful, womanly movements. She was a delicious bonus, he thought. A living mermaid. So lovely, so unspoiled, and so artlessly susceptible to flattery. It was a pity he didn't have more time to explore her charms fully. He consoled himself with the thought that he would have plenty of time for that after his plan and his financial backers were in place. Business, he smirked silently, had to come before pleasure.

"Lady Sophia, Miss Ashton," Bentley said, setting his cup aside and rising, "I fear I have imposed upon your hospitality long enough. It grieves me to say that I must return to London at first light. Pressing business matters."

A rustle of surprise stirred through the room. Cherrybottom suggested that he wait until the afternoon so that they might share a coach. Bentley declined, saying that he had calls to pay while traveling back to the city, and had already arranged with the local livery for a horse. Then he paused before Celeste's chair and asked if she would care for a turn about the garden before retiring.

She looked up at his gentlemanly form, fair hair, and handsome features, and felt strangely disappointed to accept.

He took her elbow as he escorted her out the front doors and down the path to the garden, and he did not release her until she paused to pick some daisies. After watching for a time, he impulsively reached for her elbow and pulled her to her feet.

"My dear Celeste, do you have any idea how you have overturned my world?" He gazed with heartfelt intensity into her eyes. "Words cannot express the tumult and the joy you have brought into my life this day."

She tensed as his hands closed over hers, crumpling some of her daisies.

"Watching you, seeing your devotion to your dolphins, witnessing your special bond with them, I realized how purposeless my life has been. I see now that my love of the sea is—has always been—my true calling, my cause, my vocation. Emboldened by the example of your courage, I dare to say that today I conceived of a collaboration between us. A partnership. A blending of talents and intellect and effort, in the service of a much greater good." His hands moved to her shoulders and tightened. "Celeste, you dream of bringing people and the sea together. I want to help you do that."

She was dumbstruck. "Pet—Mr. Bentley—I don't know what to say."

"Then let me speak of the dream I have for us," he hurried on. "Let me paint for you a picture of the noble venture we could embark upon . . . educating the world, bringing our love of the sea to people everywhere. We could work side by side, researching, lecturing—"

"Please, Mr. Bentley"—she put up a hand to stop him—"go no further." She searched for words. "I am only now getting my feet under me. I have much work yet to do here, and my grandmother to care for. I am not at all prepared to enter into such a . . . *collaboration*."

For a moment he seemed as if he would press his idea, but as he studied the tension and determination in her face, his hands fell away.

"Forgive my impetuousness, dearest Celeste." He backed

a step, trampling a delicate aster. "Or better, cast it as my noblest flaw . . . to err by eagerness in the interest of a great and noble cause."

"There is nothing to forgive, Mr. Bentley. I am heartened that my work helped you to make such an important decision. And I hope that my inability to accept your offer will not interfere with our friendship."

Disappointment darkened his handsome eyes briefly, but he mastered it to give her a wistful smile.

"Then I shall count myself fortunate indeed to be your devoted friend."

SOME TIME LATER, Mr. Bentley bid both Celeste and her grandmother a good night and a gracious farewell. She rubbed the spot he had kissed on her hand as she watched him climb the stairs for the final time.

She had just received her first and very likely her last offer of . . . what? What had she just refused? A partnership? There had been a hint of something more personal, but only a hint. If she had encouraged him, would Peter Bentley have courted her on a personal level, too?

It had been years since she thought of such things with regard to her life. Courtship, marriage—the usual womanly aspirations—seemed so foreign to her experience and so unlikely in her circumstance. But if she were to think of such things, would she ever think of them as part of a "collaboration" with P. T. Bentley?

The praise and admiration he heaped on her made her feel awkward and self-conscious. His constant agreement sometimes weighed on her nerves. No, if she were ever to take a partner—whether in research or in life—it would have to be someone who stimulated and challenged her thinking and her conclusions about her work, someone who made her heart pound and her thoughts race and her lips ting—

She looked up and found herself staring into Titus Thorne's forbidding scowl.

•   •   •

THE DARKNESS WASN'T dark enough . . . the bed wasn't soft enough . . . the night wasn't passing quickly enough. Celeste lay in her bed, staring at the sagging canopy overhead and watching the moon shadows lengthening slowly across it, inch by wearisome inch, thread by tedious thread.

At length, she gave up and went to the seaward window of her corner room to see if it would open a bit wider. Folding her arms, she stood in the faint breeze and leaned her head against the frame of the window.

As she stared out over the water, letting her mind drift over the momentous events of the day, her gaze caught on something down on the beach. Something—someone—was on the beach, moving toward the water. She leaned out on the windowsill, trying to make out who it was.

Taller than not, she deduced, and wearing a white shirt and trousers. She squinted and made out dark hair. That combined with a certain nuance of movement to align the tumblers of her mind and unlock recognition. It was Titus Thorne.

On the beach in the middle of the night?

Watching him moving along the shore, she thought of the water, the moonlight, and that first night on the dock. In a heartbeat she was fumbling for her sailing smock in the darkened wardrobe and feeling along the floor with her feet for her slippers. By the time she reached the stairs, she had managed to shove her arms into the sleeves and was fastening buttons.

What was he doing down there in the dead of night? Her pace quickened along the moonlit path to the edge of the cliff. The nearly full moon bathed the beach in silver light, silhouetting his form and movements. As she felt her way down the shadowed steps of the cliff, she watched him walking purposefully, with a springy tension in his step, his hands jammed into his pockets and his face turned toward the water. As he neared the path leading to the dock, he turned abruptly and retraced his steps, still staring at the water.

Pacing, she realized. Then he halted in the middle of the beach and began to remove his shoes and stockings with jerky, impassioned movements. He threw his footgear back up onto the sand with some force, rolled up his trouser legs, and faced the water again with his hands planted at his waist.

"HOW HARD CAN it be?" Titus muttered to himself. "Ducks do it. Frogs, fish, and salamanders do it. All it takes is holding your breath and lying down in the damned water . . . flailing your arms and legs about like some overturned sea turtle." He rolled his shoulders. "The human body is naturally buoyant in salt water . . . it's not possible to sink. For long, anyway."

Taking a deep breath, he strode out into the water until it reached midcalf, where he froze. For a long moment, he stood there, his fists clenched, feeling his determination eroding the same way the sand was washing away beneath his feet. He shuddered through another bout of self-loathing, then turned and stalked back up onto the beach. He stood there, staring at the water with his chest heaving.

The frustration that had been building in him since late that morning finally erupted in an anguished groan. It was out there, somewhere. A real, living dolphin. He had seen it, been given a chance to touch it. And he had been dying to touch it . . . to look into its eyes, to feel it move, to listen to its forceful breathing.

Dandified Bentley had bounded out there without a second thought, and Cherrybottom—who couldn't even reach the ties of his own shoes—had gone barreling into the water, footgear and all, to experience the thing. But *he*—the upholder of science and logic and objectivity, the quintessential "rational man"—had stood on the shore, alone, with his heart in his throat.

The water. That damnable water. It had plagued him his

entire life, robbed him of chances too numerous to mention. Tonight, the sound of it lapping against the shore had drifted into his room and robbed him of sleep as well. He was supposed to get into the water tomorrow with Celeste and her dolphin, and the thought of walking out into that water made him break out in a cold sweat.

During that interminable evening, he had nursed the hope that perhaps, since his seasickness seemed to have miraculously abated, he might be able to—

"Well, well, Professor." Her voice startled him and he jumped visibly. "What brings you down here in the dead of night?"

He whirled and found Celeste standing behind him with her arms crossed and her chin raised. She was wearing her seagoing smock and her light hair hung loose about her shoulders.

"I . . . wasn't sleeping." He matched her determined stance, hoping that his inner turmoil didn't show in his face. "So, I decided this might be as good a time as any to test your observations . . . of . . . about . . . dolphins not sleeping." He raised his chin higher to look down his nose at her. "I have to begin somewhere."

"Indeed you do." Her smile contained a satisfaction that escalated his anxiety. When she began to unfasten the buttons of her long smock, he felt the first, tiny trickle of panic.

"Just what in blazes do you think you're doing?" he demanded.

"I can't sleep either, so I may as well help you." She paused with her smock gaping open, the hem raised so that she could reach the lower buttons. He looked up from the provocative slice of white cotton widening down her front and found his gaze caught on a torrent of soft, wavy hair that glowed golden in the moonlight.

"Any excuse to throw off your clothing, eh, Miss Ashton?" He turned his head as her smock fell completely open and she shrugged it from her shoulders. "What is it . . . some bizarre taint in the Ashton blood that makes you and your grandmother incapable of enduring normal female garb?" When she didn't answer, he continued with a sharper edge. "You do realize that this is the third time you've stripped to your 'mustn't-mention-'ems' in my presence?"

She halted halfway to the water and leveled a narrow look on him.

"You're keeping count?"

He felt heat creeping up his neck. "Collecting data."

"On what?" she asked, shifting her weight subtly so that the curve of one hip was now exaggerated.

Damn good question, he told himself.

"Mermaid behavior" was all he could come up with. "Up-and-coming field, mythological females. Considerable interest in it of late. The big disadvantage, of course, is that good specimens are so dashed hard to come by."

" 'Good specimens.' " She pondered that with narrowed then headed for the water. "You're swimming in that?"

"Who said I was going to swim?" He stiffened.

"Well, it's the only way you'll learn what dolphins do at night."

"Actually," he said, thinking fast, glancing toward the dark outline of the boathouse, "I was thinking of taking the boat."

"The boat?" She laughed. "I thought it was against your principles to set foot in a boat in the dead of night." When he didn't move, frantically trying to think of a way to avoid the water, she added: "Don't worry about your clothes. Take them off and swim in your 'mustn't-mention-'ems.' "

He stood frozen, feeling his mouth going cottony and that same icy dread stealing up his limbs. "It wouldn't be proper, Miss Ashton. Both of us, unclad . . . in the same—"

"*Ocean?*" she said, sinking down onto her knees so that only her head was above the water. "You must have been fed nothing but prunes and proverbs, when you were a boy, Titus Thorne. You are, without a doubt, the primmest, most prudish man I have ever encountered."

"An unimpressive distinction," he muttered, "considering my competition is a half-wit blacksmith, a pair of senile fishermen, a Napoleonic war relic, and a devil-dodger who thinks dolphins keep secrets from him."

"Get into the water, Professor," she ordered, smiling.

"On the other hand, there is something to be said for waiting until daylight. Wouldn't want to go surprising the creature in the dead of night. Dolphins do have *teeth*."

"But dolphins don't *bite*." She began working her way toward him as he stood on the beach.

"How do you know? Just because they've never bitten you doesn't mean that they might not bite someone else. Someone new. Someone with . . . bigger flippers."

"Dolphins aren't jealous of the size of each other's flippers." She halted not far from him, bracing in the sand to keep from being washed up by the waves. "Are you coming in, or am I coming out to get you?"

Ten

WHEN TITUS HESITATED, she did come up out of the water to get him. He stumbled back a step, scrambling wildly for an excuse—any excuse.

"R-really, Miss Ashton."

"Really, Professor." She planted herself before him in the sand with her arms crossed strategically over her breasts. She nodded to his garments. "You'd better take those off. You will need dry clothes when you come out of the water."

He couldn't think properly, couldn't control his gaze or his body heat with her mere inches away, half naked and dripping wet. When she reached for his shirt buttons, he grabbed her hand and held it, and she looked up.

"First you strip off your clothes—now mine," he said, his voice oddly hoarse. "Abandoned creature."

"I am not. Any serious student of 'mythological females' should know that mermaids live by a different set of rules."

He finished the buttons himself and tossed his shirt up onto the dry sand just as she grabbed him by the arm and headed for the water.

Terror gripped him. But before he could resist, he was ankle-deep and being dragged deeper. Halfway up his calves. Another step . . . then two more. Water lapped at his knees and wet his trousers. He dug his heels into the sandy bottom, but she pulled harder and suddenly he was in up to his hips.

His throat was so constricted, he couldn't speak. Cold and darkness billowed up around him, setting his heart pounding wildly, making him feel light-headed and panicky. He couldn't seem to move his arms or legs. It was as if rigor mortis were already setting in!

"Come on, Professor, don't be a stick about this." She gave him a tug. When he didn't budge, she apparently sensed something deeper at work and turned to search his stiff face and rigid body.

He watched, choked with humiliation, as she waded back and stood looking up at him until he lowered his chin enough for their gazes to meet. Her eyes were remarkably blue in the moonlight. Insightful blue. Penetrating blue.

"You can't swim, can you?" she said quietly.

He wasn't certain if he actually made some affirming motion or if she just read a confirmation in his stiff face and helpless silence.

"You really do hate the water," she said thoughtfully, as if studying the ramifications of it. The taunting laughter he dreaded never materialized. What he got was a thoughtful nod. He remained braced, unwilling to trust her seeming calm, but she merely continued to study him, as if waiting for him to say more.

"Ironic, isn't it." His smile carried a twist of bitterness. "The fish scientist who can't go near the water. Enjoy it, Miss Ashton. The laugh is on me."

But she didn't laugh.

She understood.

It was all so clear, she thought . . . visible in his guarded eyes, etched into his defensive frown, proclaimed by the tension he wore like a cloak. The word had not been spoken; there was no need to speak it. He was *afraid*. Suddenly it all made sense: his attitude, his behavior in the boat, his stubborn doubts that her dolphins existed, and even his refusal to inspect Prospero firsthand. Fear, her grandfather had often said, made a person put up walls to keep things out. And Titus Thorne had put up more walls than anyone she had ever known.

"Well, that can be remedied," she said in an even tone. "Who better to teach you to swim than a mermaid?" She took him by the hand and caught his gaze in hers. "Come with me."

He looked into her eyes and felt her certainty dissolving some of his tension. Somehow, with her in the water beside him, the prospect of being engulfed by water didn't seem quite so menacing. He made himself focus just on her, resisting the urge to predestine this "swimming lesson" to failure. He hadn't much hope for it, but as he watched her soft smile and sinuous movements, he vowed to do whatever was necessary to have these moments with her.

When she reached for his other hand, he gave it up, drinking in the sight of her glowing features and moon-brightened hair. Taking a fortifying breath, he waded back with her to water that was only up to his knees.

"Sit," she ordered. Taking his hand, she sat down on the shifting sand in the shallow water and pulled him down with her. By the time he made it onto his rear, he was as stiff as a day-old mackerel.

"The key to swimming is relaxation. Accepting the feel of the water and letting the water do what water inevitably does. Just sit down, take a deep breath, and let the water lift and support your body."

He tried. He sank farther into the shifting water, feeling it surging and rushing around his body, and was soon as tense as a watchspring. She made a judgmental "tsk," then moved around behind him and sat down with her legs on either side of him. "Lean back."

"Why—what are you going to do?" he gritted out.

"Help you relax. Now, lean back on me. I'll support you."

"This is ridiculous. I'm never going to learn to swim this way."

"You won't learn any other way. Now, lean back on me."

Inch by agonizing inch, he managed to lower his shoulders until she supported them with her hands and upper shoulders. Her face was beside his ear. "Better. Now take deep, slow breaths. That will help you relax."

Soon she was breathing with him, drawing him into a calmer rhythm, and after a while, he did indeed feel more relaxed . . . until he felt her shifting beneath him, withdrawing. "No, stay as you were. I'm going to sit beside you."

He held his breath, but released it when she continued to cradle his head in her hands, keeping it out of the water. Soon he was lying back in the surging water, feeling it rushing over him, then pulling on his body as it returned to the sea. "Doesn't it feel like a touch?" she said into his ear. "Like a hand sweeping up your body?"

It did indeed. And it wasn't long before he felt himself responding to that cool, liquid caress. Heat began to curl through his veins once again.

"Look up at the night sky," she murmured. "The moon, the stars, the occasional cloud. Everything above you and everything below you is really part of one great creation. You're part of it, too, whether you are immersed in air or water. Can you feel that you belong to it, in it?"

Then her face, cast in shadows by the fall of her hair, appeared over his. "Relax now and let the water do what water does best. Let it lift and envelop you. Close your eyes and let it caress you."

It felt like her hands, washing up his feet and legs, then rising over his shoulders and chest. It felt like her body pressed against his, lapping softly and erotically against his legs, his chest, his loins. The pull and slosh of the water increased for a time, but with her steady litany of reassurance, he gradually allowed it to buoy him and began to trust her quiet authority. Then he let his head rest on her hand, until it lay half in the water.

The squeezing in his throat and the chill in his limbs were almost gone. Each wave that rippled gently up his body reduced his terror another degree. Soon he was floating entirely, except for her hands under his head and the small of his back. He abandoned himself to her direction. It was a curiously pleasant sensation, floating in water.

After a while, he opened his eyes to tell her so and realized she wasn't seated, but standing beside him, chest-deep in water. Instantly, he felt his lower half sinking. He panicked and began to flail.

"Where's the damned bott— Aghhh!" He ceased thrashing and came upright when his feet hit the sandy bottom. He was slightly more than waist-deep in water, well beyond the breaker zone. "What am I doing out here?"

"Floating, Professor. And very nicely, too." She grinned. "That proves you can do it. It's just a matter of practice, from here on. Now turn around and lie back in the water, again. I'll see that you don't sink."

He scowled, but she seized his arms and turned him away from her. The sight of her bright eyes and the soft swell of her breasts beneath her thin garment came with him. After some reassurance, he summoned every scrap of determination he possessed, held his breath, and leaned backward. Just when he started to panic, he felt her hands at his shoulders. It took several attempts and some coaxing for him to regain his former comfort level, but Celeste was soon towing him on his back, around in the water.

It was surprisingly liberating. Shockingly simple. He didn't have to think about it; in fact, the more he thought about it the worse he did. Slowly he relinquished control, giving himself over to absorbing the sight of moon and stars overhead and the soft caress of the water.

His fragmented thoughts gradually collected around the initiator and interpreter of this sensory banquet. Sleek, strong, supple body, delicate features, shining, sun-streaked hair . . . she was a bachelor's dream. Curious, wise beyond her years, and deliciously sensual . . . she was an odd combination of knowledge and innocence, girlish impulse and womanly deliberation. And she hadn't a shred of false modesty or coquetishness about her. She had an eye for him and she was both brazen enough and artless enough to let it show.

He bent suddenly at the waist, found the bottom with his feet, and took her by the shoulders. She looked up with surprise, but no trace of annoyance or alarm. In that moment, her eyes were windows onto a luminous soul and he saw into her depths. There was no deceit or manipulation in Celeste Ashton. She dealt with everything the way she had dealt with him just now: honestly, forthrightly. She truly wanted to help him swim, just as she wanted to share her love of the sea and of her dolphins with him . . . with the rest of the world.

A wave of inexpressible tenderness swept through him. Whatever she had concluded, whatever she had written, it hadn't been from idealism or arrogance or ignorance. It had been from a genuine desire to share her discoveries, to make a contribution to the world. A sweet, pulsing ache of desire roused in him, and before he could think better of it, he drew her to him and lowered his head.

She met his kiss with gentle caution, testing, searching his mood. Then as his arms closed around her, she seemed to find the answer to her concerns and her arms slid around his bare waist. He pulled her close, reveling in her response, wrapping her in his rising warmth.

He delved into her mouth, teasing, luxuriating in her salty sweetness. She pressed hard against him, molding herself to his larger, harder frame, and in the way of passion, gentled his strength to shelter her softness. Desire ignited in him as he ran his hands down her back, cupping her buttocks, lifting her against his aching body as he savored the taste of her.

Her kisses caught fire as she responded to the feel of him against her body and parted her legs to seek closer contact with him. Feeling her weight pressed intimately against him, he started with her toward shallower water. She broke that kiss to whisper, "Wait . . . not yet."

She fitted her lips to his again and began to lean backward, drawing him over her. Bending her knees, she sank farther and farther into the water, using the strength of their kiss to pull his head down over hers. Soon she was floating on her knees, her back arched, her face up. As the water lapped around her head, she abandoned herself to her most impassioned response yet, and he could do nothing but follow where she led.

When he felt the water against his nose, he opened his eyes in surprise and lifted his head to look at her. Her face was now submerged in water, all but her chin and mouth. She wrapped a hand around his neck and urged his head down again . . . kissing him from under water. The warmth of her mouth made a stunning contrast to the coolness of the water lapping against his face. Gradually the water spread over his face and seeped around their joined lips, flavoring their kiss with salt.

He closed his eyes and, with his heart pounding, refused to release her to the sea. Held by the power of that contact with her, holding his breath, he followed her down into the water. There was no panic, no dark, encroaching circle of memories. There was only the warmth of his mouth on hers, the coolness of the water, and his trust that she would not lead him where he could not bear to go.

When his breath ran out and he raised his head and wiped his face, it was to a sense of disbelief. He looked at her face, still half submerged but smiling. And as if to prove to himself that it had been real, he lowered his head again and, a second time, sank into the water with her.

This time, he traced her face with his fingertips and found her hair floating around her in the water. He explored its sinuous feel as it wrapped around his hands, and drank in every possible sensation, prolonging that contact. When he finally had to surface, she came with him. After he wiped his face, he looked at her and found her smiling with an irresistible radiance.

"You just learned to hold your breath under water, Titus Thorne."

"That's not all," he said hoarsely, pulling her toward him.

"Oh?" She laughed softly, sliding her arms around his bare ribs. "What else did you learn?"

It wasn't possible to put it into words. It was a jumble of impressions, reactions, and feelings. How could he express the way familiar boundaries of conduct and ethics seemed to be shifting, expanding, dissolving, and rearranging themselves? He could feel it, could identify the anxiety it generated in him, but right now he didn't want to think about all that. He only wanted to feel this closeness, this warmth with her. He lowered his head, drawing her onto her toes, drawing her into the center of his desire for her.

"That mermaid kisses are salty." He covered her lips with his and abandoned himself to the pleasure of both wanting and having.

Suddenly something struck them from the side, sending them both crashing into the water. Celeste scrambled up, wiping her eyes, and whirled to search the water around them.

"Prospero! Where are you?"

A silver head popped up out of the water not far away, grinning that perpetual dolphin grin.

"I'm sorry, Professor," she said, making sure Titus was all right. "But I suppose here is your proof that dolphins don't sleep at night. Come, meet Prospero." Taking his hand, she pulled him toward that grinning face.

Titus suddenly found himself in chest-deep water, face-to-face with Celeste's dolphin. It was larger than he had imagined, at close range.

"Say hello to Professor Thorne, Prospero," she said, nodding her head in an exaggerated fashion.

The dolphin nodded, then paused as if to look Titus over.

Then it gave its head a violent flip and shot a stream of water square in Titus's face.

He lurched back.

"Prospero! That wasn't nice!" Celeste exclaimed. She gave a hand signal, ordering the dolphin to go. It obeyed, but then it came right back.

"Oh, so you want to play, eh?"

She directed a retaliatory splash at the dolphin. But by this time, Titus was already halfway to the beach.

"See here, I don't bother you when you're playing with Ariel or Echo," Celeste muttered. "Now shove off!"

She went after Titus. By the time she reached him he had already donned his shirt and collected his shoes and stockings.

"I suppose I should thank you," he said, giving a shiver in the light breeze.

"Tomorrow, Professor," she said. "After you've had your second lesson."

She saw his shoulders ease and realized she had just answered a question he hadn't known how to ask. Taking a deep breath, he gazed intently at her and offered her his given name. "Titus. Call me Titus."

"Titus," she repeated, pleased but feeling the need for more reassurance. "You do believe in my work, now, don't you? I mean, you've seen Prospero and me with your own two eyes."

"There can be no question that you have had significant experience with a dolphin," he said, ushering her toward the house. "It is clear you've developed a strong bond with the creature."

"But . . ." She supplied the exception she heard coming in his words.

"But you've also made a number of claims about dolphin interactions . . ."

She stopped on the path, folded her arms, and glared at him. "Ever the skeptic," she charged, stung by his answer after what he had seen and what they had shared just moments ago. "You'll get your proof, Titus Thorne. I promise you. I only hope you'll be up to handling it when it comes."

P. T. BENTLEY LEFT before breakfast the next morning, with no one but Stephan there to see him off. But Edgar Cherrybottom delayed his departure until he'd had yet another look at Celeste's dolphin. After breakfast, she took Titus out to the middle of the cove in the boat, with Cherrybottom looking on from the dock, and once again made introductions between man and beast.

Prospero bobbed his head, at Celeste's urging, and rose up out of the water enough to offer a polite flipper. Warily, Titus put his hand out to "shake," but after a brief touch, Prospero sank back into the water with a splash, rocking the boat. Celeste called him back to the boat for Titus to pet and the dolphin finally turned onto his side and let himself be stroked.

"It's so smooth," Titus said with surprise. "And cool." Then he felt the dolphin's flipper and broke into a boyish grin. "It feels like a sleek, hard rubber," he observed. "Most of the ones I've seen have been limp and—" He shoved that memory aside and stroked Prospero's side. Celeste explained that the rake marks on his skin had probably come from other dolphins.

"They play and tussle with their mouths open . . . sometimes nip each other in the process. It can leave nasty marks. The males are sometimes aggressive with each other. But they often travel in pairs and I've seen them work together . . . help each other mate." She reddened under his shocked scrutiny, then hurriedly gave a sharp whistle and tapped the edge of the boat. Prospero dove into the water headfirst, presenting his tail flukes for inspection. Titus touched the flukes and traced their nicked edges. Then Prospero swam off and came up a few yards away, producing a series of clicks and screeches.

"He wants to play," Celeste said, looking around in the

bottom of the boat for one of the painted floats she had brought from the boathouse. She tossed it as far as she could in the water. Prospero submerged and went for it.

"How do you know he's playing?" Titus asked.

"I cannot think of any other purpose such behavior could serve."

They watched raptly as the dolphin seized the pear-shaped float and rose half out of the water. With a jerk of his head, Prospero tossed the float some distance away, retrieved it, and threw it again.

"When his friends aren't around, he plays 'fetch' with me." She laughed. "When we're in the water together and I throw it, he retrieves. When he throws it, it's my job to bring it back. If I forget and leave it out in the cove, he and the others will play a game of 'keep away' with it."

After a while Prospero grew bored with his toy and just let it bob on the surface of the water. She gave a sharp whistle and rattled a metal bucket and the dolphin raced just under the surface to the boat. She knelt and leaned over the side to talk to the creature.

"One of the Bass brothers heard you were back and came by this morning with some treats," she said to him. "Are you ready?" She stuck her hand into the bucket and came up with a couple of small, silvery herring. Prospero made a series of laughterlike sounds and opened his mouth in a gaping grin. She tossed the fish into Prospero's mouth, then shaded her eyes and looked up at Titus.

"Want to try giving him a treat?" He hesitated and she added: "It will probably make him your friend for life."

"The beast has teeth. A bloody headful of large, pointed teeth," he pointed out.

"Which he uses only for grabbing. From what I can tell, dolphins rarely eat anything they can't swallow whole."

"Feeding is *my* area of expertise, thank you, and you would bloody well be surprised what sorts of things I've found in—"

"Well, I've seen dolphins feeding in the wild for some

years now, and I've yet to see one snap at anything attached to a human." She realized they were treading on delicate ground and held up a hand to call a truce. "There is a way to settle this. When you're ready, you'll come diving with me and see for yourself. Now"—she stuffed a fish into his hand—"make Prospero your friend."

He gave the fish in his hand a dubious look. Then, following her instruction, he held it up by the tail. Prospero came alert and opened his mouth, with its big, pink tongue and jaws lined with conical teeth. Titus tossed him the fish, and he caught and swallowed it.

"Good! Very good!" she called out. Titus couldn't tell if she was talking to him or the dolphin.

His jaw dropped when Celeste leaned over the side of the boat with her lips pursed, and the dolphin rose up to meet her mouth with the end of his beak.

"Good Lord—you just—just—" He seemed unable to say it.

"Go on," she said, giving his shoulder a shove. "Let him kiss you, too."

He seemed to find his voice. "The hell I will."

"Go on—don't be a stuffed shirt," she chided.

"Absolutely not. I am a scientist, a professor, an expert on marine . . . the very idea is perverted. Imagine if it got out I was seen *kissing* a fish!"

Prospero settled the argument for them. He rose up out of the water toward Titus and sprayed him with a huge mouthful of water. Titus blinked and wiped his dripping face, clearly affronted. Celeste fell over in the boat laughing. When she could finally get her breath, she struggled up to meet his outrage with strained sobriety.

"I don't think he really wanted to kiss you, either."

CHERRYBOTTOM LEFT JUST after luncheon. Lady Sophia retired to her library to work on her current artifact, and Celeste took Titus for a walk along the cliffs above the cove.

Near the farthest point of land, they encountered several standing stones in a flower-strewn field. Titus was drawn instantly to the large, upright rocks, examining them from all sides, running his hands over their weathered surfaces.

"Fascinating. Old standing stones, like the henge on the plain at Salisbury," he said. "I didn't realize there were such stones in this area."

"There are a few," she said, looking a bit uncomfortable. "My grandfather was quite interested in them. He wondered if they might be connected to the history of Atlantis. I don't think he ever formed definite conclusions about it."

Her grandmother, however, had . . . as she well knew. To Nana these stones—in fact, all standing stones in Britain—were proof that Britain had once been an outer province of the great civilization of Atlantis.

"I brought you here to see the view." She pointed out the Bass brothers' dock in the distance, the church steeple of the village of Cardamon, nestled in a wrinkle of green velvet, and the fishing boats plying the deeper waters of the larger bay. It was all wrapped in an idyllic summer haze.

"It's beautiful. The sort of place everyone should have fond, childhood memories of," he said, seeming a thousand miles away.

"Where were you brought up, Titus? Tell me about your home," she said, leaning back against one of the stones and enjoying the warmth it radiated.

"I wasn't exactly 'brought up,' as you put it. At about seven years, I was sent away to school, where I simply 'grew.' " His face darkened as he stared out to sea and into memory. "Woolen undershirts, breaking ice on the basin to wash of a morning, porridge twice a day until fourth form . . . lining up for the weekly dose of castor oil. The one good thing about the place was old Fenstermacher. He taught Latin and rhetoric, and an occasional bit of humanity with stories from his wayward youth. Quite a fossil, we all thought. But he made life there bearable."

"When did your parents die? Was it when you were seven?"

Still looking out to sea, he took a slow breath. "My mother died not long after I was born. It was my father who died when I was seven. We were out in a boat, when—" He halted and looked out to sea.

"A boat?" She came alert. "Your father died in a boating accident?"

"A sudden squall. The storm blinded us and whipped the waves into a fury. He tied me to the mast while he tried to . . . a rogue wave broke over the boat and I saw him fighting to hang on . . . to live . . . and watched him being dragged under by a wave. One minute he was there and the next . . ." He abruptly pushed off from the stone and started for the path. "Shouldn't we get back?"

Frowning, she watched him fleeing both the memories and the revelation of them. His reason for hating the water was suddenly all too clear. His father died at sea, before his eyes, when he was seven years old. She thought of her parents, of how she couldn't understand why they were never coming back to her. She could only imagine the anguish that not only losing his father but actually seeing him swept overboard must have caused.

Then, as if that weren't enough of a horror, he was promptly sent away to a strict, regimented public school, where his bewildered heart was ignored, his anguished face lost in a sea of faces . . . housed in a cold dormitory, fed porridge twice a day, and probably caned for the slightest infraction of rules. No watercolor lessons, no collecting shells, no cocoa and stories at bedtime, no toasty warm rugs by the fire on rainy days . . . no Nana's hugs . . .

She followed for a moment, then veered from the path toward the cliff. "This way," she called, beckoning. "A shortcut down to the beach."

When he peered uncertainly at the narrow path, she seized his hand and gave it a squeeze. "Time for your swimming lesson."

This time, she had brought blankets and towels and her voluminous smock. While removing her skirt and blouse, she looked up to find him wearing a formfitting gray combination garment made of knitted wool. It had short sleeves and legs that ended midthigh.

"I've decided to swim in my Jaegers," he said, lifting his chin.

"Very practical," she said, feeling her cheeks reddening, and something in her veins began to hum. It was all she could do to make herself look away.

Once they were in the water, she had him repeat last night's lesson, substituting clouds for stars as a focus for concentration. It took less time and coaxing for him to begin to relax. She stayed with him for a while with her hand under him, watching his body floating, memorizing the broad mounds of his chest, the ridges of his ribs, and the elegant taper of his long, muscular legs. Then she changed her hold on him to cradle his head and surreptitiously slid her fingers through his hair as it spread in the water like a dark halo.

She finally withdrew and allowed him to float by himself. When he began to kick his feet and move his arms back and forth, sculling about, she couldn't help feeling proud that he'd come so far in so short a time.

Titus was just getting comfortable with floating facedown in the water, when something crashed violently into the water nearby, and he and Celeste both came up coughing and sputtering.

"What the—"

Titus reeled and staggered back, blinking and wiping his face, trying to clear his vision. Celeste stood several feet away, scowling down at the still-swirling water. Up, out of the middle of that disturbance, came a gray bottle-shaped beak with a grinning dolphin attached.

"You really are the most ill-mannered creature," she told Prospero. Little chastened, he gave a series of laughs like crows, bobbed his head, and then swam off toward the middle of the cove. He disappeared, then a moment later he was back, leaping through the air, headed straight for them. They separated and scrambled back, just as he landed between them with a monumental splash.

"I think he's bored," Celeste said apologetically. "If the others were here, he wouldn't bother us at all. Perhaps I'd better swim with him a while."

It took some time for Prospero to spend his excess energy, but he finally calmed and came to the shallows with her to let Titus finally have a closer look.

Being in the water with the dolphin was an altogether different experience than being in a boat beside one, Titus learned. Prospero was at least three feet longer than him and probably outweighed him by two hundred pounds. Titus watched that sleek dorsal fin cutting the surface, remembered bony jaws filled with teeth, and felt his stomach knotting as the dolphin swam around him. Twice, Prospero chose the moment he passed Titus to exhale, blowing air and water and who-knew-what all over him.

"That's the second time he's done that," he said crossly, wiping his face and ducking under the water to wash off. "What does he have against me? I've never done a thing to him. How could I? I just met the blasted beast!"

Celeste grinned at Titus's righteous indignation. "Ill-mannered and unreasonable of him, I know. One would certainly expect a higher standard of conduct from a dolphin." She folded her arms as she waited for that to sink in.

"Expecting logic of a mere animal," she said wryly. "Really, Titus . . . those 'scientist daydreams' of yours."

He turned crimson, caught red-handed crediting human motivations to a creature that only two days ago he would have dismissed as an air-breathing fish. He ran his hands over his face. In a mere forty-eight hours he had been cured of seasickness, shaken "flippers" with a dolphin, set foot in the ocean for the first time in decades, had two memorable swimming lessons, and seen Celeste Ashton do things that he hadn't imagined anyone could do.

Celeste. Just now, she stood in knee-deep water with her

arms crossed and her thin garment drawn taut across her hard-tipped breasts, looking infinitely more alluring than Botticelli's *The Birth of Venus*. She was warm and bright and determined and clever and earnest and insightful. And she kissed like a white-hot dream.

Suddenly, he was thrown forward into the water and scrambled to regain his footing. An instant later, Celeste was there, helping him up and glaring at the force that had knocked him over.

"All right, that does it," she declared. She dived into the water and returned a short while later, steering Prospero straight toward Titus.

"It's time you two made peace. Pet him," she ordered Titus. "Stroke him. Tell him how beautiful and strong and handsome he is."

Titus's horror gave place to annoyance, then determination. "I'll do no such thing." He glared at the wary gray dolphin eye staring at him, wondering what the beast was planning next.

A moment later he was stewing in confusion, scarcely able to believe he had just credited the beast with cognitive ability.

"May I remind you, Titus Thorne," Celeste said calmly, "that your task is to repeat my methods in an effort to repeat my results."

His huffing reminiscent of one of Prospero's "blows," Titus gave in and approached. After some coaxing, he stroked the animal just as he had from the boat. Standing in the water on equal footing with the dolphin, that contact seemed infinitely more risky . . . and more personal and profound.

As he relaxed, he used more gentle strokes, heeding Celeste's advice to avoid Prospero's sensitive eye region and powerful tail flukes. With a delicate but thorough touch, he investigated the rake marks on the dolphin's head and sides and the deep scar on the animal's lower jaw. After a while, Prospero turned onto his side and Titus took this as a sign that the dolphin was warming to him. He began to rub the dolphin's belly and Celeste, who had backed away to allow them to get acquainted, came to attention.

"Titus, I don't think you want to rub him there," she called.

"Don't be silly. He seems to like it," Titus called back, thinking of the way puppies roll to offer their stomachs for a good scratching and assuming it meant the same in dolphins. "In fact, we're getting along rather well here. Aren't we, old man. Just us fellows . . . having a good old-fashioned belly rub. You know, I believe he has a bit of pink on the underside, here. Interesting, actually . . . the difference in coloration from upper to lower. I wonder what the infamous Mr. Darwin would make of such a thing, what purpose he would say it—" He froze, his hands on Prospero's belly, his eyes fixed on a slit at the beginning of the dolphin's tail and what was suddenly protruding from it. "What the hell is—"

His eyes widened. "Aghhh!" He lurched back with a grimace and his hands spread in horror on either side of him. Prospero rolled onto his side and tried to rub against Titus as he lurched back toward the beach. Celeste rushed to intervene, withstanding a bit of the dolphin's misdirected enthusiasm herself. At her adamant rejection, Prospero sped off toward the center of the cove and executed several jumps and acrobatic turns before disappearing.

Pausing a moment to compose herself, she headed for the beach, where Titus stood like a colossus, dripping seawater and indignation.

"Did you see that 'thing'? I mean, it was what I thought it was . . . wasn't it? Well, what else could it be?" he said, embarrassed at having to ask her for confirmation in such a matter. When he glanced up and saw her knowing smile, he realized that she had been trying to warn him. "Do you, have you—"

"I thought you said you had read my book," she said as she proceeded to the blanket and wrapped herself in a large towel. She then handed him one.

He stiffened, feeling awkward and naïve and more than a little foolish. "Of course I read it."

"Then you must have skipped parts, because I described in detail that very behavior."

He looked nettled. "You most certainly did not. Being accosted and savaged by a rut-maddened dolphin—you never said that."

"I believe I used somewhat more 'romantic' language," she said with laughter in her eyes. "A peculiarity of style you have denounced on a number of occasions. Perhaps I should rephrase it. Something on the order of: 'Beware of randy dolphins. If you pet or stroke one on the belly, he's likely to try to make you his next amorous conquest.'"

He turned away, rubbed his face with the toweling, and then turned back with fresh horror blooming. "It's happened to you, too, hasn't it? Why, that is monstrous—a young woman subjected to such indecencies—"

"Titus, he's a dolphin." She came to stand near him. "It's what dolphins do. It's not rude or disgusting or an outrage." She saw in his eyes the objection he was about to raise. "And it's not immoral of me to have seen it and reported it. It's just a dolphin's way of making certain there will always be dolphins."

She freed the grin she had been holding back. "Look at it this way: you've just verified my assertion that it is not difficult to distinguish males from females."

Giving up a lifelong prejudice was a rather disorienting process. Titus suddenly felt a little weak in the knees. He stalked over to the blanket and sat down hard. Distracted by troubling new thoughts, he dried his hair and then wrapped the toweling around his neck.

Young women weren't supposed to see such things or even know such things existed. Conventional wisdom had it that women who knew about such things were crude, immoral, and dissolute . . . the mere knowledge of such things tainted their weaker minds and made them susceptible to all manner of vices. They couldn't help it. It was just in women's delicate natures to be easily ruined.

He looked at Celeste and found her sitting on her knees with her smock wrapped demurely around her, watching him with a hint of anxiety. He realized he was scowling fiercely. And with good reason. He was as confused as hell.

Celeste Ashton was about as "weak-minded" and "susceptible" as Admiral Horatio T. Nelson. She knew a great deal about sex and about mating and it didn't seem to have corrupted her overly much. In fact, she was probably the most temperate, moral, and compassionate person he'd met in his entire life. She carried the responsibility of her household, supported and protected her grandmother, studied her dolphins and wrote about them, capably defended her work before two royal societies . . . and gave swimming lessons to an annoying, hidebound professor who had doubted and insulted her at every turn.

He studied her, surprised anew by the maturity she had shown in designing, conducting, and recording her work. He saw now that his prejudice against her work had been aroused, in large part, by her use of feminine terms, analogies, and allusions. Ironically, it was that very sort of language that had softened the shock of the startling content of her work and made it palatable for a moralistic and often hypocritical public.

Thinking of it now, in a more rational and objective light, he saw that her use of a feminine viewpoint had nothing to do with the validity of her observations. And how absurd of him to have ever believed that it did! He felt suddenly as if he'd been struck by a brickbat and rendered *conscious* for the first time in his life.

"I am a bit of a prig, aren't I?" he said, his voice suddenly thick.

She nodded with a wistful smile.

He winced, embarrassed by the clash of his rigid moralism against his highly touted scientific objectivity, and shamed by her gift for accepting and understanding these animals for what they were. She hadn't tried to make them into "little humans" subject to human feelings and human morality . . . *he* had.

He groaned silently and focused on her. Those blue eyes . . . whole worlds of experience seemed to be revolving just beneath their surfaces. That golden hair . . . sunbeams probably vied for the chance to illuminate those tresses. And those lips . . . gentle and stubborn . . . desirable in both modes.

She was nothing short of extraordinary.

And she was here. With him.

"I want you to show me," he said, his voice low and resonant. "I have to be able to see it for myself. I'll learn to swim . . . hold my breath for hours . . . whatever it takes. I want to see what you see." He nodded to the water. "Under there."

She burst into a smile that left him feeling a bit dazzled.

"I thought you'd never ask."

Eleven

THE NEXT MORNING, Celeste helped Titus add the arm movements to his floating technique, transforming it into true swimming. After some practice, he tried swimming to the dock and back and made it with no difficulty. When they paused to rest, Celeste noticed the way the salt water had reddened his eyes and produced two pairs of her goggles.

A new world opened to him. Peering through the round glass of the rubber-rimmed goggles, he could see with startling clarity under the water. He sat on the bottom in the shallows, staring at his hands and feet . . . then at her hands and . . . other interesting parts. Having his eyes open under the water made swimming a much more productive endeavor, and made the repeated transition between air and water much easier to bear. But the first time he looked up and saw Prospero bearing down on him, he scrambled up out of the water.

"What is it? What happened?" Celeste surfaced just behind him.

"Did you see that?" He pointed frantically.

"It was just Prospero," she said, bewildered until she recalled her first experiences with goggles and understood the reason for his shock. "The water makes everything seem larger at first, including dolphins. Come with me. I want you to see how Prospero swims under the water as well as on top."

Together, they ventured out into water that was slightly over their heads. At first Titus had to fight his uneasiness at barely having a bottom beneath his feet. But with Celeste's reassurance and reminders to breathe calmly and let the water buoy him, he gradually relaxed and was able to alternate treading water and touching bottom. She swam off and returned shortly with Prospero. Pointing under the water, she dove with the dolphin and Titus groaned, telling himself it was now or never.

Summoning every shred of self-control he possessed, he drew breath, held his nose, and sank below the surface. And he entered an environment that few humans in his part of the world had ever seen.

The water was relatively clear and an eerie blue-gray light illuminated everything, overlaying all colors with a wash of blue and silver hues. As the bottom sloped away, toward the center of the cove, there were boulders sticking up through a mixed bed of sand and rock. Brown seaweed and nondescript algae covered every available space. There were nooks and crevices in the rocks, around which occasionally something elusive would dart into view and be gone before it could be identified. After several brief glimpses, he realized they were small, quick shallows fish that used their speed for protection. He surfaced, took another breath, then submerged again, focused now on the riveting spectacle of a woman and a dolphin swimming in concert with one another.

It was nothing short of astounding . . . the sight of Prospero's seemingly effortless motions propelling him through the water . . . the sight of Celeste hanging on to the dolphin's dorsal fin and using her feet much like flukes. Her sleek body moved with graceful undulations beside the dolphin, following it into turns and rolls that seemed to have no aim except the pleasure of the movement.

Titus could scarcely get to the surface and back down

quickly enough. He watched her break off and head to the surface herself, her legs scissoring effortlessly, poising motionless near the surface as she filled her lungs, then snapping powerfully to send her shooting toward the bottom, where Prospero waited. The pair swam in a narrowing circle, gathering speed, and he sensed what was about to happen. He broke the surface even as they did and watched them leap into the air together and then dive separately back into the water.

His heart nearly stopped as he sucked in a breath and plunged back into the water to see where they were and what was happening. They were already swimming together again, preparing for another jump. This time he ducked back under in time to see them enter the water like living arrows, pulling white plumes of air and bubbles in after them.

If he lived to be a hundred, he would probably never see anything that was further from the realm of his experience than the sight of that small piece of ocean. It was a magical world, a place of serenity and beauty, a place that humans could glimpse only for the length of a breath. All humans except Celeste Ashton, that is. It was clear from her masterful movements that she was as at home here as she was walking down a village lane.

By the time they climbed out of the water, dried, and collapsed on the blanket, Titus was reeling. His head was stuffed with sensations and his chest felt tight with conflicting emotions. He was excited, terrified, pleased, appalled . . . felt both tremendous satisfaction at having witnessed such unique events and dismay at how disturbing this new view of the ocean was. He lay back on the blanket, staring up at the clouds drifting overhead, feeling the midday sun's rays pricking his skin and grappling with the subtle but pervasive tension in him.

"What did you think of it?" she asked.

He raised his head and looked at her. She was lying on her back, too, staring up at the clouds. She had taken her hair out of its braid and spread it on the blanket around her to dry in the sun. He shifted up onto an elbow to look at her, and for a few moments simply absorbed the beauty of her.

"I don't think I could have even imagined anything like that," he said finally. "It is another world down there."

"Yes, it is," she responded, her eyelids heavy with fatigue and the sun's drowsy warmth. "Everything about it is different, at first: the light, the colors, the animals and plants, even the way you have to move around in it. But after a while you get used to it and it begins to feel like . . . just another room in the house you live in."

"I've never lived in a house with rooms like that," he said, appreciating the feline contentment radiating from her, half expecting her to begin purring at any moment.

"Then perhaps it's time you changed houses." She laughed softly and he was seized by the most irresistible urge to *make* her purr.

Steam trickled up from his loins, condensing on the underside of his skin, warming it. He was instantly aware of every part of his body in proximity to every part of hers. Her smock draped her body so that he could clearly see the outlines of her legs, the curves of her hips, the hard-tipped mounds of her breasts. She had seemed striking when they first met; now she was nothing short of beautiful. She glowed with a unique radiance that came from clarity and self-assurance deep within. Her accumulated effect on him was nothing short of devastating, but just now there was no place on earth he'd rather be than on this blanket, beside her.

Every time he looked at her he glimpsed mysteries and intrigues. It was as if Lady Sophia's ancients had taken a hand in putting her together, specifically to humble the likes of arrogant mortals who believed—as he had—that they knew everything. The sages of creation had knitted secrets into the very fabric of her being . . . the boldness of the human heart, the depths and range of the human mind, the dimensions of human courage. He suddenly wanted to know everything she had seen, everything she had thought, observed, and concluded.

"Tell me"—he channeled his urge for her into a safer area—"about all the fish you've seen under the water."

"If I do, we may be here until Christmas," she said.

He leaned an inch closer and captured her gaze in his.

"I'm not going anywhere."

Her countenance brightened with a smile.

They lay side by side, looking up at the sky as she spun stories for him of her encounters with sharks and porpoises, squid and crabs, and massive schools of sardines and jacks. She spoke of seeing schools so dense they were like a wavering wall of flesh, of watching the mating dance of the clown anemone, and of witnessing the sea turn cloudy with the milt of spawning sardines.

He couldn't resist tossing in a tidbit or two about the structure of fish scales as seen under a microscope. She brightened instantly and began asking questions. His descriptions of the laboratories and libraries at Oxford, including his wry descriptions of the academics who worked there, delighted her. When she learned that they had hundreds of specimens preserved and on display in the science hall, she moaned and closed her eyes.

"What I would give to be able to go to the university and see all of that."

"It is quite an impressive display," he said. "However, a goodly number of our finer specimens are on loan just now, to the Natural History Museum in Knightsbridge. I personally have preserved over two hundred specimens . . . and have a rather astonishing collection of items taken from the bellies of fish. You would be surprised what the buggers swallow. Gives us a clue as to just how indiscriminate some fish are in their feeding . . ."

". . . of course I had no proof that they were human bones, but I had the professors and fellows at Christ's Church look them over and they concurred that the things probably were from a human hand." He realized she had been silent for some time, and found that her eyes were closed and her breathing was slow and shallow.

Asleep. He reddened. It was true that his sort of science might not be glamorous or thrilling, he thought defensively, but did she have to fall asleep? He sighed. It was probably his own fault . . . rambling on and on about the contents of fish guts. He hadn't a decent story to tell that didn't involve stomach contents or somebody being "caught out" for defrauding the public with some absurd invention or idea, neither of which would probably endear him to her.

But as he studied her and saw around her eyes evidence of the fatigue that had claimed her, he felt a protective tenderness invading him again. Swimming, diving, dealing with cantankerous dolphins, and giving cranky professors swimming lessons in the dead of night . . . she had every right to be exhausted.

He lay back on the blanket beside her, shading his eyes and listening to the rhythmic sloshing waves and the caws of the gulls circling overhead. He felt strangely tired himself.

Celeste awakened, some time later, to discover the sun going down and Titus asleep on the blanket beside her. It took a moment for her to orient herself, then she smiled and propped herself up on one elbow beside him, absorbing him with her eyes and finding that he had quite an impact. His tousled hair and sun-bronzed features made her lips grow sensitive and the pulse at the base of her throat begin to flutter erratically. How long would it take for him to finally come over to believing in her sort of research, so that they could get on with more enjoyable pursuits? On impulse, she leaned closer, intending to brush his lips with hers, and his eyes popped open.

"What are you doing?"

She sat bolt upright, scrambling for an excuse. "There was a . . . a fly on your face and I was merely brushing it off."

He gave her a look that was accusing, but his charge was

hardly what she expected. "You fell asleep on me. And you snored like a bear in winter."

She clamped a hand over her nose, sounding quite nasal. "I don't snore."

"Since it is categorically impossible for a person to listen to herself sleep"—he managed a professorial tone even while lying down with his arms behind his head—"you cannot say, with any reasonable certainty, that you don't snore." He looked rather pleased with his logic and turned his head toward her with a smug expression. "I thought it rather rude of you, actually, nodding off just when I was getting to my story about the tar who lost his wooden leg to a shark."

"I'm sure it would have been enthralling," she said tartly.

"I'll have you know, my lectures at Cardinal College have always been considered a cut above the usual academic drone. I might even say, without boasting, that I am something of a favorite amongst the undergraduate crowd." He turned his face away and sniffed. "Now that you're awake, I ought to make you listen to every last word."

He made it sound like a dire fate indeed.

"Very well, then, tell me." She lay back down, wriggled to get comfortable, then folded her hands. "Every last word. I want to hear it all."

"You do?" He seemed a bit puzzled by that. "Why?"

"Because I might never have another chance to hear a university lecturer."

Acknowledging her logic, he settled back with his hands under his head to tell his tale of a sailor with a wooden leg who worked on a fishing trawler.

As he talked, she watched with a warm light in her eyes, grateful that he wasn't looking at her just then. It wouldn't be wise to let him see how much she had enjoyed going to sleep to the sound of his voice and waking up to the sight of him sprawled on the blanket beside her. Even now, listening to his somewhat predictable story, she found herself drawn to every word.

She liked listening to him speak about the university and

the characters who inhabited his world every bit as much as she enjoyed telling him about the things she had seen and discovered. It had been a long time since anyone had sat down to listen to her stories or to share the joy of her discoveries with her. Nana was immersed in her own work; the other members of the Atlantean Society were either too aged or too rheumatic to go near the water; and Ashton House was so off the beaten path that they never had visitors. It struck her forcefully that until now, her life had been astonishingly solitary.

It had always been that way. She had grown up an only child in a house of adults, and she had come to terms with it early on, accepted it. But without anyone near her own age to talk with, without someone to share her ideas and concerns with, it had been . . . was still . . . *lonely*. And she hadn't realized just how lonely until Titus Thorne had come doubting and scoffing his way into her life.

There was not another living soul who had seen what she had seen . . . off the coast of the Azores, under the waters of the cove, and in the wider bay. By all accounts, there wasn't another person in all of Britain who swam with and studied dolphins . . . or who dived in ocean waters to glimpse living things in their natural settings. But there was one person who wanted to share her underwater visions. Titus Thorne. An ichthyologist who hated the water, but intended to brave it in her company, so that he could see what she had seen.

". . . and there the blessed thing was, smack in the middle of the shark's belly," he declared with a dramatic flourish. "It was covered with blood and guts, but otherwise none the worse for wear. We pulled it out, washed it up. The fellow stuck it back on and stomped out . . . without so much as a word of thanks." He turned with a defensive scowl to collect her reaction to his rather grisly tale.

She was beaming.

•   •   •

THE FISH WITH the spectacular tail was back in Titus's dreams that night. This time he was digging his way through the water after it, half running, half swimming, trying desperately to catch it. He gradually closed the distance and just as he put his hands on it, he realized he was totally submerged, panicked, and popped to the surface like a cork. He still had the tail in his grip, however. All he could think was that if he could just get it back to his laboratory . . .

Suddenly, he *was* in his laboratory with that fish on his dissection table. Beautiful colors in its tail . . . light coming through prismlike scales again. It was an exotic new species, he was certain of it. He picked up his scalpel and, with a pang of regret, cut into that marvelous tail.

There were ripping, popping sounds, almost as if he were cutting through fabric. Puzzled, he cut more. Then more.

Peeling back the outer layer, he saw legs inside. A woman's legs. He groaned, sensing what came next.

The fish sat up, glared at him, and gave him a powerful smack across the face with its heavy, ornate tail. Then it hopped off the table, gathered its droopy flukes, and stalked indignantly out the door on two human legs.

He awakened to his heart pounding wildly and grabbed his chest, only to find that part of the pounding he was hearing was coming from the door. "Titus—wake up!"

When he flung open the door, Celeste was standing there in her long smock clutching a stack of toweling. "They're here," she declared, invading his room and rushing to the window, pointing. "The whole group—they've finally come!"

He hurried to look down at the cove and—sure enough—spotted two or three dolphins leaping out of the water at a time. He blinked, then looked at her. "I don't know why this should surprise me. Nothing you do should surprise me."

"Quickly—get into your swimming clothes." She smiled as she headed out the door. "We have work to do!"

Nearly an hour later, he stood on the dock staring at a

veritable orgy of jumping and splashing going on in the cove. The water was teeming with dolphins. Celeste tried to count them, but kept losing her place as they continually submerged and reappeared in another part of the cove. Then she dragged out the logbook in which she kept descriptions of the markings of specific individuals, and tried to identify some of the creatures. Making notes in the margins near some drawings, she went on to write a brief summary of the group's appearance and general behavior.

Titus watched, reading over her shoulder and trying to identify them from her drawings, but soon gave up. He had difficulty even picking out Prospero among that boisterous group.

"Every year the group changes. Some don't return and there are always a few new ones," she explained, watching their rowdy play with an indulgent eye. "I can't see Charlie or Thunder, who were here only three weeks ago, and there are three or four new ones I don't recognize."

"How can you tell?" he asked, shaking his head. "It's all one huge twisting, turning mass of fins and flukes."

"Time and patience," she said. "Over the years I've seen and recorded quite a number. As I wrote in the book, the ones you see frequently take on characters of their own and you can spot them more easily. Come on—" She tucked her journal under her arm, grabbed him by the hand, and started for the boat.

When he saw what she intended, he dragged her to a halt. "We're not going out there?"

"We have to get close enough to see who is here." She flashed a mischievous smile. "Unless, of course, you'd rather climb right into the water . . ."

They nudged the boat out into the cove and dropped an anchor line. Soon a dozen dolphin heads were sticking up from the water around the boat, and Celeste was talking and stroking them as she greeted old and new friends. He was grateful to be seeing it with his own eyes, because he would never have believed it possible otherwise.

By the time they pulled up anchor and headed back to the dock, he had seen dolphins nuzzling and bumping each other, dolphins playing what appeared to be a game of tag, and dolphins batting and tossing cork floats as if they were cricket balls. The beasts clearly enjoyed socializing with each other and were either curious enough or fond enough of Celeste to stay close and investigate both the boat and her.

One by one his last, desperate exceptions to her claims were being demolished. He had come here to determine the truth, but his attitude and behavior since the day he arrived had been that of an iconoclast, not a scientist. He had come here with appallingly fixed ideas and was having to rethink them, one by one. What would happen when she had dismantled every one of his objections to her work?

"Ariel and Echo both have new babies," she said as they tied up the boat and climbed to the dock. "We shall have to think up names. Any suggestions?"

He looked a bit put out. "Hardly my area . . . naming infants."

She swayed a bit closer as they reached the beach. "All right, I'll do it. I believe I'll call Ariel's baby Titus." He paused and gave her a censuring look.

"I'm not sure I fancy having a dolphin with my name on it, running amuck out there . . . indiscriminately doing . . . 'what dolphins always do.' "

She laughed. "Then we'll use Titan instead. Would that make you feel better? And I think Echo's baby should be—"

"Celeste?" he proposed, with one eyebrow raised.

"After myself? Hardly. I was thinking of Edgar, for Mr. Cherrybottom."

"How do you know if they're males or females?"

"I caught a glimpse of the slits on their bellies. I think they're both males. But, as you recently learned, time and observation usually removes all doubt."

Smiling at the way his ears reddened, she took his sleeve and pulled him toward the cliff, the house, and a bit of luncheon.

•   •   •

THAT AFTERNOON, CELESTE insisted on another swimming lesson.

"The water is thick with dolphins, out there," Titus argued unsuccessfully, as she dragged him by the arm toward the steps down the cliff. "There probably isn't any room."

As it happened, there was plenty of room. Several of the new dolphins in the group had satisfied their curiosity about the cove and its resident humans and departed. By the time they reached the water, only three or four dolphins heard them splashing into the water and came to investigate.

Celeste watched Titus staying in the shallower water with his hands on his hips, and after she greeted each of the dolphins by name, she herded one into the shallows and beckoned to him. "There's someone here I want you to meet."

Warily, he waded deeper and soon found himself staring at a perfect miniature of a dolphin, barely four feet long.

"It's one of the infants," he said with surprise, watching her stroke its pale, unmarred skin and observing the little dolphin's enthusiastic response to her touch. He knew just how the creature felt.

"Titus, meet Titan," she said with almost maternal pride.

"This is my namesake?" He came closer and put out a hand to stroke the baby's back. The skin was smooth and soft; it seemed thinner and more tender than that of the adult dolphins he had touched. He began to stroke and examine little Titan in earnest. When the little dolphin opened its mouth and made a series of squeaks and high-pitched screeches, he laughed with delight.

The other dolphins responded to the baby's cries, inserting themselves around the baby and ushering it back to deeper water. "That one"—she pointed to Ariel—"is the baby's mother." Then she indicated another, lighter-colored dolphin. "That female is Echo, who also has a baby."

Titus stood staring after them with a lingering air of wonder.

When Celeste collected their goggles from the blanket and insisted Titus see the dolphins interacting underwater, he was less than enthusiastic.

"All you have to do is what you did yesterday," she explained. "Hold your breath and submerge for a while, then come up for air." She smiled. "I'll be there, too."

Remembering the marvels he had witnessed the day before and considering the promise of seeing dolphins interacting in their natural habitat and association, he donned the goggles and moved carefully toward deeper water. She put her goggles on, then took his hand, and soon they were in over their heads, literally.

As on the day before, the landscape beneath the surface was blue-tinged and otherworldly. But now, in the depths of the lagoon, there were more than half a dozen dolphins, swimming close together, romping, and stroking each other. With each arch and turn, their bodies flashed in the sunlight that penetrated the water, making them seem as if they were made of living quicksilver. Titus rose to the surface, took a breath, then submerged again. It was hard to believe that this world existed just steps away from the mundane, cluttered world he usually inhabited.

They watched in awe as the dolphins executed a few jumps and paired for various instinctive acrobatics. For a time, Prospero herded Ariel aside and rolled her over onto her back. For a brief time they were belly to belly, then they broke apart and Prospero shot around the cove at a remarkable speed before jumping forcefully into the air. When the disturbance cleared, the others were carrying on as usual, including Ariel and her baby, who sought her out for a feeding.

Titus pushed his air supply to the limit, each time, to be able to continue watching. He had to make for the surface, once, and Celeste went to see if he was all right. When he nodded, his grin was almost as blinding as the sunlight on the water.

They dived again, and it wasn't long before Prospero and

one of the others came over to investigate them. Since, where one dolphin goes, others usually follow, the rest soon swarmed around the visiting humans, making clicking sounds that Titus found a bit unnerving under water. When Celeste joined him at the surface for air, Titus suggested they put a bit more bottom under their feet.

When they reached a level where he could stand with his head above the surface, Titan swam near and brushed against Titus. The little dolphin darted quickly away, but soon circled back to brush against him a second time.

"Did you see that?" Titus said with animation. "He's investigating me."

As little Titan continued to circle and brush against Titus, each time with a bit more familiarity and duration, they realized that the baby was indeed exploring them. After several of these passes, Titus ventured to stroke Titan's back as he came around again. The dolphin baby slowed and seemed to enjoy the attention. Shortly, the others came to retrieve their offspring. Unlike before, however, Titus felt a sudden and overwhelming exhilaration at being in the midst of that group of powerful and fascinating animals. It was clear they were beginning to acknowledge and accept his presence, even to interact with him in a personal way.

When they headed for deeper water, Titus reseated his goggles on his face and went with them. Plunging under water and locating a rock to dig his feet under, on the bottom, he watched the adults stroke and investigate Titan and Edgar and play with them, flipping them over gently and rubbing their fins and bellies. He was so absorbed in their interactions that he almost forgot about breathing. When he returned, Titan noticed him and once again ventured close to him, poking and wriggling against him.

When Titus shot to the surface again, Celeste hurried after him. He was panting and gasping, but grinning. "Did you see? Did you feel them swimming around us? And the baby—he keeps coming back to me—did you see that?"

He dragged in a supply of air, clamped his nose, and

headed back to his observation point. But the sight of his glowing face and the compressed pleasure in his voice left Celeste dangling in the water, speechless.

He had just caught it, she realized. The enthrallment, the insatiable curiosity, the joy of the sea . . . he had just discovered some part of the passion she had lived with for more than a decade.

She dived under water and settled beside him, watching with him the commonplace interactions of that small group of dolphins. Seeing it through his wonder brought her a fresh appreciation of just how remarkable it was to see them like this.

It was some time later that she noticed his lips tinged with blue and his teeth beginning to chatter when they surfaced. He couldn't stop talking about the dolphins and fish they'd seen, so it took some work to convince him that he was getting too cold and needed climb out and get warm. He didn't seem to feel the cold of the water at all, but finally bowed to her experience. With a longing look over his shoulder, he began paddling toward the beach.

"Do you realize what we just saw?" he demanded as soon as they emerged into waist-high water. He removed his goggles, wiped his face, and seized her shoulders in a tight grip. "They swim and play with the infants like . . . *parents.* And they are always rubbing and touching one another. They're familiar, almost as if they're a family. Mother, father, children—who would have thought it?"

In his excitable but fatigued state, he couldn't seem to talk and navigate at the same time, so she pulled him to the beach and shoved a towel into his hands with orders to dry. He obeyed mechanically, then put on his shirt, and stood motionless, staring out at the water, his eyes wide and glazed with wonder. He turned to her in the light of early evening, looking as if he might explode if he didn't get it all out.

"Celeste, it's magnificent—it's all just—*magnificent!*" He impulsively grabbed her shoulders and pulled her against him, staring down into her eyes with unabashed wonder.

"This is only a small cove. Imagine"—he made a sweeping gesture across the ocean's horizon—"the treasures waiting to be found and explored in the rest of the ocean. You're a pioneer—a visionary—a genius!"

He was delirious, wonderfully, ecstatically so. Celeste felt his excitement stirring her emotions and understood, with a uniquely feminine intuition, that the door that had just swung open was inside him. The man who stood before her now, with his hair dripping, his shirt hanging open, and a fire in his soul, was a far cry from the starched and priggish academician who had arrived on her doorstep a week ago. With some coaxing and some prodding, he had overcome his fear of the water and his narrow-minded approach to science, and had entered a realm of possibilities that he had never imagined existed.

There, her thoughts were interrupted by her being picked up bodily and swung around and around until she was dizzy. She collapsed on her knees in the sand beside the blanket, feeling her own world spinning wildly.

"I probably shouldn't do this." He went down on his knees before her and leaned over her, his face dusky, his eyes shining with sensual anticipation.

"Do what?" she asked breathlessly.

"This." Lowering to his knees, he pushed her back onto the blanket and brushed his lips against hers. "It's probably against the 'scientist rules.'"

"Well, then we'll just have to play by 'mermaid rules.'" She raised her head and ran her tongue along the generous curve of his lower lip. "Because in mermaid rules"—she pressed her parted lips fully against his, muffling the rest—"this sort of thing is definitely allowed."

Laughing against her mouth, he pressed her down onto the blanket and lowered himself beside her, teasing and tasting her lips, exploring the various kinds of kisses that made helpless, hungry noises come from deep in her throat. After a while, he shifted his chest above hers, rubbing against her breasts and forcing a sigh from her that sounded like an invitation to more.

More came as she wrapped her arms around his neck and abandoned herself to a seemingly endless stream of kisses—long and intense in a way that spoke to parts of her not accessed by mere words. He ran his hands up her sides, causing her body to ripple, following his touch as waves follow wind. She opened to him, responding eagerly, as if the passion they were discovering were something new and wonderful, something invented just for them.

He lowered his kisses and caresses down her throat. By the time he reached her buttons, she was aching with a new sort of curiosity, hungry for a new kind of knowledge, eager to feel his hands on her the way they had been that day in the boat. Every sensation—the gradual slide of her smock, the pressure of his body against her breasts, the hard-soft demand of his mouth on hers, the scent of him invading her head, her lungs—was a sip of pleasure that seeped through her very flesh like heated brandy. She stilled and drank them in, trying to hold and savor each.

Gradually she gave in to her growing need to explore him and learn what would pleasure him. She ran her hands up the middle of his back then out along his shoulders, learning the tactile dimension of the shapes she had long since explored in her mind. He was so lean and hard and deliciously heavy against her. She could feel the working of his muscles beneath his skin, could make him shiver by raking her nails across a certain spot on his back, and learned that his neck and ears were just as sensitive as hers. He groaned and flexed his lower body against her whenever she applied her mouth to his bare throat.

Moments later she felt the fabric sliding from her breasts, exposing them to the cooling air and his heated attentions. She closed her eyes as he traced the mounds of her breasts and lavished hot, wet strokes on their tightly budded nipples. The resulting burst of sensation stopped the breath in her throat.

As pleasure built upon pleasure, she felt a silken cord of anticipation drawing tighter in her loins, and soon discovered that the press of his body against hers had the power to relieve that peculiar tension. Seeking relief, she instinctively held him tighter, and pressed her body into his. He responded to her need by sliding more of his body over hers, bracing above her, concentrating his weight so that she parted her thighs and welcomed him closer. Every movement brought a new discovery, every discovery brought a pleasurable new movement.

"So this is what it feels like," she said, hardly aware that she spoke aloud. "No wonder Prospero and Thunder and the others enjoy it so much."

He looked up from nibbling her throat . . . her words and her dewy, passion-warmed face focusing in his mind at the same moment. He began to chuckle, his body went slack, and he slid over onto the blanket beside her. "You watched them mating and pairing for years, and wondered how it compared to—"

" 'Human mating rituals' I believe you called it." She retreated into her scientist persona, refusing to give in to her embarrassment. "Until now, I haven't had anyone to help me investigate them. It takes two, you know."

"Yes, it does." He grinned and leaned closer with a wicked glint in his eye. "I've had a modest bit of experience in the field. What say we"—he waggled his eyebrows—*"collaborate."*

"Collaborate." She smiled. "Yes. Let's." The glint in his eye migrated into hers. "But only if we share any and all important discoveries."

"Done," he said, hooking a hand around the back of her neck and moving closer to her. "And to show good faith: I must announce that I have already made one major discovery."

"Oh?" She caught the hint of mischief in his broadening grin.

"Humans are better kissers than dolphins."

As he leaned closer to provide proof, she raised her eyebrows.

"You think so?"

Her response halted him just long enough for her to surprise him with a laugh and a playful shove that sent him toppling. While he scrambled to recover, she jumped up, laughing, grabbed the blanket and pulled it from under him, sending him rolling onto the sand. In a heartbeat he was on his feet and chasing her toward the steps of the cliff.

ON THE ROOF of the old tower, high above the beach, Lady Sophia and her Atlantean sisters stood in the dying rays of the sun, watching with wistful pleasure as the Man of Earth and their Woman of Sea embraced their passion for each other, far below.

"Luv-ley bit of man, that," Anabelle declared, with a wistful sigh. "Alwus said so."

"A match made in Heaven itself," Miss Penelope said, fumbling in her cuff for a handkerchief and dabbing at her eyes. She sniffed and glanced at Lady Sophia, whose eyes were filled with mist and hopes for the future of the union being begun on the beach below. "What do you think, Sophie?"

"I think," her grandmother said in a voice filled with equal parts joy and wistfulness, "it is time to begin preparing our dolphin ceremony."

Twelve

"COLLABORATION" WAS A pale term for the compelling attraction that drew Titus and Celeste together in a haze of sensation and discovery. Each evening they dined with her grandmother and occasional members of the Atlantean Society, exchanging glances that fairly crackled across the dinner table. But their passions were no less evident when they rushed down to the cove each morning, eager to swim and study Celeste's dolphins, or when they pored over her logs and journals, discussing at length her interpretations of the various behaviors both now had witnessed.

"I don't see how their clicks and screeches and vocalizations can be seen as anything other than a sort of language," she insisted. And when he looked doubtful, she rubbed the furrows of doubt from his forehead with her fingers.

"Communication, certainly . . . but a language?" Titus kissed each and every one of her fingertips, almost losing his thoughts in the process. "Language implies discrete units with agreed-upon meanings. Do the dolphins always make the same sounds in the same situation? More importantly, do they attach a specific meaning to a given sound they make?"

She propped her chin in her hand and gave him a suggestive smile. "Do you?"

"Of course I do." The heat stirring between them was suddenly palpable.

"Ummm. Then what do you mean when you make that growling noise, deep in your throat, when we're kissing?"

"Interesting question," he said, moving to sit close to her and nuzzle her hair aside. "And which noise would that be? This one?" He produced a light, playful rumble as he dropped a kiss on the nape of her neck, then a deep, hungry growl when he consumed her throat with a ravenous kiss. "Or that one?"

"Interesting," she said, dragging her scattered wits back together. "Two different sounds. But I could swear they meant the same thing."

He looked up, his eyes darkening. "Tricky thing, language."

"Ummm. Perhaps you'd better try that last one again. I believe I need more data . . ."

Thus, Titus's discovery of dolphin society and the world beneath the water's surface blended inseparably with his sensual discovery of Celeste and her discovery of him. They would charge into the water, splashing and chasing, and end up at the side or bottom of the cove, observing the dolphins and interacting with them. Then later, as they lay on the blanket in each other's arms, a sensation would stimulate a thought and between experimental kisses they would discuss and analyze her ideas about the dolphins' clicks, or plan an experiment to test the dolphins' ability to distinguish shapes or colors.

He could feel the change it was working in him, but had no need or means to examine it, until the afternoon they saw Prospero and Thunder separate one of the females from the group and take turns rolling her onto her back in what he recognized as the traditional mating posture. Soon after, the pair of males did the same with another female. Then, before the humans' gazes, the other dolphins began to do the same things . . . taking turns rolling each other over, as if parodying the mating taking place nearby.

Titus's shock was profound when they surfaced for breath. "Were they all doing what I think they were doing?" When she nodded, he shook his head. "It's a regular orgy . . . the beasts will mate with anything in flukes. And Prospero is the worst of the lot!" There he paused as if listening to and hearing for the first time his all-too-human moralizing, and he looked a bit unsettled. "Or, I suppose, from a dolphin's standpoint . . . perhaps the best of the lot."

By the time they swam to the dock and climbed out for a rest, the arguments and explanations she had prepared were largely unnecessary. He collapsed beside her on his back, and declared with great insight: "There has to be a good reason for such frequent and enthusiastic sexual activity . . ."

"There is." She raised onto an elbow and looked down at him with an Eve-like smile. "It's fun." She took the fact that he didn't dismiss her suggestion as a positive sign and leaned over to lavish a passionate kiss on him. "Isn't it?"

HE APPARENTLY THOUGHT about it a good bit, for that night, as they were spiraling into a haze of sensual pleasure under the pristine night sky, he raised his head and said, "It's a big ocean out there. And there isn't exactly an eligible dolphin on every corner. Maybe they have to be ready and willing to mate with whatever dolphin they can find, at every opportunity they have. So nature has bred a bit of excess in them to make sure the deed gets done and more dolphins get born."

She stared at him in bewilderment, before she caught the flow of his words, recognized the topic, and the revolution it represented in his thinking. "Titus Thorne, if you could hear yourself talk . . ."

"I would be scandalized?"

"No." She gave him a look that left no doubt of her sincerity. "Proud."

·   ·   ·

TWO . . . THREE . . . FOUR . . . they lost track of
the passing days. A midsummer haze descended, and in the
closeness, the nightly ocean sounds were joined by the
chirping of crickets and the rustle of tall grass in the nearby
fields. But inland, where the weather was not tempered by
the sea, those affluent and idle enough began to flee toward
the water. And as they came to the southern coast and the
fashionable resorts of Brighton, they brought with them
small blue-green books with dolphins embossed on the
cover, and a vague recollection that the Lady Mermaid was
reported to live somewhere along that coast.

When Stephan opened the door one afternoon, he was
surprised to find a pair of well-dressed gentlemen standing
on the step, a hint of dust on the brims of their hats and on
the shoulders of their nattily striped summer coats. Behind
them in the gravel yard were two fine black coaches, covered
with the dust and mud spatters that spoke of miles traveled.

"Is this the house where Miss Celeste Ashton lives?" they
asked. When answered in the affirmative, they glanced at the
sagging house with dubious expressions, then headed back
to their coaches and began to unpack their wives, children,
and nannies.

CELESTE AND TITUS had spent all morning in the water and
enjoyed a picnic lunch on the dock. They were preparing to
build a new set of cork floats for the dolphins to play with,
when they heard a jumble of voices coming from the top of
the cliff and looked up to find a stream of brightly clothed
humans starting down the stepped path. They looked at each
other in surprise, then back at the striped coats, frilly para-
sols, and flock of children in smocks and short pants that
were descending on them.

Celeste quickly snatched her long smock together and
tidied her braided hair; Titus hastily finished buttoning his
shirt and rolled down his trouser legs. They reached the

center of the beach just as the first of the children were spilling onto the sand and running to and fro.

"Ho, there!" one of the men in striped coats called from above. "Miss Ashton, we presume! We've come to see the dolphins!"

Shortly Celeste and Titus were inundated by fashionable Londoners and their rambunctious offspring. The gentlemen tipped their hats and marched by them to the edge of the water while the ladies collapsed on nearby rocks, fanning themselves, the nannies stood together out of the way, and the children ripped off their shoes and stockings—or didn't bother—and went charging into the water.

"Please, children—come out of there!" Celeste jerked up the hem of her smock and waded out to shoo the children back up onto the dry sand.

"Why?" One boy of about seven years refused to comply without a reason. "Do the fish bite?"

"You mean they might harm the children?" One of the mothers was instantly on her feet again and charging down to the water, her parasol bobbing. She gave her husband a dark look on her way past him. "I thought you said these fish were tame. Ce-cil," she shouted to the boy, "come out of there this minute!"

"They're not vicious," Celeste told the nearest man, feeling roundly put upon. "But they are large animals, and un-used to children."

"Well." One of the men glowered at the water, searching for some sign of the dolphins. "I promised the children a look at the trained dolphins and—by thunder—I intend to deliver!"

"Please, miss, we've traveled for hours," the other fellow explained, stepping forward. He dabbed his forehead with a handkerchief and resettled his hat as he approached. "Took us quite a while to find you. The children have had their hearts set on seeing the dolphins—been drawing the beasties on their slates since we left London. It would mean a great deal if you could help them have a bit of a look-see."

She looked at Titus, who stood with his legs spread and his arms crossed, scowling at the children jumping and jiggling and pleading for a "look-see." It was up to her, she realized, gazing into those upturned faces filled with excitement and hope. In their eyes she glimpsed the curiosity she herself had felt as a child and the interest and appreciation she hoped to stir in people for the things that live in the sea.

"It seems your audience has found you," Titus said, strolling to her side. "They've read your book and you've got them interested."

Her own reluctance left her a bit baffled. This was indeed what she had said she wanted: a chance to introduce others to the joys and wonders of the sea.

"Very well. I'll help the children see the dolphins." Then she looked down into seven pairs of widened eyes. "You'll have to do just as I say . . . no adventuring on your own."

Before long, she had gathered parents, nannies, and children into a group and was explaining a few facts about dolphins to them. Then she introduced Titus as a visiting professor and, while she went to get the boat and bring it near the shallows, he related parts of his experience with meeting dolphins.

The children squealed when they saw the first dolphin's head sticking out of the water. The adults joined in the gasps and exclamations when Prospero made a few leaps out of the water. From the boat, Celeste got Prospero to jump through a hoop and to retrieve a float. Then in a spectacular finish, she got him to rise mostly out of the water and "walk" on his tail flukes.

The children crowded the edge of the water waving and begging to come out in the boat with her, to see them up close. Titus had to roll up his trouser legs and retrieve one or two intrepid youngsters who couldn't seem to stay out of the water. By the time Celeste returned to the beach, it was clear she had only succeeded in whetting their appetite for dolphins. They begged, bargained, and finally demanded to see one up close.

Celeste relented. She gave a whistle and Prospero soon appeared. She waded out into the water, smock and all, to direct him into the shallows. The fathers had to carry the little ones in their arms, ruining their trousers in the process. With Celeste's tutelage and coaxing, they all petted Prospero and got to touch his flukes and "shake flippers" with him. When he opened his mouth to make a series of cawing sounds, the fathers spotted his teeth and drew the children back. Other dolphins soon arrived and looked over the little humans as eagerly as the little humans stared at them.

Then one intrepid little traveler spotted Titan and called out—"Look, there's a little one!" The children migrated to where the dolphin baby had edged farther into the shallows and soon dolphin offspring and human offspring were splashing and playing happily together. All of the dolphins, in fact, seemed quite interested in the children, darting into the shallows to see them, repeatedly calling to them and splashing them gently. Periodically, one of the adult dolphins would break away and go far enough out to execute several jumps, then come racing back to enjoy the squeals and laughter of the children and the attention that resulted.

It was a memorable two-hour visit; a wonderful first encounter between dolphins and humans. By the time the visitors climbed the steps of the cliff, had a bit of Maria's wonderful lemonade, and climbed back into their coaches, Celeste's initial misgivings about their intrusion into her world had been dispelled. She waved to the children from the step as the coaches bumped and jostled their way down the rutted drive, toward the lane.

But as she reentered the house and headed for the kitchen to heat bathing water for Titus and herself, she felt an inexplicable but growing sense of loss.

After dinner that evening, in the parlor, they took turns reading from one of her grandfather's classic books about the people and culture of India. But it was clear her heart wasn't in it.

"What has you so serious this evening?" he finally asked,

setting the book aside. "Those people today? I thought, considering all the possibilities, that it went very well."

"It did go well," she said. "But . . . I suppose I hadn't really considered what it would really involve for people and dolphins to mix." She matched his frown. "It has taken me years to learn about Prospero and Ariel and the others. And still, sometimes they surprise me. They're big animals and fast and smart, and today I realized . . . I mean, I know they aren't aggressive by nature, but to see them with those children . . . I wasn't sure what to expect. It turned out well, but it could have been quite different. I suppose I just realized that there are lots of aspects to introducing dolphins to the rest of humankind."

"Well, think of it this way: you learned something about dolphins today that you couldn't have learned by yourself."

"Oh?" She looked up and felt her worries melting in his warm smile.

"That dolphins—at least your dolphins—seem to like children."

"They seemed to, didn't they. They made regular show-offs of themselves over the children. Do you suppose they really understood that the children were the equivalent of their babies?"

"It's not impossible. They did single them out for special attention," he offered. "And we've both seen how they dote on their own babies." He slipped an arm around her waist and she shivered with pleasure and laid her head against him. He chuckled wryly. "This whole business would be so much easier if we could learn their wretched language and just have a good long talk."

THE CLOCK IN the entry hall was striking half past eleven when Celeste sat up in bed and punched the pillow one final time. For more than an hour she had lain in bed, her head buzzing and her body heated and yearning. She thought of Titus lying in his bed not far away . . . his long, elegant body draped with sheets, his hair sleep-tousled, his lips parted in sleep. And she slid from the bed to go sit in the window seat overlooking the beach.

The unseasonable warmth didn't help. She lifted the tail of her gown and fanned herself with it, then struggled to open one of the side windows a bit wider. Movement on the ground below caught her eye. It was Titus, strolling from the house, clad in shirt and trousers, with his hands in his pockets. He was headed for the beach and didn't seem to be in a hurry.

She pulled a robe from her wardrobe and slipped out into the hall and down the stairs, without noticing the slice of light coming from her grandmother's doorway, or the silvery head that bobbed up at the creak of the floorboards under her feet.

Her heart beat faster as she sped along the path to the cliff. The moon was waning—a mere quarter now—but there was still enough light for her to make her way down the familiar steps toward the beach. There Titus sat on one of the boulders at the edge of the sand, staring out at the moon-brightened sea. She slowed and stopped, watching him stare at the waves coming in to the shore.

Titus had picked up two pale, rounded rocks along the path down the cliff and now sat tumbling them over and over in his hands as he watched the waves meeting the shore. They were like his thoughts, going around and around. Like Celeste, he had resented the visitors' intrusion into their snug, sheltered world. And like Celeste he had been reminded of a wider world outside of Ashton House and the dolphin cove. Once admitted, that first thought made way for a flood of others . . . thoughts he hadn't realized he had been denying. Now they were going around and around, unanswered questions and disturbing impressions that he wanted to keep in motion . . . to keep them from settling in his mind.

So much had happened in the last week and a half. He had finally checked the date and discovered that twelve days had passed since he arrived at Ashton House. The count and feel of "lost time" surprised and unsettled him, but not nearly as much as the realization that he had temporarily forgotten that he was an Oxford professor who would some-day have to return to the university and his colleagues.

He had spent all of his adult life at Cardinal College, first as an undergraduate, then a graduate student, and now as a full faculty member. It was all he had known, and in less than a fortnight, all of that seemed to have happened to a stranger who lived a largely incomprehensible life. It was remarkable how this place, this woman, could have opened his vision and ideas of things and had introduced him to a new view-point and methodology in so short a time. For the first time in his life he was experiencing things, venturing into un-known territory, seeing things that no one had ever seen— except Celeste. He stared out at the dark horizon of the moonlit ocean, feeling suddenly awed and unsettled at the thought that there was a whole, unseen world out there—

"Having trouble sleeping again?"

Her voice startled him. Whirling on his seat, he found her standing nearby, dressed in her night robe, her hair flowing free about her shoulders. He felt slightly guilty, as if his thoughts had somehow conjured her here.

"A bit," he replied, moving aside on the rock and patting the place he had just vacated for her. "You must be having trouble, as well. Come, sit with me."

She did sit beside him and at first he made no move to touch her. It felt strangely as if they were friends, meeting in the most ordinary of circumstances. They watched in silence as the waves of the evening tide came in. But then he looked at her, searching her profile in the moonlight, and felt a sudden and powerful surge of emotion . . . part desire, part desperation. He reached for her hands and pulled her up with him.

She didn't question him or resist as he led her to the water's edge and took her face between his hands. In the dim light she looked up into his face with hope and desire shining in her eyes. He rubbed his thumbs across her warm cheeks and absorbed the sensation of her soft skin yielding to his touch. And he somehow sensed that he was holding his future in his own two hands.

"Swim," he said thickly, when he could speak. "Let's swim together."

She seemed to know what he wanted, because she wanted it, too. She nodded, smiling, and slid her hands up his chest to unfasten the buttons of his shirt. He pulled the ribbon ties of her robe and peeled it gently down her shoulders. His shirt came next, then shoes and trousers, and her nightgown.

She stood in the moonlight as bare as the Almighty made her, every curve a sculptor's dream, every inch a man's desire. He ran his hands reverently inward, along her shoulders then down her chest to trace the soft mounds of her breasts. He could feel her responding, warming to his touch, and closed his hands around her. Her eyes closed, and after a few moments, he lowered his hands to her waist and pulled her close to press a gentle kiss on her lips.

She slid her hands down his sides and beneath the waist of his one remaining garment. "For this collaboration to work, things have to be equal," she whispered. When she slid her hands down the sides of his hips, his drawers went with them and he stepped out of them. He released her waist to take her by the hand and lead her into the surf.

She couldn't have counted the times she had spontaneously shed her clothes for a starlight swim with her dolphins. But never before had she felt the water like this, filling every pore, caressing every inch of her skin . . . enlivening primal instincts, awakening the awareness of her sex within her. It was his presence, she understood, that had changed it all. The look and feel of him enlivened her senses and the possibility of him aroused her desires.

The intimate contact of the days just past had built a debt of need between them. Each time they had stopped, each time they had swallowed back their desires and reasserted propriety and control, they had merely added the weight of that unspent pleasure to sensual imbalance inside them.

As they waded into the cool water, each stole glances at the other, sensing what was to come and savoring every movement, every delicious moment. The water swirled around them, encircling their waists, surging between their legs, caressing their limbs as they stretched out to swim. The water became an erotic bridge between them, connecting them as they glided quietly through the dark water into the uncharted territory of realized desire.

"A WOMAN DON'T shed her 'mustn't-mention-'ems' unless she's ready t' take the plunge," Anabelle observed quietly from the top of the tower. She and Sophia, sharing the second watch of the night, each had peered down the spyglass to glimpse a heap of clothes and two pale, bare-bottomed figures on the beach disappearing into the water.

"You're right, of course," Lady Sophia said, her eyes filling with moisture and her face lighting with a wavery smile. "It's going to happen, I can feel it in my bones." She hurried to the figure wrapped in a blanket and snoozing peaceably by the steps. "Stephan, wake up! It's time. Go fetch Ned and the reverend and Daniel and tell them to hurry. Things are moving quickly now."

While the old servant disentangled himself from the blanket, she turned to Anabelle. "You go waken Penelope and the brigadier—I'll get the torches and garlands and the sacred puzzle, and meet you in the entry hall."

As the others hurried down the steps, she couldn't resist turning back for one last moment. Peering out at the beach, made indistinct by the age of her eyes, she let one tear fall. "Love well, my children." Then she looked up at the night sky. "Make sure it's beautiful for them, will you, Martin?"

·   ·   ·

TITUS AND CELESTE swam to the far side of the cove, where rock gradually replaced the sandy beach, and found footing beside some of the smooth, tide-washed boulders. The chill of the water was noticeable on her bare skin and she shivered as she swept her hair back. He noticed and circled her with his arms, pulling her against his body for warmth. She raised her face to him and luxuriated in the salty warmth of his kisses, wrapping her arms around his neck, opening to him. She felt the strength of his desire, pressed against her belly, and felt her body both swelling and tightening in anticipation. Closer, she wanted to be closer to him, to feel him hard against every inch of her skin. The closer she pressed, the tighter his arms clamped around her and the hotter the waves of sensation that broke over her senses.

He kissed and touched her feverishly, lavishing attention on her throat, her breasts, her sensitive nipples . . . recalling and reclaiming each pleasure they had shared these last few days. He slid his hands down her buttocks and lifted her against him, thrusting gently, rubbing her rhythmically with his hardness, finding the sensitive center of her pleasure. She moaned softly and parted her legs, abandoning her weight to him. He carried her back against one of the rocks, setting her partway on it.

With both hands he stroked and caressed her while suckling her nipples, nipping her shoulders, nibbling her neck. When she began to slip, he laughed softly and set her back farther on the rock . . . pausing to adore the erotic picture she made with her wet hair swirling around her, her breasts and nipples swollen with desire and stimulation. She was woman, beauty, pleasure . . . all things generative and good . . . worthy of worship . . . a goddess of desire.

Beginning with her feet, he kissed his way up to her knees. It tickled and she squirmed, but he refused to be dissuaded from adoring every possible inch of her. He nibbled and licked and kissed her knees, wringing giggles and gasps from her . . . which transformed into half-uttered moans as he proceeded up the insides of her thighs. Sensing where he was headed, she closed her eyes; after all, her dolphins did this and seemed to enjoy it. Moments later, she felt his kisses reach the center of her desire and shuddered with every delicious flick of his tongue.

Her breath came in short gasps, the muscles of her legs drew taut, and her body arched to meet those breathtaking sensations. She sank back on the rock, abandoned to the tension that gripped her, spiraling higher and clenching tighter . . . released suddenly in a blinding, white-hot climax of pleasure. She could scarcely breathe as successive aftershocks of pleasure rumbled through her. As she sat up, she felt the tension still heavy in her limbs and that odd, expectant hollowness prominent in the core of her . . . and knew what more she craved.

Here, now, she slid down the edge of the rock, into both his arms and the water. Wrapping her legs around his, she mated her body to his and savored the hard prominence of his desire riding against her sex. She understood what would come next, wanting it, needing it. As the water lapped around them, he drew back slightly and began the joining of their bodies. Bit by luscious bit, he parted and invaded her yielding flesh, forcing the breath from her in soft moans. And when she felt the fullness of him in her, she sighed and relaxed closer against him as lush trills of heat and pleasure vibrated along her nerves.

The water lapped and surged around them, adding to the myriad sensations drenching her awareness. She felt herself being propelled along a now-familiar spiral of tension and delight. Giving herself over to it, she met his thrusts and responded to his voracious kisses with all the passion in her. And as she felt that spiral tighten and strained against him, she felt his hands clamping on her shoulders and heard his groan of release. Moments later, she joined him, contracting around him, holding him tightly, feeling the fabric of her inner being tearing, opening, welcoming a part of him that would never again reside anywhere but in her heart.

He found a submerged rock nearby and sat down, holding

her astride his lap, sheltering her against him as they both recovered. He stroked her hair and she ran her hands up and down his sides. With her ear pressed against his chest, she heard him swallow and clear his throat. He was trying to work up the nerve to say something, she realized and she sat up and stroked his face.

"Perhaps we should not have done this here. I mean, without a proper bed or . . ." He lowered his gaze to her bare breasts, which were half covered with water, and reacted strongly to the erotic sight. She felt that reaction in the place where their bodies were still joined and smiled.

"My adorable Professor Prude. Where better for a mermaid to make love than in the water?" The smile in her voice brought his gaze up. "I'm sure Prospero and Ariel and the others heartily approved."

His jaw dropped, he sat up straight, and looked at the water of the cove in horror. "Oh, my God—you don't think they were watching, do you?"

Thirteen

CELESTE LAUGHED, SLID from his lap, and pulled him to his feet.

"They don't sleep at night," he recalled, "and their hearing is probably phenomenal under water." His eyes widened and he braced, refusing to budge until she answered. "You don't really believe they . . . ?"

"You've watched *their* mating rituals for days now," she said teasingly. "Don't you think turnabout is fair play?"

He sputtered and even in the moonlight she could see his face reddening. With a wicked chuckle, she plunged into the water and began to swim for the beach. "Wait!" he called, then pushed off after her.

They raced toward the shallows of the beach and Titus caught her by the foot just before she popped out of the water. He dragged her back, causing her to inhale water and come up coughing. He stopped instantly, coming up out of the water to see if she was hurt and she took advantage of his concern to jerk one of his feet from beneath him while giving his shoulders a powerful shove. Then he was the one coughing and flailing.

"Why, you—" Clearing his face, he bounded after her through the water, and she laughed and dived under the surface to get away. His revenge thwarted by darkness, he stalked back and forth in the water, searching the surface for a glimpse of an elbow or heel. "Cele-este," he called in a conciliatory tone, but with a far from conciliatory glint in his eye. "Celeste . . . sweetness . . . where are you?" He waded out into chest-deep water and braced with his feet apart, planted firmly in the sandy bottom. Hearing what he would have sworn was the sound of a splash behind him, he whirled, but saw nothing. "Come, come, Celeste. Don't be a naughty mermaid."

He felt something brush against his leg and smiled, getting ready to pounce. Whirling, he plunged his arms into the water to grab her and came up empty-handed. She was swift and agile under water, he knew, but determination counted for a great deal. Especially when one of them was under water and had to come up to breathe. All he had to do was wait.

Then he felt it: something sliding up the back of his leg. He stiffened and the hair prickled on the back of his neck. It was her, of course, he thought, suppressing a shiver. Playing mermaid games. Fresh heat surged in his loins and his eyes widened. Damned effective mermaid games. The feeling ceased and he held his breath, waiting—hoping—for it to return.

A minute later, something trailed up the inside of his other leg and it was all he could do to stand still. Chills raced up his thighs and gooseflesh appeared on his arms and shoulders. This time he couldn't stop the shiver or the sensual lightning that flashed through his body. That mesmerizing touch continued up and up, to his most sensitive area, and he held his breath as it circled him slowly and withdrew. Heartbeats later it returned . . . gliding along the inside surface of both legs at once . . . as if something were sliding between them. He closed his eyes and groaned with erotic delight. A second later—no more than that, he was sure—he heard a laugh from some distance away. He opened his eyes to see Celeste's head sticking up out of the water.

"How did you get over there?" he called, his smile dying

as he realized it wasn't likely she could have gone so far, so fast, under water. And if she had been over there, then what had . . . He froze, concentrating on the lower half of him and realizing that there was only one other possibility. A *dolphin*? Good Lord—he'd been goosed by a dolphin?

Frantically, he searched the waves for any hint of an ovoid head or a bottle-shaped nose. It was too dark to see well and when he looked up, Celeste had disappeared again. Stiffening, he stalked backward toward the beach, scanning the water frantically as he went. Then he felt a brush against his leg and halted, opening his hands wide, intending to grab whatever it was. When it came again, tickling the inner surface of his calf, he made a grab and felt hair sliding through his fingers. Silky hair that he knew in the light of day would be the color of golden wheat.

Relief poured through him and, grinning, he walked slowly back out into deeper water to spread his legs again. This time when he felt that erotic tickle up the inside of his thigh, he slid a hand down his side and found the water filled with silky hair. She was drawing her hair between his legs, past his . . . Then he felt the rest of her gliding sinuously against the sensitive skin of his inner thighs. His arousal returned instantly. He closed his eyes and heard her surface in front of him. There was a small sound from the surface closing, and he felt her again, swimming between his legs, caressing him, teasing him. This time when she swam back through she came up against his front, rubbing against his body, heightening his arousal. When he opened his eyes she was there, her arms gliding around him, her eyes shining in the moonlight.

He pulled her against him and growled. "You had me worried for a minute. I was afraid Prospero had taken a rather peculiar fancy to me."

She laughed softly. "That's not beyond the pale of possibility. But, if he does, he'll have to deal with one very annoyed mermaid."

"Ummm." He seemed satisfied with that. "It's good to

know I enjoy your stalwart protection as well as your . . . your . . ."

"Love" was the first word that came to her mind, and she just managed to keep it from coming to her lips as well. Shocked, she looked up into his angular face and light eyes and finally put a proper name to the powerful combination of passion and emotion that had been growing in her since the day they met. Love. The thought staggered her. She was in love with Titus Thorne.

"Adoration?" she supplied weakly. "Admiration? Affection? Passion?"

"I'm crazy about you, too." He dipped his head to kiss her. "I don't know when I've ever been this . . . happy." He looked as if the word startled him. "Happy." He smiled as he turned it over in his mind. He was *happy*. He couldn't recall being "happy" in years.

"We make a good team, Professor Thorne," she said, rubbing her cheek against his bare chest. "Who would have thought when you came here that we'd end up in such a perfect *collaboration*?"

"Is that what we're doing?" he asked. "Collaborating?"

"*Tsk.* You academics." She wagged her head. "Pay attention, Professor . . . this may come in handy someday. What we're doing right now is *making love*. It is a process by which a male and a female of the human species—"

He put a hand over her mouth to silence her. "Just show me, sweetness. I have it on very good authority that experience is the best teacher."

"There, I'm afraid I have to differ."

"Oh? Recanting your own theory, Miss Ashton?"

"I've researched the topic thoroughly and discovered that experience is the *second-best* teacher."

"And the first is . . ." he prompted.

"Mermaids."

As their kisses deepened, she wrapped her legs around his and he braced and bent slightly to support them both. Then they kissed and caressed until the heat of their bodies threatened to evaporate the water in the cove. They joined a second time, buoyed by the water, cloaked in the darkness, urged on by the rhythms of the sea surging around their bodies and in their veins. It was a long and luxuriant exploration of each sensation and nuance of loving. When they reached their climax of pleasure, the wind and the water seemed to sigh approval.

For a while afterward, they floated together on their backs, hands joined, looking up at the stars. But as passion's heat drained, a chill slowly crept in and they had to leave the water. He dried her with his shirt, but when she would have dried him with her gown, he protested and gave her his shirt instead. She wiped the water from his body, then let him dry what he could of her hair. She slipped her nightgown back over her head and he slid his drawers and trousers on, then together they spread her robe on the sand and lay down on it.

Wrapped in each other's arms and in the lingering glow of passion wisely spent, they drifted to sleep.

HOW LONG THEY slept, neither had any way of knowing. But it wasn't long enough. It was the sound that first aroused Titus. He pushed up onto one elbow to look around, a bit disoriented at first, and saw a wavering line of yellow lights moving down the side of the cliff. Sitting up, he squinted against the darkness and rubbed his eyes to clear his vision.

"Celeste." He gave her shoulder a nudge. "Celeste, look." He pointed as she sat up and she too rubbed her eyes and squinted.

"What on earth?" The lights were bobbing and moving down the face of the cliff and she detected a droning of some sort. "That's the path up to the field on the point, where the standing stones are," she said, rolling up onto her knees.

He pushed to his feet and stood watching intently. "Torches," he announced. "It's people carrying torches and . . ." His eyes widened as the figures carrying those torches materialized from the dark. They seemed to be dressed all in white. "And singing."

Celeste watched the procession down the cliff path with tension collecting in her stomach. Torches . . . people in white . . . singing . . . coming from the field of standing stones. She groaned audibly and stood up, beside him. "It's Nana and the Atlantean Society."

He took her hand and pulled her toward the edge of the water, where they could get a better view.

"What in blazes are they doing out here in the dead of night, running around with torches?" He paused to listen. "And *drums?*"

"Coming from the field on the top of the point, they must have been—" She stopped. She didn't want to imagine it, much less say it. They had been performing a ceremony. And from the fact that they were headed for the beach, she guessed just what sort of ceremony they had been conducting.

"Good Lord," Titus said as they neared, "they're all wearing bedsheets."

"Chitons, actually," she said limply. "And the 'bedsheets' wrapped around them are himations, borrowed from the dress of the ancient Greeks."

By the time they arrived at the center of the beach, the full horror of it had descended on Celeste. They were dressed in their Atlantean garb and carried torches and two "standards" on poles . . . one a stylized dolphin figure and the other the twelve-sided orb Titus had helped them assemble. They were singing of the glories of Atlantis and the wonders of the sea in sundry wavery keys, accompanied by the haberdasher, Daniel Tucker, pounding a drum and Anabelle Feather clanging away on a set of thumb cymbals.

Lady Sophia led the group, bearing rings of flowers in each hand. She was wearing a golden circlet and a huge gold necklace made of leaping dolphins. Behind her came Miss Penelope and the Reverend Altarbright jointly carrying a large garland of flowers.

"Greetings, my children," Nana said in her best "high priestess" tone, raising both hands and the rings of flowers she held in a beatific salute.

"Nana, what on earth are you doing down here at this time of night . . . dressed like that?"

The old lady's reply was a knowing smile and a pointed look at Celeste's own clothing. Celeste felt her face reddening under the group's scrutiny and was suddenly aware of the fact that she stood in the circle of Titus's naked arms, against his naked chest, wearing only a thin nightdress.

"We are here, dear children, to bless and consecrate the union you have entered into this night. For, according to the prophecies of the ancients, your joining—the union of the Man of Earth and the Woman of Sea—is the event the world has waited for in toil and travail. From your union, a new era has just been born upon the earth . . . an era of promise and understanding . . . an age of restoration and hope."

"Prophecies? What prophecies? Nana, what are you talking about?" Celeste felt Titus stiffening beside her and her heart began to beat faster. Union? She made herself look from face to familiar face, and in each she saw that same knowing look. *Joining?* The realization crashed over her like an icy wave: they knew that she and Titus had just made love!

"For a long time now, Celeste, we have known that you were our Sacred Virgin, who would someday become our Woman of Sea. The tablets your grandfather and I translated before he died spoke of the prophecies of Atlantis . . . the coming destruction of their world and the promise that their knowledge and understanding would someday be resurrected in a new world, a new society. And the new order would begin with the joining of a man of the earth and a woman of the sea. You, Professor, are our long-awaited *Man of Earth*. We welcome you into our midst and into our society."

Nana came forward and placed one of the wreaths on her head, proclaiming something about the blessings of all creation being upon her. Then she turned to Titus and stretched up onto her toes. Celeste felt him bending and looked up to see her grandmother settling the second ring of flowers on his head and repeating the same words.

He looked a bit stunned. When he straightened, he looked down at her with an expression of dismay and confusion.

"What *is* this nonsense?" he uttered. "Man of Earth . . . prophecies . . . us joining something together?"

"I've never heard any of this before," she said, alarmed by the way his arm withdrew abruptly from her waist.

"And now," Nana continued, "Reverend Altarbright will bless and consecrate your sacred union." She stepped back and the reverend and Penelope Hatch came forward with the large garland, holding it up for all to see.

"Dearly beloved, we are gathered here to celebrate and consecrate your 'joining' as man and woman. This garland is a symbol of your chosen union, a blending of the ocean's marvelous riches and the earth's magnificent bounty."

"It's seaweed," Titus said, not entirely aware he was speaking his thoughts aloud. "With flowers and stalks of grass tied on it."

"The flowers symbolize the beauty and fertility and plenty of the land. And the seaweed symbolizes the richness and stability and abundance of the sea. In joining them together, as you have chosen to join yourselves together in body and spirit, we have created for you the sacred Circle of Life."

The reverend and Penelope placed the garland on the sand in a circle, around Celeste and Titus, then the reverend took his place before them.

"My God—he's wearing a clerical collar," Titus said audibly.

Celeste groaned. The good reverend was indeed wearing a cassock and clerical collar beneath his chiton and himation. "Then that means—"

"I am here in an official capacity, as well as an Atlantean

one," the reverend intoned, having heard their exchange. "For as much as you, Titus Thorne, Man of Earth . . . and you, Celeste Ashton, Woman of Sea . . . have seen fit to join your bodies and spirits in holy and blessed union . . . I can and must, by the authority vested in me by the church and in the name of the Almighty, declare you to be joined hereunto and henceforth, forever and ever."

Then Nana stepped up and the reverend relinquished his place to her. She raised her hands and smiled radiantly upon them. "As High Priestess of the resurrected holy Order of Atlantis, I bless your union, consummated this night in joy, love, and peace. Through its blessedness the rest of the world will be blessed. I now pronounce you"—she nodded to Titus—"the new Adam"—then to Celeste—"and the new Eve. May the Great Creator give you strength and understanding and courage to lead us well into a rebirth of our society and our natural world."

Celeste glanced up at Titus, who was scowling, and her heart skipped a beat. Forever and ever? She looked wildly about the group. They were all beaming. They knew she and Titus had made love and were using that as the basis for declaring them to be . . . joined forever and ever . . . like Adam and . . .

"Dearest Heaven," she mumbled in horror, "they think they've just m-married us." Titus must have heard her, for he grabbed her by the shoulders and turned her to face him. His eyes were dark-centered and intense in a way she hadn't seen in days. "Titus . . . I . . . I'm—"

A sudden blast of sound startled them, and they whirled and found Hiram Bass standing at the water's edge with a huge conch shell to his lips. The old fisherman drew a huge breath and blew again, producing a low, half-musical blast that was loud enough to rouse Poseidon himself. The other members of the society hurried down to the water's edge behind Ned Caldwell, who was carrying a pole with a dolphin figure on it. He planted it in the sand and stood at attention, steadying it, while the others arrayed themselves behind him, chanting something about "brother dolphins" and "coming forth from the deep." They waved their torches and chanted ever louder, while Hiram produced blast after blast.

"This is where it begins," Nana said reverently, coming to stand beside Celeste and Titus and nodding to the ceremony in progress.

"What the hell are they doing?" Titus demanded. "Singing praises to the fish?"

"Not exactly," Celeste said weakly, feeling light-headed and a little sick, unable to believe what was happening. This ceremony she did recognize. "I believe they're calling the dolphins."

"They're doing what?" His scowl deepened as his features tightened.

"We're calling our brothers the dolphins," Nana reiterated. "Watch."

Celeste felt a part of her withdraw to a safer, saner place inside herself. The torches, the ceremony, the horn, the flowers and seaweed, the dolphin on a pole . . . Anabelle's finger cymbals . . . all here in the dark, after she and Titus had . . . She could only hope this was all a bizarre dream from which she would soon—oh, please, let her wake up!

In horrified fascination, they watched as swaying was added to the chanting, and listened to more blasts from the shell horn. After a while she looked up at Titus, reading in his face the tumult in his thoughts and emotions.

"I've seen them try to call dolphins before," she said, forcing each word past the lump of humiliation in her throat. "It doesn't ever—"

Abruptly, the chanting and horn blowing stopped. The silence over the cove was so profound that the gentle slosh of the waves sounded like storm-whipped surf. Her heart sank at the hopeful way they stared at the water. She should have known it would come to this—should have never let her grandmother's absurd notions about the dolphins go this far. Her grandmother was staring out to sea, smiling through prisms of tears. The sight was like a knife in her heart. She had only herself to blame.

Suddenly, Nana began to walk toward the others, and as Celeste followed the old lady with her eyes, she glimpsed a disturbance in the water at the center of the cove. It was almost as if the water were boiling. It took her a minute to realize that it wasn't water at all, but *dolphins* . . . wriggling, sliding over each other in a tightly packed group. The hair on the back of her neck prickled.

Suddenly, up out of the water rose a dolphin, onto its tail flukes. Her jaw went slack. Prospero? Hiram sounded his horn again and another dolphin, and another rose up out of the water on its tail flukes, "walking" on the water.

She blinked and shook her head to clear it, but they were still there. Now there were at least a half-dozen dolphins "walking," more with each passing second. Soon there were a dozen dolphins, all mostly out of the water, moving along the surface on their flukes . . . then a dozen and a half . . . then two dozen—all doing what she had always believed she taught to her one special dolphin, Prospero.

Finally, one by one, the dolphins sank back into the water. Even as they disappeared, she was already beginning to deny the reality of what she had seen . . . making excuses, conjuring logical explanations.

Hiram sounded his horn once more. They rose again . . . one by one . . . answering that call with a behavior whose significance was known only to them and the Creator who made them. After a long walk, they sank back into the water again, a few at a time. Only, this time, they swam *en masse* for the beach, making caws and screeches and all manner of vocal sounds. They were in grave danger of stranding themselves on the wave-washed sand when Celeste realized they were too close and charged into the water to herd them back to safer depths.

Frantically, she called to Titus and the others to help. Titus came running from the beach, and soon he and the society members were helping to push the determined dolphins out of the shallows and back into deeper water. But even when they were back at a safe depth, the dolphins continued to linger, screeching, singing, and giving barklike yelps.

The noise was horrendous. Celeste put her hands over her ears. Titus stood not far away wearing a pained expression. Just when they thought they couldn't bear much more, the dolphins began to slip away. As suddenly and mysteriously as they had come, one or two disappeared back into the water at a time. Before long, there wasn't a dolphin in sight.

Silence descended once again over the beach. Celeste looked warily over at the Atlantean Society, standing in the shallows. Suddenly, as if someone had snapped fingers to end their trance, they all began to shout and hug each other, bobbing about like children.

"We did it!" Nana cried and the others echoed her joy.

Only heartbeats later, the celebration halted as they turned to look at Celeste and Titus, who were wading in from the waist-high water.

"Well?" the brigadier demanded. "What did they say?"

"What did who say?" Celeste asked.

"The joining ceremony changed everything," Nana said excitedly. "This time when we called them, they came and they spoke. Oh, do tell us what they said!" She grasped Penelope's hands and together they fairly jiggled with excitement. "What are we supposed to do?"

"Yea," Ned Caldwell spoke up. "Ye heard 'em roight enuff. We all did. Now, tell us wot they said."

"I haven't a clue what they said," Celeste said, shaking her head.

Titus stared at them, seeing only a group of daft old-agers wrapped in droopy bed linen, running around in the dead of night performing mystical rites of some sort . . . declaring that he was a second-generation Adam because he'd made love to . . . Oh, God.

He was reeling; he hadn't a clue if he was dreaming, feverish, or just plain delusional. None of it made any sense.

And he was a man who needed things to make sense . . . had to make things reasonable and logical and . . . *safe.*

"You're mad, the lot of you," he said, coming to life, "conjuring up a herd of dolphins, expecting them to bring you the secrets of Atlantis and the answers to mankind's problems . . . with me as go-between."

"But it's all in the prophecy," Lady Sophia said, wading toward him. "After the Man of Earth and the Woman of Sea 'join,' their ears will be opened to . . ." She looked from him to Celeste with the realization dawning. "You mean, you didn't understand what the dolphins said?"

Confusion broke out in the Atlantean Society ranks and Lady Sophia found herself beset on all sides. The members were still under the spell of the startling response of the dolphins to their call and couldn't understand how Celeste and Titus could have missed hearing the dolphins' message. It was plain as day, they declared. They all heard it; they just needed to know what it meant.

Titus watched it all from a small island of reason in his reeling, unreliable mind. At that moment, in that place, he could scarcely have told anyone his entire name, much less make sense of what had just happened to him. He looked at Celeste, who seemed equally bewildered, and his gaze caught on the garland around her head. Reaching up, he felt the flowers of the matching ring of vegetation on his own head.

"What the hell is going on here?" he demanded of any-body who might be listening. Dragging the garland from his head and staring at it, he heard echoes of "forever and ever" in his mind. His mouth began to dry and his heart began to pound.

Throwing the garland onto the water, he stalked up onto the beach, past the arguing Atlanteans, past the place where he and Celeste had lain together, and straight up the path along the cliff. He didn't stop until he reached his room and slammed the door.

．　　　．　　　．

CELESTE WATCHED TITUS charging up the path along the
cliff and felt the fragile trust they had built over the last
several days falling to pieces around her.

Feeling like a stranger in her own body, she crossed the
same beach, picked up her robe and the shirt he had left
behind, and climbed up the cliff. Once in the house, she
went straight to her room and sat in the window overlooking
the cove.

How much time passed, she wasn't sure. But eventually
the thoughts circling in her mind began to settle and she
realized that more than anything else, she had to talk to
Titus. Slipping down the hall, she knocked on his door.

"Titus, I think we need to talk."

The looming silence from the other side of the door sent
her back to her room with dragging steps. She collapsed on
the window seat, wrapping herself in his shirt and drawing
her knees up under her chin. She stared down at the cove
and let the tears come.

Fourteen

"HE'S LEAVING," STEPHAN wheezed out, leaning heavily on the door handle of Celeste's room the next morning. "The professor . . . going . . . right away."

The clock in the entry hall hadn't even struck eight o'clock, the next morning, and already calamity was descending on Ashton House. Celeste rushed down the stairs, her hands trembling as she tried to put combs in her hair. She stopped dead at the bottom of the steps, staring at the valise sitting by the front door. He really was leaving? She pressed a hand over her heart, feeling an awful sense of emptiness.

Titus was standing by the seaward-facing windows in the drawing room, looking out over the cove. The early-morning light spread around him like a golden fan, highlighting his dark form and even darker mood. He turned when she entered, squared his shoulders, and tugged his vest down into place.

She couldn't keep the edge of distress from her voice. "You're leaving?"

"I am," he said with emphatic calm. "I came here to verify your observations of dolphins and I have certainly done that. There is no need to prolong my presence here. And I do have a position . . . duties and obligations."

"I don't want you to go"—she tried to meet his gaze but he avoided that contact and she shrank a bit more inside— "away angry. The 'joining' they performed—it's not a real marriage, or valid or binding in any way. You're not—we're not—obligated to anything."

"I understand the situation," he said stiffly. "I assure you that it will have no impact on my estimate of your work or your competence."

"And the dolphins. I've seen Nana and her friends conduct their dolphin ceremony before, but it never worked until last night. I've never seen that many dolphins together in one place, before. And the way they rose up out of the water . . . I haven't a clue what it means. I know all of this must be confusing."

"Confusing?" He gave a short, hard laugh. "Confusing? It's nothing short of *confounding*! I came here on a simple scientific mission to verify a few observations, and last night I found myself half naked on the beach in the dead of night, being sung to by a group of senile, torch-wielding old people in togas . . . who proclaimed me the second coming of Adam, wrapped me in seaweed, and married me off to their Sacred Virgin in some pagan ceremony . . . after which I was witness to what very well may have been the world's first 'fish ballet' . . . which, I learned afterward, was intended to somehow induce in me the gift of fluency in 'dolphinese' so that I could learn the secrets of a three-thousand-year-old civilization and then charge off to save the world from disease, deprivation, and depravity!" He ran both hands back through his hair, tugging on it as if considering tearing it out.

"You make it sound so . . . crazy," she said in a small voice.

"Do you think it sounds sane? Or perhaps it's me that's gone around the bend—which wouldn't surprise me in the least, after a fortnight in this place. I can't be sure of anything just now—up or down, day or night, land or water—I haven't a clue what's real and what's not any more! I have to get away from here or risk losing what is left of my mental faculties!"

There he halted, staring down at the misery in her face and feeling it migrating into his own heart. He wanted nothing more than to pull her into his arms and hold her until all of the pain and uncertainty faded and there was nothing left in the world but the feel of her and—

He gritted his teeth and backed away, retrieving his hat and gloves from a nearby table. "I will make a verbal report as soon as possible to the secretaries of the two royal societies, confirming your research. I expect to have a full copy of my written assessment on Edgar Cherrybottom's desk by month's end."

She looked up at him with her heart in her eyes, but he was already in motion. He paused briefly by the door. For a moment it seemed he would speak, but he turned and strode out in silence.

She reached the front step in time to watch him climb into the cart with Ned and see the pony lurch into motion. Arguments and denials battled for expression, and she watched in mute anguish as the cart swayed down the rutted drive. It was some time before she could clear her vision and her throat.

"But what about our 'collaboration'?"

"HE'S GONE?" REVEREND ALTARBRIGHT asked breathlessly, as he, Daniel Tucker, the Bass brothers, and Ned Caldwell clambered out of the smith's cart the moment it stopped, and made straight for the steps.

"He left this morning," Lady Sophia said anxiously. She, Penelope, Anabelle, and the brigadier had seen them coming from an upstairs window and hurried down to meet them at the front doors.

"Said 'is propers pretty as ye please, an' wus out the door like a scalded hound," Anabelle said, with dark emphasis on the word "hound."

Sophia led the group into the dining room, where Stephan was laying out plates on the sideboard and lighting the warmer under the coffee server. The society members settled into the chairs around the table, looking forlorn, indeed. They were so preoccupied, in fact, that they actually failed to notice the smells of buttered crumpets and cinnamon-rich muffins wafting from the sideboard.

"What do we do now? This isn't turning out at all as we planned," the reverend said, seeming both surprised and distressed by the fact.

"Is it possible we got the wrong Man of Earth?" Penelope asked.

"Oh, I don't think so," Sophia said, shaking her head. "Celeste is absolutely mad about him. And we couldn't have found a bigger 'landlubber' in six counties—he said so himself. No, he's our Man of Earth, all right."

Silence descended for a time as they each wrestled privately with their dashed hopes and the failure of their long-awaited revelations.

"Well, what the prophecy says has to happen, right?" Daniel Tucker looked around the table. "And if it's going to happen, then he'll be back."

That brought them to attention and they looked at the little haberdasher.

"Won't he?" he said.

No one had an immediate answer but the question caused a number of heads to rise and brows to furrow in speculation.

"Is it possible," the reverend said thoughtfully, "that we may have expected too much too soon? I mean, it may take a while for things to develop. The prophecy says what will happen, not necessarily when or how."

"Mebee we rushed 'em a bit?" Anabelle asked, looking around the table. "They wus only just married up, an' folks take a while to settle in. Mebee it was too much . . . expectin' their ears 'ould open up after only one good hard—"

"Mebee," Hiram interrupted, "they'll have to *learn* that dolphin talk."

" 'At could take a right good bit 'o time," Bernard said, nodding earnestly.

"Took dashed near forever for me to get on with that Latin business," the brigadier put in. "Pesky things, declensions. Demmed lot of trouble."

Sophia brightened and her eyes began to dart over visions in her mind. "You know, Daniel and the reverend may be right. It's just possible that we've misjudged the timing of it all. You all saw them together . . . he's mad about Celeste. Yes . . . the more I think on it, the more certain I am. He just needs some time to sort out his thoughts and start to long for her." She straightened in her chair, seeming confident once again that things in her corner of the universe were proceeding according to plan. "He'll be back." Then she glanced at the sideboard. "Now would anyone care for some breakfast? I see Maria has made her lovely cinnamon buns . . ."

SMOKE DENSE ENOUGH to bring tears to his eyes, steam whistles so piercing they made him wince, the booming yells of porters that could be heard all up and down the platform, the genteel shoving and umbrella pokes that had to be endured in the rush for the best seats . . . Titus had never been so glad to be miserable in his life.

The train station at Paddington was bustling and noisy and reassuringly hectic. The ride up from Brighton had been filled with families heading back to the city after a holiday by the sea; even in first class restless and annoying children were rampaging about, underfoot and climbing on every available seat and surface. What did people pay nannies for, anyway? He grumbled and buried his nose deeper in the newspaper he was trying in vain to read.

He categorically refused to let the little wretches remind him of that day in the cove with the children and the dolphins and Titan and Celeste with her smock buttoned up all the way to the neck and her hair coming out of her braid. Nor did he allow the *shush*ing of the wind, when he stepped out onto the rear platform of the car for a little air, to remind him of the continuous slosh and slap of waves against a beach. And in Paddington Station, while purchasing a ticket for his trip to Oxford a few days hence, he forbade himself the memory of dolphins' squeals and screeches when he got stuck next to an excessively fashionable woman with a horrendous, high-pitched laugh.

He was doing very well, thank you, at not recalling anything that had happened to him in the last two weeks . . . until he boarded an omnibus bound for Knightsbridge and had to ride on top. A few seats down he spotted a young girl with yellow hair that glowed like spun gold in the sunlight and felt his eyes begin to burn and a surge of pure anguish erupt in his chest. Suddenly he was struggling for breath.

Stumbling from the omnibus at Harrods, he managed to navigate the familiar streets of Knightsbridge and to locate the venerable Bolton Arms Hotel, where Cardinal College faculty always stayed when in London. The desk clerk greeted him, registered him, and with a wince of concern, asked if he was feeling "quite all right." He produced a taut facsimile of a smile.

"Of course. Never better."

If only that had been true when he had tipped the porter and closed the door to his room. Then, he crumpled over as if his guts were killing him and groaned until he grew lucid enough to be shocked by the sound of his own pain.

Falling into a stuffed chair, he clasped his stomach and tried to breathe, tried to reassert some control over the pain. For the first time in his life he couldn't do it; as he sat there in the chair, writhing, he realized frantically that he had no way to fight it. The more he tried to resist, the more painful it became. Exhausted from the tension and pain, and terrified by the maelstrom of emotion that accompanied it, he finally heard a whisper in his mind: "Let it wash over you, let it do what pain must do." Groping toward that bit of hope, he surrendered, letting it wash over him, searing his chest, clearing away the clutter to expose his conflicted soul.

He began to breathe again, slowly, painfully, as if his lungs—the whole inside of him—were raw. Sweating and exhausted, he lurched to the bed and fell facedown across it. He didn't know who or what he was. He couldn't even tell what was real any more, and Celeste and what had happened to him at Ashton House were to blame. The conflict between the things he experienced with her, in that place, and his usual understanding of the world had built a dangerous tension within him.

Everything in his life had been based on solid logic and intellect, and everything in his work, on impersonal manipulation of scientific data and specimens. But in her world, there were few boundaries between personal and objective, between investigation and encounter. She didn't "do" her work, she lived it. It was a way of being and thinking so far outside the sphere of his own experience, that he had no frame of reference to deal with it.

He certainly had tried at first . . . forcing each experience through the grid of his intellect, dissecting, categorizing, and cataloging it in his neatly ordered mind. But eventually, there were too many experiences, too compelling to all fit inside the narrow confines he allotted them. They began to spill over, then to take over. Before long he was wandering around in an intellectual fog, drunk with sensation, greedy for new sights, sounds, experiences, and pleasures . . . no longer able to discriminate between what was fact and what was created out of the tantalizing attraction between him and Celeste.

The thought of her sent a wave of longing through him that renewed the hurting in his gut. Was that the source of the pain? Wanting her? He had never before had someone to talk to the way he could talk to her, never before trusted someone with the terrors of his heart and shared the shame of his fears. He had never experienced tender and playful physical pleasures the way he had with her. She hugged him, held him, laughed with him, teased him, listened to him . . . even when he was as boring as mold on pudding. She had excited every nerve in his sensation-starved body and satisfied every impulse to sensual exploration and discovery he possessed.

He rolled onto his back and laid his arm across his forehead. Staring up at the ceiling, he began to admit more of his surroundings to his awareness, and heard the sounds of vehicles and horses and people in the street outside the window. She suddenly seemed a thousand miles away. She belonged to another man in another life . . . to someone he could never really be.

He knew well what he was, had known for years. He was a scientist, a professor, a man of letters . . . steeped in tradition and connected to every touchstone of scientific correctness that existed. He was a detail picker, a carcass poker, a quintessential "laboratory man." One short, idyllic stay at the seaside with a bright, delectably uninhibited young woman couldn't change all that.

He had to put the memories of her and his time with her away; not to be opened until someday far in the future, when they would be so faded and brittle that they wouldn't have the power to wound him any more.

Rising, he washed his face and penned a note to Sir Parthenay and the rest of the faculty, saying he was in London and intended to complete his written report on "the dolphin matter" and drop in on the secretaries of the royal societies before returning to Oxford. Purposeful activity made him feel considerably better. It would take some time, no doubt, for this new emotionalism of his to fade, but he had no doubt that it would happen. He just had to get this writing over and return to his routine as quickly as possible.

To that end, he made reservations to dine at the Athenaeum Club in St. James that evening. The atmosphere there was always intellectual and restrained and the food was good by his standards. Most important, there would be nothing there to remind him of the sea or Celeste.

He sent his coat and trousers down to be pressed and had the porter bring him a paper to read while he waited. Thankfully, there was nothing in it about mermaids or dolphins. He examined every inch of every page; he would have seen it if it were there. Feeling considerably more himself, he changed his shirt, dressed, and had the doorman call him a cab.

THE ATHENAEUM CLUB, in the Pall Mall, was the most aesthetic gentleman's club in London, both in its classical architecture and in the intellectual bent of its members. Its serious tone and impressive subscription list made membership in the Athenaeum a sought-after commodity in academic circles. Titus had received notice of his election to the club at about the same time he was invited to join the Royal Oceanographic Society and was gratified to be able to call himself a member.

The dining room was only half full when he arrived, and he was seated promptly with a pair of older members. The wine was exceptional, the food acceptable, and the company forgettable. It was a mercifully dull interlude, until he strolled into the long drawing room and found himself being hailed from the far end by none other than Sir Gregory Finnes, the general secretary of the Royal Zoological Society. Portly, thick-whiskered Sir Gregory waved to him and, when Titus hesitated, barreled down the length of the room to seize him by the arm and drag him back to a small group of society members clustered around a tray of drinks. He was soon greeted, seated, treated to a glass of vintage port.

"What say—did you 'clean and scale' the Lady Mermaid, Thorny old boy?" Sir Gregory demanded with a wine-warmed grin.

"Details, man!" Sir Thomas Edelson ordered, giving the table a thump.

"Did you teach her a thing or two?" the dapper Herbert Margrove asked with a sly smile. "Or did she teach you?"

Titus looked from face to avid face, in the group clustered around him, and felt his stomach tightening. "I spent a fortnight at Ashton House, yes. And I do have a report for the secretaries of the societies."

"Well, then, make it, man, make it!" Sir Gregory said, grinning. "Unless, of course, it is something better told over a hand of cards and a bottle of scotch—in which case, we should move this gathering to the bar at White's and have at it!"

The others laughed and the heavy aromas of wine and old cigars blended powerfully in the stuffy atmosphere.

"I was able to verify virtually every aspect of her work . . . with the possible exception of the frequency of the dolphins' behaviors. Frequency was not within the scope of my charge, I felt, given the limited time available."

They stared at him as if he'd just spoken in a rare Albanian dialect.

"Beg pardon?" Sir Gregory gave a short laugh and glanced at the others. "I thought I heard you say you *verified* her work."

"I did say that," Titus answered. "That was my task, was it not? To determine the truthfulness of her claims? Well, I did so."

"Good God," Sir Thomas said, in genuine shock, "I think he means it."

"Surely not," Margrove insisted. "That blond bit of fluff?"

"That choice piece of muslin . . . swimming in the ocean . . . riding around on the backs of dolphins?" Sir Gregory snorted. "Impossible."

"Not on the *backs* of dolphins," Titus said. "She merely swam *with* the creatures. Interesting sight. I observed her swimming submerged with the creatures for two and three minutes at a time. She has taught one to jump a hoop and to play fetch with a cork float. Prospero even lets her stand on his head and launches her out of the water into dives."

"Prospero?" Sir Gregory said, scowling.

"One of the dolphin's names," he responded, feeling them shifting focus now to scrutinize him.

"On a *first-name basis* with the beasts, are you, Thorne?" Sir Thomas glanced at Margrove and Sir Gregory.

Titus looked from one wine-reddened face to another, sensing that more depended on his answer than he realized. "Actually, the names are as good a way as any to refer to the specimens. One has to be able to tell the creatures apart and identify them somehow . . . in order to keep track of which dolphin does what."

"Sounds as if you were quite thorough in your investigations," Sir Gregory observed.

Then Margrove snatched up his glass of port and swirled some around in his mouth before asking, "And what position were you in when you made your *quite thorough* observations, Thorne? Vertical or *horizontal*?"

His interrogators all thought that remark quite witty and went off in spasms of laughter. Titus felt his face heating and gripped the stem of his glass tighter.

"If you're asking how I acquired my opinion of her work . . . I'm afraid I had to swim for it," he said with hard-won aplomb. "That too was in my charge, I believe: repeating her methods and observations personally."

They sobered and studied him, clearly displeased by his answers. His full report, when it was tendered, would please them even less. It hadn't occurred to him that his professional credibility and integrity as a researcher might be called into question, for simply reporting the *truth*.

"Well, of course. You discharged your obligation. We all credit that," Sir Thomas said very deliberately, looking to the others. "Verified the woman's claims in the sum and the particulars. Report made . . . eh, Finnes?"

Sir Gregory caught his intent and nodded judiciously. "Report made and duly noted." Then he burst into a grin and sat forward like an eager schoolboy. "Now give us the slick and skinny of it, Thorne. Did she practice her special 'breath-holding' techniques on you?"

"What did the minx wear to swim in?"

"How intimately did you *probe* her knowledge of 'mating behaviors'?"

"Gentlemen, really." He forced a smile while scrambling mentally for a way to answer without revealing his irritation or further inflaming their imaginations. "Like my colleagues at Cardinal College, you seem to see a potential for adventure in everything. The reality of my stay was far more mundane than it might sound. For the first three days all I did was sit around in a boat and on a dock, watching Miss Ashton calling the beasts. As to what she wore swimming . . . she employed a rather unflattering smocklike garment in my presence. And however knowledgeable she may be about dolphin mating habits"—he steeled himself to appear unfazed by the final topic—"she appears to have had little opportunity to expand her field of inquiry to humans. Her grandmother and a passel of aged family friends avidly supervise her time and activities."

Disappointment darkened their expressions. But they continued to ask questions and he continued to relate a judiciously censored account of his experiences at Ashton House. He admitted his early doubts about her leaky boat and makeshift tin drum. He told of his astonishment at seeing her swim with the creatures by holding on to them and at seeing her leap and dive with them. By the time he got to his own firsthand experiences and impressions, his three inquisitors were scowling in open irritation.

"So, in short, you intend to write that this Ashton creature's observations are true," Sir Gregory summarized.

"I must report what I saw," Titus answered tautly, his tension turning to anger at the intimation that he would—or *should*—consider doing otherwise. There was a pregnant pause.

"Well, where's the harm in that?" Margrove poured himself another glass of port and spoke with a patronizing air. "I mean, after all . . . just what did he see? A woman who swims like a fish. While uncommon, such a thing is hardly remarkable. And a dolphin swimming around with a bit of cork in its mouth . . . there's nothing earth-shattering about that. A dog will grab onto a bone and run with it, and we certainly don't call that science. Swimming around in the ocean, watching dolphins play a bit of 'rumpy-pumpy' . . . it hardly *proves* anything, does it?"

"I say. Leave it to Margrove to put it all in perspective," Sir Thomas said with relief. "Interesting little episode. Fodder for the penny press, certainly, but hardly *science*. By all means, Thorny old boy, you must write about it. Put it in perspective for the masses, and put this clever-nell 'mermaid' in her proper place."

By the time he exited the club, twenty minutes later, Titus was ready to take something apart . . . preferably something very large and made of brick. His muscles were aching, his shoulders swollen, his fists clenched, and his jaw ached from keeping it clamped against a dozen furious responses that very nearly escaped him. He had come within a hairsbreadth of laying Margrove out flat on the drawing-room floor. The wretch had smirked and suggested he was remiss in not investigating what sort of noises mermaids made when they got "stuck" in the tail.

These were men at the top of his field, in authoritative and highly prestigious positions. He had begun that sticky interview believing he could ill afford to antagonize them, and their skeptical attitude toward him reinforced his instinctive caution. But their sneering insinuations and leering quips offended his most fundamental sense of decency and eroded his respect for them as men and as scholars. Nothing intelligent or worthwhile, they believed, could come from anyone wearing *skirts*. Their attitude was so arrogant and unrepentant that it truly appalled him.

Unbidden, Celeste had risen in his mind. Out of hand, they dismissed her ingenuity, integrity, and strength of character. They didn't know the first thing about her or her work, but they were positive, even insistent, that she was a greedy, loose-living female who would wheedle, bribe, and seduce to get what she wanted. For all their degrees and honors and high-minded talk of scholarship, they were more than eager to violate the first principles of inquiry . . . discounting even the possibility of truth in a work if it was authored by someone who did not fit their notion of an "acceptable" researcher. A woman.

He stopped on the street in the deepening gloom, watching people hurrying by in pairs . . . realizing that nearly one of every two was a woman. It struck him forcefully that fully half of the human race was female. What were the mathematical odds that *all* of them had substandard or defective brains?

He shoved his hands into his pockets and struck off for Knightsbridge, hoping to walk off some of the angry energy generated in him by that infuriating exchange. It was somewhere along Piccadilly that it hit him with the force of a runaway milk wagon: *two weeks ago, he had not only admired them, he had agreed with them!*

THE WAVES LAPPED gently around Celeste as she waded into the cove waters and stood, watching her dolphins jump and frolic nearby. The rise and fall of the water against her skin reminded her of Titus's touch, of the rhythms of his breathing and his walk, of his body moving against hers. It had been more than a week since he left and, still, she looked up at the sound of footsteps, expecting to see him, still held her breath at each distant sound, desperate to hear his voice, still prayed that she would wake up and find that his leaving was only a dream.

But it wasn't and she didn't wake up. She paced her room and stared off into space and sailed halfway to Plymouth and ate a whole bowl of Maria's chocolate-cake batter. She swam until her body ached, read books from Brighton's lending library until she was bleary-eyed, and walked all the way to Cardamon with the last of their money to pay the butcher's bill. Each evening, she sat silent at the dinner table, avoiding her disappointment in Nana and her anger at the disastrous effects on her life of the Atlanteans' lunatic ideas. Each night, in the quiet darkness, she wrapped her arms around a pillow and released her tears into it.

He wasn't coming back.

It was a simple fact. And she was much too rational to ignore facts.

Her heart might be sore and empty, she told herself sternly, but the rest of her was still functional. She couldn't go on this way, wanting, aching for something that had passed forever out of her reach. She had work to do . . . dolphins to observe . . . another book to write . . . bills to pay. If the events of that fateful night had taught her anything, they had taught her that there was no one to depend on but herself.

SQUARING HER SHOULDERS, she gave the whistle she wore around her neck three short, hard blows. Several dolphins responded and she gave each a stroke and a murmur of greeting before singling out two dolphins to work with.

"Hello, Prospero, old boy." She stroked her favorite dolphin's head and gave him a good rubbing under his bony "chin." He rolled back and forth in the water as if reveling in the attention. "At least I have you, don't I?"

Unbidden, the memory of Titus meeting Prospero rose in her mind. The consternation he had shown when Prospero spat water at him . . . the joy that shone in his eyes when he began to look at Prospero and the others as individual beings rather than just "specimens" . . .

Banishing those bittersweet thoughts, she sent Prospero out to make a circuit of the cove while she turned her attention to little Titan. He and his friend Edgar were the first dolphin babies she had seen at close range and she was curious to find out how quickly he would pick up the behaviors Prospero, Ariel, and the others had learned. It was a tribute to the dolphins' acceptance of her that she was allowed to play alone with young Titan.

She brought out her bag of tricks, which included cork floats and hoops and a leather ball that was filled with air for surface play. She was just introducing Titan to the float when Prospero darted in to give the little dolphin a nudge from below that sent him tumbling. When Prospero stuck his head out of the water with his impudent dolphin grin, she waved him off.

"Leave us alone for a while, Prospero," she ordered. "I need to find out how quickly Titan can learn this." She introduced the float to Titan and Prospero darted in again, this time grabbing the float and racing off with it.

"If I didn't know better, I'd swear you were jealous," she chided when he brought the float back into range. She grabbed for it, but he threw it purposefully into the center of the cove, where it bobbed tauntingly on the water. And then he laughed.

Ha ha . . . ha, ha, ha, ha, ha, ha, ha . . .

"Why, you—" Now roundly irritated, she headed for the float. He raced past her, grabbed it, and plunged beneath the water. "Give it back!" she yelled, smacking the surface with a hand. The other dolphins apparently thought she was calling them and arrived in a heartbeat to begin a mad game of keep away. "Stop this, right now! I have work to do!"

The dolphins raced and splashed and suddenly began a contest to see who could leap the highest and make the biggest splash upon reentry.

"Stop!" Awash in spray, heaving waves, and confusion, she had to struggle to keep from inhaling water. "Stop—stop it!"

They ignored her demand, continuing their raucous play until she yelled in frustration, "Stupid dolphins—maybe you really are dumb brutes!"

She swam hard for the beach and, as soon as she reached

waist-high water, stood up to walk. But she was trembling so that she halted before she reached the edge of the water. Sinking to her knees in the surf, she felt her anger and frustration bursting through the walls of self-sufficiency she had built these last several days. A wounded cry worked its way up from deep inside her and she dropped to a seat in the water and let it come. The incoming waves washed around and over her . . . as if the sea were embracing her . . . absorbing her tears.

Those first explosive waves of emotion gradually subsided and she began to feel the comfort of the water around her, seeping into her awareness, reaching into her in ways too deep and complex to put into words. With a shuddering breath, she finally looked up and wiped her eyes.

Prospero lay not far away in the shallows, watching her. There was a dark, almost troubled aspect to his eyes.

"I'm sorry, boy." She sniffed and wiped her cheeks, looking at his strangely baleful expression. "I didn't mean to get angry with you. It's just that I'm so . . . so . . ."

He opened his beak and uttered some odd sounds, things she had heard only once or twice before. He went over the sounds again and again, as if he were trying hard to communicate something to her. She trapped those plaintive sounds in her head, alert now, listening with every particle of her being. And suddenly she heard it.

Cele. Cele. Play? Cele play?

"No," she responded, her heart beginning to pound. "Cele no play, Prospero. Cele is sad. Cele is very *sad*."

Aad. Cele aad. Cele sad. Sad. Sad.

"Yes," she said in a whisper. "Cele sad."

Rolling up onto her knees, she went to him and wrapped her arms around him, laying her cheek on his cool, sleek surface, drawing solace from his presence. He nodded again and again, then rolled slightly to loosen her grip and rubbed his beak against her arms and shoulders, stroking her as he would one of his own kind.

"Saaad," he said in his peculiar crylike voice. "Cele saaad."

A chill suddenly raced through her at the recognition of what was happening. It was a long, electric moment before she released him and lurched to her feet, staring at Prospero, realizing the words she had heard weren't just interpretations in her own head. "You talked! Prospero, you talked!" She staggered back and forth, laughing, shouting to the world at large, *"He talked!"*

Her delirious first impulse was to hug Prospero, but when she sprang at him, he seemed confused by the abrupt change in her mood and shot off toward the center of the cove. She laughed, twirled around in the hip-deep water until she was dizzy, and was seized by the impulse to share her amazing discovery. She headed for the beach and dragged her towel frantically over her dripping body.

Sweet Heaven, it was wonderful! No, not just wonderful—*miraculous*! She couldn't wait to tell—

She froze. Who? Who could she tell about talking to a dolphin and understanding what a dolphin said in response? Nana? She thought of her grandmother's eccentric notions about her and her dolphins. Only half an hour ago, she was regretting that she had ever even listened to Nana's beliefs.

Then she thought of Titus, wishing he were here to hear it and to tell her what he thought of it. In his stead, she resurrected his opinions from memory. *"That is a great deal to believe on the word of a young woman who has no scientific training"* . . . *"it is impossible to separate reality from your romantic imaginings"* . . . *"the possibility of dolphins speaking of anything at all is exceedingly remote . . ."*

Icy reason poured over her, chilling her excitement. She halted in the middle of pulling on her smock. It sounded crazy. The very sort of "crazy" that Titus had fled Ashton House to escape.

She looked out over the cove, spotting a dorsal fin here and there, and an occasional dolphin floating at the surface, resting. What had she truly heard, just now? She recalled the sounds and pieced them together, concentrating, trying to make them clearer. Imbedded deep within the familiar dolphin caws and cries, she still heard sounds that approximated human words.

Were they real, meaningful communication, or had she constructed them out of her need for comfort and companionship? The more she tried to analyze those memories, the more elusive they became. There was only one way to be certain of what she had heard. She hurried back into the water and called her dolphins again.

Three hours later she collapsed on the blanket and wrapped her arms around her knees, staring at the water. Not a word. Not a single meaningful syllable. If Prospero had spoken to her before, he wasn't talking now. Perhaps she *had* just imagined it all.

Climbing the steps up the cliff, she felt more empty and isolated than ever before. Two weeks ago, she would have rejoiced to hear even a hint of meaning in Prospero's vocalizations. But now all she could think about was how isolated she was . . . professionally as well as personally. There was no one to help her test her hypotheses, no one to help her examine her conclusions or temper her enthusiasm with reason. Perhaps she was just imagining things.

Without the grounding that came with an honest "collaboration," how could she possibly be certain that what she saw and heard were true?

CONFUSED AND DISTRAUGHT, she spent the next afternoon helping Nana clean the flower garden. Several times she considered telling Nana about hearing Prospero speak. But each time she thought of the disaster unleashed by the Atlanteans' beliefs that night on the beach and kept her experience and her doubts to herself. There was no telling what they might do if they thought she and Prospero had actually had a conversation.

It was late afternoon, nearly time for tea, when a horse

and rider turned up the lane and headed for Ashton House at a fast clip. Surprised, Celeste shed her apron, smoothed her hair, using Nana's approval as her mirror, and then ran for the front of the house. But when the rider dismounted and removed his hat, it was a blond head and a fair face that greeted her.

"Mr. Bentley. How lovely to see you again." She was surprised by the depth of her pleasure at his return. It *was* good to see him. When he pressed gentlemanly kisses on both her hands, she felt an unexpected surge of pleasure at the arrival of a friendly and understanding presence. She found herself saying: "You're just in time for tea."

Nana was pleased to see him, of course, and they chatted amicably all through tea and Maria's cucumber sandwiches and apple-raisin tea cakes. By the time tea was cleared away, Peter Bentley was an invited guest for the night . . . given the room recently occupied by Titus Thorne.

After a cold supper that evening, Celeste led Bentley to the top of the cliff overlooking the cove, where the standing stones kept their silent vigil. Together they watched the moon rising up out of the sea, crimson at first, gradually more golden, then cool silver. Bentley quoted some of Blake's and Shelley's poems. And when she shivered in the rising breeze, he removed his elegant coat and placed it around her shoulders, using it to pull her close.

She looked up into his face, feeling his warmth surrounding her, invading her tension, touching her need for companionship and closeness.

"I confess," he said softly, "I expected to find Thorne still here."

It was a question as much as a statement, she sensed. He was inquiring about the state of affairs between her and the professor.

"Professor Thorne completed his work here and returned to Oxford . . ." After almost ten days, the mention of Titus's departure still caused a contraction around her heart. ". . . where he belongs."

Bentley broke into a captivating smile and used the excuse of tucking a strand of her hair back into place to touch her face.

"I cannot see how he could bear to leave," he murmured. "What could there possibly be in Oxford to compare with the sight of you in moonlight?"

She was so busy trying to cope with the sudden emptiness she felt, that it was a moment before she realized his head was bending. When his lips touched hers, it was a mild surprise. His kiss was so warm and firm and gentle, she couldn't bring herself to pull away. Just now she desperately needed warmth and strength and gentleness.

"Ah, Celeste. How I've longed to be here with you again." With a smile warm enough to thaw even the frostiest feminine heart, he put an arm around her to urge her farther down the path.

And she couldn't help wondering what he would say if she shared with him the fact that she had heard Prospero talk and had actually understood him.

Fifteen

"THORNY, M'BOY . . . so, you are here." Sir Parthenay stood just inside the paneled lecture hall, wearing his black academic gown and a look of confusion. "Milton said you showed up this morning and insisted on taking back your lecture. I didn't believe it. I thought you'd be in London for at least another week."

Titus dismissed with a nod the students who had stayed after the lecture to ask questions.

"I decided there was no need to stay in London just to finish up a bit of writing." He began to collect his lecture notes and drawings into his briefcase, avoiding Sir Parthenay's perceptive gaze. "And I was eager to get back to my laboratory work and lectures."

"Oh? How did it go?" Sir Parthenay asked. He smiled but his lively gray eyes searched Titus with an air of concern. Behind him a number of black robes suddenly appeared and filled the doorway, bumping and jostling at first, then drawing back adamantly to defer to each other.

"Oh, for God's sake—" Sir Mercer finally thrust himself through the pack with a grunt of impatience and led them into the room. "By all means, my boy . . . how did you get on with that frisky little mermaid creature?"

"Did you manage to tickle her fins a bit?" Sir Isaac asked with a grin.

"Well, I have to say . . ." Titus was more than a little annoyed. He hadn't a clue what he had to say. He'd been trying his damnedest not to think about any part of the experience since he arrived back in Oxford, three days ago. "It was a most . . . *educational* . . . experience."

"Details, boy, details!" Sir Isaac demanded, tottering over to the lectern and grabbing hold to steady himself.

"By all means, the sum *and* the particulars," Sir Harold Beetle demanded, joining the group forming around Titus.

It was precisely those "details" that Titus had fled London to escape. But before he could think of a way to squirm out of this command performance, Reggie Witherspoon, Sir Milton, and Sir Eldred Harvey barreled through the door, crowded with the others around the lectern, and insisted he wait until Sir Benedict Bush arrived so they all could hear "every fascinating detail."

Titus reluctantly complied, hoping that when this lecture and the damnable article he was still struggling to write were both finished, he would never hear the word "dolphin" again as long as he lived. When old Sir Benedict arrived and the old boys were seated, he delivered a neat, dispassionate, and largely juiceless account of his experiences. The group quizzed him on his opinions of Celeste's work and he answered as objectively and noncommittally as possible. Afterward, he excused himself to his laboratory, saying that he was afraid his assistants might have let things go to rack and ruin in his absence.

The old boys sat for a moment, staring after him in bewilderment.

"What in blazes happened to him down there? He looks awful." Sir Mercer broke the silence.

"Liverish color—eyes all bloaty!" Sir Isaac said, loud enough for even himself to hear. "Th' boy needs a good physic!"

"Looks as if he hasn't slept in days," Harold declared, scowling.

"Didn't seem to think much of sea air. You don't suppose he 'caught' something down there, do you?" fastidious Reggie Witherspoon asked, putting a handkerchief over his nose, just in case.

"He's wound tight as a watch spring," Sir Milton said, shaking his head.

Sir Parthenay rose and began to pace. "I had such hopes for this little adventure. I was so certain that Miss Ashton and her dolphins would loosen him up. But he seems more rigid and narrow-focused than ever. What are we going to do with him?"

Sir Mercer dragged out his pipe and clamped it between his teeth, offering sagely: "Not much you *can* do with a boy who fails a course in 'beautiful mermaids.' "

HE HAD THOUGHT it would be easier here in Oxford, back in his own element, back in his own Spartan bed, back in the hallowed stone walls that had always seemed to resonate reason, and integrity, and truth. He had left London hoping to immerse himself in his work and his sane and sensible life and recover his sense of self and his sense of truth. But the floor of Titus's living quarters was littered with crumpled paper and the bed was piled with rumpled sheets. He had scarcely written a coherent page since he arrived back at Oxford and he was still barely sleeping at night. If only he didn't have this cursed summary of his experiences at Ashton House to write, he could put all of this nonsense behind him and return to normal.

For more than two weeks, he had grappled with the problem of how to unpack his volatile memories, one thought, one sentence at a time. He had tried letting impressions re-form briefly in his mind, then quickly slamming the lid on them again, before any of the emotions attached to them could visit themselves upon him. But it was a tedious process that required far too much self-control and quickly exhausted him.

Worse still, he was once again plagued by those "fish" dreams he dreaded so. For the last two nights he had awakened in a cold sweat to the sound of sobbing, and was relieved to find that it was not his own. It was that fish with the glorious tail; sometimes with legs, sometimes without. Again and again he wrestled it onto his laboratory table and was confounded by its sad, accusing eyes and by his own reluctance to pick up a scalpel and do what had to be done. Increasingly, he found himself moved to comfort the creature, and last night he went so far as to take the damnable thing into his arms to rock it and pet its drooping fins and sadly lackluster scales.

When he reached his laboratory on the ground level of the college quad, he opened the narrow ceiling-level windows to air the dankness and disperse the preservative alcohol smell, and then cleared a space on his worktable, in the midst of the jars and beakers and drying racks and wax-filled dissection pans. He pulled the report he was trying to write from his briefcase and sat down to look it over. He shook his head at the huge blanks he had left under every topic heading. His gaze was gradually drawn to the words themselves.

He had really done such things? Gone to sea in a boat? Learned to swim? Explored life at the bottom of a lagoon? Swam with dolphins?

It didn't seem possible, except for the fact that he had a wealth of powerful, compelling memories of such things. That was all they were, he admonished himself yet again—*memories*. It had been a brief and absorbing encounter with the power of primal human urges and the seductive lure of emotionalism. For a few short days he had been transformed into someone else.

But the truth of it was that who he had been, who he was now, didn't matter. What he had to do was write the truth about her and her dolphins. And just how did he do that?

Again and again Celeste's words to him in the garden

came back to haunt him: "The truth wears many faces, Professor." Now he saw how accurate an observation that was. In this situation alone, it wore at least three faces: the truth of what he personally had observed . . . the ultimate, objective "scientific" truth of her work with dolphins . . . and the "truth" that would be assigned to her work through his writings.

But, when he reached this point, he realized that his troubles with *Truth* had only just begun.

Truth, he was beginning to see, was an alarmingly subjective commodity, even in the supposedly objective world of science. The powers of the Royal Zoological Society viewed her work and the outcome of his observations through a set of assumptions and attitudes that had nothing whatsoever to do with science or logic. And they had made it clear that their assumptions and attitudes must prevail. In his conversation with them at the club, even the barest facts of his experiences had been seen as subversive to the established order.

If he wrote his real opinion of her work—that she had done substantial and even potentially groundbreaking work—he would pay a price for it. The old boys at the Athenaeum Club had made it clear that his credibility and career were on the line as well as hers. He had always prided himself in being a rational and devoted servant of scientific truth. How could he tell their twisted and contorted "truth" and still be true to his own intellect and reason, his ethics, his heart?

It was at this point that he always remembered that group of sexagenarians on the beach, wearing bedsheets and waving torches, singing and swaying and blowing on shells. Then he remembered that startling dolphin ballet and being asked to interpret dolphin speech because he had just been anointed the "new Adam" because he had made love to a "sacred virgin."

It was at this point that he began to distrust his own senses and judgment and sanity.

And it was at this point that he began to feel a terrifying emptiness that reached all the way down to his bones.

SUNDAY MORNING CELESTE and Lady Sophia invited Bentley to join them for services at the village church in Cardamon. He declined, saying he was not a religious man, but he insisted on escorting them. It would do him good, he said, to visit the local pub and see what was happening in the London newspapers.

That afternoon, Celeste took Bentley for his first swim with dolphins. He seemed most enthusiastic at first, wading straight into the water and scanning the surface for signs of dorsal fins. Celeste called the dolphins with her whistle and two or three arrived and swam around and around. She managed to corral the female, Echo, to let Bentley meet and investigate her. He stroked and touched her, brushing her sensitive eye with his hand, causing her to yelp and shoot off toward the center of the cove.

"You have to be very careful of their eyes, Peter," Celeste told him, looking after the dolphin. "They're very sensitive."

"I'll remember. I'm terribly sorry—I certainly didn't mean to hurt her." He was the very picture of contrition.

She led him into deeper water and gave him a pair of goggles to let him see how they swam beneath the surface. Then she whistled again and four or five dolphins answered her call to meet Bentley. As he began to touch and explore them, Celeste felt Ariel nudging her, bidding for attention, and turned to pet her. A shriek and sudden violent thrashing broke out behind her, and she whirled in time to see the young male named Charlie thrashing and struggling to get away from Bentley, who had his fingers over Charlie's blowhole.

It was as if a lightning bolt went through the other dolphins; they raced to rescue Charlie, churning the water vigorously, obscuring his escape with foam and spray. Bentley lurched toward Celeste, and she rushed to grab his arm and pull him out of the way.

"What did you do?" she demanded.

"All I did was touch the top of its head," he said with great dismay. "It let out a howl and started to thrash."

"They're extremely sensitive about their blowholes," she said, with an anxious look out at the cove. "I'm sorry . . . I thought I had warned you."

It took some time to coax the dolphins back into the shallows, and this time Prospero came with them. When he was introduced to Bentley, he spat a stream of water in Bentley's face. Celeste laughed. Bentley didn't. Not even after Celeste chided Prospero and made him come and offer a flipper in peace.

She tried to get baby Titan to come and meet Bentley, but Ariel always intervened and sent Titan sulking away. Celeste frowned. That wasn't like Ariel. When she finally managed to get Titan alone to introduce him to Bentley, Prospero leaped and fell with a smack just behind Bentley, sending a wall of water over the American that knocked him facedown into the water. He came up coughing and furiously wiping his face.

"Damned beast—" he growled, then caught sight of Celeste's shock and checked his reaction. "Sorry. The thing just caught me unawares."

For the rest of the afternoon, Prospero made it his mission to catch Bentley off guard again and again, whenever, however possible. He began to bump Bentley over, to surprise him by leaping and crashing into the water next to him, and to swim at him at full ramming speed and turn aside only at the last second.

Celeste watched in distress as Prospero and the others not only rejected Bentley's overtures, but harassed him until he declared through clenched teeth that he had "learned" quite enough for one day and stalked from the water.

That evening, Celeste kept going over and over the afternoon's events in her mind. She had never seen her dolphins react to anyone the way they reacted to Peter Bentley. Again and again, she recalled her glimpse of Bentley's hand by Charlie's blowhole. It bothered her because she had brushed and even grabbed that sensitive region on numerous dolphins and had never gotten such a pained and frantic reaction. Had Bentley actually stuck his fingers into Charlie's blowhole and interfered with his breathing? Surely he knew better.

Nana was quieter than usual that evening and retired early, suggesting Celeste do the same. But Celeste chose instead to do some needlework in the drawing room and keep their guest company for a while longer. Nana scowled, but withdrew. After a few moments, Bentley deposited his cup on the coffee tray and transferred to the settee beside her.

"I cannot tell you how much it meant to me to meet your dolphins and be in the water with them today."

She lowered her gaze, struck by the disparity between his annoyance that afternoon and his professed pleasure tonight. But then, she chided herself, he truly might have enjoyed *some* of what they had done with the dolphins.

"Since this afternoon, I have thought of little besides those graceful and noble creatures of the sea. I share your great admiration for them and your desire to present them to the world. I have given it some thought, my dear Celeste, and I've just had the most splendid idea."

He smiled warmly at her surprise and plucked her hand from her lap to hold reverently in his. As he spoke he began to drop kisses on her fingers.

"The greatest barrier to understanding our beautiful sea creatures, my dearest, is simply distance." He paused and raised to her a gaze filled with heated admiration. "People cannot remove to the seacoast to encounter sea creatures . . . but they would be more than willing to see and learn if the creatures were brought to them."

She frowned, mulling that over, and he tightened his grip on her fingers and used them to draw her closer.

"I can see it so clearly, Celeste," he said, pressing a pas-

sionate kiss on the inside of her wrist and edging closer to
her on the settee. "An educational exhibit. A chance for
people to encounter and experience dolphins and possibly
other sea creatures." He pressed the palm of her hand against
his chest so that she could feel his heart pounding. She
looked up into his handsome blue eyes and saw there a light
she recognized. Desire. It rattled her so that she had difficulty concentrating on his next words.

"We could do it, Celeste. You and I. We could build a
place—say, in London—to house and exhibit Prospero and
the others. You could show people the tricks they can do
and talk to them about dolphins. If you'd like, you could
even climb in the water with them . . . show people what
they can do."

She realized his arm was around her when he began pulling her against him. The heat of his chest beneath her hand
and his moist breath along her cheek stirred in her the memory of another's heat, another's passion. Titus. Peter Bentley's loving seemed strangely cool and mechanical by
comparison.

"I shall never forget the spectacle of you being borne up
out of the water on the dolphin's head." He closed his eyes
as if to hold and savor that image, then opened them to look
down at her with passion rising red under his fair skin. "I
want everyone to see you like that. And everyone who
comes will be touched by the magic of you and your dolphins, as I have been. You have touched me deeply, sweet
Celeste . . . deeply." His mouth closed over hers.

She was suddenly pressed back against the arm of the
settee with nowhere to retreat. He pressed himself against
her and kissed her with extravagant passion, taking her
stunned lack of response for permission. He slid his hands
feverishly over her sides and waist as she braced her arms
between them, against his chest. She was so busy thinking
about whether she should put a stop to his rampant adoration, that she scarcely gave a thought to what he was saying.

"Will you join me?" he murmured earnestly. "Will you help me to share our mutual love with the world?"

"Peter . . . I . . . I really don't know . . . I need time . . ."

He paused and searched her, his breath hot, his body insistent against hers.

"Then you shall have it, sweet Celeste," he said with a husky, sensual laugh that defused the tension. "But be warned. I am determined to win you over completely."

He released her with a seductive smile, helped her extinguish the lamps, and escorted her up the steps, where Nana stepped out into the hall and bumped into them on the way to the kitchen for a warm posset.

Celeste had the strangest feeling that Nana had purposely waited for the moment when they would arrive at the top of the stairs, to go for her sleeping aid. The dark look Nana gave her lingered in her thoughts as she lay in her bed some time later. Her meaning was as plain as if she spoke it aloud: Celeste had no business accepting P. T. Bentley's attentions . . . not when she was already joined to the society's Man of Earth.

Joined, Celeste thought, with tears welling. How could that be so, when she'd never felt so alone in her life?

Bentley was all attentiveness and blue-eyed smiles the next morning, and when Celeste suggested taking the boat out he readily agreed. They had a lovely morning of sail and sea, of watching her dolphins play in the open water. Twice Bentley tried to broach the idea of what he now called "our collaboration," and twice she spotted something—a fishing pelican and then a cliff filled with nesting terns—to divert the conversation. She could see him struggling with his disappointment and felt a twinge of guilt at her reluctance to discuss his ideas. But she couldn't help being a little annoyed by his persistence in the matter, when she had already indicated she was undecided about her work and her future plans.

Then a large fishing boat appeared in the middle of the bay, and Celeste thought of her curious dolphins and decided to lead them back into the cove, away from that boat. Halfway in, Bentley asked for the tiller, saying it had been some time since he'd handled a boat and that he was afraid his sailing skills were getting rusty. Knowing him to be an accomplished sailor, she handed it over and sat back with her eyes closed, enjoying the feel of the sun on her face and the sounds of the wind and waves and seagulls.

Twice he pointed out that the dolphins were following the boat and she opened her eyes briefly to see them. Then she heard the waves breaking on the barrier rocks that formed the mouth of the cove and realized they were nearly home. She sat up and looked around, seeing that they were indeed in the cove and headed for the dock . . . but at an alarming speed. Bentley was distracted, looking off toward the center of the cove where the dolphins were leaping and playing.

"You're going too fast!" she called, pointing at the dock and scrambling for one of the oars stowed in the bottom of the boat, intending to use it to push away from the dock. "Hard to port! Steer hard to port!"

Bentley reacted out of shock and, inexplicably, shoved the tiller hard to starboard instead, setting the bow of the boat on a collision course with the dock's wooden piers. She dropped the oar. "No! Port not starboard!" She lunged at the tiller and began to pull frantically back the other way, trying to turn the boat enough to soften the coming impact.

The aged tiller groaned and two of the rusted bolts securing it ripped free of the degraded wood around the pivot. The bow of the boat rammed straight into a piling, splintering ancient boards and crushing one whole side of the bow. Everything happened in a flash: water rushing in through the broken boards . . . the boat filling and swamping . . . Bentley pulling her through the water to the ladder and urging her to climb. Her gaze fastened helplessly on the sight of the sail trapping air as the boat rolled and slowly settled toward the bottom.

"My boat . . . my poor boat . . ." she said over and

over, as she stood on the dock, dripping water and staring at the ghostly gray outline beneath the water. She felt as if her heart had gone down with it. When Bentley pulled her into his arms, she accepted his offer of comfort and cried into his lapel. With her head pressed against his shoulder she couldn't see the way he looked down at her sunken boat and smiled.

By the time they reached the house, the magnitude of the loss had settled fully on Celeste. Maria rushed to tell Nana and get the dripping pair some blankets, while Stephan quickly fetched a bottle of sherry from the cellar. Sitting in the warm kitchen wrapped in a blanket, Celeste tearfully recounted what had happened. Nana hugged her and began to cry as well.

"It was Martin's boat . . . his pride and joy." Nana dabbed Celeste's eyes with a handkerchief and then her own. "Are you sure it cannot be repaired? Perhaps if we had Bertrand and Hiram Bass look at it—"

"Half of the bow is gone, Nana," Celeste said, facing the awful fact anew. "The wood was so old it just splintered everywhere."

Bentley apologized yet again for his inattention to how fast they were going. "I was so busy watching the dolphins . . ." He seemed quite distressed. "And I suppose I must be more out of practice at a tiller than I imagined."

Celeste could scarcely look at him, so she focused instead on her grandmother. "Why don't you have a lie-down, Nana. I must change into dry clothes—come, I'll help you upstairs."

By the time she returned to the drawing room, Celeste's shock had subsided enough for the scope of the calamity to become clear. She went to the seaward windows and stood looking out over the cove. Bentley entered, wearing dry clothes himself, now, and came to stand behind her.

"It's not just the boat, it's my work," she said, trying to contain the bitterness she felt. "How can I continue to work with my dolphins if I have no boat?"

"I'm embarrassed to admit," Bentley said, running his

gaze speculatively over her back and waist, "that I currently have no excess funds to help remedy your situation. But surely the proceeds from your book . . ."

"I've received very little from the book yet, just enough to pay off a few debts and—" She halted, appalled that she was speaking of such personal things, and escaped to the settee. He followed.

"You mustn't despair," he said, seating himself beside her and taking her hands in his. "I'm your friend and, if you'll let me, I'll be your partner, as well. I can help you get another boat, Celeste, a bigger, even better boat. With your help, I can find the funds to support your research and to realize your dream—*our dream*—of bringing the glory of the sea to the masses."

He smiled at her confusion and smoothed away her frown with his fingers. "You must trust me, dear Celeste. I have a way to provide for you and your dolphins. I have some very wealthy friends . . . men who want to invest wisely and see good done with their money. If I go to them, tell them of the exhibit we plan, ask for their support . . . I know they'll be more than eager to help us."

"The exhibit we plan?" Celeste roused from her misery to register what he had just said. She looked up. His face was flushed and his eyes were glowing with the same sort of hunger she had seen in them last night. He was pressing her about his exhibit idea *now*?

"Our plan to bring the beauty and mystery of dolphins into the dreary world of the city," he said. "Last night I told you of it. My idea to take your dolphins to London, to build a facility for them . . . a special facility for training and exhibiting them . . . a place where people can come to see them and you can explain all about them."

"You want to take Prospero and the others to London? But they're creatures of the open sea . . ." Who ranged over hundreds, perhaps thousands of miles. How could he possibly think of putting them in a pool or tank of some sort, in a big, noisy, smelly city?

"I know it will be an undertaking, but with your help, I will soon have the financial backing I need."

"A facility? It would have to be something at least the size of our cove, to care for dolphins properly." The thought staggered her. Did he honestly believe he could build such a place? "It would have to be filled with seawater and kept fresh at all times. And dolphins always migrate elsewhere in winter—they would have to be able to get back to the open sea. Then, there is the problem of handling a group of dolphins . . . they live in groups . . . you couldn't separate them and expect them to live for long, much less thrive."

Each statement contained an insurmountable obstacle, to her thinking, a reason such a project would end in disaster, but she could see from his face that he didn't understand that. He was taking her comments as participation in his plan. If he didn't understand the seriousness of her objections, then he certainly didn't know much about the sea.

"Oh, I'm certain we can find a way to cope." He gave her an adoring smile meant to pacify her, then kissed her fingertips for good measure. "We can capture as many dolphins as you want and keep them together. They will be so happy, they'll forget all about going anywhere else for the winter."

"It would take a fortune to—"

"Oh, I'll have the money, lots of money, dear Celeste. Besides, people will pay good money to see exhibits like this. We'll have lines from Covent Garden all the way to Putney Bridge." He released her hands to pull some papers from his inner coat pocket and unfold them before her. "The possibilities are virtually limitless. There would have to be souvenirs—children will all want a toy dolphin of their own—and they and their parents would all want a treat or a meal. We could build a tearoom or a restaurant and have another source of . . ."

Her disbelief turned slowly to anger as she stared at the papers he held. His carelessness was responsible for wrecking her boat, she realized, and now he magnanimously offered to replace it . . . *if* she was willing to join him in some half-baked scheme to capture and exhibit dolphins. His smile bore a trace of smugness, as if he believed her participation was assured, as if she didn't have a choice, now that her boat was—

A chill coursed through her. There was nothing careless or slipshod about P. T. Bentley. His every movement, every expression, every comment seemed to be made for effect. She suddenly could see the calculation behind his handsome face and sly charm and it took her breath.

He had done it on purpose. He had sunk her boat so that she would have to agree to a partnership with him. There was the proof, in black and white—he'd had those wretched papers in his pocket all along.

Making money was the entire motive behind his grandiose ideas of a "collaboration" and his fawning attentions to her. However little he knew about the sea, he knew even less about *her*!

"I took the liberty of putting a few things down on paper. And to save time, I drafted a letter saying that you intend to participate in the venture. I will need that when I speak to my financial friends about funding the facility." He looked around the drawing room. "Is there a pen in here?"

"No," she said with fierce control.

"Well, perhaps there is one in the library." He rose and she shot to her feet to face him.

"I mean: *no,* I don't want to be involved in such a loathsome venture."

He stared at her, caught off guard by her resistance.

"I don't think you understand, Celeste." His purposeful, lubricating smile bloomed again. "The plan I am proposing will replace your boat . . . yes . . . but it will do much more. This is a magnificent venture that will enlighten the rest of the world as to the life of dolphins and the importance of the sea." He set the papers down on the settee to reach for her hands, but she kept them folded tightly against her.

"But Celeste"—his voice filled with entreaty—"I need

you to be involved, to share my vision and work alongside me. You've been my inspiration, all along. Our *collaboration,* my dearest, will insure its success."

His use of that particular word infuriated her.

"You ran my boat into the dock . . . and I'm supposed to trust you with my future? I will tell you, Mr. Bentley, in terms you have to understand—I would never permit my dolphins to be used in a tawdry scheme such as you propose."

"Tawdry?" His face abruptly hardened. "Before you reject my proposals out of hand, I suggest you think about your future . . . here at Ashton House." He swept the room with an ill-disguised sneer. "And think about your boat on the bottom of the cove—the boat you have no means to replace. *I* can replace it. If you sign with me, I can make you wealthy. I can make you the toast of London."

"I'd rather do without a boat than buy one at the expense of my dolphins . . . and my self-respect," she declared furiously. "How much plainer must I say it? I want nothing whatsoever to do with your miserable venture. Or with you."

He looked as if he had just been slapped. His face reddened and he shoved to his feet. Gone were the smooth, boyish looks and the engaging blue-eyed charm. In their place was a crackling hostility that said she had no right to refuse him. The change was so quick and so complete, that she realized this attitude must have been there all along, just beneath the surface.

"That is your final word on the subject?" he asked in cold tones.

"It is."

The smile that came over him had nothing to do with pleasure.

"Very well. I shan't trouble you further, Miss Ashton." He stuffed the papers back into his pocket and strode out.

Celeste heard him storm up the stairs. Shortly he reappeared with his valise and strode out the door without another word to her, headed for their dilapidated stable. She went to the front door and waited until she saw him ride down the lane, giving his horse a vicious spur. A shudder went through her at the thought of his determination and of the disturbing greed she glimpsed in him.

What if he had managed to get his hands on her dolphins and exhibit them? She thought of Prospero imprisoned in a small pool or tank . . . unable to swim or jump, trapped without friends or proper food or his precious freedom . . . and shuddered to think what it would be like for him.

Nana hurried downstairs, to find Celeste. "Where was Mr. Bentley going in such a hurry?"

"I don't know and I don't care." Celeste was adamant. "I don't think we'll be seeing him again any time soon." She told Nana what had sent Bentley from the house in such a huff, and her usually soft-spoken grandmother was outraged.

"Capturing and exhibiting our sacred dolphins—why, the wretch ought to be horsewhipped!" She took Celeste by the shoulders. "We'll find a way, Cele. We'll find a way for you to get on with your work, mark my word." She put an arm around Celeste and drew her along into the drawing room.

Things had been strained between them since Titus's departure nearly two weeks ago. Neither had wanted to broach the subject of the Atlanteans' part in driving him away from Ashton House. Now, strangely, the outrage of Bentley's behavior seemed to have broken the tension between them. Nana led her to the settee and drew her down on it.

"I've been thinking," the old lady said tentatively, as if unsure of how Celeste would receive her words. "I've been holding on to your grandfather's artifacts for a long time. Perhaps it's time to go through them . . . make some space in the library and morning room. Some of the artifacts are really quite rare. They could bring a tidy sum." She gave Celeste a hopeful look. "Perhaps even enough to replace your boat."

Celeste's heart melted.

"Oh, Nana." She slid her arms around her grandmother

and held on for all she was worth. "I could never let you do that." After a long, painfully sweet moment, she gave Nana a tighter squeeze, then sat back with wet eyes and a beaming smile. "But it means the world to me that you offered."

THAT VERY EVENING, P. T. Bentley sat in a dingy dockside tavern in Brighton, refusing the blowzy waitress's attempts to interest him in a mug of ale or, failing that, a bit of fleshier fare. Facing the proprietor's edict of "drink or get out," he ordered a tankard of rum. But it was cut with filthy water and virtually undrinkable. By the time he spotted the man he was waiting for, coming across the tavern toward him, he was more than ready to leave.

"Well?" The grizzled middle-aged fellow in a frayed captain's coat and sagging hat slid onto the planking bench beside him. "Wot happened?"

"The bitch won't do it." Bentley glanced around and spoke in low, tightly clipped tones. "We'll have to do it ourselves."

"But I tho't ye said she wus ripe fer the pickin'," the captain snarled. "Ye said ye could get her to lead them dolphins straight into th' nets."

"I said, she's *out*," Bentley snapped.

"What'll we do now?" the captain demanded, looking around them to see if anyone was close enough to hear.

"We'll have to take them by ourselves."

"Us? How d'we do that?"

"It won't be that difficult." He smiled at the captain's skeptical look. "She's trained the damned beasts to come to her call. But they don't have to know that she's not the one doing the calling."

Sixteen

THE NEXT MORNING Celeste made herself go down to the dock to get her training equipment, even though it meant passing the skeleton of her sunken boat. With her arms full of floats, balls, hoops, and her journals, she paused to stare down at it, feeling that its demise somehow marked the passing of an era in her life. Being out on the sea in that boat was more than a way to study dolphins. It had been a link with her deceased parents and her beloved grandfather. As long as she could sail in the same craft they had sailed and enjoy the same coastline and savor the same wind, sun, and sea . . . she could still feel their presence and they had stayed alive for her.

Now, the means for that special communion was gone, and she couldn't help feeling that the innocence and joy of her youth was gone with it, thanks to Bentley. She was a woman now, with responsibilities and duties and work to do.

She headed for the beach, set out her equipment, donned her whistle, and stripped her smock. There weren't any fins visible in the water this morning, but she waded into the water and blew her whistle anyway. The group was often out of the cove in the morning, feeding, but they sometimes left an adult female behind to look after the babies. Since it was the babies that interested her this morning, she continued to blow her whistle and to scan the surface for a sign of them.

Half an hour later, she donned her smock again and headed for the boathouse to get her tin "drum." An hour of intermittent calling produced no dolphins. Puzzled, she took her spyglass up the cliff to the promontory where the great prehistoric stones stood. From that vantage point she could see the cove, and the coast on either side for some distance. There was no sign of dolphins, but she did spot that fishing boat she had seen yesterday as she and Bentley were coming back to the cove. It was under full sail, heading toward the channel, and she was relieved to see it go.

Through the afternoon she called Prospero and the others, with no success. Her dolphins seemed to have vanished. She thought of their migration patterns in previous years. According to her data, it was more than a month before they would leave for more favorable winter climes.

Nana heard her repeated calling and came down to the beach to see what was happening.

"I can't seem to raise them at all," she explained, trying to suppress the alarm rising in her. "Perhaps they ventured farther out than usual while feeding and got distracted. Perhaps they met some other bottlenoses and stopped for a bit of fun." She looked at Nana with a question in her eyes.

"They'll come, dear," Nana said, putting an arm around her and turning her toward the house. "You'll see. You'll wake up tomorrow morning and the naughty beasties will be all over the cove."

But they didn't come the next morning. Or the morning after that.

Every day for the next week Celeste called and scanned and searched. The Bass brothers took her out in their boat to look for them. Pained by the sight of Celeste's worry, the Atlanteans even tried one of their dolphin-calling ceremonies, hoping to raise them. Nothing seemed to work.

"How could they all have disappeared without a trace?" she asked the Atlanteans who had gathered to consult on the problem and commiserate. No one had an answer, or at least an answer that wouldn't deepen Celeste's worries.

That night, Celeste went down to the dock by herself and called her dolphins for hours, praying they would return to the cove. But between rounds of calling, on the dock, she scanned the waves with burning eyes and realized that they might not come again for a long time . . . if ever.

It was almost too much to bear. She pulled her knees up and buried her face in her arms, sobbing and feeling abandoned once again. It seemed as if everyone she had ever loved had abandoned her—her parents, her grandfather, Titus, and now even her beloved dolphins.

OXFORD SLOWLY WORKED its stultifying spell on Titus's overburdened senses. With all the black robes, tweed coats, monochromatic classrooms, and somber libraries, there was nothing to stimulate his memories of Celeste and her dolphins, or his regrettably emotional reaction to them. With each tedious, passing day, he felt himself returning a bit more to the man he had been.

Thus, a fortnight after he resumed his duties at Cardinal College, he was finally able to sit down with pen in hand and commit to paper the particulars of his experiences with Miss Ashton's dolphins. He adopted a spare, scientific style and listed the basic, incontrovertible facts, making no comment on *her* claims and offering neither condemnation nor praise for her work. He simply left it to the readers to draw whatever conclusions they wished.

It was either a stroke of diplomatic brilliance or a pathetic capitulation to the powers that be. At this point he didn't care which. It was over. Finished. And he had learned a valuable lesson in scientific writing. All one had to do to be scientifically acceptable in print was to remove everything but subjects and verbs from the page.

Sir Parthenay came rushing into his lecture hall a few days later, waving a telegram, his face flushed with alarm. "Awful news, Thorny!" He paused to catch his breath. "There's been a fire at the Natural History Museum and our specimens—*your specimens* . . . There's been some damage, I'm afraid."

Titus was on the train down to London that very afternoon. He arrived just as the museum was closing and, luckily, caught the curator of the aquatic-life section on the way out of his office. The harried curator delayed his departure to show Titus the damage, which fortunately had been confined to one exhibit hall, two preparation rooms, and a storage area.

In a sooty, smoke-stained exhibit hall, Titus found a number of broken jars and smashed and ruined specimens. There were his prize squid, his puffer fish, and some of his baby sharks, lying on the floor. He felt his stomach sink.

"It could have been much worse," the curator said. "If the preservative alcohol in your specimens had caught fire, the entire museum might have gone up in flames."

With that small consolation, Titus promised to return in the morning to help the curator move and clean the remaining specimens; then he headed for the Bolton Arms.

The minute the porter set his bag down in his customary room, Titus felt an unwelcome rustle of memories of his last stay here. Turning on his heel, he went straight back down to the lobby, asked for a change of rooms, and had the doorman call him a cab. He proceeded to the docks, where he located one of the fishing-boat captains who secured his specimens, and gave him a list of creatures he would need to replace the damaged specimens. Then he sent a note to the School of Medicine to ask if they would have an operating theater free for his dissections.

Midway through the next morning, he strode down the second-floor hallway of the Natural History Museum holding a two-gallon specimen jar in each arm. He had removed his coat, rolled up his sleeves, and donned a rubber apron to help the curator and his assistants clean the specimen jars, evaluate the damage, and transfer them to a holding area.

Up the main stairs came a small herd of children—more than a dozen—accompanied by a pair of gray-clad women of middling years. He groaned silently, wishing the museum hadn't decided just to carry on and remain open to the public. Try as he might, he couldn't make it past the stairs before the children poured into the hallway and blocked his passage. He had to pause and wait while they received orders and fidgeted, eager to be off exploring.

Two intrepid young boys spotted him and the large jars he held. "What's in there, mister?" they asked him.

"A puffer fish and a small moray eel," Titus said, deciding to clear his own path. The boys followed and then raced around in front of him to get a look at the contents of the jars. They recoiled from the sight, their freckled faces puckering.

"E-e-ewww, yu-u-uck," one of the little barbarians declared.

"Looks like somebody ate 'em and then puked 'em up!" the other crowed with atavistic delight. The pair broke into enthusiastic and disgustingly authentic imitations of vomiting.

The little Philistines raced off to spread their gleeful disrespect elsewhere, and Titus was left standing in the hallway with their words echoing in his head—*Yu-u-uck. Somebody . . . puked 'em up.*

He stalked into the temporary storage room with his face like a thundercloud, and placed the jars on a shelf. Then he backed a step and surveyed the collection. Heat shot through his veins as he studied his prize octopus, baby sharks, and eels and tube worms. He hadn't "puked 'em up," he had *disgorged* them from the bellies of large fish. It was a perfectly legitimate investigatory technique.

And these were perfectly splendid specimens. What if his urchins were a little bleached from the alcohol? You could still see *some* of the colors they had been. And his sunfish specimens—only a few scales and fins had fallen off and drifted to the bottom. Eels and worms *always* shriveled when taken out of seawater. The small rays and baby sharks—he had even inserted wires to make certain they wouldn't curl up in the jars.

"Magnificent specimens," he declared, crossing his arms tightly. "I'd like to see *anyone* keep a large squid from deflating in a bath of alcohol!"

That afternoon, he went down to the docks to meet the boats and collect his specimens. The captain had canvassed the other fishing captains and had come up with virtually his entire list. The fish were loaded into an ice wagon and hauled across town to the medical college.

On the stone floor of the wood-paneled operating theater, Titus rolled up his sleeves and put on his rubber boots and apron. He laid out his knives and saws and scalpels, placed the metal "gut" buckets beneath the operating table, and prepared the jars of alcohol. This was his element, he told himself firmly. It would be just like old times. He would find a few specimens, make his customary measurements and notes, and have replacements back to the Natural History Museum by tomorrow evening.

"Whar d'ye want it, guv?" The old sailor who had driven the ice wagon stood at the side door of the operating theater with a good-sized shark over his shoulder and dangling down his back.

"Over here, on the table." Titus's stomach contracted at the sight of the smooth gray skin and sleek body. When the old fellow plopped it onto the table, he took measurements from nose to tip of tail fin, wrote a brief description in his open journal, then picked up a hefty butcher knife and sharpened it on the leather strap hanging from the table. His heart was thudding faster and he looked down to find his hands shaking.

"Wot are ye gonna do, Perfesser?" The old sailor winced as Titus made the first cut.

Puke, Titus thought as the first wave of blood and half-digested gut smells hit him. Clenching his teeth, he fought down the nausea and a rising bit of panic. He'd never had this trouble before. What the hell was the matter with him?

"I'm looking for specimens . . . evidence of what sharks eat."

"Aww—I ken tell ye that. They eat everthin' wot gets in their way," the old fellow declared, holding his nose and watching as Titus began sorting through the contents of the shark's stomach. "I seen 'em eat hunks of wood th' ship's carpentur tossed overboard. Ye know, I seen a man's guts before. They kinda look like that there shark's. Funny, ain't it? I guess parts is parts."

Parts is parts. A faint ringing began in Titus's ears as he held his breath and pulled out the shark's last meal. A few small fish . . . a cod or two . . . and the bleached remains of a bony beak—a leftover from a former meal. It was the remnants of . . . a small dolphin's head.

Suddenly, the blood on his rubber gloves, on his apron, in the pool around his feet, looked too vividly, sickeningly red. He stared at the shark . . . limp and splayed before him, stripped of its ferocity, its dignity, its very life. He picked up the bony skull of the little dolphin and his ribs seemed to crowd his lungs. He was suddenly struggling for breath.

"Nothing worthwhile here," he declared, dropping the skull into the gut bucket by his feet. Frantically, he cleared away the debris and ordered the old sailor: "Help me get this carcass back to the cart."

As they dumped it into the wheelbarrow waiting outside, he managed to gulp a few breaths of fresh air and swallow his panic.

"You all right, Perfesser?" The grizzled old tar frowned at him.

"Fine. Never better." He straightened fiercely. "If you'll carry the next specimen inside, I'll be there in a moment."

But, moments later, as he strode back into the operating theater, dread settled over him like a blanket. His heart pounded heavily and his mouth was dry. He told himself he was going to pick up a scalpel and cut open the specimen just as he had done a thousand times before. And he was going to complete the dissection this time . . . find a few "parts" to preserve. Eyeballs were always good. He should be certain to get the eyeballs . . .

He was so busy pulling on his large rubber gloves and selecting a sharp knife that he didn't see what lay on the table before him until he started to make the first cut. He froze.

Gray, with a silvery white underbelly. A curved dorsal fin and a bottle-shaped beak. It was a dolphin. Small. Probably fairly young. It looked almost identical to little—

He couldn't move, could scarcely breathe. He stood there, his gaze blurring, his chest aching, his whole body beginning to tremble.

His mind somehow superimposed the image of baby Titan over the dead dolphin . . . his vibrant little body, so smooth and quick, his eyes that seemed to twinkle with mischief. Titus felt as if he'd been dealt a blow to the solar plexus, dropped his knife on the floor, and bent over, trying to draw in air.

When he opened his eyes, he found himself looking down into a bucket of entrails . . . parts of a living thing . . . that he had pronounced "nothing worthwhile." *Parts is parts* . . . it had never occurred to him that a shark's entrails might look the same as a man's. Were a man's guts, his inner workings, not worthwhile?

He whirled and stared at the jars of alcohol nearby, remembering his precious preserved specimens, with their drooping fins, bleached bodies, and flat, lifeless eyes. They were all just hunks of dead tissue that bore little relation to the living things they had been at one time. Equally shocking was the fact that until just over a month ago, that was what he had thought the creatures really looked like—would have argued with anyone claiming otherwise.

He had spent his entire adult life up to his elbows in the bellies of dead animals, and everyone in the academic world, especially him, had called it *science*.

He ripped off his thick gloves and apron and grappled

with his rubber boots, while trying desperately to remain upright. He hadn't a clue what was "worthwhile" or what wasn't. How could he? He'd been stuck away in a laboratory for half of his life, sorting through fish guts . . . telling himself he was searching for the key to understanding the workings of life! The raw truth of it was that he didn't know the first thing about *life* . . . not even his own.

He grabbed his coat and blew from the operating room with his soul on fire. How could he have been so narrow-minded as to believe that his laboratory contained the truth about life? He thought of his colleagues on the Cardinal College staff, of the way they had encouraged him to get out of the lab and do field studies, and of the defensive way he had rejected their advice. Each time it came up, he returned to his laboratory with renewed intensity, packing a little bit more of himself in each of those jars along with his specimens.

He stalked along the streets, heedless of the pedestrians who had to step out of his way or the vehicles that had to pull up to keep from hitting him.

He hadn't chosen the laboratory; he had fled into it. Since he was offered the chair in ichthyology, he had lived in dread of having to confront those painful memories of seeing his father drown before his eyes. He had grown up loathing the water, had arranged his education, his work, his whole world, to avoid all contact with it. And if that wasn't enough, he had developed a whole philosophy of science to defend his fear-spawned research technique, to defend himself against risk and hurt and passion and discovery . . . against living . . . against life itself.

Something intruded powerfully on his thoughts and he halted, looking around to discover where he was and what had jangled his senses. Just down the street he spotted the trademark green awnings of Harrods and—

"Dolphins—come an' see real o-cean dolphins—li-i-ive—in the flesh!"

See dolphins? He felt a powerful surge of longing in his

chest. Hell, yes, he wanted to see dolphins—he was absolutely desperate to see them again!

Locating the source of that cry—a boy in knee breeches and a ragged cap, not far away, handing out flyers—he hurried over and took one.

LIVE DOLPHINS! was printed in huge, hastily inked letters, followed by smaller lettering: "If you have wanted to see the LADY MERMAID'S DOLPHINS, come and see these magnificent creatures of the sea! Admission £1."

The name at the bottom of the paper startled him. *P. T. Bentley, Impresario.* Dolphins? P. T. Bentley an "impresario"? He thought immediately of Celeste, but as he hailed a cab and ordered it to the address in Covent Garden, he quickly discounted the idea that she would be there, or have anything to do with such an exhibition. The wording of the handbill was cannily ambiguous. It was possible that Bentley had gotten his hands on a dolphin or two and was trying to exploit both the beasts and Celeste's fame . . . the little weasel.

In a quarter of an hour, he disembarked beside a shabby market building just west of Covent Garden, in one of the areas of London where livestock exchanges and livery stables still flourished. The aged brick structure was emblazoned with a large banner in red and white advertising it to be the home of: "Dolphins! Like the Lady Mermaid Rides!" Titus shook his head in puzzlement.

The line of customers extended outside the front doors and all the way to the nearest cross street. When he approached the door, a number of those who were waiting shouted irritably for him to go to the back of the line. A pair of beefy fellows at the door pointedly ignored his assertion that he was a "friend" of P. T. Bentley's, and he found himself trudging back down the length of that line and waiting his turn to buy an overpriced ticket. He was sure it would be some pathetic ruse: "dolphins" one would have to view via mirrors or through glass so uneven that it distorted the image. He had seen plenty of fraudulent exhibits in his time and wouldn't put it past Bentley to have hatched just such a scheme.

Half an hour passed before Titus was able to purchase his ticket and file into what surely must have been a livestock auction at one time . . . the smells of that trade lingered strongly in the place. To accommodate more visitors at a time, a catwalk had been built along the top of two large metal tanks, and a window had been installed on the lower level of each tank, so that some could view from the bottom, while others viewed from the top.

Leery of the rickety steps and walkway, Titus chose to stay on the ground and was eventually able to get close enough to the leaky window not only to hear the gasps of surprise and curious comments of the other patrons, but to see the creature inside the tank for himself.

He stared at a long, gray body suspended in water that looked a bit rusted and brackish. The creature inside was swimming restlessly back and forth, surprising spectators by banging into the side of the tank near the window. Each time it did this, the crowd gasped and backed away, allowing Titus to squeeze in closer, to get a better look at what was clearly the silhouette of a dolphin.

When the creature banged into the tank wall again, and then swam frantically up to the surface, Titus caught a clear glimpse of its head.

To his shock he saw what looked like a fresh gash on the dolphin's beak, along with evidence of an old wound on the dolphin's lower jaw. That and the rake marks on the beast's head made it look just like . . .

He began knocking frantically on the window, trying to get the dolphin's attention. Desperate for a better look, he rushed up the steps and squeezed his way past the people on them, apologizing profusely along the way. At the top, a single board formed a railing along the edge of the round tanks, and he burrowed and "pardoned" his way over to it.

He knelt as close to the edge as he could, hanging on to the plank that formed the railing and stretching down with his other hand to try to feel the side of the tank. He couldn't reach and had to let go of the board and crouch on all fours at the platform's edge. He couldn't see what was beneath the platform, but he could feel the metal wall of the tank. He began to rap on it with his knuckles . . .

. . . five raps in sequence, a pause, then a single rap . . .

He did it several times, ignoring the protests of his fellow patrons.

Suddenly, the dolphin shot to and through the surface, rising up half out of the water, sending water and squeals of horror flying. A few of the more skittish patrons scrambled down the steps.

"Prospero? Prospero, is that you?" Titus called, wiping the water from his face and leaning as far over the tank as he dared. The dolphin seemed dazed. Titus was horrified to see the cut on his beak wasn't his only injury. There were fresh rake marks on his skin and what appeared to be dark bruises on his pale underside and around one of his eyes.

"Prospero!" Titus cried, recognizing the battered visage with its scarred jaw as clearly as he would any human face. "It's me, old boy . . . your old friend."

Titus stretched out a hand and managed to hit the surface of the water. Prospero headed for the sound. A moment later, Titus lay cantilevered out over the edge of the platform, running his hand over the dolphin's scarred head.

"It is you—I knew it!" Titus said, feeling a sudden constriction in his throat. "It's me, Titus! Don't you remember me?"

Prospero managed to spit a small stream of water at him.

"You old devil, it is you," Titus said, aching with wonder as he wiped his face. "How did you get here? In this awful place?" He glanced at the other tank, where he could just glimpse another gray beak in the foul water. "And who is that with you? One of your friends?"

He raised his hand to get the dolphin's attention and then smacked the water a few times, the way he had seen Celeste do it. Prospero rolled onto his side and waggled a flipper weakly in response. There was yet another bloody gash on that waving appendage. Prospero sank back into the water and lay floating on his side as if exhausted . . . his injured eye visible . . . staring . . .

"Dear God—what have they done to you?" He could scarcely breathe.

"Out o' the way—comin' through!" The pair of toughs that had been posted by the door came barreling through the crowd and spotted Titus lying on the platform. "Here— what the hell d'you think yer doin'? We don't allow no triflin' wi' the fish."

"I'm not 'trifling.' I know this dolphin, and it doesn't belong here," Titus declared. "I insist upon seeing Bentley—the owner!"

Before he could move, he was grabbed by the legs and pulled back up onto the platform. "Stop—wait—" he demanded as they wrenched him to his feet. Above the noise of their orders and the patrons' gasps and murmurs, he heard Prospero calling. He gave a violent twist and freed himself long enough to grab the railing and spot Prospero. The dolphin was lying limply in the water, calling to him.

Ti . . . ti . . . ti . . . elp . . . elp . . . help . . . Tita . . . help . . . Tita help . . .

Titus held the railing in a viselike grip, staring frantically at Prospero, hearing, within those pathetic cries, unmistakable words. A spoken plea.

Help, Titus. Help.

Shock loosened his grasp on the rail and in a moment he was being dragged down the steps. "Stop—you don't understand—I know that dolphin—it belongs to Celeste Ashton!"

"Won't have no troublemakers in 'ere, Jack-o," one declared.

"I'm not a troublemaker, I'm a professor from Cardinal College and a member of the Royal Oceanographic Society—" He resisted, but he couldn't get solid footing on the stairs, and was thrust forcefully along until he reached the ground. There, he was propelled straight to the door and shoved out into the street. He managed to keep his feet and whirled, furious now. "Bloody mindless oafs—I want to see Bentley—your 'impresario.' Where is he?"

"Oafs is we?" the other said through the gaps in his rotted teeth.

They both came at him at once. He reacted with an instinct he hadn't known he possessed, landing a blow before they wrestled him around the corner, out of the view of the other customers. There, they each landed a blow or two before turning him loose and returning to their posts.

He leaned against the wall to clear his vision. There was a nasty pain in his jaw and side, and he wondered if this was what broken ribs felt like. Taking a deep breath, he got his feet under him, and looked around for his hat . . . which hadn't made it out the door with him.

"Bentley." He had to see the wretch.

He made his way around front, where the line was even longer than before, and went straight to the ticket seller. "I've got to see P. T. Bentley—the proprietor. Where can I find him?"

The man selling tickets shrugged and remained sullen and silent. Then the exhibit's muscular security system appeared at the door and spotted him, and he was forced to beat a hasty retreat.

He turned back to look at that garish red and white banner. The dolphins weren't "just like" the Lady Mermaid's; they *were* the Lady Mermaid's!

Celeste. He felt her presence stirring powerfully in his memory and thought of how devastated she would be to see her beloved dolphins cooped up in tanks, abused and injured. He came to attention. In fact, she must know Prospero was missing; she was probably frantic.

On his way back to Covent Garden and the nearest cab stand, Titus felt an increasing anxiety for Prospero and the other dolphin. How long would they last in those dirty, confining tanks, injured and getting banged about and cut and bruised?

Celeste. He had to let her know what had happened to Prospero, had to be with her . . . see her . . . touch her. A smothering wave of longing engulfed him and he stumbled into the nearest cab and sank back in the seat. He felt as if he were drowning in emotions. In his mind that voice came again . . . "just relax and breathe and let it wash over you." He took one labored breath, then another, and another.

Suddenly he knew the source of that voice in him and focused on her face as he continued to breathe, feeling her presence strongly, trusting her words and her warmth. The terror eased; that oppressive, smothering weight began to lift.

A powerful new sense of peace stole over him, an emphatic sense of direction. He knew just what he had to do.

When he reached the Bolton Arms, it took only a few minutes for him to pack. He stopped by the desk to retain his room and reserve another, then caught a hansom cab and headed for the Paddington Station and the last train of the day to Brighton.

EVERYTHING WAS DISMAL at Ashton House, including the weather. It had done nothing but rain since her dolphins disappeared and everything was so waterlogged that now even the gravel path in the garden squished underfoot. The clouds that had rolled in thick and low made it feel like dusk at midday, and forced them to light lamps to read in the early afternoon.

Celeste's spirits had slid to a new low. Hours dragged by as she sat in the window seat of her room, peering through the trickles on the glass at the cove below . . . wishing she could see Titus, wishing her dolphins would come back, and disappointed on both counts.

Finally, the rain stopped and the clouds shredded and blew away. She hurried down to the dock to call her dolphins again. Sophia and the brigadier saw her from the drawing-room windows and looked sadly at each other.

"They've been gone a full week now," Sophia said. "She's so miserable."

"Breaks my heart to see her like this," the brigadier said, tucking his chin. "Ought to go after her. See she's safe."

Sophia nodded and went for her shawl. Shortly, they were making their own way down the cliff to the beach. By the sound coming from the dock, they realized she was pounding the tin, calling her dolphins. They paused to look at each other regretfully and shake their heads. Moments later, as they reached the dock, Celeste came rushing around the side of the boathouse, her face flushed and her eyes alight.

"They've come back—they're here!" She pointed excitedly to the center of the cove. Sure enough, there were the fins and beaks of several dolphins. They rushed down to the beach, and soon she was stripped to her swimming clothes and running into the water. When she swam toward them, they didn't swim away. They let her swim among them stroking them, welcoming them the way she always did.

She swam to the dock and brought out a cork float for them to play, but when she tossed it, not one dolphin went to get it. She treaded water, watching the thing bob along untouched. She tried a second time without success, and then swam in toward the beach and called to Nana and the brigadier.

"Something's wrong. They're behaving oddly . . . as if they're upset."

As she spoke, little Titan swam up and bumped into her. Recovering her balance, she stroked him and asked him where his mother was. His cries and vocalizations sounded strangely plaintive. Scowling toward the others at the center of the cove, she realized that she couldn't recall seeing Ariel.

"Come on, I'll take you back and we'll find her," she said, sensing as she said it that something was wrong. Dolphin babies seldom ventured far from their mothers. Under the water, she couldn't locate Ariel, and finally had to surface. When she went down again, she saw Titan go to Echo and nudge her underside. The nursing female stilled and permitted Ariel's baby to nurse.

The sight shocked Celeste. She had never seen a dolphin nurse a baby that wasn't her own. But Echo was allowing little Titan to nurse and that could mean only one thing; Titan's mother wasn't around and Echo knew it.

She dived with them one last time to take attendance and see who was there. Thunder, Echo, Edgar, Charlotte, Henny, old Adelaide, and two juveniles she knew as Sassy and Rollo. No Ariel. And no Prospero.

She swam to the beach, where Nana and the brigadier waited. "Ariel isn't here and neither is Prospero!" She waded out and wrapped up in her shawl. "I'm worried. Ariel wouldn't have gone anywhere without little Titan. I'm afraid that something has happened to her. If so, that might explain why Prospero isn't here." She looked out toward the sea. "Where could they be?"

There was no answer to her question or to the puzzle of the dolphins' doleful mood and lackluster behavior. It was the first time she had seen a group display what she had to call "sadness" . . . behaving as if they were mourning their missing members. If only Prospero were here, Celeste thought miserably, perhaps he could *tell* her what had happened.

Celeste, Nana, and the brigadier set up a vigil on the beach that afternoon, that continued into the evening. Other members of the Atlantean Society came to join them, and Maria sent their dinners down to them on the beach. Periodically, Celeste would climb out on the dock and rap out her dolphin signal on her tin drum, searching the responding heads for Prospero and Ariel.

The next morning they resumed their vigil, calling and waiting while Celeste spent as much time as possible with the motherless little Titan. By dusk, the group of humans was as dispirited as the group of dolphins.

"We may as well go in," Nana said, putting an arm

around Celeste who was seated on a boulder. Celeste looked up at her and smiled.

"You go on. I want to sit here for a while."

The sky was purple, the night gulls were making their first round of the evening high above, and the waves lapped rhythmically against the beach. In the center of the cove the smooth gray shapes of resting dolphins broke the regular pattern of the waves. She had seen the cove like this a thousand times.

But for all its comforting familiarity, she sensed that something was different tonight. She thought about it for a while and produced a pained smile as she realized that the sea was probably the only thing at Ashton House that hadn't changed in recent weeks, the only thing that would never change. Dolphins would come and go, boats would sink, lovers would leave . . . but the sea would still be here, calling to her . . .

Celeste—

She straightened, hearing her name, so lost in the depths of thought that for a moment she wondered if the sea truly were speaking her name. She stood up with her eyes widening, listening hard. It came again, from behind her.

"Celeste!"

She whirled. Coming toward her, materializing out of the cliff shadows and just possibly her fevered longings, was Titus Thorne. She heard rocks crunching and then heard the soft *shush* of sand under his feet. Her heart began to beat erratically. Her knees went weak.

He stopped a few feet away, looking rumpled and wind-blown—much too disheveled to be a proper dream.

His expression spoke of strong emotions, tightly reined.

"Titus—" She could scarcely get his name out past the constriction in her throat. "What are you doing here?"

"Prospero is missing," he said, searching her with his gaze.

"Y-yes. How did you know?" Her voice sounded small and breathy.

"I've seen him. In London."

"London? How on earth did—" The fact that Titus had seen him there quickly collected other facts and knitted them into a chain of deductions. She knew who was responsible before he even said it.

"It's Bentley. He's somehow captured Prospero and another dolphin and has them in an exhibit near Covent Garden."

The blood drained from her head and she swayed. "Peter Bentley. I hadn't even thought of him." She put a hand to her head, trying to steady it. "How stupid of me not to think of him . . ." She looked up at him with a pricking sensation in her eyes. Titus's expression was grave and his bearing rigid. He was once again the detached, deliberate scientist who had arrived at Ashton six weeks ago.

"You came all the way from London to tell me this?"

"Yes." He stiffened visibly.

"Why?"

Seventeen

IT SEEMED LIKE a small eternity passed before he answered.

"Because Prospero needs help—the sooner the better." He paused and his shoulders relaxed ever so slightly. "And . . . I knew you would be worried."

"I've been frantic—we all have." She took a step toward him but stopped, reading in his restraint that he had more to say, some of which would be difficult to hear. "Dearest Heaven." She clasped a hand to her mouth. "What has Bentley done to them? Are they hurt?"

"He has them in tanks of a sort and they seem to be miserable. I didn't see the other dolphin, except at a distance. I'm not certain if it's one of yours."

"I think it's Ariel—it must be. They're both missing and they're often together. Once Bentley had one of them, it was probably easy to take the other." She took another step toward him, clasping her hands tightly. "You didn't answer—are they hurt?"

He directed her back to the nearby boulder, indicating that she should sit. She did so, bracing for what was to come.

"Prospero has a few cuts and what look like bruises. The tank is fairly small and the water isn't good. I haven't a clue what Bentley is feeding them, but at least the place smelled like fish. I don't want to upset you, Celeste, but I think it's important you know the truth about their situation and how urgently they need help."

She looked down at her tightly clenched hands and then out at the dolphins resting peacefully in the light of the rising moon. Prospero should be out there with them . . . playing tricks on the youngsters . . . courting the females in the dark. Ariel should be with little Titan . . . feeding him . . . teaching him the ways of his kind and the ways of the sea . . .

She looked up at Titus, who stood a yard away with his coat back and his hands propped at his waist, looking toward the dolphins. He had come all this way to tell her about Prospero; he must care something about her dolphins. But she thought of the way he had withdrawn from her that night on the beach, not long after they had made beautiful love, and warned herself that this was a man who was not swayed by mere emotions.

"How did you know they were missing?"

"I didn't."

"Then how did you find them?" she asked, aching to ask more important, but far riskier questions.

He glanced at her, then looked back out over the cove. "I was in London to collect some specimens . . . I went for a walk . . . and heard a street crier say something about seeing dolphins." The words came haltingly at first, as if he were sorting through a much denser memory; condensing it, abstracting it, making it transferable.

"I took one of the boy's fliers and saw Bentley's name listed as an 'impresario.' I went immediately to the address given and had to stand in line and pay to get inside. Bentley wasn't there . . . but I saw the dolphins . . . and they looked so pathetic . . ." His voice hardened in a way she had never heard before.

"He has no right to treat intelligent creatures that way. Dolphins belong in an ocean, not a tank. They belong in the sea, where they can swim and leap and play and explore . . . where they can eat what they want and mate whenever they please." He turned and strode back to her. "Dammit, Celeste—they belong with *you*. They need to be here with you, so you can observe them and teach them and learn from them and swim with them—"

"What did you just say?" she said, rising, searching his moon-shadowed form for evidence of what she thought she'd just heard.

"They belong with you—"

"Before that." She took two steps toward him and stopped herself.

He scowled for a moment.

"I said, it's not right to keep intelligent creatures . . . *beings* . . . locked up as if they're freaks or curiosities or dumb brutes. Because they're not dumb . . . and they're not just beasts." He produced a rueful smile and wrestled with something internally before continuing. "I've experienced their intelligence firsthand. They're creatures with brains and courage and feelings . . . they communicate with language and they make attachments very like ours."

He searched her face desperately. Was it for confirmation of his conclusions? Understanding? Compassion? Forgiveness?

"An old man recently said to me, 'parts is parts.' " His voice lowered and thickened as new emotion boiled up in him . . . a starved wonder mingled with newfound conviction. "It took me a long time to see it—I must be the slowest man alive. We're more alike than different, we living things. We breathe, we eat, we reproduce . . . we die. A shark's insides don't look so very different than a man's, and there's a reason for that. We're made of the very same stuff."

He gave a humorless laugh and ran his hands back through his hair. "I've spent my professional life poking around in other creatures' guts, without the slightest clue what was in my own."

The need to touch him was like an ache that began in her core and radiated all through her. He was a man who had changed . . . a man who spoke as if he had just seen himself as being a part of the natural world, for the first time in his life.

He was a man who processed everything through his intellect first. The tremendous changes in him had begun in his ideas and concepts and had finally worked their way down to his values and convictions. But there was no evidence, as yet, that those changes had penetrated all the way to his heart.

As she struggled for self-control, he took her by the shoulders.

"You were right, Celeste. About all of it." He nodded toward the water. "There's a huge world to explore out there. And science *is* about risking and discovering, about observing and experiencing. It was you and your dolphins that made me see it." He drew his fingers down the side of her cheek. "That's why I had to come, Celeste."

She could barely see him for the tears collecting in her eyes.

"I want to help you get Prospero back." He cradled her face in his hand and she felt her resistance slipping. "You need him. I need him." He laughed ruefully. "Who knows, maybe the whole blessed world needs him."

Her defenses crashed. Tears rolled down her face and he pulled her against him and held her securely as she cried. His warmth, his wool and starch smells, the strength of his arms around her . . . everything about him comforted her. In the midst of her cry, he managed to reach into his pocket and pull out a handkerchief for her. After a few moments she looked up, feeling raw and exposed . . . vulnerable to the need within her.

The night, the rhythm of the waves, and the moonlight conspired with memory. She looked at his lips. So near. So far.

"Thank you." Her smile trembled. Her heart was pounding. His presence invaded her blood like a potent drug, heightening her senses. She could barely remember what she had meant to say. "F-for caring enough to come all the way from London to tell me about Prospero. For understanding how much my dolphins mean to me."

His head lowered toward hers. When he abruptly checked that motion and stiffened against her, she realized it had been an instinctive motion left over from another time, another set of feelings.

She forced herself to step back, feeling strangely warmed and chilled all at once. She had helped to change his thinking and his life. But that didn't mean he belonged to her, any more than her dolphins did.

"We'll get them back, Celeste, I promise you," he said thickly. Then he reached for her hand and together they climbed the path up the cliff.

"PROSPERO IS A little battered, but he's alive," Titus reported to the Atlanteans, who were gathered in the drawing room when he and Celeste reached the house. The group had sent Titus down to the beach to find Celeste, then had scurried up the tower stairs to watch their reunion. Even from such a distance they had observed the tension between their Woman of Sea and their Man of Earth. It was far from the joyous reunion they had hoped for.

"I didn't see the other dolphin—Ariel—except at a distance," Titus continued. "I got tossed out on my seat before I could get that far. I demanded to see Bentley, but he either wasn't there or didn't want to be seen."

"Bounder," the brigadier said. "Ought to be drawn and quartered."

"Scheming, conniving heathen," the reverend proclaimed.

"Bully," came from the Bass brothers' corner.

"I thought about it on the way down from London." Titus's hand slipped over Celeste's on the chair arm between them. The Atlanteans looked at one another. They sat straighter and their eyes widened with pleasure. "Celeste, I'm afraid you're the only chance those dolphins have. You have to go to London . . . talk to Bentley . . . reclaim Prospero and Ariel as yours.''

Celeste looked anxiously from her grandmother to Titus. "But Peter Bentley would never listen to me. He came to visit two weeks ago and harangued and wheedled to get me to join him in a scheme to exhibit Prospero and the others to the public. He spoke of building a place to house and show them and of making a lot of money. When I turned him down, he—well, he was furious when he left."

Titus frowned. "But you're the one who discovered and trained and wrote about these dolphins. That has to give you a prior claim to them."

He was right, she realized. There was no one else to intervene on their behalf . . . no one else with the claim or interest she had. The strength of his hand around hers gave her the encouragement she needed. For the first time in a month she didn't feel as if she were alone.

"We have to try it," she said, straightening, setting her resolve. "That means we'll have to leave for London first thing in the morning."

"I'll come, too," Nana said, her eyes shining.

"Might need an extra pair of hands. Count me in," the brigadier declared, putting his arm awkwardly around Nana's shoulders to give her a bracing pat.

"We need to get some rest. It will be a long day tomorrow," Nana said, rising. "You can have your old room, Prof—Titus." She gave him a smile that said his former attitude and behavior were forgiven. "Brigadier, you can stay the night, to save you the time of traveling back and forth."

They received advice and wishes of "Godspeed" from the other Atlanteans, who departed for their respective homes. Then Nana showed the brigadier upstairs, directing him to one of the little-used guest rooms. Celeste and Titus remained in the drawing room tidying up and dousing the lamps for old Stephan. They climbed the stairs in a silence that grew more intense with each step.

As they reached the upstairs hallway and parted, Titus

seized Celeste's hand and held it, looking down at her for a long moment. Her pulse fluttered. Her skin came alive with heightened sensitivity . . . instantly yearning, hungry for the pleasure of his touch. Was the light flickering in the depths of his eyes truly desire? Or just the reflection of the lamp he held?

Abruptly, he pulled her into his free arm and lowered his mouth to hers.

It was electric. Her entire body was suddenly charged, tingling, drawn to that promise of sensual lightning. That deep, penetrating kiss went on and on, like a "falling dream" in which the dreamer never hits bottom.

Their bodies pressed hard together—his knee finding the space between hers, her breasts molding against his ribs, her hands clutching the sides of his coat. Rising heat reached the flashpoint.

Then, without warning, it was over, stopped just short of conflagration.

He staggered back and she turned and wobbled toward her room, steadying herself against the wall. When she finally closed the door behind her, she sank back against it and felt her kiss-swollen lips through a haze of wonder. Steam and fire and liquid sensation . . . her whole body seemed to be melting into one huge, hot puddle of need.

She smiled. He still wanted her. Every bit as much as she wanted him.

There was hope.

AT SUNRISE THE next morning, Nana rapped on Celeste's door. Celeste knocked on Titus's shortly thereafter, asking if he wanted to come down to the cove with her to say good-bye to her dolphins. She wouldn't leave them ever again, she told him, without telling them good-bye and making provisions for them in her absence.

As they climbed down the cliff, Celeste told him about Bentley's visit, about the dolphins' reaction to him, and their week-long disappearance just afterward. When they reached the beach, she started to remove her smock, but paused and looked out to sea, holding her garment together over her heart.

"That must be when he caught them," she said quietly. "Prospero and the others were out in the bay for a long time. It's strange . . . I always worried that they were too friendly with boats." She took a deep breath, fighting the despair settling over her shoulders. "I should have worried more about land-based perils . . . like human treachery. I was so pleased by the interest Bentley took in them. I thought he really cared."

He reached for her shoulders and turned her to him. "You can't be expected to know what is in the depths of a man's heart, Celeste. You're not responsible for Prospero's plight."

"I wish I could believe that," she said. "Prospero is special. I've worked more with him, and he's the leader of the group." She looked up at Titus's strong, serious face and sea-green eyes and wished she could tell him about hearing Prospero speak . . . if indeed she really had heard it. But she didn't dare go that far. The thought that Prospero might be one of only a few special dolphins who could perform such a feat sent her spirits lower still. "I talked about him constantly to Bentley. I can't help feeling that it wasn't entirely a coincidence that Prospero was the one taken."

"And Ariel," he reminded her.

"And Ariel. She always spends so much time with Prospero, it was probably inevitable that they'd be together when—"

"Blaming yourself won't help them, Celeste," he said. For once his dispassionate logic proved to be the compassionate response. When he smiled as if hoping to coax her to do the same, she gave him a rueful nod.

"Come on. Let's go see your dolphins." He began to shed his shirt and trousers as if he intended to climb into the water, too. When she had shed her smock, he held out his hand, and together they walked into the surf.

Celeste whistled several times and began to smack the water to attract their attention. They approached warily at first, but let down their guard as they recognized her. She stroked them and talked to them as they swam past, assuring them that Maria and Stephan and Ned Caldwell would be seeing them daily in her absence.

Titus noticed their wariness and watched Celeste's mood becoming more somber. Bentley's treachery had already driven a wedge between Celeste and her dolphins. He would have liked nothing more, at that moment, than to plant a fist in the wretch's face. He began to search the fins and bodies in the shallow waters, looking for one special dolphin.

"Where is Titan? I haven't seen him yet." When she looked up with a worried expression, he braced for bad news.

"Titus, he's not doing very well," she said gently. "He's taking Ariel's absence hard. Echo has been letting him nurse, but he doesn't seem to eat well without his mother."

"I—I hadn't thought of—" He looked frantically around for the little dolphin. "Where is he?"

Celeste ducked under the water and swam through the dolphins to the edge of the group, where Titan usually could be found. She grasped his flipper and dorsal fin and directed him into the shallows.

"Here he is!" she called. "He's all right."

"Thank God." Titus went loping through the water to meet them and ran his hands over the little dolphin. "So, there you are." Titan's skin felt oddly slack; not as firm and plump as before.

"I thought of you a thousand times," Titus said to him. "You have to eat better, little fellow. You have to keep up your strength, so when your mother comes home . . ." He looked into the dolphin's eyes and was transfixed by what he saw there. He dropped to his knees and cradled the little dolphin's head in his hands, putting his face close to it.

"I know what it's like, growing up without a mother. I know it's hard, but you'll have to be strong for a little while longer." His voice thickened with feeling. "I'll bring her back to you—I swear it."

Celeste watched him stroking Titan until the sight of them blurred. She turned back to the beach, leaving them together for a moment longer.

They were quiet as they climbed the cliff steps together. At the top, she paused and looked out over the cove, feeling a quiver of fear that she might never return to it. It was silly, she told herself.

"We'll get them back," Titus said with quiet fierceness. "Don't worry, we'll get them back."

When they had washed and dressed for travel, they found Nana, the brigadier, and a hearty breakfast waiting in the dining room. A sober mood descended as they finished eating and assembled their luggage by the front door to wait for Ned Caldwell and his cart. Instead, two hired coaches pulled up before the house. When they went out to investigate, they discovered the reverend and the Bass brothers already inside.

"What on earth?" Titus looked at Celeste, who looked just as surprised.

"We're going, too," the reverend said, tipping his hat. "Can't have our sacred dolphins in danger and not do something about it."

"But surely—" Celeste began.

"Surely," Nana said, taking their side, "you need all the help you can get."

"An' it's *our* job t'help ye," Hiram Bass put in, while Bernard nodded.

Titus looked helplessly at Celeste, whose moist-eyed smile would have melted granite. As he helped her up into the coach, he leaned by her ear and muttered: "Well, at least they're not wearing togas."

·   ·   ·

THE TRIP TO BRIGHTON by coach, then on to London by train, took the entire day. Twice they made unplanned stops and had to wait for something to clear the tracks. Here and there, Titus pointed out landmarks to take Celeste's mind off what the delays might mean to Prospero's and Ariel's welfare. Across the car, the Atlanteans nodded off for their customary afternoon naps.

It was evening when they arrived at Paddington Station, and it fell to Titus to secure cabs for the lot of them. He made certain everyone's bags were loaded and directions were given to the drivers. By the time he led them into the Bolton Arms Hotel and negotiated rooms for them, he had a feeling that now he knew what the nannies he had so frequently disdained were up against.

The Bass brothers were awed by the comparative elegance of the hotel and kept wandering off, the reverend objected to having to sleep with the brigadier on account of a shortage of rooms, and Nana pestered Titus and the desk clerk about whether it was still possible to get cucumber sandwiches and tea.

Celeste watched Titus struggling with the arrangements and with his temper, and tried to help. But inside she was growing steadily more desperate and anxious. By the time they had found their rooms and deposited their bags, it was dark out and the exhibit, Titus told her in some frustration, was closed. She would have to wait until tomorrow morning to see her dolphins.

She nodded, holding back tears of tension and worry, and Titus smiled tiredly and gave her cheek a caress. "It will be all right, Celeste."

What followed seemed to be the longest night of her life. She tossed and turned beside Nana; not truly sleeping, but not quite fully awake. In her mind she kept imagining that she heard dolphin cries and kept seeing the confused and dispirited little Titan swimming aimlessly around the cove.

Next door, Titus was having no better time of it. The reverend's and brigadier's vigorous snoring from the next room kept him awake and for the first hour or two he silently cursed the surprisingly thin walls. When he eventually did fall asleep, he saw fish—thousands of them, all shapes and sizes—staring at him in despair, their eyes plaintive and entreating.

Just before dawn he awakened to fading sobs and found himself cradling a pillow against him, trying to comfort . . . It took a moment for him to realize that it was that fish again, the one with the marvelous tail. Only this time it had arms as well as legs . . . and hair . . . lots of long blond hair . . .

They were all relieved when the porter knocked on the door to awaken them. Everyone gathered in the hotel dining room for breakfast, but Celeste couldn't make herself eat a thing. Titus reached for her hand and she looked up with her heartache visible in her eyes.

"I have to see Prospero and Ariel."

Titus signed for their breakfast and ushered her toward the door. As they hurried across the lobby, Titus glanced back to see a line of Atlanteans trailing behind them. "They're our sacred dolphins," Nana said stubbornly when Titus questioned the wisdom of their coming along. "We've a right to see what those awful men have done with them."

It took three hansom cabs to carry them all to Covent Garden, where they disembarked into a throng of people patronizing the shops and stalls and street entertainment. From there, they had to traverse a few blocks to come to the building where Bentley housed his dolphin exhibit. They stopped across the street, staring at the building and the long line of people waiting to get inside.

A few blandishments had been added to attract new customers since Titus's last visit. Red and white striped bunting now draped the front of the building, and a barker's platform had been added beside the ticket booth. There were two life-sized painted cutouts amid the cloth drapes; one a dolphin and the other a blond mermaid wearing a bodice made of two large mussel shells.

It was supposed to be *her,* Celeste realized. The Lady Mermaid. Humiliation burned her cheeks. There was no mistaking the place for anything but a cheap sideshow. This was Bentley's idea of an important educational experience? An encounter between man and dolphin?

She started for the door, but Titus grabbed her hand and brought her up short. "They won't just let you in," he said. "We'll have to buy a ticket."

"I will not," she declared, pointing at the place, her countenance blazing. "They have my dolphins in there— they're trading on my name, my work, and my book—the least they can do is *let me in!*"

She pulled from his grip and headed for the door. The Atlanteans bustled along after her, huffing and puffing, while Titus groaned and ran to catch up with them. They charged straight past the indignant looks and glares of the people in line and nudged through the crowd at the door.

"Tickets," the burly doorkeeper demanded.

"I don't have a ticket," Celeste said stubbornly. "And I do not intend to purchase one to see my own dolphins."

"This is Celeste Ashton," Titus hastily explained. "She is the Lady Mermaid . . . the owner of these dolphins."

The fellow stared at him through narrowed eyes, as if recalling him. "These here dolphins"—he jerked a thumb over his shoulder—"belongs t' Mr. Bentley. And don't nobody get in fer *free.*"

"Well," Titus said adamantly, "there is always a first time." He started to push through the door with Celeste, but the fellow brought an arm as thick as a tree trunk down across the door opening.

"Naw, there ain't."

"Oh, but there is." Nana's voice came clear and strong. "Isn't there, Brigadier?"

There was a clamor from the rear, and in a moment the streetwise tough was inundated by the Atlantean Society . . . chiding, shaking fingers and fists. No amount of cargo hauling or alley fighting or barroom bullying could have prepared him for dealing with a determined gang of sex-agenarians, led by a silver-haired grandmother, a brawny brigadier, and a scripture-spouting reverend.

Behind her back, Nana waved Celeste and Titus through, and they backed away and hurried down the entry ramp into the arena. Bentley's minions had added lime and sawdust to the floors, hung a few canvas partitions to blot out some of the more unsightly areas, and draped more of those garish buntings on the railings. As before, there were the two large tanks and a platform along the top for viewing. But, unlike before, there was a rotten smell coming from the exhibit, and it worsened the closer they got.

Celeste headed for the platform, and Titus was hard put to keep up with her as she squeezed through the crowd and headed up the steps. All around her there was grumbling about the smell and the fact that the dolphins couldn't be seen. Burrowing past elbows and ducking around shoulders, she made her way to the front and pressed against the board railing. She was stunned by what she saw.

There were the two large tanks Titus had described: crude metal contraptions, rough-edged and rusty in spots, filled with dingy-looking water that had an oily film and floating pieces of fish around the edges. With her heart pounding, she leaned out as far as she dared and searched the water for sign of a dolphin.

"Prospero? Ariel?" she called out, frantically. Then she thought to try a sharp whistle. The other patrons scowled, made comments on her manners, and even threatened to report her to the owner.

"The owner?" She felt bile rising up the back of her throat. "Go right ahead and call him. I have a few choice words for that despicable man."

While the other patrons glowered and gave Celeste a wide berth, Titus worked his way through the press of bodies toward her. "Rap on the tank," he called. "Get down on your knees and knock on the side of the tank!"

She ducked under the rail and stretched down to find the

side of the tank. Locating it, she used her knuckles to rap out her call. It wasn't long before she got the response she had hoped for. A gray dolphin beak soon appeared and a head and eyes came after it.

"There it is!" a nearby patron called, from behind a handkerchief.

"Ooooo—it's ugly!" declared another.

"What's wrong with it? Is it bleeding?" came still another voice.

There were gasps and mutters as more of the dolphin appeared. One of the gasps was Celeste's. The gash on Prospero's beak and the bruiselike darkness around his eye both looked terrible and she could swear his skin looked thinner and duller than when she last saw him.

"Prospero?" she called, forcing his name past the tears collecting in her throat. "Here, boy! It's Celeste—" She stretched out a hand as far as she could, but he didn't respond. When she rapped again on the tank, he rallied and tried to follow the sound. "Prospero," she moaned softly, "what have they done to you?"

He opened his mouth and gave a few caws and squeaks, and she sat up on her knees and looked wildly about for Titus. She spotted him nearby and looked over the edge of the platform, outside the round tank. It was at least ten feet to the floor. "I have to get down there with him," she called, looking with dismay at the crowd blocking her exit.

"Wait." He slid down the edge of the platform, grabbed the railing, and lowered himself over the edge. Then he dropped the last six feet to the floor. Dusting himself off, he hurried over to help her down. Together, they crept around the edge of the tank to the canvas partition that now formed a backdrop for the exhibit. Another platform stood at the rear, between the tanks, partly constructed and not yet connected to the ground by steps. Titus spotted a wooden ladder lying to the side and carried it to the platform.

There was commotion among the patrons when they saw her and Titus climbing up onto the half-finished catwalk.

The other patrons weren't certain if this was meant to be a part of the "show" or not. Titus went first, walking along the planks that had been laid in place, then reaching for Celeste's hand.

Soon, she was kneeling on the planking beside the tank, calling Prospero. The dolphin came to her rhythmic slap of the water and she rubbed and stroked his head with both hands, inspecting his battered eye and the cut on his beak. She couldn't speak, could hardly see for the tears welling in her eyes. As Prospero pressed against her hands and tried to get closer to her, she struggled to swallow the lump in her throat. She stroked and reassured him, speaking to him in calm, earnest tones, telling him that she would find a way to free him.

Then she leaned over the tank, smacking the surface of the water, and Prospero rolled onto his side and waved his flipper. His injured flipper. Her heart stopped when she saw the gash, which seemed to be going bad in this putrid water. "They *have* hurt you," she choked out. "Oh, Prospero."

Titus took hold of her shoulders from behind. "Over here. I think this is Ariel." She managed to turn and slide across the narrow platform to the other tank. Titus had rapped on the tank and brought the second dolphin to the surface.

"It *is* Ariel," she said. She smacked the water and held her breath as Ariel swam listlessly toward her, then veered off at the last moment. "Here, Ariel, it's me . . . Celeste."

Again and again, Celeste called and coaxed her and she finally edged close enough for Celeste to touch. She stroked Ariel to reassure her, but the more she touched the dolphin, the more alert and frantic the dolphin became.

Suddenly Ariel began to dart around the tank . . . this way and that . . . bumping into the walls, disoriented and unable to right herself. Celeste called repeatedly, but when Ariel finally came to the surface again, she made strange little yipping cries that sounded like a lost child's. Then she resumed her erratic swimming and banging into the walls.

Celeste looked up at Titus, her breaking heart visible in her eyes.

"She must be sick . . . she keeps bumping into the walls . . ."

Titus took her hands in his, keenly aware of the scores of eyes trained on them. "I'm sorry, Celeste. We'll do everything we—"

"You up there!" an irate male voice shouted. "Come down from there this minute or I'll have the constables on you!"

Surprised, they looked for the source of that voice and finally peered over the edge of the catwalk to the ground below. There stood P. T. Bentley in his dapper gray suit and silk top hat. Beside him was one of his hulking employees and a uniformed constable brandishing a nightstick stood at his back. When he saw Celeste, his eyes widened with what could only be called pleasure.

"Well, well . . . if it isn't the Lady Mermaid herself."

Eighteen

"MR. BENTLEY." CELESTE clung to the edge of the platform to steady herself and watched Bentley stroll over to the bottom of the ladder and hold up a nattily gloved hand.

"Allow me to help you down, Miss Ashton. That really is no place for a lady." His sardonic tone rasped her already frayed control. She jerked her skirts out of the way and climbed down the ladder without his assistance. Her feet had scarcely touched the ground when she turned on him.

"How dare you come to my cove under the guise of learning more about the creatures of the sea . . . in order to steal my dolphins?"

"Your dolphins?" He took a step back, affecting dismay at her accusation. "My dear Miss Ashton, I assure you, I have stolen nothing from you. After you declined my offer of a lucrative and mutually beneficial partnership, I merely entered into an agreement with another party and went in search of my own dolphins. These specimens were caught fairly . . . in open sea."

"These *specimens* are called Prospero and Ariel . . . two dolphins from my group." She felt Titus at her back, strengthening and supporting her. "I know their markings and their faces as well as I know my own. Even Titus— Professor Thorne recognized Prospero."

"This is unconscionable, Bentley," Titus said, his voice low and angry.

"What is unconscionable, Professor?" Bentley said, crossing his arms and raking them with a desultory look. "That I am making money hand over fist, despite Miss Ashton's high-and-mighty rejection of my idea?"

"Money? That is what you're after?" Titus's mind began to race.

"And what is wrong with money, Professor? You British bear a curious contempt for anything that smacks of 'commerce.' Odd sentiment for a nation of *shopkeepers,* don't you think?"

"Very well. If money is all that matters to you, then how much would you take to turn the dolphins over to us?" Titus said. "Five hundred pounds? A thousand? Two thousand?"

"A provocative question, Professor. However, I don't recall saying that money was *all* that mattered to me." Bentley strolled a bit closer to Celeste, running his gaze over her. "I intend to keep these dolphins."

"Only to mistreat and abuse them, the same as you did the friendship Miss Ashton and her grandmother extended to you," Titus said.

"The dolphins are getting sick in that filthy water," Celeste said, pointing to the tanks with a trembling hand. "There are rotting fish parts floating in it—dolphins eat whole fish, not chum. They're starving, Mr. Bentley, *starving.* Both have gashes and cuts that need attention or they will never heal in that foul water."

Bentley edged closer to her, his handsome eyes now hard with purloined power. "Perhaps you could do something about that, Celeste. I might be persuaded to cosset the beasts . . . if the Lady Mermaid would come and appear with them . . . to enhance the educational aspect of the exhibit, of course."

"Appear with the dolphins?" Celeste was stunned.

"As the Lady Mermaid," he clarified. "I can see you now . . . in a sequined tail and delectably discreet mussel shells

. . . your hair swirling about bare shoulders." A chilling smile appeared as he watched the desperation in her face. "If you made them do a few tricks for my customers, I might be willing to improve the beasts' food . . . perhaps find money to build them larger tanks . . ."

"She'll do no such thing, Bentley." Titus stepped in, pulling her against his side. "That's blackmail."

"No, Professor"—Bentley smirked, eyeing Titus's protective impulse and her acceptance of it—"it is business."

"Please, Peter," Celeste said, pushing from Titus's protective hold. "You must know that they're not faring well. How long do you think you can keep them like this? Poor Ariel has banged into the walls of that cramped tank so often she cannot even remember who she is, much less who I am!"

"Perhaps she cannot recall who you are because she doesn't know you, Miss Ashton," Bentley said with disdain. "One dolphin looks very much like another. But I would have expected you, as an 'expert,' to know that. These are not *your* dolphins. I can produce the sea captain and fishing crew who helped me catch these dolphins, to prove that I caught them myself. I have bills of lading for their transportation and the testimony of the workmen I employed, to prove that I had them hauled here at considerable expense."

"You know these dolphins are mine," she charged.

"What proof can you offer, Miss Ashton, that these dolphins are the ones you say they are? Or that they belong to you?" He dropped all pretense of civility. "*None.* I must insist that you leave the premises, both of you. You and your aged cohorts outside have put me to considerable inconvenience. Count yourself fortunate that I do feel a debt to you. After all, you taught me just what I wanted to know about dolphins: *how to call them.*" His smile was positively malicious. "I would never have known how to catch these magnificent specimens without you."

His words struck Celeste like a slap. Shocked to the depths of her soul, she couldn't respond on any level.

"You haven't heard the last of this." Titus's voice dropped

to a menacing rumble. "If any harm comes to these dolphins, I promise you, you will pay for it."

Titus pulled her through the canvas partitions and up the wooden ramp to the exit. Outside, they found the members of the Atlantean Society huddled under the watchful eyes of two more constables. When they appeared, the Atlanteans came to attention and demanded to know what had happened. It fell to Titus to tell them that the dolphins were not faring well and that Bentley had threatened to set the law on them if they didn't leave peacefully.

With a meaningful nod to Celeste's anguished expression, he suggested they go back to the hotel to regroup and get some rest.

Once in the cab with Titus, Celeste could no longer contain the tears that had been building in her from the moment she saw Prospero.

"How could anyone be so vile and inhuman? Stealing my dolphins and then threatening to set the law on *me* for trying to see to their welfare," she said, wiping away tears with bare hands. "He thanked me for making his theft possible, for teaching him how to 'call dolphins' . . . knowing all the while that if they came to that call, they must be *my* dolphins."

Titus watched her eyes darken with recriminations and self-loathing, and felt as if he'd been kicked in the gut. There wasn't a more earnest and caring heart in all of England than Celeste Ashton's, and now that loving heart was paying the price for another's callous disrespect for life.

"It's not your fault, Celeste," he said, reaching for her hands.

"Yes it is." Fresh tears rolled down her burning cheeks. "If I hadn't published my journals and writings to tell people about dolphins, Bentley would never have known about them. I was so isolated . . . I grew up with Nana and Grandpapa and Ned and the Basses and Miss Penelope and the reverend and Anabelle . . . It never occurred to me that people in the rest of the world would be different . . .

would see my dolphins as mindless 'fish' and try to own them or exploit them or harm them. All I could see was the beauty, the joy and wonder they had brought into my life. All I thought about was sharing that goodness and knowledge with the rest of the world. How could I have been so stupid?"

He lifted her chin on his hand and caught her gaze in his. The suffering in her face caught his breath. "Celeste, you did nothing wrong," he declared hoarsely. "You tried to bring something fine and wonderful to the world."

"And look at the results." Every word etched the sorrow deeper into her heart. "Don't you see? I taught Prospero and the others not to fear humans. I taught them to come to my call, to see me and other humans as their friends. A dolphin's only defense against humans is to avoid them altogether, and I took that away from them." Her eyes closed and tears squeezed through her lashes.

"Worse—I introduced them to humans who would capture and abuse and mistreat them." She pulled away and turned her face as if she couldn't bear to have him look at her. "I took Bentley out in my boat and taught him how to call my dolphins . . . I helped him *practice* it." She stared out the window, seeing into the recent past, remembering Bentley's first visit. "He quizzed me about what they were like and how they behaved and how dangerous they were. I was so flattered . . . I shared everything I could . . . so eager to teach . . . so eager to . . ."

She crumpled on the seat and, without an instant's hesitation, he pulled her into his arms and held her. Moments later, the cab stopped in front of the Bolton Arms. Hoping to spare Celeste a walk through a lobby full of gawking strangers, Titus had the driver pull into the alley that ran behind the hotel. There, he paid and lifted Celeste from the cab. He helped her up the stairs to her room on the third floor, and sat her down on the bed while he closed the door.

When he turned back, she had dragged her hat from her head and let it fall from her fingers to the floor, where it rolled away. For a long moment, she just sat there . . . her shoulders rounded, her eyes downcast, looking as if the spirit had been drubbed from her. When she spoke, her voice was a hoarse whisper.

"It was wrong. It was all *wrong*."

Titus felt her anguish seeping through him, her sense of loss invading him, and against all reason and logic, he welcomed those feelings into his emotion-starved heart. If he could, he would take more of them—all from them—from her—bear them for her. When he called her name, she raised her head and his heart stopped at the pain visible in her.

With sudden clarity, he understood her last words. It was not only her dolphins she was grieving; it was the death of her lifelong dream.

"No, Celeste, you're *not* wrong," he said, going to her. "And your dream isn't wrong. It's not wrong to want to share goodness and wonder with the rest of the world. If you let the likes of P. T. Bentley take from you your faith in humanity, your passion for discovering and sharing . . . if you let him kill your dream without a damn good fight . . . then he and all the other cheats and bullies of this world have won."

He sat down beside her and took her by the shoulders, forcing her to look at him.

"It's true that we humans plod along, safe and smug in our illusions, convinced that we know everything there is to know . . . when what we really are is woefully, willfully ignorant that a whole, magnificent world lies submerged at our feet . . . a world that doesn't operate by human rules or human ideas of superiority or morality. I know, sweetheart"—he smiled ruefully—"because I was chief among those smug ignoramuses.

"I also know that some of us can overcome our narrow minds and prejudices. Some of us can learn to see the world as a whole . . . made up of land and sea and all the life that is in both of them. But we need someone to teach us . . .

someone special . . . someone with a foot in each . . ." He raised her hand between them with a wry grin. "Or a flipper.

"You mean too much to me, Celeste, to let you give up now."

He lowered his mouth to hers, offering back to her the strength and healing and hope she had first given him.

When he raised his head and gazed into her eyes, she realized every word of his confession was true. The turbulence that had so often clouded his gaze was gone. In its place she saw new clarity of being, a new inner peace, a new sense of purpose.

"You aren't a failure, Celeste Ashton. I'm living proof. You and your love of the sea and your dolphins gave me back a part of me I had lost many years ago. My heart." He stroked her cheek with awed gentleness and she felt that touch as if it moved across her very soul. "But I didn't have much of a chance to get used to having it back, before I lost it again. To you."

"Oh, Titus . . ." She bit her lip, her eyes luminous with pained hope.

"The jury is probably still out on whether I've gone totally around the bend . . . but I do know that I'm mad about you. You're everything I could have wanted in a woman—if I had ever had the sense to want a woman. I want you, Celeste Ashton, Woman of Sea, more than anything else in my life."

Tears salted their next kiss, but couldn't overpower its sweetness.

Somewhere in the midst of that steamy embrace, they sank backward onto the bed. And somewhere in the next two or three kisses, buttons twirled and hooks unsnapped and garments slid . . . all undone by her fingers. When he raised up onto his arms above her on the bed, his face was bronzed with desire and his eyes were dark with need. He grinned at the picture she made lying beneath him . . . her jacket and blouse open, her skirt unhooked, and her breasts looking as if they might spill from her corset at any moment.

"I take it this means you would be in favor of a renewed 'collaboration'?"

She gave his leg a stroke with her foot. "I think you'd better lock the door."

When he returned to the bed, he had shed most of his clothes and Celeste had managed to rid herself of shoes, blouse, skirt, and petticoats. He helped her undo her laces and peeled her corset and stockings from her . . . pressing hot, urgent kisses on every inch of skin he exposed. She writhed and shivered and finally ended that delicious torture by pulling his head down and giving him a long, sultry kiss.

She surprised even herself with her hunger for sensation. Giving as freely as she took, she used her hands, her lips, and her body to pleasure and caress him. She wanted to know every part of him, to match and mate every part of her to the corresponding part of him. Soon she was trembling, taut, and hollow with need.

They rolled, entwined, and pressed their bodies hard together, absorbing the potent new feelings each shift of positions brought . . . until he came to rest between her thighs and deep, compelling hunger took control. He joined their bodies and they moved together, in instinctive synchrony . . . sea lapping earth . . . earth cradling sea . . . until every heated promise of pleasure had been fulfilled.

Afterward, they lay together, looking at each other in the rosy light coming from around the heavy curtains. She ran a finger down his nose and over his smiling lips.

"Say it again," she said. She wanted to hear again what he had whispered to her at least a hundred times, over and over, like a caress, a prayer, a plea, and a celebration of rebirth.

"I love you." He savored the strange mixture of satisfaction and pleasure that suffused him. He had never been this content in his entire life. It was her. She produced this curious mélange of emotion in him . . . especially when she smiled at him like that . . . and rubbed her foot up the inside of his leg like that . . .

"I love you, too, Titus Thorne." She beamed. "There is no one on earth I'd rather 'collaborate' with."

A SHORT WHILE LATER, they descended to the lobby and found Nana, the brigadier, the reverend, and the Bass brothers seated in an out-of-the-way window nook, waiting for them.

"There they are!" The reverend was on his feet in a flash.

The others turned anxiously to greet Titus and Celeste, and all were struck by the new attitude between their Man of Earth and Woman of Sea. Whatever he had done, their Man of Earth had managed to stuff the heart back into Celeste and the Atlanteans beamed smiles of gratitude and approval as they quickly reseated themselves to make room for Titus and Celeste together on the settee.

"We have to decide what to do . . . and soon," Celeste announced. "Prospero and Ariel don't have much time."

"Perhaps if we offered him more money," Titus said, contemplating the idea.

"More?" Celeste stared at him in surprise. "Where would we have gotten two hundred, much less *two thousand* pounds?"

"I . . . have money." He looked embarrassed to admit: "My inheritance. It was a considerable sum then, and has been accruing since I was small. I haven't touched it." He smiled ruefully. "I never needed it. Until now."

"That's wonderful of you, Titus." Her eyes shone briefly as she slid her hand over his. "But you heard him say money wasn't his entire point. I'm not sure he can be persuaded to let them go by any amount." Then her expression darkened as if a shadow had fallen over it. "Keeping our dolphins captive is his way of punishing me for not helping him with his ugly little scheme."

They thought of—and discarded—the possibilities of going to the newspapers, attempting to buy the dolphins' freedom through a third party, and even appealing to influential persons who might intercede. All of those would take time. And it appeared that time was the one thing that was in critical supply. They would have to take matters into their own hands.

"We have to go to the law," Titus announced. "It is our only recourse."

"Titus, there isn't time," Celeste said. "Prospero and Ariel aren't eating, they're kept in filthy water . . . they need to be released now."

"Short of storming the place with troops, we can't release them without legal intervention," he said. "Bentley will just call in the constables."

"Lawyers require money," the reverend said, his eyes widening.

"Money isn't a problem," Titus said firmly.

"But time is. And court judgments require weeks," Celeste said.

"Sometimes years," the reverend put in.

"Anyone know a solicitor or a justice?" the brigadier said. "Knew a fellow who had been at Temple before he was forced to join the army. Cashed it in at a skirmish in India. Good chap. He'd have taken it up for us."

"I've been thinking about that," Titus said, stroking his chin. "The father of one of my former students sits on the bench in the criminal courts. Sir Charles Tweetum, a sensible and reasonable fellow. His son was one of my outstanding pupils. I know that justices can issue 'bench orders' in some cases . . . perhaps he can make Bentley release them. At the very least he could tell us how to proceed. What time is it?"

The brigadier pulled out his timepiece and declared, "Just past noon."

"We'll have to hurry—the courts will be dismissing for dinner. Perhaps we can catch him before he leaves." He rose, pulling Celeste up.

"What about Prospero and Ariel?" she asked. "They need help *now*."

"We'll take care of that," Lady Sophia said, gesturing to her Atlanteans. "We'll get some fresh fish and smuggle it inside the exhibit . . . keep an eye on them . . . make certain they're at least fed." When she saw Titus's frown, the old lady smiled. "We'll change our clothes. *And* we'll buy tickets this time. They won't recognize us."

Thinking that was doubtful, but in no position to argue, Titus grabbed Celeste's hand and headed for the doors. In moments they were in a cab, racing toward the Strand.

The Courts of Justice had indeed just recessed for dinner. The corridors of the court building were clogged with solicitors, litigants, witnesses, spectators, and sundry hangers-on. Titus and Celeste had to negotiate the virtual tide of humanity that was heading for the exits.

"Where can we find Sir Charles Tweetum?" Titus asked a uniformed bailiff. "It is a most urgent matter."

The bailiff looked from Titus's harried expression to Celeste's anxious face. "Ye'll have to go round to the side door where the justices come an' go t' their chambers . . . see if ye can get 'im a message thru there."

After thanking him, they got directions to the justices' entrance and hurried around the block. At first, there was no response to their repeated knocks on the door. Finally, a pallid, clerkish fellow appeared and scowled at their request to see Justice Sir Charles Tweetum.

"The justices don't see people in chambers."

The door closed and just as Titus was preparing to knock again, it reopened and two well-dressed gentlemen exited. "Pardon, but could you tell me if Justice Sir Charles Tweetum is still inside? We've come on a matter of . . . family business . . . and the clerk won't admit us."

"Tweetum?" One gentleman looked Titus and Celeste over, assessing the urgency in their faces as he donned his gloves. "Tweetum is often here through the dinner recess." He glanced at the other gentleman, who shrugged.

"Come with me, I'll show you to his chambers. This will only take a minute," he told his companion. "Hold the carriage."

Sir Charles was indeed in his chambers, but he was putting on his coat, preparing to go to dinner. He looked up with a frown.

"Sir Charles, you may not remember me," Titus said, removing his hat, "but I am Titus Thorne . . . I was your son's tutor in the natural sciences at Oxford. I was a guest at your country house in Coventry."

The justice's studious, bespectacled face brightened with recognition. "Ah, yes. So you were. Quite a surprise, seeing you here, Professor."

"I would never presume upon you in ordinary circumstances. But this is no ordinary matter and there is no time to lose. Lives are at stake."

"Lives?" Sir Charles looked questioningly from Titus to Celeste.

"Permit me to introduce Miss Celeste Ashton, the author of *The Secret Life of Dolphins*."

The justice took her hand, obviously bemused.

"You may recall," Titus prompted, "she is the young woman who has befriended and studied dolphins in the wild."

"Oh, *this* is the one." The justice stared at her in surprised admiration. "Well, it is little wonder they call you 'the Lady Mermaid.' "

"Please, Sir Charles," she said anxiously, "we need your help. Two of my dolphins have been stolen and put on exhibit here in London. They're ill and are being kept in intolerable conditions. Unless we do something soon to release them, I'm afraid they will die."

The justice scowled. "Dolphins? I know nothing about seagoing matters. My area is the criminal courts. I doubt I could be of much help to you, Miss Ashton."

"We have nowhere else to turn on such short notice, Sir Charles," Titus said. "We were hoping perhaps you could issue an order . . . make the wretch turn the dolphins over to Miss Ashton so that she could get them back into their rightful environment."

Sir Charles went back to his desk and waved them into the pair of chairs set before it. "Well, if the creatures were stolen . . . perhaps I could consider it a case of common theft." He templed his fingers and turned a thoughtful look on Celeste. "Do you have papers of some sort . . . bills of sale, cargo manifests, breeding papers, titles of some sort . . . showing your ownership of these animals?"

"No, not really," she said, frowning, looking at Titus. "I mean, I befriended them and they adopted me. What sort of 'papers' would there be?"

"Hmmm." Sir Charles tried another tack. "Then what about ownership markings . . . brands or ear notches, that sort of thing? Have you marked them physically, in any way, as belonging to you?"

"N-no." His questions brought home to her the enormity of the difference between her love and respect for the creatures of the sea and the rest of society's expectation that the sea life was to be captured, branded, owned, and disposed of as suited human whims.

"Then you have no real proof that they belong to you?"

"There never was any need for proof. These are intelligent creatures, Your Honor." She felt her heart sinking under the weight of her new insight. "In truth, they probably don't belong to me, either. Or to anyone but themselves."

"Miss Ashton trained and cared for these dolphins over a period of years, Your Honor," Titus put in. "I was sent by the royal societies to confirm her work and can attest that she did indeed train and observe and care for them. Surely that has to give her a prior claim of ownership to them in common law . . . in much the same way that the law recognizes common law rights in ownership, inheritance, and marriage. It isn't a matter of papers and registration, but of fact of belonging. These dolphins recognize Miss Ashton as their mistress. They come to her call, they perform tricks for her, and they return to her cove year after year in summer."

"Hmmm." Sir Charles rose and went to his shelf, searched the spines of leather-bound tomes, and pulled down a heavy volume. He looked up several references, pacing as he read. Then he rubbed his chin and came back to his seat behind the desk.

"The rule of common law has been infused into our statutes, but not always in ways one would expect. Possession, as it is often said, is nine-tenths of the law. In disputations arising over property, with no refuting evidence of ownership, whoever has possession of the property in question is given the benefit of the doubt. If this party has your dolphins, where did he get them? Did he encroach on your home or lodgings to take them from you?"

Property. Her dolphins were now considered *property*. Celeste felt a huge emptiness opening inside her. "He claims to have caught them in the bay outside my cove. There was an accident and one of the dolphins was hurt and they all withdrew into the bay. They were gone for several days or so before they returned. He must have taken them then."

"So, he caught them in open water." Sir Charles sighed and lifted up the book in his hand. "It's been quite a while since I read maritime law. But apparently the statutes haven't changed. If they were in open water, then they are subject to maritime law. And maritime law makes very clear distinctions in such matters. Any fish that is lashed or tethered to a ship in any way is considered a 'fast fish' . . . property of that ship and company. Any untethered, unlashed fish, swimming in the ocean is considered a 'free fish' and is fair game for capture."

"But these aren't *fish,* they're mammals . . . intelligent creatures with a language and a society of their own," she said passionately, coming to the edge of her seat. "They aren't just any sea creature. Fishermen don't hunt them . . . they're not sold in fish markets as food . . . whalers don't even take them."

The justice shook his head sadly. "I'm sorry, but that is the statute. The law doesn't differentiate between fish and mammals . . . both are considered game. You have no proof of your prior claim to them, Miss Ashton, and that means there is no basis in law for removing them from their present owner. I am very sorry." He did indeed look pained. "If you like, I can speak with my colleagues this evening . . . we're having a Law Society dinner. I cannot hold out much hope, but I can ask their opinions. Perhaps if you come back tomorrow morning . . ."

Celeste heard Titus ask something about Sir Charles's son and the justice respond that he was in London just now, and staying at a club of some sort. He encouraged Titus to pay his son a call, saying that William would love to see him. When Titus and Sir Charles rose, Celeste pushed up from her chair, too. She managed a polite nod when the justice came around the desk to take her hand. As she and Titus wound their way to the street, she slipped her hand in his and told herself they would find a way . . . legal or not.

IN THE LOBBY of the Bolton Arms, Lady Sophia, the brigadier, and Hiram Bass sat brooding over the deepening muddle of their prophecy-gone-awry.

"Jus' seems t' go from bad to worse," Hiram said, shaking his head.

"I cannot believe we won't find a way to save our beasties," Sophia said. "Do you think this is all a part of the way things are supposed to go? Is it possible that this horrible episode is something that has to happen?"

"Dashed awful way to start a new age." The brigadier scratched his muttonchops. "Sacred dolphins dying. Bloody awful."

"At least th' perfesser come back," Hiram said.

"That's true. Maybe we just have to have faith that everything will work out for the best," Sophia said with a mist in her eyes. "Though I don't think I could bear it if our dolphins didn't survive. They're almost like family."

The brigadier reached across the settee to pat her hand as it lay on her lap. Swallowing back his own misery, he looked up at Hiram, who was misting up, too, though he tried to cover it with a loud blow into his handkerchief.

"There they are!" Miss Penelope Hatch's voice broke into their somber gathering. She, Anabelle Feather, and Daniel Tucker hurried across the lobby and were soon enveloped in Lady Sophia's hugs and Hiram's and the brigadier's grateful welcome.

"We had to come. We couldn't bear to think of what might be happening to . . ." Penelope said as the threesome shifted to make seating room for them.

"Lord, ye look like ye been rode hard and put away wet," Anabelle said, then halted in the midst of straightening her enormous, feathered hat.

"It's bad news, isn't it?" Daniel asked.

Lady Sophia nodded gravely and tapped the brigadier's arm, indicating that he should relate what had occurred. The three were horrified to learn the state of their beloved dolphins.

"Something must be done!" Penelope declared.

"Bernard an' the rev'rnd, they're over there now, watchin' the beasties, seein' they get fed," Hiram informed them.

Penelope, Anabelle, and Daniel debated whether they too should go to the exhibit, but in the end decided to secure a room at the hotel and wait for Celeste and Titus to return. The group sank into dismal small talk of how Ned and Maria and Stephan were faring with the other dolphins—"roight fine, thank ye"—then into utter silence.

That was where Celeste and Titus found them, including the newcomers, napping peacefully in the warmth of the out-of-the-way window nook of the hotel lobby. Celeste's eyes were rimmed with tears, but she couldn't help grinning at the sight of them . . . nestled, sprawled, and propped

. . . snoring with varying degrees of gentility. There wasn't one of them that didn't have a number of the aches and complaints that accompanied aging, but not a word had been said about their discomfort or inconvenience. They were here to help their beloved dolphins. She looked up at Titus who wagged his head with a smile.

"Nana." Celeste knelt by her grandmother's chair and gave her a gentle shake. When she looked up, startled, Celeste reassured her. "It's just me. We're back from the courts."

The others woke at the sound of her voice and quickly roused and collected themselves to ask what she and Titus had learned. She remained on the floor beside Nana's chair and Titus perched beside her, on the arm of the settee. There was no reassurance in what they had to relate.

"In short," Titus summarized, minutes later, "there doesn't seem to be anything we can do through the courts. The law favors the person or persons in possession of a disputed property. Bentley has possession of Prospero and Ariel, and as far as the law is concerned, he can do what he wants with them."

"Humph," Hiram said contemptuously. "If th' law ain't figured out yet that dolphins an' mackerel ain't the same thing, they ain't too bright."

"There has to be something else we can do," Nana said.

"Not within the bounds of the law, I'm afraid," Titus said, feeling strangely on edge, as if alerted to a thought lurking at the edges of his mind, working its way toward his center. He listened with half an ear while Daniel said something about the reverend.

". . . he was here, he'd say that we all answer to another law, a *higher* law. And in that law, dolphins have a right to live, undisturbed, in their own home."

"Law ain't justice," the brigadier opined with a raised finger. "Sad fact."

"True 'nough," Anabelle said. "Justice would be if th'

dolphins took Bentley an' kept him under th' water in a tank of air."

"Except that dolphins would never bother with something as wasteful as vengeance," Celeste said dismally. "In the sea, they do what's necessary to survive . . . no more. The laws of the sea are mercifully pragmatic."

Titus sat listening, feeling the words collecting and resonating all through him in a new way. Dolphin justice. Pragmatism. The laws of sea and laws of land. A higher law. Titus's world took one last dizzying tilt, and then settled into final position with a jarring mental thud that struck Titus with the force of a swinging sail boom.

His mental and experiential world had just doubled . . . enlarged . . . changed forever by a new vision of reality. The world was so much larger than he had known. Earth and sea were a part of a whole . . . joined, inseparable, interdependent. And yet estranged. The doors of his thinking swung open wide. The inrushing air of fresh thoughts and ideas was momentarily staggering.

"Here we sit," he declared, "thinking like *humans*."

"Beg pardon?" the brigadier said, looking around for confirmation. "Ain't that what we are?" The others looked at Titus as if he'd lost his mind.

"We've been going about this all wrong," he said, testing ideas mentally at the speed of a runaway locomotive. "We've tried it the land way . . . human rules. And the right thing can't be done. Perhaps it's time we borrowed some of that seagoing pragmatism. Who says we have to play by human rules?"

Celeste blinked. "Titus, what on earth are you talking about?"

"Just that I finally understand what it is to have one foot in the ocean and one on the land." He grinned. "A broader vision, a bigger scope, greater freedom. *Mermaid rules*."

Celeste was the only one who didn't scowl, shrug, or scratch a head.

"Mermaid rules," she echoed, and suddenly she was smiling, too.

"What are we wasting time with the courts for?" Titus declared. "Why not just go steal Prospero and Ariel and set them free?"

It was probably a credit to their collective character that they didn't instantly applaud his larcenous proposal. But it didn't take much more than a minute for them to ask themselves that same question, and come up with a marvelously liberating answer. Why not?

"Steal 'em?" The brigadier looked at Hiram, who broke into a grin, then back at Titus and announced: "I like it."

"Stealing?" Nana said, looking at Penelope and Anabelle, who were looking at her. "If it will keep our dolphins alive . . ."

Titus wasted no time getting down to business. "We'll have to get them to water right away. There's only one possibility in London: the Thames. Downriver, it's tidal . . . brackish . . . mostly saltwater. They'd be able to swim from there to the Channel and freedom." Backtracking, they came to their first problem. "Now how do we get them from the exhibit to the Thames?"

"Have t' ferry 'em," Hiram said, catching on, brightening. "Have t' find a good spot to get 'em down t' the water."

"Carts of some kind," the brigadier put in. "Carriages . . . lorries . . . have to find somethin' to carry the beasts."

"What about getting them into the vehicle?" Celeste contributed, glancing around at the silver-haired Atlanteans. "We'll need help lifting them. Do we know anyone in London who might help?"

"Tactical situation, really." The brigadier caught the flow and rose to the occasion. This was his area. "Have to get inside the place, first." He sat forward, thinking of their objective. "Likely have a watch posted. Guards, maybe. Best to attack at dawn. Catch the sentries napping."

"Can't ferget th' bobbies," Anabelle said with an authoritative nod. "Wouldn't want 'em to hear a tussle an' come runnin'."

"And a disguise of some sort," Daniel said. "Some way to get through the city with two dolphins in tow . . . without anyone taking notice . . ."

Nineteen

MUFFLED HOOVES STRUCK the damp paving bricks and padded harnesses creaked like rasping whispers, challenging onlookers to lower their eyes and heads. Out of the gray mist and gloom of early dawn, two massive black hearses materialized on Piccadilly, each drawn by four soot-black horses whose flaring nostrils and stabbing hooves called up unsettling visions of the relentless and implacable onslaught of mortal demise. The heavy pillars at the corners were crowned with tall black plumes and gold-leaf finials, and the insides were hung with black satin drapes that turned the glass walls into a mirror in which anyone who ventured too near would see his own eventual fate.

Behind those grim carriages walked a somber procession: three women in long black capes and veils, an aged military officer in regimental dress and black armband, a man of the cloth in collar and cassock, and two husky, if somewhat elderly looking fellows wearing the sign of mourning on their sleeves.

In the eerie, murmuring quiet, the lamplighters dousing the lamps along the street paused, removed their hats in tribute, and averted their eyes as the entourage passed. In so doing they failed to notice that one of the women wore what looked like a white bedsheet beneath her cloak or that there was an odd sloshing sound and a small trickle of water coming from the bed of one of the hearses.

Periodically, the clergyman would open the book in his hands and begin to recite dolorous liturgy about the brief, troubled, and transitory nature of life—apparently intended as comfort for the bereaved. One of the women was subject to periodic frissons of emotion that caused her shoulders to shake and compelled her to put a hand over her mouth. A hand wearing a wine-red glove. At such times, one of the other women always came to put an arm around her and often began to quake a bit herself.

The dolorous procession crossed Haymarket Road, with its stalls and costermongers and greasy smells and gritty pavement, and seemed to pick up its pace as it neared the Covent Garden district. More people were about in that shabby, working-class area that surrounded the markets. But, as before, those who noticed averted their eyes and experienced a shiver of relief that the procession had nothing to do with them.

By the time those ominous hearses disappeared into the narrow streets just east of the Covent Garden market halls, there was no one abroad. No one saw the vehicles turn gingerly down an alley near a former livestock auction house that was now draped with gaudy red and white bunting. No one saw the hearses stop or the mourners hurry to the back of one hearse and release a man and a woman from confinement inside.

"Thank heaven we got here without being stopped," Celeste whispered, shaking out her skirt and examining its wet areas. "The water sloshed about so much, I was sure someone would see it dripping out." The others peered into the back of the hearse, where a large galvanized metal horse trough filled with water lay in the middle of the slatted bed.

"Is there enough water left?" the reverend whispered, craning his neck.

"Plenty," Titus said, scowling at the drips still coming from the bottom of the hearse. "Good thing we took out the carpets, though." He consulted his pocket watch and then glanced up and down the alley. On the other side of the hearses, two figures materialized out of the darkness, creeping stealthily toward the group and finally surprising them with a: "Here we are."

Half of the Atlanteans grabbed their hearts, startled by the sudden sound and movement. Celeste grabbed Titus's arm. After an hour of tense whispers, normal voices sounded like shouting.

"And right on time." Titus smiled at the manly young faces that appeared around the corner of the hearse. "Tweetum. Good to see you." He put out his hand and called their names as he recognized each of them. "And Exeter. Of course, Marsh and Suddesby are here, too."

The two drivers of the hearses climbed down to greet their old classmates. That made a total of four former students who had answered Titus's call—on short notice and without a qualm—for able-bodied help in "rescuing" dolphins.

"It's been a while, Professor," Tweetum said. "I was surprised when my father mentioned he had seen you . . . even more surprised to get your message."

"I was surprised to get your message, too." The one called Suddesby grinned with gap-toothed charm. "I thought it would be at least a few years yet, before you'd need one of my father's bone-rollers."

"I pray today will be the last time I am forced to ride in one of these miserable things," Titus said, "for a very long time."

"Odd," Suddesby responded, "we don't usually get complaints."

Tweetum cuffed him good-naturedly then looked at Celeste. "I say, Professor, is this the one? The Lady Mermaid?"

"The very one," Titus said with more pride than heat. "Put your eyes back in your head, Tweetum. She's spoken for."

He gathered everyone together and went over the rest of

the plan. Door opening and "distraction" were assigned to Miss Penelope and Anabelle Feather. The brigadier and the Basses were the rush and "knock out" detail. The reverend, who was a bit squeamish about violence, was their "look-out" in front and Daniel would see to the hearses and "look-out" duties in the rear. Two of the students, Suddesby and Marsh, would drive the hearses, and the other two, Tweetum and Exeter, would help with subduing the guards, if neces-sary . . . but, otherwise, would proceed straight to the tanks with the nets and poles. Celeste and Titus would su-pervise the loading and calm the animals while they were being wrapped in the net slings and transported out the rear door.

The plan wasn't exactly watertight; there were a thousand things that could go wrong. But they were running out of time. And there were occasions, Titus reminded them, when a body just had to close his eyes and take a plunge. When he looked her way, Celeste was beaming at him.

At Celeste's nod, Penelope and Anabelle took off their cloaks and every male jaw in the alley dropped. Underneath, they wore the tawdriest, most suggestive red dresses any of them had ever seen. Anabelle plopped a wildly feathered hat on her head and Penelope giggled and tugged her bodice upward around her ample bosom. Titus leaned toward Ce-leste in shock.

"Aren't they a little long in the tooth for soiled doves?" he muttered.

"It was Anabelle's idea," she whispered back. "It just has to get them in the door. She still has lady friends in the East End. That's where she got the clothes. And did you notice? Not a constable in sight . . . courtesy of those same friends."

"Good Lord," he said, deciding not to question the workings of fortune . . . or of soiled doves . . . ever again. Then he turned to the Basses and the brigadier.

"Are you ready?"

Nodding, the Basses enthusiastically brandished long

black truncheons that looked exactly like constables' billy clubs. "Where did you get— Never mind, I don't want to know."

Somewhere out there, a bobby had been relieved of his billy club and was being distracted from duty within an inch of his life.

They split into two groups. The brigadier led the Atlanteans around the front, while Celeste, Titus, and Titus's students crept to the alley door and waited to be let inside. "Let's just hope," Titus muttered fervently, "that the guard's eyesight is very, very bad."

They crept to the door and waited. And waited.

Penelope got cold feet at the last moment, and Anabelle had to coax her to do her part. Finally, arm in arm, they approached the door and tried the handle. Then they tried a little knocking, and finally a bit of banging. A ruddy, unshaven fellow answered and, rubbing his eyes, asked them what in blazes they wanted.

"Well, ain't this the roight place?" Anabelle said, stepping back for a look up at the colorful buntings outside. "Yeah, this is it. 'At oth'r bloke sent us. Said we could get a peek at them fancy fish . . . if'n we wus real nice to ye."

"Ollie?" He squinted against the morning light. "Ollie sent ye over?"

"Yeah, that were him. Come on, sweets. We ain't got all day." When Anabelle gave the door a shove, the fellow fell back to admit them, scratching his head and edging closer for a better look. Anabelle dragged Penelope farther in, so that the fellow would have to follow and turn his back to the door. "You alone here?"

"My mate'll be back soon." He rubbed his chin, staring at Penelope.

"Is that them?" Anabelle walked a bit farther, pointing toward the tanks. "Phew—stinks loike fish in 'ere. *Bad* fish."

"Them fish is as bad as it gets. Half dead, I reck—"

A truncheon came down on his head with a smack, and that was the last thing the guard would "reckon" for at least another hour. Bernard Bass looked at the beefy fellow sprawled at his feet and rocked up onto his toes, grinning. "Alwus wanted t'do that."

The others darted in, closed the door, and hauled the guard off for a nap in a sawdust pile. Hiram Bass went running to find the rear door, while the brigadier bolted the door and the reverend posted himself in an upstairs loft window as sentry.

The stench was worse than the day before. Despite the Atlanteans' attempts to help them, Prospero and Ariel seemed considerably weaker. Both dolphins lay floating on their sides in the water, looking blanched and still, expending the least amount of energy possible. Celeste gasped when she saw them, but quickly stanched that reaction and forced herself to get to work. They found the ladders, climbed the platform, and set to work positioning the rope-net slings around them.

The dolphins' passivity made securing them in the nets easier than expected. Celeste spoke soothingly to them, stroking their heads and praying that they didn't suddenly revive and begin to struggle the moment they were lifted from the water. When the slings were in place, one of Titus's students suggested using the rafters overhead to help hoist the animals. It proved a valuable suggestion, and Ariel was already up in the air in her rope cradle when the reverend gave a soft whistle, which was relayed by the brigadier . . . only seconds before a banging erupted on the front door.

Everyone froze. Thinking fast, Anabelle grabbed Penelope and headed for the entrance. Motioning to the Bass brothers to get behind the door as she opened it, Anabelle straightened her hat and unbolted the door. "Wot the— Who are you?" a voice came from the doorway. Anabelle fell back before the fellow's determined entry and pulled Penelope back with her.

"Umm . . . we come for a look at the fish. That other fella let us in. His friend Ollie sent us."

The hulking brute scowled. "I'm Ollie. An' I ain't never

seen you before." Glancing up, he caught sight of the rope and the net and the dolphin. "Hey—wot's goin' on—"

His hard head made a satisfying *crack* under the billy club. Hiram tapped his palm with the club and looked at his brother. "Yer right, Bernie. It is fun." Together they took the fellow to join his comrade on the sawdust pile.

Reprieved, they were instantly back at work hoisting, straining, lowering. Everyone had to get into the effort, hauling on the rope or keeping Ariel from swinging and banging into the tank or platform. The dolphin didn't struggle as she was lowered to Titus and three of his students on the ground. Celeste rushed to untie the rope and the first phase of the transfer was done.

It took six of them to actually lift and slide her into the tank in the hearse. She was a bit longer than the tank, but with her body bowed, they managed to close the velvet curtain at the rear of the hearse over her flukes.

Celeste sagged against the lacquered pillar at the corner of the vehicle and looked at Titus with cautious optimism. "That's one."

Prospero was nearly two feet longer than Ariel and considerably heavier. He also had more fight left in him. Several times, they thought they had him secured, only to have him flop and twist the ropes and net into a tangle. Celeste finally succeeded in reassuring him, and had to stay by his head, stroking and talking to him, while he was lifted out of the water. The Atlanteans groaned and winced, straining on the rope until they finally succeeded in hoisting him up and lowering him over the side.

Since he was heavier than Ariel, they had to rush to help Titus and his students carry the dolphin outside. Getting Prospero into the tank was a backbreaking task that strained every muscle they possessed. Celeste had to climb into the hearse beside the tank and reassure Prospero continually, while Titus and the others padded the edge of the tank for his long tail flukes to rest against. Even with his body bowed his tail flukes stuck out the rear of the hearse, beneath the black velvet curtain.

"Come on—get your cloaks. We've no time to lose," Titus said. Then he put Lady Sophia and Daniel into the hearse with Ariel, and climbed into the rear hearse with Celeste and Prospero.

Reverend Altarbright hurried down from his post and paused over the two sleeping guards to reassure himself that they were not dead. At his touch, the bigger fellow stirred. "Come on, Reverend!" the brigadier bellowed, not knowing that his volume would penetrate the fog in their victim's head. The fellow's eyes opened and the reverend lurched up and headed for the rear door at a run.

The hearses were already halfway down the alley when the reverend caught up with them. He seemed worried and kept looking back over his shoulder. "What's the matter, Reverend?" Penelope asked.

"The big fellow was waking up," he responded. "What'll we do?"

"Walk faster," Penelope said, and passed that worrisome news along.

At the brigadier's whistle—their prearranged signal—the drivers picked up the pace. Now that they had the dolphins, every minute that went by prolonged their risk of discovery. They had to get Prospero and Ariel back into the water and to do it soon. Prospero's caws and screeches would attract attention, especially coming from the inside of a hearse.

The drivers hurried through Trafalgar Square as quickly as they could and headed down Thames Street toward the location on the riverbank that the Bass brothers had scouted for them the previous afternoon. The place was one of several old docks east of the Isle of Dogs. It served only a few ill-kept boats and had stone steps and a ramp down to the water nearby. At that point, the river widened slightly and boat traffic was not as dense. If all went as planned, they would reach the place at high tide, and the dolphins could reach open water faster.

There were more people about on the streets now and the dripping and noise from the hearses were reaching embarrassing levels. The mourners bustled along behind, breathlessly trying to keep up and to block any onlooker's view of Prospero's tail flukes protruding from the curtain, waving and flopping in agitation.

IT WAS HALF PAST EIGHT, and P. T. Bentley was lingering over coffee and a copy of the *Times* in the Clarendon Hotel dining room, savoring the comfort funded by his latest scheme. When a commotion broke out by the door, he ignored it, spooning another bit of sugar into his coffee with determined leisure.

"I said, you can't come in here!" The headwaiter raised his voice, a serious breach of decorum in such an elegant establishment. Bentley looked up at the sound of scuffling. A second later his newspaper was being dragged from his hands by the sweating, steaming longshoreman named Harold, whom he had hired to guard his exhibit. Bentley shot to his feet, furious at the oaf's intrusion.

"What the hell are you—"

"They're gone, Mr. Bentley," the fellow panted out, still fending off the maître d'. "Yer dolphins. They whacked me an' Ollie o'er the head and jus' took 'em."

Bentley seized the wretch's arm and shoved him out the door, intent on minimizing the embarrassment of being linked publicly to the oaf. Once outside, he pulled the thug behind a thick column and demanded to know: "When?"

"A bit ago. Ollie—he woke up an' saw 'em takin' off down the alley. In bone-rollers."

Bentley's eyes narrowed. "What the hell are 'bone-rollers'?"

"Them fun'ral wagons. Ollie, he woke me up and sent me to fetch ye, whilst 'e follered 'em."

"Damn and double damn them!" Bentley cursed with quiet fury. "I should have known." He glared up at the longshoreman and gave him a vicious shove. "Stupid bastards—you're fired—both of you!"

A quarter of an hour later, Bentley was in the local constabulary, pouring out his tale of loss and outrage to the sergeant in charge who was impressed by the well-dressed, drawling American. In minutes, the sergeant was calling for the police van and three constables to come along with him in pursuit of the stolen dolphins.

There was only one place for the thieves to go if they intended to free the animals, Bentley and the sergeant agreed. The Thames. But which direction? East, Bentley finally decided; they would have to head toward the brackish tidal region, toward more open water. There was only one major road along the Thames between Covent Garden and the Tower: Thames Street. By deduction and process of elimination, they gradually closed in on the route Celeste Ashton and her "gang" had used to transport the dolphins to water. Their theory was confirmed when, on lower Thames Street, Bentley spotted one of his henchmen, lumbering along—winded from running—heading back toward the exhibit.

" 'At way, sarr." Ollie pointed behind him, gasping for air. "Follered 'em . . . a ways. Big black . . . bone-rollers . . . some walkin' b'hind."

Without a second's hesitation, Bentley smacked the sergeant's shoulder then pointed to the road ahead. "What did I tell you? Let's go."

THE CLOSER THEY got to the dock where they would release the dolphins, the faster the hearses traveled and the more the mourners on foot lagged behind. Finally the brigadier struggled up to the back of the second hearse and called to Celeste and Titus to hurry on without them: "Got to call a halt. Troops all fagged out, back here." They were passing through an area of crumbling buildings and aged docks, and

Titus, peering out the side curtains, rapped on the roof and ordered a halt.

He slithered out of the back and helped the Bass brothers hoist Anabelle and Penelope up onto the seats beside the drivers. Then the Basses, the brigadier, and the reverend climbed up onto the pallbearer steps on the sides.

"We may as well run for it," he called to the drivers. As soon as he was back inside, they slapped the reins and the hearses lurched and began to race along at a breathtaking pace.

Within minutes they were turning down a rutted side street that led to a set of dilapidated docks. There, the Atlanteans disembarked and helped the first driver turn and back his vehicle slowly down the long stone cargo ramp until the back wheels were submerged. They braced the front wheels with wooden blocks and threw open the rear curtains. Titus and Celeste slid to the back and exchanged nervous smiles at the sight of the water at their feet.

"So far, so good." Celeste dropped into the water, skirts and all.

"Now if we've calculated correctly," Titus said as he beckoned the Basses, the brigadier, and the reverend into the water with them, "we should be able to slide the tank out into the water and let the tank drop away. Prospero, here, should be able to float without it. Then we just peel off the net and give him a shove in the right direction."

The scent of the water, the strange angle of the tank, the sudden movement . . . all startled Prospero. When the tank was halfway into the water, he began to thrash and cry out. Celeste tried to calm him, but he was too panicky and before the tank slid off the hearse bed he flexed powerfully and keeled over onto his back in the water. Celeste screamed as he hit with a tremendous splash.

For a moment afterward all fell silent, as the group held their breaths in horror and expectation. The only sound was the violent sloshing of the water where he had disappeared.

Celeste felt as if she were falling slowly down a well,

watching disaster approaching at one-tenth normal speed. To come so far—to get him to the very edge of the water and then—

Suddenly his pale, rope-covered body rose to the surface and as they watched, stunned, his blowhole opened and shot a tremendous spray of water into the air. They shouted and grabbed each other and jiggled and hugged, while Celeste and Titus rushed to remove the cargo net from him.

"One down!" Titus cried, grinning at Celeste as he pulled the now useless tank from the hearse and dragged it aside.

They had to help push the hearse back up the ramp and the going was slippery on the wet surface. But soon it was done and the driver, Marsh, gave Titus a salute and drove off. Next, they helped Nana and Daniel from the second hearse so it could begin backing down to the water. At the bottom they halted, braced the wheels, and gathered around to pull the tank from the back.

Ariel was visibly weaker and lay quietly in the tank, except for an occasional toss of a fluke. This time, they struggled to support the tank as it slid into the water and then let the water of the Thames flood into it and surround Ariel. She wriggled some when the tank dropped from under her, and Titus and Celeste supported her as they worked quickly to remove the net. Suddenly she was free. Celeste gave her a few strokes along her head and sides, hoping to stimulate her, and felt her give a series of little jerks. When she thrashed her flukes once, Celeste retreated into shallower water, beside Titus, who put his arm around her. The Atlanteans gathered at the water's edge watching the dolphins floating aimlessly in the water and, after a few moments, began to look at each other and Celeste and Titus, with concern.

"Wot's wrong with 'em?" Hiram asked quietly.

"They aren't swimming, aren't going anywhere," Lady Sophia said.

Alarmed, Celeste waded out into chest-high water, feeling for footing on the slimy bottom. "Go on, boy," she said, stroking Prospero gingerly, and gave him a gentle push in the right direction. "Go on, you're free now. Head for the sea." She pointed. "That way."

She went to Ariel and stroked her, relieved to see she seemed a bit more alert. The dolphins floated into deeper water, occasionally bumping into each other and seeming as if they were having difficulty waking up from the week-long nightmare they had endured.

Celeste headed back to shore, where Titus helped her out of the dark water. "What if they're too sick or disoriented to find their way?" she said, looking up at him, then around at the others. She looked out into the main channel and it seemed that the number of ships and boats had multiplied just since they arrived here. Some of the ships headed for berth were huge, and in places there were so many of them that the river seemed to be covered from bank to bank with decking. "There are so many ships . . . the water is so muddy and dark . . ."

Titus was already eyeing some of the aged boats tied up at the dock nearby. One was a small catboat, not unlike the one Celeste had always sailed at home. "We'll have to lead them down the river—show them where to go." He pointed to the boat. "Think you could handle that boat?"

She looked it over quickly and nodded. In moments they were racing up the ramp and onto the nearby dock. She and Titus climbed down into the boat and she inspected and pronounced it seaworthy. With trembling hands she unlashed the aged sail and tried the ropes. They were half rotted, but she only needed them to last another hour or two. Carefully she and Titus nudged the boat out into the water, and as she worked the lines and tiller, Titus leaned over the side and began to beat out her dolphin call on the hull to get the dolphins' attention.

They were just catching a bit of wind when shouts and the sound of running came from the street above them. They looked up to see Bentley in his elegant gray morning clothes and a number of black-clad constables running down the steps and ramp toward them.

Galvanized, Celeste flung the boom around to fill the sail and they began to move. "Prospero and Ariel . . . are they coming?" she shouted above the angry voices on shore.

"I can't tell," he called. "I can't see them."

"Keep pounding out the call," she said, glancing frantically over her shoulder at the shore, where the startled horses were rearing and straining against their harness, trying to drag the hearse up the ramp; the Atlanteans were scattering all along the dock, steps, and street; and Bentley was shouting at the constables, demanding they give chase.

"Don't you dare let those damned thieves get away!" Bentley's fury rolled across the water toward them.

"Head for the hills, men!" the brigadier bellowed, leading the Bass brothers and the reverend down the street after a fleeing hearse.

"Don't let 'em take you alive, sisters!" Lady Sophia cried, leading Anabelle and Penelope the opposite way, forcing the constables to split up to pursue both groups.

"Damnation!" Bentley stormed up and down the end of the dock, glowering after the boat. "Don't just stand there—go after them!" The constable with the stripes on his sleeve said something, and Bentley roared back: "Well, I can. Get in a damned boat and I'll do it!"

They were well out in the channel before Celeste could turn to see what was happening. Apparently the first boat Bentley and the constable climbed into was leaking badly. Cursing a blue streak, Bentley had to climb out and search for another, more seaworthy craft. As the distance between them and Bentley widened, Celeste turned her attention to the water behind the boat, praying for the sight of a dorsal fin. But in the dark water, being stirred and churned by the wake of passing steamers and trawlers, there wasn't a fin anywhere in sight.

"Where are they? Do you see them?" she called above the increasing drone of boat engines and the slap of wakes breaking against the hulls of boats. As they neared the main channel, their small boat began to roll and yaw in the heavy wash of the larger vessels.

"Hold it steady!" Titus called, lurching this way and that.

"I'm trying!" she yelled back. "Where are Prospero and Ariel?"

It seemed like an eternity before his exultant shout erupted. "There they are! They're coming—they're right behind us!"

Celeste glanced back and saw them, off to port, their dorsal fins bobbing up and down in the water. That motion, so very familiar to her, caused her heart to skip a beat. And suddenly she saw everything through a haze of moisture.

They didn't have long to relish the sight. Titus soon called to her and pointed behind them. Bentley had located another boat, raised a sail, and was headed straight for them. She hauled up every inch of canvas they had and set the sail at the optimal angle.

"Where are Ariel and Prospero? Are they keeping up?" she shouted.

"They're coming!" Titus pointed briefly, and went right back to banging, giving the dolphins a signal to follow in the murky water of the Thames. As their boat picked up speed, the dolphins did indeed keep up. But Celeste's worry intensified when she saw two large ships running hard down the center of the channel, shoulder to shoulder, as if in a race. She would have to try to skirt them and pray that their wash didn't swamp her borrowed boat.

Setting her course and her jaw, she steered hard to port and had to lean every bit of weight she possessed against the tiller to get it to respond. Slowly, the boat started the turn and she realized she was probably going too fast to take the wash of the boats smoothly. But, looking back, she found Bentley gaining steadily on her and realized she couldn't lower the sail until they reached water that was deep enough to provide Prospero and Ariel protection.

For a moment, she glanced to the port side, and was

heartened by the sight of those fins still rising and falling in the water, keeping pace with the boat. They were shaking off the numbing effects of their captivity and their energy was returning.

But while she was absorbed in watching her dolphins, she missed the sight of a schooner straight ahead, cutting hard to starboard, impatient to get around those large ships before the channel narrowed. She was still running under full sail when she looked up and saw the schooner bearing down on her. Sailing regulations said she should head starboard, but she wasn't sure if the captain of the schooner would count on her to do that. Worse still, a starboard turn would put her smack in the turbulent waters between the schooner and one of the large cargo vessels. Indecision gripped her, just as Titus turned and saw they were headed for a collision with the schooner.

"My God—turn, Celeste! Turn right, left . . . anything!"

She threw herself hard against the tiller and the bow began to turn starboard. The schooner's captain saw her maneuver and came hard to starboard as well. The schooner was headed into clear sailing; she was headed into high waves and chop. She barely had time to call to Titus "Hold on!" before the turbulence hit and the little boat was tossed around like a jackstraw on the water.

Titus was sprawled in the bottom, and grabbed a seat board and hung on. But Celeste was standing in the stern, fighting with the tiller. She couldn't brace sufficiently to deal with the wild pitching and rolling, and lost her balance.

With horror-slowed clarity, Titus saw her lurch, then snap backward to compensate . . . at the very moment the boat gave a sharp roll. She seemed to strike her head as she fell overboard. Titus heard a horrible howling "No-o-o-o!" and realized it was coming from his own throat.

The boat tossed wildly in the clashing wash of the two ships and, for a time, Titus could scarcely hold on himself. Then the craft shuddered, rolled back, and smacked the last

heavy wave, bow first. It stayed upright this time and minutes later everything miraculously calmed. Titus scrambled
up to search the water for Celeste and she was nowhere to be
found. Frantically, he called to her and lunged from one side
of the boat to the other.

He began to tremble all over, feeling that old, familiar
iciness creeping up his limbs and spreading through his body.
His blood congealed in his chest, forcing his heart to pound
violently as he repeated his calls.

"Celeste?" She had to be here, he thought. She had to
still be alive. The water was her second home. "Celeste—
where are you?" He couldn't lose her just when he was
learning to live and to love— "Celeste!"

He saw her floating, her face half in the water, her eyes
closed. Panic gripped him. Old fears and memories surged
up from the deepest regions of his soul. She was dying . . .
or dead . . . and he would be alone again . . . always
alone . . .

In one stark moment, the misery of a lifetime flashed
before his mind's eye. And the pain of it seared through the
chill closing around his heart. He had to do something—
anything. Acting on pure instinct, he began ripping off his
coat and shoes.

"Dammit, I'm not going to lose you—do you hear—"

And he dived into the water. The cold and darkness
closed in again, only this time, they were real and he was an
adult, not a seven-year-old boy. This time, he knew how to
deal with both water and fear. He wasn't going to lose Celeste and his life with her before it started. Forcing himself to
concentrate on how to swim, he held his breath and began
to move his arms and legs in the way she had taught him.

It worked! He moved through the water toward Celeste
and finally reached her. She was still breathing, but he
quickly realized that he didn't know how to hold on to her
and swim for shore at the same time. In desperation, he tried
to roll her over onto her back and succeeded, clamping a
hand beneath her chin to hold her head up. With his other

arm he pulled toward shore, but made little progress in the cold water and was tiring fast.

"No, no—" he panted. "It can't end here—I won't let it." But the next instant, it became a prayer. "Please, God—don't let it end here—not like this— Swim, dammit—move—move—"

Then he felt something nudge him in the water and looked wildly around. He saw nothing, but the push came again . . . moving him a yard or so toward shore. His hand had found a sleek, hard surface next to him, bumping into him. "Prospero? Is it—*it is you*!" Struggling to keep both his head and Celeste's above the water, he caught a glimpse of the dolphin's body in the dark water. Spotting Prospero's dorsal fin and remembering Celeste's mode of travel, he wrapped his hand over the front edge of the fin and held on.

The dolphin whipped its tail flukes again and again; he could feel its sleek, muscular body flexing and straining, shuddering with determined effort. They began to move. Soon they were cutting through the water with surprising speed.

Near the riverbank, the dolphin slowed, and Titus found he could touch bottom. He released Prospero and stood up. He collected Celeste into his trembling arms, then carried her out of the water. There were weedy patches of grass here and there. He laid her down on one, sinking down on his knees beside her.

"Celeste?" He rubbed her shoulders and felt for her heartbeat. It seemed weak but still there. Hot brine filled his eyes. "Wake up, sweetheart. Are you all right?" He gave her a gentle shake and patted her face. "Celeste—"

She moved her head, then opened her eyes. She began to cough as if she had swallowed or inhaled half of the Thames. Smiling foolishly, half delirious with relief, he pulled her upright and gave her several bracing thumps on the back. When she waved a hand, he stopped and wrapped his arms around her. His heart beat wildly as he held her and let her cough and spit out the foul taste of the Thames. He'd never seen her more beautiful. His Lady Mermaid.

"We did it, Celeste." He tilted her pale face up and caressed her cheek. "They're free. Really free. And for the first time in twenty years, so am I."

Her eyes filled with tears. She buried her face in his chest and slid her arms around him, holding him as if she would never let him go.

That was where Bentley and the constable sergeant found them: on the muddy bank of the Thames, dripping wet, exhausted, and holding each other. Bentley headed the boat into shore, pointing at them, his eyes silver with fury.

"There they are, Sergeant. The dolphin thieves." Bentley charged forward in the boat and gave an imperial snap of his arm to order the sergeant out to get them. "In my country we *hang* people for stealing livestock."

"Fortunately, Sergeant," Titus said, looking up with a tired smile, "we are not in his country. What is this nonsense about 'livestock'?"

"He's lying," Bentley declared to the sergeant. "We saw the dolphins in the water. We could see their fins sticking up. These two took them and they're damned well going to pay for it."

"Dolphins?" Celeste said as Titus rose and then helped her to her feet. "What dolphins?"

"Those dolphins!" Bentley pointed to dorsal fins in the water some distance away, heading down the Thames. "You stole those dolphins from my exhibit!"

"You had better be prepared to defend those accusations, Bentley," Titus declared, drawing himself up to his full height, formidable despite his drenched appearance. Then he turned to the constable sergeant. "I am Professor Titus Thorne, of Cardinal College of Oxford. I am holder of the Regents' Chair in Ichthyology and a fellow of two royal academies of science. I am not a thief, and I certainly have no need to steal fish. The idea is ridiculous."

"Then how do you explain being caught red-handed with my dolphins?" Bentley demanded.

"How can you say they were your dolphins?" Celeste said calmly, coming forward. "It is well known that river porpoises and even dolphins can be seen in the Thames. Professor Thorne and I came down to investigate those stories. Those creatures out there are merely dolphins we happened upon and hoped to study."

"She's lying," Bentley said, seething. "You saw my dolphins, Sergeant."

"Really, Mr. Bentley, this is beneath even you . . . trying to embroil me in a scandal simply because I refused your . . . *offer*." She left the nature of that offer to the constable's imagination and turned to him with a sympathetic smile. "Everyone knows it is virtually impossible to tell one dolphin from another, Sergeant. Mr. Bentley knows full well that *all dolphins look alike*."

"That's n-not true," Bentley exploded. "Just yesterday, she yammered on and on about how she could tell one from another, claiming they were her dolphins and I'd stolen them from her!"

"Have you ever seen Mr. Bentley's dolphins, Sergeant?" She winced and shook her head. "Pathetic creatures. Scarred and malnourished and abused. He keeps them in tanks of putrid water where they desperately fling themselves against the walls of the tanks trying to escape. When I saw them last they were half dead. They probably are dead by now, poor creatures, and he's trying to place the blame on someone . . . or find dolphins to replace them."

The sergeant had heard enough.

"Everyone into the boat," he ordered. "We won't straighten all this out standing here." He offered Celeste his hand and escorted her to the boat and helped her in as Bentley fumed.

"Dammit—can't you see what they're doing? I demand—"

"I believe," the long-suffering sergeant barked back, "I

have heard quite enough of your demands, Mr. Bentley. Be so good as to keep them to yourself until we get back to the constabulary!"

WHEN THEY ARRIVED back at the dock, the other constables were waiting, with the Atlantean society in custody. The broad smiles on Celeste's and Titus's faces told the Atlanteans that their mission had been a success and they hugged each other, smiling all around, as they waited for the police vans that would carry them off.

By the time they reached the constabulary office in Kensington, Celeste and Titus were wrapped in blankets and gazing raptly into each other's eyes, Bentley was red-faced with fury, and the Atlanteans—to a person—were leaning exhaustedly on one another in the van, napping.

Once in the constabulary offices, Bentley resumed his harangue of the sergeant. Titus, Celeste, and the Atlanteans, by contrast, were as genial and cooperative as it was possible for a group of humans to be. They gave their statements politely and were careful to thank the good constables for their offers of tea and blankets. They had to wait for the constables to search out Bentley's employees so that they could identify Celeste and Titus and the Atlanteans as their attackers. Bentley paced and Titus and Celeste held hands and smiled at each other, determined to face whatever happened, together.

Fortunately, when Harold and Ollie were brought in, they had been tipping a bit of ale—having just been sacked—and were in no mood to verify their former employer's story.

"But you saw them," Bentley charged, pointing at the Atlanteans.

Harold turned on Bentley with a sneer. "I ain't n'er seen them b'fore in my life."

"Me, neither," hulking Ollie declared.

"Tell the truth, damn you!" Bentley roared.

"We jus' did. I don't remember none o' them," Harold said vengefully. "I jus' remember that ye sacked me an' Ollie."

"But . . . but . . ." Bentley wheeled on the sergeant, thinking desperately. "The hearses! You saw the hearses they used to carry the dolphins."

"We checked into that," the sergeant said with a hint of pleasure. "The mortuary owner said they were borrowed by his son. Some harmless prank, he said, on some of the lad's friends from the university."

With no witnesses and no physical evidence of stolen property, the sergeant was forced to declare that "person or persons unknown" must have stolen Bentley's dolphins . . . if indeed they had been stolen. He flatly refused to reopen his investigation of the matter, stating that he had wasted far too much of his and the professor's valuable time. He released Celeste and Titus and the Atlanteans with an official apology for inconveniencing them.

Bentley stormed out of the constabulary and they exited close behind. Once on the street, Celeste called to Bentley, and after a volatile moment, he turned to face her.

"You think you've won," he declared coldly.

"I *know* I've won, Mr. Bentley," she said with a calm smile.

"I'll only find more dolphins."

"I doubt you'll do anything quite so foolish," she said firmly, "and I'll tell you why. You're far too practical a man to pursue vengeance at the expense of profit. Dolphins don't do well in captivity, Mr. Bentley. They're ocean creatures . . . they need room and they need to feed and migrate and explore in order to thrive. If you capture more, they'll only get sick and die on you, just as my dolphins would have if we hadn't rescued them. Let me give you a piece of advice."

He bristled. "I don't need your advice, Miss Ashton."

"Import something from your own country to exhibit," she said anyway. "Bring over some of your 'cowboys' . . . hire some of your American sharpshooters and trick riders.

Or ship over some of those 'buffaloes' we hear about. At least those creatures are all native to land. And I doubt they'll give you half the trouble you'll get from us if you attempt to exhibit dolphins again."

Bentley stood glaring at them as they climbed into cabs and headed back to the hotel. When they were out of sight, he turned and walked purposefully back toward the Clarendon Hotel, muttering: "Cowboys and Indians . . . sharpshooters . . . the Wild, Wild West . . . and *buffaloes* . . ."

Twenty

THE SUN WAS WARM, the sky was a pristine blue, the cove was tranquil, and the old house was filled to capacity with guests and laughter and joyful expectation. Two weeks had passed since their daring dolphin rescue, and Celeste and Titus were being married that afternoon in a beachside ceremony. Nana was in her element, directing preparations and enjoying the energy generated by such life-giving happenings in the house. The Atlanteans were bustling about, setting tables and arranging flowers and seeing to the needs and entertainment of the guests who had arrived yesterday from Oxford.

Titus was the first Cardinal College faculty member to marry since the university rescinded its prohibition on marriage for dons. The old boys of Cardinal College had canceled classes and tutorial sessions in honor of the nuptials and had traveled *en masse* to the south coast to be present for the wedding.

Celeste and Titus spent the morning showing the old professors their dolphins and demonstrating a wide variety of dolphin behaviors. The professors were especially taken with little Titan, who followed Titus around whenever he was in the water. And even old Sir Isaac got into their borrowed boat and rowed out into the cove with them to greet the dolphins firsthand.

"Marvelous. Simply wonderful. You make me a proud man, Titus," Sir Parthenay said, putting his arm around Titus's shoulders as they followed the others up the path to the house to get ready for the ceremony. Ahead of them, Celeste was helping Sir Isaac up the cliff steps and coping diplomatically with the old boy's frisky behavior.

"She is truly a wonder, your Miss Ashton. And this place . . ." He turned to look out over the cove. "It's almost magical. I can see why you fell in love with them both." After a moment, he chuckled. "I must be getting old, Thorny, I'm starting to talk like a poet."

As they proceeded up the path, Titus chuckled, too. "If you live to be a hundred, you'll never be as old as I was before I met Celeste. Have you given any thought to what we spoke about last night?"

"Your idea for a program in marine science and conservation?" Sir Parthenay nodded. "I'll have to take it up with the faculty council and the other college heads, but I think it's a marvelous idea. A program of studies that joins lecture and laboratory with field experiences here on the coast . . . I think after today I could even get Reggie Witherspoon to vote to make your Celeste an adjunct professor!"

In a few hours, just as the sun was beginning to set, filling the sky with a palette of delicate roses, reds, and golds, they proceeded back down those cliff steps to the beach. Titus and his Oxonians went first, then Edgar Cherrybottom, who had arrived less than an hour before, and Maria and old Stephan descended the steps. There was a pause, then voices floated out over the beach . . . singing of the glories of the sea and the beauty of the union of earth and sea. The Atlanteans appeared, dressed in their best togas, once again carrying their standards and garlands.

Behind them, Celeste appeared at the top of the cliff, dressed in sheer flowing silks, styled on the order of the classical Greeks. Nana and Anabelle had labored for more than a week to make certain Celeste's wedding dress would be worthy of her exalted status as the Lady of the New Age of Humankind. And she was radiant . . . crowned in flowers, carrying a wreath of blossoms for her beloved's head. The sea breeze billowed her airy garments, making it seem that she floated down the side of the cliff to join Titus on the beach.

There, at the edge of the water, the Reverend Altarbright waited in his best clerical garb, eager to perform the ceremony. Nana took the matron of honor's place beside Celeste and Sir Parthenay took the best man's place beside Titus. And as the sun bathed the cove in golden light, the Man of Earth and the Woman of Sea exchanged eternal vows of love and hope and peace. There wasn't a dry eye in the place as the reverend spoke of their love, their joy, and their unique destiny to care for and protect the sea and its marvelous creatures.

But just as everyone dabbed their eyes and the reverend prepared to pronounce them husband and wife . . . there was a sudden motion behind them in the cove and a sleek silver-gray body shot high up out of the water and landed with a tremendous splash in the shallows. Water sprayed everywhere and sent the guests and bridal pair scrambling back from the water's edge. Celeste lifted her head from the shelter of Titus's chest, glowering at the ill-mannered dolphin who had dared interrupt her wedding.

Then she straightened and pushed from Titus's arms, staring, listening to that mischievous laugh. *Ha, ha . . . ha, ha, ha, ha, ha, ha, ha . . .* She spotted the scar on the jaw . . . the one over the eye . . . and her heart lurched.

"Prospero! It's Prospero—he's come back!"

She grabbed Titus by the hand and together they rushed out into the water, wedding clothes and all, to greet their beloved old friend. Soon they were waist-deep in the water, stroking Prospero and making a fuss over him, laughing with him. Farther out in the cove, little Titan leaped out of the water with another dolphin, and they realized Ariel was back in the cove as well.

After the excitement settled a bit, Titus pulled Celeste against his side and turned her toward the reverend.

"You'd better finish quickly, Reverend, before something else happens." With a chuckle, he looked down at Celeste's rosy, beaming face. "I've got a mermaid on the hook and I don't intend to let her get away."

The reverend pronounced them husband and wife and instructed Titus that he might kiss Celeste. They stood in waist-deep water, kissing to the collective "ahhh," of their guests, until they were forcibly parted by a sleek gray beak and head. Prospero seemed determined to be the first in line to kiss the bride.

Afterward, the dolphins led by Prospero put on an ebullient display of jumps and aerial acrobatics. And then Prospero came into the shallows to serenade Celeste and Titus, ending with a repeated series of yips and screeches that stunned the bride and groom.

They looked around them at the guests, who were applauding and happily talking to each other . . . completely unaware that the dolphin had just spoken to all of them . . . in plain English.

"Did you hear that?" Celeste asked urgently, staring up at Titus.

"You heard it, too? Thank God—I thought I was losing my mind!" Titus wilted with relief. "He said 'happy . . . happy . . . happy . . . people.' "

"He did not," she said, bewildered by her new husband's faulty hearing. "He said 'many . . . many . . . many . . . babies.' "

Titus looked at her in horror. "He did not."

"Did, too."

"Did not."

"Did, too." She stepped back and looked at him through playfully narrowed eyes. "I see Nana still hasn't told you the rest of the prophecy . . ."

When she turned with a twinkle in her eye and headed up onto the beach to greet their friends, Titus stiffened and headed after her. "What prophecy? What's all this about babies? Good Lord—many babies? *Celeste*—"

IN THE WEE HOURS of the next morning, as Titus and Celeste lay together in their marriage bed, wrapped in warmth and each other's arms, Titus slid into a familiar dream. He was in water . . . lovely blue water that seemed warm and deliciously caressing. Suddenly, out of the distance came a veritable wall of fish of all sizes, shapes, and descriptions. They were coming straight at him and he braced, knowing what they intended and telling himself that he probably deserved it. But when they surrounded him and closed in, they began to smile . . . sunny, adoring smiles that melted the tension in him. And when they turned their tails this time, it was to stroke and caress him. Then the little fish parted to admit a newcomer . . . an old friend . . . his big fish with the marvelous tail.

As it swam toward him its face transformed into a human one, its scales became long hair, and its fins became soft, graceful arms. His fish was really a rather familiar-looking mermaid, who wasn't wearing anything but a few scales. He stood in awe, watching her stop in front of him, watching her sultry blue-eyed smile, feeling her silky hair floating and wrapping around him.

When she unbuttoned his shirt, he let it slide down his arms. When she sank before him and unbuttoned his trousers, he had some difficulty stepping out of them. He looked down at himself and saw scales all over his lower half . . . and a tail, a beautiful multicolored tail like hers. Then she pulled him along and he found himself swimming with her, exerting only the slightest effort.

When they came to a beautiful place of blue water and colorful fish and coral, he pulled her into his arms and luxuriated in the sensation of her warm breasts pressed against his chest in the cool water. When he kissed her, she tasted like salty honey, warm and vibrant . . .

He opened his eyes a moment later and found himself kissing that very mermaid in real life. Her bare breasts were pressed against him, her mouth did indeed taste like salt and honey. He suddenly groaned, broke that kiss, and quickly threw back the covers to stare at his lower half. There were his belly and legs and the evidence of his rising passions, all in reassuringly human form.

"Oh, thank God," he said, dropping his head back.

"Titus?" she said, laughing. "What's gotten into you?"

His face reddened, but he pulled her over him bodily, relishing the feel of her legs against his. "You know, there is something to be said for *not* having your dreams come true."

Author's Note

I HOPE YOU enjoyed Celeste and Titus and the Atlantean Society.

These characters and this story will always be special to me because in the course of researching it, I went to the Florida Keys and "swam with dolphins" myself. My intention was to gain firsthand information about what dolphins are like and what it is like to be in the water with dolphins. I had imagined swimming freely and joyfully with these wonderful sentient creatures . . . communing mystically . . . absorbing impressions and ideas for Celeste's point of view. Instead, I found myself stuck squarely in Titus's wary and unwilling mind-set . . . unnerved by how big the creatures are up close . . . reluctantly being towed around a lagoon by two very patient dolphins named Sherry and Thunder.

I did eventually relax, however, and I have wonderful photos to prove it. One small step for writerly authenticity, one giant step for a wary writer.

My heartfelt thanks to Matthew and Linda Stone, of the Deep Six Dive Shop in Stuart, Florida, whose patience in giving me scuba instruction and in arranging for my dolphin foray went above and beyond the call of familial duty. Much thanks also to my editor, Wendy McCurdy, and my sister, Sharon Stone, for their encouragement and assistance.

Celeste's experiences with her dolphins are based solidly on current-day understandings of dolphins and on human-dolphin experiences. But that is not to say that many of these characteristics and behaviors could not have been observed earlier. Over the long history of humankind's adventuring on and in the sea, dolphins have occasionally been curious enough about humans to seek us out. "Friendly dolphins" have appeared in bays and coves in virtually all areas of the world—England, New Zealand, Australia, the United States, Costa Rica, Spain, France, Norway, South Africa, Italy, Ireland, and the Bahamas—to investigate and play with the human residents of the nearby land.

In England in the early 1800's, people flocked to the seashore to see a friendly dolphin dubbed Gabriel, who played with children, accepted food from humans, and splashed and played with swimmers. Since the 1950's there have been at least thirty-five documented cases of friendly dolphins, worldwide. Who knows how many more have gone unreported, except in local lore? Thus, it is not beyond imagining that a young woman with a great love for the sea might make friends with such a dolphin, or even several such dolphins, and study them.

In two areas, however, I did take a bit of license. Dolphins in captivity work for food rewards much of the time. For the purposes of the book, I decided against having Celeste carry a bait bucket wherever she went. Secondly, while Titus thought of the dolphins of Pevensey Bay as a family, dolphin groups are loosely structured and often-changing. Such groups are primarily females and juveniles or boisterous groups of "adolescent" dolphins. In the wild, many male dolphins lead fairly solitary lives, temporarily linking up with group-living females for reproductive purposes and social interaction.

Strangely, the Atlantean Society's success in "calling the dolphins" has a real-life counterpart. Arthur Grimble reported in his book *A Pattern of Islands* that the Pacific islanders of what is now Kiribati (formerly the Gilbert Islands) have people among them who reportedly can "call" the dolphins. These hereditary "dolphin callers" enter into a dreamlike state where, the story goes, their spirits leave their bodies and seek out dolphins. In a ceremony, which Grimble once witnessed and found quite disturbing, the dolphin dreamer leads the entranced dolphins to strand themselves, *en masse,* on the beach. So it is not unthinkable that the Atlanteans might have found the right combination of sound and "spirit" to call dolphins to the cove of Ashton House . . . to a more humane end.

And one more bit of information. Like so much of our twentieth-century culture, the ecological movement that burst onto the American scene in 1970 had its roots in the conservancy movement in Victorian England. The "natural world" became a major focus of interest for all segments of society, and for the first time, the delicate ecological relationships of living things to their environment were studied and understood in a larger scientific framework.

And as to what happened to Celeste and Titus and their research . . .

One year later, the racket of hammers and saws and the noise of workmen filled Ashton House. With the money from Celeste's book and Titus's help, the roof of the old house was being replaced and the floors were being reinforced. Celeste and Lady Sophia stood in the front court, discussing the work with the foreman, when Titus came out of the house with his hands over his ears and a look of exasperation on his face.

"I can't get a thing done," he declared. "I can't hear myself think."

"Well, after all, it was *your* idea to replace the roof and do all the inside work at once," Celeste said, but with a sympathetic smile.

"Sheer lunacy on my part," he grumbled. "Must be the salt air. Seeps into my brain and makes me say and do things that don't make the slightest sense."

"I've never met a person who makes more sense than you

do." She slipped her arm through his and drew him toward the garden. "You just need a change of pace. Come with me."

"But we still have to prepare that talk for the Wiltshire Conservancy Society," Titus protested. "And there is a small mountain of correspondence, and our first student will be arriving in three weeks. With the state of the house, I'm not certain we'll even have a bed for the fel—"

"Titus." She pressed her fingers against his lips to halt him and dragged him to a seat on the garden bench.

"Who knew that being a mermaid's husband would prove to be so much work?" he said, as she positioned herself behind him and kneaded his shoulders and neck until he began to relax.

She laughed and her eyes twinkled. "If you think keeping up with a mermaid is hard, however are you going to cope with a 'merbaby'?"

He straightened, then whirled on the bench to stare at her.

"A baby?"

She smiled and nodded, and he joyfully wrapped both arms around her and held her tight. Moments later she pulled back from his embrace and suggested going for a swim to celebrate. He was more than willing . . .

"But you have to promise you won't tell Prospero for a while." With a wry grin, he placed a hand on her midsection. "The big oaf will probably insist we name it after him."

A lot had happened in the last year. Together, Celeste and Titus had begun a conservancy newsletter, compiling news, ideas, and discussion of conservation issues and sending it to all of the nature-conservation societies in England. Titus elected to give up his chair in ichthyology, but to keep his position on the faculty of Cardinal College. He intended to teach only selected terms, so that he might collaborate with Celeste to create a curriculum to help carefully screened students gain a broader understanding of the world under the sea.

In addition, they had begun to help citizens in several communities organize conservancy societies of their own. They traveled and appeared together, speaking to groups and helping local people contact whalers, fishermen, land owners, and political figures to lobby for support for better stewardship of the earth's resources, especially the marine mammals.

P. T. Bentley, as it happened, had taken Celeste's advice and imported a number of his fellow countrymen and American animals to produce a "Wild West show." His buffaloes, armadillos, and longhorn cattle had been the curiosity of London for a time, and recently word had drifted back across the Channel that they were an even larger success in Paris. It reassured Celeste to know he was far away and apparently no longer interested in dolphins.

The Atlantean Society continued to meet and to study the old artifacts and perform an occasional ritual. But more and more, their focus had shifted to enjoying the dolphins and helping Celeste and Titus with their conservation activities. It was Celeste's and Titus's task, the society had decided, to protect dolphins and the knowledge of dolphins until the world was ready for the lessons the marvelous creatures would bring . . . about the connectedness of all nature and the interdependence of all living things.

IT IS MY THOUGHT that a long time in the future . . . say, a hundred and fifteen years or so . . . a pair of dolphin researchers, on their honeymoon in the Florida Keys would stop for a cappuccino at a quaint little bookstore on Taverner Key. While he chats with the proprietor and waits for the coffee, she sorts through a box of old books that the proprietor says were just purchased from an estate sale. At the side of the box is a worn blue-green volume with a faded dolphin embossed on the front. She leafs through it and her eyes widen at what she sees.

"Look at this, sweetheart." She brings it back to her new husband. "Published in *1884*. Apparently there was a woman in England who swam with dolphins and wrote a book about it."

And the proprietor gives it to them as a wedding present.

ABOUT THE AUTHOR

Betina Krahn lives in Minnesota with her two sons and a feisty salt-and-pepper schnauzer. With a degree in biology and a graduate degree in counseling, she has worked in teaching, personnel management, and mental health. She had a mercifully brief stint as a boys' soccer coach, makes terrific lasagna, routinely kills houseplants, and is incurably optimistic about the human race. She believes the world needs a bit more truth, a lot more justice, and a whole lot more love and laughter. And she attributes her outlook to having married an unflinching optimist and to two great-grandmothers actually named Pollyanna.

Enter to win in Bantam Books'

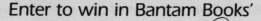

Romance Readers Never Go to Bed Alone!

SWEEPSTAKES

You could win ...

Grand Prize Dream Getaway for Two to

BRACO VILLAGE RESORT, JAMAICA,

courtesy of Empress Travel with round-trip coach air travel on American Airlines!

or one of 3 sensational First Prizes ...

A Touch of Enchantment "Year of Flowers" delivered to your home or office!

∎

The Silver Rose custom-designed sterling silver charm!

∎

The Mermaid Weekend Getaway for Two!

or one of 10 terrific Second Prizes ...

A trio of romance novels and a custom-created **"ROMANCE READERS NEVER GO TO BED ALONE!"** nightshirt!

NAME: _____ AGE: _____

ADDRESS: _____

CITY: _____ STATE: _____ ZIP: _____

PHONE:(DAY) _____ (NIGHT) _____

ENTRIES MUST BE RECEIVED BY NO LATER THAN SEPTEMBER 1, 1997

🐓 **Bantam**

Grand Prize Dream Getaway courtesy of

 EMPRESS TRAVEL   **Braco** *village resort*   **AmericanAirlines**

BANTAM BOOKS ROMANCE READERS NEVER GO TO BED ALONE! Official Entry Rules

HOW TO ENTER

1. No purchase is necessary. Enter by completing the ROMANCE READERS NEVER GO TO BED ALONE! SWEEPSTAKES entry coupon or by printing your name, address, age and phone number on a 3 x 5 card and sending the coupon or card to: BANTAM BOOKS ROMANCE READERS NEVER GO TO BED ALONE! SWEEPSTAKES, BANTAM BOOKS, DEPT. RR-1, 1540 Broadway, NY, NY 10036

PRIZES

2. One (1) Grand Prize:

A 7-night Dream Getaway for two to BRACO VILLAGE RESORT, Jamaica, the luxurious all-inclusive resort and round-trip coach air travel on American Airlines, courtesy of Empress Travel. The Dream Getaway at BRACO VILLAGE includes all meals and beverages plus use of all water sports facilities with instructions, and resort facilities including tennis (night and day), bicycles, and fitness center. Estimated value of Grand Prize: $3,700.00

Grand Prize bookings must be made through Empress Travel, and travel arrangements and resort accomodations are subject to availability. Grand Prize trip must be taken within 12 months of date awarded. Blackout dates may apply. Winner will be responsible for any expenses involved in traveling to the nearest airport serviced by American Airlines. The winner and his/her guest must each have a valid passport or a photo I.D. and proof of citizenship. Once travel arrangements are made, no changes will be allowed. All expenses not mentioned are the sole responsibility of the winner.

Three (3) First Prize Awards:

a) The Touch of Enchantment "A Year of Flowers" mailed monthly to winner's home. Estimated value of First Prize: $350.00

"A Year of Flowers" First Prize arrangements will be made by Bantam Books marketing department for winner. Shipments will be made once per month to one address.

b) The Silver Rose Charm, custom created for this sweepstakes, in sterling silver. Estimated value of The Silver Rose First Prize: $300.00

c) The Mermaid "Weekend Getaway" for two. Estimated value of The Mermaid First Prize: $325.00

The Mermaid Weekend Getaway First Prize arrangements will be made by Bantam Books marketing department for winner. Weekend must be taken within 12 months of date awarded. Blackout dates may apply. Winner will be responsible for any expenes involved in traveling to "Weekend Getaway" Package. The winner and his/her guest must each have a valid passport or a photo I.D. and proof of citizenship. Once travel arrangements are made, no changes will be allowed.

Ten (10) Second Prize Awards:

A package consisting of 3 Bantam backlist paperback romance novels and one 100% cotton, One-Size-Fits-Most "Romance Readers Never Go To Bed Alone!" nightshirt, custom-created for this promotion. The three paperbacks will be chosen by Bantam marketing for the winner. Estimated value of Second Prize: $28.00 each.

ELIGIBILITY

3. Entrants must be 18 years or older at the time of entry. There is no limit to the number of entries. Entries must be received by Bantam no later than SEPTEMBER 1, 1997. The winner will be chosen in a random drawing by the Bantam marketing department from completed entries received and the winners will be notified on or about OCTOBER 1, 1997. Bantam's decision is final. Each winner has thirty days from the date of notice in which to accept his/her prize award or an alternate winner will be chosen. Odds of winning depend upon the number of entries received. No prize substitution or transfer allowed. Only one prize per entrant; one prize per household.

4. The winner and his/her guest will be required to sign an Affidavit of Eligibility and Release supplied by Bantam Books. Entering the sweepstakes constitutes permission for use of the winner's name, likeness and biographical data for publicity and promotional purposes, with no additional compensation.

5. **Prize awards are subject to the rules of entrant's employer.** Employees of Bantam Books, Bantam Doubleday Dell Publishing Group, Inc., Empress Travel, American Airlines, Braco Village Resort, their subsidiaries and affiliates and their immediate family members are not eligible to enter this sweepstakes. This sweepstakes is open to residents of the U.S. and Canada, excluding the Province of Quebec. Canadian winner would be required to correctly answer an arithmetical skill testing question in order to receive his/her prize. Void where prohibited or restricted by law. All federal state and local regulations apply. Taxes, if any, are the winner's sole responsibility. In the event that these prizes become unavailable, Bantam Books reserves the right to substitute with prizes of equal value.

6. For the name of the prize winners, available after December 1, 1997, send a stamped, self-addressed envelope entirely separate from your entry to BANTAM BOOKS ROMANCE READERS NEVER GO TO BED ALONE! SWEEPSTAKES WINNER, Bantam Books, 1540 Broadway, Dept. JL, New York New York 10036